# THE BLUE MOUNTAIN

MEIR SHALEV, one of Israel's most celebrated novelists, is the author of three other works of fiction – *Four Meals, Esau* and *The Big Woman* – all of which have been notable literary and commercial successes in Europe and beyond. His novels have been published in over ten countries. Shalev is also a columnist for *Yediot Achronot*, a leading Israeli newspaper, and is the author of five children's books, also published widely on the international front. He lives in Jerusalem.

HILLEL HALKIN has translated over fifty books from Hebrew and Yiddish by well-known contemporary Israeli and classical Jewish authors.

# THE BLUE MOUNTAIN

## MEIR SHALEV

Translated from the Hebrew by

## HILLEL HALKIN

CANONGATE
*Edinburgh · London*

First published in Great Britain in 2001
by Canongate Books Ltd,
14 High Street, Edinburgh EH1 1TE.
New paperback edition published simultaneously
in North America and Great Britain in 2002.
First published in Israel in 1988
by Am Oved Publishers.
First published in English
in the United States in 1991 by
HarperCollins Publishers.

This edition first published in 2004

*British Library Cataloguing-in-Publication Data*
A catalogue record for this book is available on
request from the British Library

ISBN 978 1 84195 242 0

Typeset by Palimpsest Book Production Limited,
Polmont, Stirlingshire
Printed and bound in Great Britain by
Clays Ltd, Elcograf S.p.A.

www.canongate.tv

*To Batya, my mother*

# 1

One summer night the old schoolteacher Ya'akov Pinness awoke from his sleep with a great start. 'I'm screwing Liberson's granddaughter!' someone had shouted outside.

High, brazen, and clear, the shout winged past the Canary Isle pine trees near the water tower. For a moment it hovered like a bird of prey before swooping earthwards to the village. The old teacher felt a familiar twinge of pain. Once more he alone had heard the obscene words.

For years he had chinked every crack, repaired every rent, stood in the breach every time. 'Like the Dutch boy plugging the dyke,' he would say as he beat back yet another threat. Fruit aphids, state lotteries, cattle ticks, anopheles mosquitoes, bands of locusts and jazz musicians swirled around him like dark waves before breaking in a slimy froth against the breastwork of his heart.

Pinness sat up in bed and wiped his fingers on the hair on his chest, perplexed and enraged that life in the village could go on as usual when such debauchery publicly thumbed a nose at it.

The little co-operative settlement in the Valley of Jezreel was sound asleep. The mules and cows in their sheds, the hens in their coops, the visionary men of toil in their humble beds. Like an old machine whose parts were used to each other, the village purred routinely in the night. Udders filled with milk, clusters of grapes swelled with juice, prime beef waxed fat on the joints of calves soon to be sent to the slaughterhouse. Tireless bacteria, 'our one-celled friends', as Pinness appreciatively called them in the classroom, laboured to fix fresh nitrogen at the roots of plants. But notoriously patient and even-tempered though he was, the old educator was determined to let no one, least of all himself, rest on the laurels of productivity and past achievement. 'I'll catch you yet, you degenerate,' he mumbled irately, jumping heavily from his iron bed. His hands trembled as he buttoned his old khaki pants and pulled on his confidence-inspiring black work boots in preparation for the fray. He was too upset to find his glasses in the dark, but the moonlight shining through the cracks in the door showed him the way.

Outside he tripped over a molehill subversively dug in the garden. He picked himself up, brushed himself off, called out, 'Who's there?' and waited intently for an answer, his myopic eyes boring into the night while his large hoary head swivelled back and forth like an owl's.

The lecherous shout was not repeated. It never was. Each time it was sounded but once.

The coarse words, Pinness brooded, were a battle cry of decadence, of mean hedonism, of individualism run wild – in short, of gross breach of conduct. Reluctantly the old teacher, 'under whose tutelage our children were reared to a life of high ideals and hard work', recalled the great chocolate robbery, in which several of his eldest pupils had raided the village co-op; the steamer trunk of Riva Margulis, which had arrived from Russia bursting with seductive luxuries and outrageous frills; and the devilish laughter of the hyena haunting the fields outside the village, 'smirking and up to no good'.

The thought of the hyena when he was without his spectacles and unable to see a thing plunged the alarmed Pinness into an all but paralysing anxiety.

The hyena was a sometime visitor to the area, a messenger unleashed from the worlds that lay beyond the wheat fields and the blue mountain. Several times in the years since the founding of the village the old teacher had heard its clear, mocking bark ring out from the nearby wadi, and a shiver had run down his spine.

The hyena's bite was highly dangerous. Some of its victims were so badly infected that they sowed penicillaria in autumn and pruned their vineyards in summer. Others took leave of their senses and became doubters, cynics, even turncoats, forsaking the land and drifting off to the city, or else dying or even leaving the country.

Pinness was beside himself with worry. He had lived long

enough to see the many fallers by the wayside, the slinking deserters re-embarking in the ports, the haggard suicides at rest in their graves. He saw renegades and deviants everywhere – 'The parasitic Talmudists of Jerusalem, the messianic millenarians of Safed, the credulous Communists, disciples of Lenin and Michurin, who were the ruin of the Workers' Brigade'. Long years of observation and reflection had taught him how easily a man was struck down once his immune system failed him.

'It especially attacks children, because their young minds are still vulnerable,' he warned, demanding that the schoolhouse be guarded around the clock when the scurrilous creature's tracks were discovered near the farmers' houses. At night he joined the posse of young men, his former pupils, who sought to track the fiend down. But the hyena was wily and elusive.

'Like other traitors we've known,' said Pinness at one of the village's general meetings.

One night when he was out hunting shrews and tree toads for the school nature corner, he saw the hyena cross the planted fields on the other side of the wadi and come toward him with the steady, distance-devouring lope of a wild beast. Pinness stopped in his tracks while the creature fixed its bright orange eyes on him and purred seductively. He could clearly make out the large, sloping shoulders, the bulging jaws, and the striped coat that swelled and bristled along the ridged backbone.

The hyena quickened its pace, trampling the tender vetch sprouts, and threw the old pedagogue a last mocking smile, baring its purulent fangs as it vanished into a wall of sorghum. Only when he realised that he had forgotten to take his gun along did Pinness understand the reason for 'that sly grin'.

'Pinness always forgets his gun,' said the farmers upon hearing of the nocturnal encounter. They still recalled how, long ago, when the village was newly founded and Pinness's wife Leah died of malaria while pregnant with twin daughters, he had risen from the deathbed of his beloved, whose body continued to exude green sweat even after it was cold and still, and taken off on the run for the copse of acacia trees in the wadi that was a popular spot for suicides. Several friends who rushed to the rescue found him lying among the golden thistles, sobbing bitterly. 'He forgot his gun then too.'

Now, thinking agitatedly of the abominable beast, of his dead wife, and of her two blue, sinless foetuses, Pinness stopped shouting, 'Who's there?', returned to his room, found his glasses, and hurried off to my grandfather.

Pinness knew that Grandfather rarely slept. He knocked and entered without waiting, the slam of the screen door waking me up. I glanced at Grandfather's bed. As usual it was empty. The smell of his cigarette drifted in from the kitchen.

I was fifteen years old. Most of those years had been passed in Grandfather's cabin. He had raised me with his own hands, the hands of a planter. Under his watchful eyes I had grown, bound tightly by the heavy raffia of his yarns. In the village I was known as 'Mirkin's orphan', but Grandfather, a man merciful, zealous, and vengeful, never called me anything but 'my child'.

He was as old and pale as though he had dipped himself in the white unguent he painted the trunks of his fruit trees with each spring. He was also short, sinewy, moustached, and mostly bald, with eyes that had slowly receded into their sockets and lost their lustre until they had come to resemble grey, nebulous rock pools.

On summer nights Grandfather liked to sit at the kitchen table in his faded undershirt and blue shorts, filling the room with smoke and good, woody, milky smells while swinging viney legs that were gnarled from work, and reliving old memories and iniquities. He had a habit of jotting down his thoughts on scraps of paper, which later flew about the room like swarms of migrating butterflies. He kept awaiting the return of whomever he had lost. 'To see them again become flesh before my eyes,' I once found written on a note that fluttered into my hand.

Many times, from the day I was old enough to wonder about it until the day he died, I asked him, 'What are you thinking about, Grandfather?' His answer was always the same. 'About you and me, my child.'

We lived in the old cabin. Casuarinas showered their needles on its roof, and I climbed up there twice a year on Grand-father's orders to brush layers of them off. The cabin floor was raised above the ground to keep the wooden walls free of insects and dampness, and the dark, narrow hollow beneath it resounded with the wars of hedgehogs and snakes and the soft scratching of skink scales. Once, after a huge, poisonous centipede crawled into the room, Grandfather bricked off this space. But the death groans and grunts for mercy coming from below persuaded him to dismantle his enclosure, and he never repeated the experiment.

Our cabin was one of the last in the village. The founding fathers had spent their first funds on concrete sheds for the cows, made vulnerable to the vagaries of the weather by long centuries of domestication that had rendered them deaf to the call of the wild. The pioneers themselves lived in tents and later in wooden cabins. Years went by before a brick house stood in every farmyard. Ours was inhabited by my uncle Avraham, his wife Rivka, and my twin cousins Yosi and Uri.

Grandfather hadn't wanted to leave the cabin. A planter of trees, he was a lover of wood.

'A wooden house breathes, sweats, and moves,' he told me. 'No two people make the same sound when they walk in it.' Proudly he pointed at the thick beam over his bed that put out a green sprig every spring.

The cabin had two rooms and a kitchen. In one room Grand-father and I slept on our iron beds, whose prickly mattresses were stuffed with seaweed. There was a large, simple clothes closet, and next to it, the 'commode', and a chest of drawers with a cracked marble top; in its uppermost drawer Grandfather kept his raffia twine and rolls of Graftex. In the pouches of a leather belt hanging from a nail on the wall were his red-handled shears, his grafting knives, and a tube of homemade black tar for pruning cuts. His other things – his pruning saw, his alembics of salves and poisons, his pots for mixing his 'Bordeaux Soup', his solutions of arsenic, nicotine, and pyrethrum – were kept in the locked storeroom by the cowshed where my uncle Efrayim had shut himself up prior to his final disappearance.

In the second room were the kind of books that could be found in every house in the village: Bodenheimer and Klein's *The Farmer's Insect Book*, blue-bound issues of *Field* and *The Planter*, a copy of *Yevgeni Onegin* in a light cloth binding, a black Bible, the Mitzpeh and Stiebel series of Hebrew literature, and the books that Grandfather loved most of all, the two greenish volumes of Luther Burbank's *Harvest of the Years*. '"Small, lithe, slightly stooped," he had "knees and elbows bent a little from long years of the hardest physical labour,"' Grandfather read to me from the introduction to the American plant wizard's autobiography. Burbank, though, had eyes of 'a deep and placid blue', while Grandfather's had turned grey.

Next to the Burbank was a row of memoirs written by people who were Grandfather's friends. I still remember the titles of some of them: *Native Paths*, *From the Don to the Jordan*, *My Earth*, *The Road Home*. These friends were the heroes of my childhood stories. All of them, Grandfather told me in his Russian accent, had been born in a faraway land that they left 'clandestinely' long ago, some in railroad cars full of *muzhiks* – poor Russian farmers – on trains that 'travelled slowly amid snow and wild apple trees' via rocky coasts, great salt lakes, bald hills, and sandstorms. Others, mounted on wild geese whose wings stretched as far as 'from the hayloft to the brooding house', soared with joyous quacks over vast fields and high above the Black Sea. Still others knew secret passwords that 'carried them off in a gale' to the Land of Israel, where they landed all in a sweat, afraid to open their eyes. And then there was Shifris.

'When we were already at the railway station at Makarov and the conductor blew the all-aboard, Shifris suddenly announced that he wasn't coming with us. Finish your tomato, Baruch.'

I opened my mouth, and Grandfather slipped a slice of tomato sprinkled with rock salt into it.

'Shifris said to us, "Comrades! To the Land of Israel we should go on foot, like pilgrims." And with that he parted from us, shouldered his pack, waved, and disappeared in a puff of steam. He's still trudging along on his way, the last pioneer to arrive.'

Grandfather told me about Shifris so that someone would

know who he was when he came. Long after all the others had given up or died without waiting, I went on expecting him. I would be the boy who ran to greet him when he neared the village. Each dot on the distant flank of the mountain was his approaching form. A circle of ashes by the side of a field was the campfire he had made to boil tea. Tufts of wool in a hawthorn tree were the remains of his torn puttees. Every unfamiliar footprint in the dirt was a sign he had left as he passed by.

I asked Grandfather to show me Shifris's route on the map, the borders he had crossed clandestinely, the rivers he had forded. I was fourteen years old when Grandfather said to me, 'That's enough of Shifris.'

'He really did say he would walk,' he told me. 'But after a few days he must have run out of steam. Or else something happened to him on the way – maybe he got sick or hurt himself or joined the Party or fell in love . . . who knows, my child? There's more than one thing can nail a man down to a place.'

On one of his slips of paper, in tiny letters, I found this note: 'The flowering, not the fruit. The way, not the distance covered.'

The books were propped against a large Philco radio that subscribers to *Field* could buy in easy instalments. Facing them were a couch and two armchairs that my uncle Avraham and his wife Rivka had moved to Grandfather's cabin after refurnishing their house. Grandfather called this room the living room, although his guests always sat at the large table in the kitchen.

Pinness stepped inside. I recognised at once the loud voice that had taught me Bible and nature.

'Mirkin,' he said, 'he's been shouting again.'

'Who was it this time?' asked Grandfather.

'I'm screwing Liberson's granddaughter,' said Pinness loudly and emphatically. Shutting the window apprehensively, he added, 'Not me, whoever shouted.'

'That's wonderful,' said Grandfather. 'A most accomplished fellow. Would you care for some tea?'

I strained to hear their conversation. More than once I had

been caught eavesdropping behind open windows, a secret listener among fruit trees and bales of hay. With a practised movement I would wrest myself free of the hands gripping me and walk away with head high and shoulders squared, silent and untouchable. Later, when the injured party came to complain, Grandfather wouldn't believe a word of it.

I heard his old feet scrape across the wooden floor, followed by the pouring of water, the tinkle of teaspoons against thin glass, and loud slurps. I had stopped being surprised long ago by the way the old people of the village could hold burning glasses in their hands and calmly swallow boiling water.

'The nerve of him!' said Pinness. 'How could he shout like that? Shooting his foul mouth off in the trees!'

'It's just someone's idea of a joke,' said Grandfather.

'But what should I do?' groaned the old schoolteacher, who took it as his personal failure. 'How can I show my face to the village?'

He rose and began pacing relentlessly. I could hear him cracking his knuckles in chagrin.

'Boys will be boys,' said Grandfather. 'Why get so worked up about it?'

The chuckle creeping into his voice enraged Pinness even more. 'Screaming at the top of his lungs so that the whole world can hear him!'

'Look, Ya'akov,' said Grandfather soothingly, 'we live in a small place. If someone goes too far, he'll be caught by the night watchmen and the Committee will take it up at a meeting. Why get all worked up?'

'But I'm the teacher,' stormed Pinness. 'The teacher, Mirkin, the educator! It's me they'll blame.'

Filed away in Meshulam Tsirkin's documentary archives was Pinness's famous declaration at the 1923 Conference of the Movement: 'The biological ability to bear children is no guarantee of the ability to educate them.'

'No one's going to blame you for some horny young ass,' said Grandfather sharply. 'You've given the village and the Movement a splendid generation of youngsters.'

'I can picture every one of them,' said Pinness softly. 'They come to the first form as tender as baby rushes, like flowers that I weave into the brocade of our life.'

Pinness never spoke of 'years', only of 'forms'. I smiled to myself in the darkness, knowing what would come next. Pinness liked to compare education to agriculture. When talking about his work, he was prone to expressions like 'virgin earth', 'an unpruned vine', 'irrigation holes'. His pupils were saplings. Each form was a furrow.

'Mirkin,' he continued emotionally, 'I may not be a farmer like the rest of you, but I too sow and reap. They're my vineyard, my orchard. It only takes one rotten apple . . .' He almost choked on his own despair. 'Yea, and it brought forth wild grapes. . . . Screwing! The issue of horses and the flesh of asses!'

Like all his pupils, I was used to his quoting from the Bible, but I had never heard verses like these from him before. Unwittingly I moved in my bed and froze at once. The floorboards creaked beneath the weight of my body, and the two of them fell silent for a minute. At the age of fifteen I weighed close to sixteen and a half stone and could grab a large calf by the horns and wrestle it to the ground. My size and strength were marvelled at in the village, the farmers joking that Grandfather must be feeding me colostrum, the vim-giving first milk of nursing cows.

'Not so loud,' said Grandfather. 'You'll wake the child.'

The child; that's what he called me until the day he died. 'My child.' Even when dark hair had sprouted all over my body. Even when my voice had changed and my shoulders had grown broad and beefy. My cousin Uri couldn't stop laughing when our voices began to crack. I was the only boy in the village, he said, whose voice went from baritone to bass.

Pinness uttered a few sentences in Russian, the language the founding fathers switched to for angry whispers, after which I heard a metallic pop that was the sound of Grandfather opening a can of homemade olives with a screwdriver. Now he would place a full saucer of them on the table. As soon as Pinness, who had a great liking for anything hot, sour, or salty, began to devour them, his mood would lighten at once.

'Do you remember, Mirkin, how we stepped off the boat, a bunch of yokels from Makarov, and ate black olives in that restaurant in Jaffa? And that pretty blonde girl with the blue kerchief who waved to us in the street?'

Grandfather didn't answer. Words like 'Do you remember . . .' left him cold. Besides, I knew he couldn't talk because he had an olive in his mouth and was sucking on it slowly as he sipped his tea. 'Either you eat or you remember,' he once said to me. 'There's only so much you can chew on at once.'

It was a habit of his to keep a cracked olive in his mouth while he drank his tea and nibbled gingerly at the sugar cube hidden in his palm, enjoying the soft, bittersweet combination. 'Tea and olives. Russia and the Land of Israel.'

'These olives are good,' said Pinness, growing affable. 'Wonderful. How few are the pleasures left us, Mirkin, how very few indeed, and how few are the things that still excite us! Can thy servant taste what I eat or what I drink? Can I hear any more the voice of singing men and singing women?'

'You seemed excited enough when you walked in,' Grandfather remarked.

'What gall!' spat Pinness. I could hear the olive stone shoot from his mouth, bounce off the table, and fly into the sink. Then there was silence, in which I knew that a new olive was slowly being crushed between Grandfather's false teeth, releasing its subtly bitter juice.

'And Efrayim?' asked Pinness suddenly. 'Have you heard anything of Efrayim?'

'Not a word,' replied Grandfather with predictable aloofness. 'Nothing.'

'It's just you and Baruch, eh?'

'Just me and the child.'

Just Grandfather and me.

The two of us. From the day he carried me in his arms from my parents' house to the day I carried him in my arms to his grave in the orchard.

Just him and me.

# 2

My eyes clouded over with longing for Grandfather. I rose from the big leather armchair and wandered through the rooms of my home, the big house I bought after growing up, burying him and his friends in the orchard, becoming rich, and leaving the village. 'Just me and the child' – I could not get these words to disappear back into their drawer. I went out to the mowed lawn and lay down facing the shore and the booming surf.

I had bought the house and everything in it from a banker who had to leave the country in a hurry. I never knew why, just as I never knew anyone of his ilk and was never inside a bank in my life. The money I received from the families of the deceased had been stashed away in some fertiliser sacks in the cowshed, next to the bedding of old Zeitser, who slept with the cows on principle.

'In the old days in Sejera I slept with the livestock too,' he declared.

Zeitser's large ears stuck out on either side of his old Russian worker's cap. He was able to wiggle them, and sometimes, when in a good mood, he gave in to the pleas of us children and showed us how he did it. Zeitser had unshakeable principles and a platform that bent reality like a clover stem. 'Zeitser,' Grandfather once wrote, 'is the only workers' party that never split into factions, because it never had more than one member.'

Busquilla, the manager of my cemetery, Pioneer Home, brought me to my new house in the same van we used for transporting coffins from the airport and old folk's homes, and headstones from old stone carvers in the Galilee.

It was a spacious white residence surrounded by a fragrant hedge of pittosporum. Busquilla surveyed it with a satisfied look before ringing the buzzer on the electronic gate. As soon as I told him that the last of the pioneers was dead, that there was no room for even one more grave, and that I wanted to shut down the business and leave the village, he went and found me a new place to live. He bought it on his own, haggling with the agents and wearing down the lawyers with his poisonous good nature.

Standing there with him in front of the big gate, I realised that I had never lived in a real house in my life. My only home had been Grandfather's wooden cabin, the likes of which the other farmers in the village had long ago turned into sheds or chopped into firewood.

I was wearing my blue work clothes. Busquilla, in a light linen suit, was carrying a sack in one hand. The banker hurried out to us, a plump, agile man propelled by flabby muscles along the polished floor tiles.

'Ah,' he called out. 'It's the undertakers.'

Busquilla said nothing. Years of ideological warfare with our village and the Movement had taught him that our cemetery was resented by whomever was not buried in it. He untied the sack and dumped the dusty banknotes on the rug, sending up a noxious cloud of ammonium sulphate. Then, stepping up to the gasping banker, he slapped him hard on the back with one hand while shaking his hand with the other.

'Busquilla, Mordecai, director,' he announced. 'It's all in cash, as agreed. Please be so kind as to count it.'

Busquilla is my right-hand man. He's a good friend too, though he's a generation older than me. A short, sharp, thin-haired, thin-bodied man who always gives off an agreeable smell of green soap.

While the banker gathered up the notes, Busquilla showed me around the large house, leading me over entrapping rugs, past fancy crystal and a collection of silver goblets. Sketches and portraits peered down at me in anger and astonishment from every wall. Busquilla stuck his head into a walk-in cupboard where dozens of suits were hanging, and fingered the fabrics with an appraiser's expertise.

'What will you do with all this?' he asked. 'His clothes will be small on you.'

I told him to take whatever he liked. He put on a record, flooding the white interior with the soprano screech of an opera singer. The banker rushed furiously over.

'Can't you wait to have your party until I leave?' he snapped.

'The faster you count, the faster that will be,' smiled Busquilla. 'It's for your own good.' He put an arm around the banker's portly waist, spun him around in a dance step, and steered him gently back toward the pile of money.

Soon the lawyers arrived with the papers to sign. The banker took his luggage and made a quick getaway, and Busquilla, a drink already in his hand, went to wish him bon voyage from the terrace. Returning, he saw I looked depressed.

'Maybe I should leave?'

'Stay,' I said. 'You may as well sleep here. We'll have breakfast together, and then you can go.'

The banker's large bed was the first in my life that my legs did not stick out of. My body was not used to the submissive mattress, the black feel of silk perfumed with degeneracy, the redolence of fancy women who had left their prurient crinkles in the sheets. And yet the walls built in me by Pinness and Grandfather were impregnable. The calloused soles of my feet shredded the soft fabric, and the scent of leather and wood panelling left no more trace on my skin than the glitter of chrome and crystal.

It was a quarter of an hour before dawn when I fell asleep, and then only for a few minutes. Grandfather's schedule was branded in my flesh like a tattooed clock. He always woke before me, put my breakfast on the table, gave me a quick, rough shake, and went out to work in the orchard. 'It's best to catch the pears before they're wide awake,' he explained to me.

Busquilla was still sleeping. I opened the large glass door and stepped outside. The banker's garden was too sweet-smelling, full of pompous flowers I had never seen before. Pinness had taught us to be experts in wildflowers and field crops exclusively.

'Dahlias and freesias are bourgeois plants,' he told us. 'Our ornamentals are the jonquil and the burnet, our gardens the vineyard and the clover patch.'

'That Burbank of yours,' he jeered at Grandfather, 'wasted good time growing chrysanthemums.'

Looking about me, I saw the sea for the first time in my life. It had always hidden behind the mountain, though I knew of it from Grandfather's stories, because its waves had borne him and my father to this country and sprayed the handsome face of my lost uncle Efrayim as they carried him off to war. Half an hour later I was joined on the lawn by Busquilla, wearing a dressing gown and carrying a tray full of toast and tall glasses of juice.

We sat at one end of the garden, where my eyes, peering into the bushes, immediately picked out a balloon spider's web still shiny with dew. Busquilla guffawed while I crawled over on all fours to search for the spider itself. It was hiding in a little tent of dry leaves stitched together with filaments, lying in wait for its prey. It was Pinness who first showed me a balloon spider, in Grandfather's orchard. Early that summer he had taken me often to 'the School of Nature' to look for insects and spiders. With astounding agility, his old hand trapped a fly on a leaf and cast it onto a web.

'Watch closely, Baruch,' he said.

The spider came running down a radial strand, wrapped the fly in white shrouds, flipped the tiny mummy this way and that between its hairy legs, gave it a little poison kiss, and carried it off deftly to its hideaway. I stood up and walked back to Busquilla.

'Well, do you feel better now?' he asked, amused. 'You'll be all right here? I had the insects especially ordered for your new garden.'

When I was five, Grandfather and Pinness took me to Eliezer Liberson's almond grove. Grandfather strode over to a tree, dug a little by its roots, and showed me signs of chewing and tunnelling beneath its bark. He ran his fingers over the trunk, pressing gently until he found what he was looking for, and then took out his grafting knife and cut an exact square in the bark. The large grub that appeared was a good four inches long, pale yellow in colour, with a broad, hard head that was much darker. Struck by the sunshine, it began to wriggle and curse.

'Capnodis,' said Grandfather. 'The foe of the almond, the apricot, the plum, and every stoned fruit.'

'Whose work is done in darkness,' quoted Pinness.

Grandfather pried the grub loose from its burrow with his knife tip and flung it to the ground. I felt a wave of anger and disgust.

'We brought you here,' Pinness said, 'because your grandfather's trees don't have pests like this. Mother Capnodis stays away from trees that are healthy and well kept. She looks for the sickliest sheep in the flock and deposits her eggs there. Let her but see a robust tree bubbling with juices and she will straightaway seek another victim that is bitter, dry, and despondent. There she lays her eggs of doubt, which soon ravage the tormented soul from within.'

Grandfather turned away to hide his smile while Pinness kept me from crushing the grub with my foot.

'Let it be,' he said. 'The jays will put it out of its misery. If the thief be found breaking in and be smitten so that he die, there shall be no bloodguilt for him.'

We went home, Grandfather holding me by one hand and Pinness by the other. Both were named Ya'akov. Ya'akov Mirkin and Ya'akov Pinness.

On another such outing Pinness showed me a capnodis beetle strolling on the branch of a tree.

'She disguises herself as a black, rotten almond,' he whispered.

When I reached for it, it tucked in its legs and fell like a pebble to the ground. The old teacher bent to pick it up and dropped it in a jar of chloroform.

'She's so tough,' he told me, 'that it takes a little hammer to drive the pin into her.'

The two old men drank a dozen glasses of tea, ate a pound of olives, and at 3 a.m. Pinness announced that he was going home and that if he ever found the Casanova, 'he'll rue the day he was born'.

He opened the door and stood facing the darkness for a

moment. Then he turned around and said to Grandfather that he felt heavy at heart because he had just thought of the hyena.

'The hyena is dead, Ya'akov,' said Grandfather. 'No one knows that better than you do. Relax.'

'Every generation has its enemies,' said Pinness darkly as he left.

He made his way home through the warm thicket of the night, treading upon 'the thin crust on which our life has been established', and thinking, I knew, of the menacing creatures of havoc that hatched and swarmed ceaselessly around him, bursting in his sombre nightmares like the bubbles of a foul, unruly past. He could sense the silent squat of the mongoose and see the blood-spotted face of the wildcat padding on its silken-pawed rampage of murder and plunder. Mice gnawed at the farmer's labours in the fields of grain, and beneath the chequered carpet of ploughed field, stubble, and orchard, waiting for the first signs of Doubt, growled the most legendary beast of all, the great swamp imprisoned by the founders. Far in the west he saw the orange-glowing lights of the big city beyond the mountain, with their seductive glitter of exploitation and corruption, of easy money, carnal baubles, and lewd winks.

It took Grandfather a few minutes to clean up in the kitchen. Then he turned out the light and came into the bedroom. He leaned over me for a moment, and I shut my eyes to make believe I was asleep.

'My little child,' he whispered, his moustache tickling my cheeks and mouth.

I was fifteen years old, over sixteen stone of raw muscle and bristly black hair, but Grandfather still made sure to cover me every night. He had done so on the first night he brought me home, and he did so now. Only then did he take his pyjamas from the linen chest under the bed. I watched him undress, undiminished and untarnished by the years. Even when I buried him in our orchard in the middle of the night, taking off the new pyjamas he had requested before dying, his body still gleamed with the same mysterious whiteness that had enveloped it all his life. All his friends were deeply bronzed, their skin cracked and crisped by molten years of light and labour. But Grandfather had never gone out to his trees without a wide-brimmed straw hat and long sleeves, and his face was still pale as a sheet, unmarked by the whip lines of the sun.

He opened the window and got into bed with a sigh.

# 3

Meshulam Tsirkin shook his head at the end of each sentence, sending a handsome ripple through his mane of grey hair and splaying the bitter lines in his cheeks. Even as a child I had never liked this master-of-no-trades who lived at the other end of the village. 'Who gave you such a big body and such a small brain?' he used to ask me with a slap on my back, breaking into his cackling laugh.

Meshulam was the son of Mandolin Tsirkin, who, together with Grandfather, Grandmother Feyge, and Eliezer Liberson, organised the Feyge Levin Workingman's Circle. Mandolin was a good farmer and a wonderful musician, and today he is buried in my cemetery.

Pesya Tsirkin, Meshulam's mother, was a functionary in the Movement and spent little time at home. Though Meshulam was fed by charitable neighbours and had to do his own and his father's washing, he adored his mother and was proud of her contribution to the cause. The most he saw her was once or twice a month, when she arrived with her big breasts and important visitors, who were always 'comrades from the Central Committee'. All of us children saw them too. My cousin Uri would be the first to spot the grey Kaiser parked by the Tsirkin house and to inform the rest of us, 'They're here again to smell the cow shit and have their pictures taken with the calves and the radishes.'

In a world in which his mother came and went, Meshulam was always on the lookout for a tolerable niche. He stayed clear of the imaginative mazes in which other children lost their way. The old pioneers wove a different web for him than for me. He devoted his keen memory and thirst for knowledge to research, documentation, and the collecting of historical artifacts, and found solace in perusing old by-laws, deciphering correspondence, and thumbing through papers so ancient that they fell apart at a touch.

Already as an adolescent he displayed several proud exhibits, each with a handwritten card: 'Liberson's Hoe', 'Milk Can, c. 1924', 'The First Plough (a product of the Goldman Bros. Smithy)', and of course, 'My Father's Original Mandolin'. As he grew older he removed his father's old spray cans and rusty cultivator blades from the toolshed, retiled its roof, filled its two little rooms with broken kitchen utensils and decrepit furniture, and renamed it 'Founder's Cabin'. Rummaging through houses and farmyards, he found corroded flour sieves and washboards, copper pots that were green with age, and even an old mud sled.

'I want everyone to know how people once lived here,' he declared. 'I want them to know that before the road was paved the carts sank into such deep mud every winter that the milk had to be brought to the dairy on sleds.'

He was especially proud of the gargantuan stuffed figure of Hagit, Eliezer Liberson's half-Dutch, half-Lebanese cow, who was once national champion in milk production and fat content. When Hagit grew old and Liberson's son Daniel decided to sell her to the glue factory, Meshulam was up in arms. Calling for an emergency session of the village Committee, he protested that 'so dedicated a comrade' could not possibly be converted into sausages and gelatin. 'Hagit,' claimed Meshulam, 'is not just an agricultural phenomenon. She is the definitive proof that pure Holstein cows were not suited for conditions in this country.'

The Committee paid Liberson to deed the cow to Meshulam and even offered to give her a small pension. That very day, however, Meshulam dispatched the dedicated comrade with a generous portion of rat poison and stuffed her huge frame with the help of the veterinarian.

For years Hagit stood stinking of embalming fluids on the front porch of the Tsirkin house, her famed udders dripping formaldehyde while alfalfa stems dangled from her mouth. Meshulam regularly brushed her coat, which had large bald spots from the rat poison, polished her bovine glass eyes, and sewed up her cracked hide to keep the sparrows from stealing blades of straw and tufts of cotton wool for their nests.

The stuffed cow revolted the entire village, and especially Zeitser, who had been most attached to Hagit and her prodigious flow of milk, which he considered to be 'a symbol of our national renaissance'. Sometimes he stole from our yard for a look at her. Each time he was face to face with her, he told us, he was seized by a combination of 'horror and longing'.

'The poor cow,' he murmured to himself. 'Meshulam Tsirkin stuffed her with more straw than Liberson ever gave her to eat in her whole lifetime.'

My irreverent cousin Uri, however, who looked down on the village from his mockingbird's-eye view, was sure that the stuffed cow had nothing to do with Meshulam's historical research.

'Hagit's udders reminded him of his mother,' he said to me. 'It's that simple.' And I looked at him as I do to this day; with love and with envy.

Our village has many visitors. Busloads of tourists and schoolchildren come to see the flourishing creation of the founding fathers. Excitedly they stroll the village streets, oohing and aahing over every pear and chicken and breathing in the smells of earth and milk. Their tours always end in my cemetery on the old Mirkin farm.

Meshulam demanded that no tourist buses be allowed into the village and Pioneer Home unless they also stopped at Founder's Cabin for a look at Hagit and the gold medal from the British High Commissioner that hung around her stuffed neck.

Pioneer Home was anathema to the whole village, but Meshulam Tsirkin hated it especially. The buses that rolled up to it, the wide-eyed children, the enchanted tourists who strolled agog among its freshly washed headstones and rosebushes, reading in whispers the legendary names in copper letters and drinking the cold fruit juice that Busquilla's younger brother sold them from a pitcher at the entrance gate – all this made his blood boil.

Meshulam Tsirkin hated my cemetery because I refused to bury his mother. I buried only Grandfather's friends of the Second Aliyah.

'I'm very sorry,' I said to him when he waved the *Trade Union Yearbook* in my face with an article about his mother's contribution to the Workers' Co-operative Credit Fund. 'Your mother came to this country after the First World War, when the Second Aliyah was over.'

'The deceased does not comply with our entrance requirements,' explained Busquilla.

When Meshulam threatened to appeal to the institutions of the Movement, I reminded him that he had already done so after old Liberson put out *The Pioneers' Album*, in which he refused to publish a photograph of Pesya for reasons similar to ours.

'Besides which,' said Busquilla, 'your father couldn't stand to have her near him when she was alive either.'

What most got Meshulam's goat were the lead coffins I brought from the airport. He knew that every new casket from America filled my old sacks with tens of thousands of dollars.

'By what right do you bury traitors who left this country, and not my own mother?' he screamed at me.

'Whoever came to this country with the Second Aliyah can buy a plot here,' I replied.

'You mean to tell me that any little fart who came here from Russia, chucked it all after two weeks of hoeing crabgrass, and went traipsing off to America can be buried here as a pioneer? Just look at that!' he shouted, pointing to one of the headstones. 'Rosa Munkin, the archfiend in person!'

Rosa Munkin, who had known Grandfather back in Makarov, was my first customer.

'Shall I tell you about Rosa Munkin?' asked Meshulam contemptuously after the outcry that arose when her pink headstone was unveiled beside Grandfather's grave. 'Rosa Munkin came here from the Ukraine, worked for a week in an almond grove in Rehovot, didn't like what the country did to her lily-white hands, and bombarded the whole world with SOSs. A brother of hers who had emigrated to America, a little bandit who became a pioneer Jewish gangster in Brooklyn, sent her a ticket to join him.'

Meshulam planted a foot on the pink marble slab in a gesture of patronising disdain.

'During the First World War, when your grandparents and my father and Eliezer Liberson nearly starved to death and Zeitser was conscripted into the Turkish army, Rosa Munkin bought her fourth corset shop in the Bronx. When the Feyge Levin Workingman's Circle was settling this village, Rosa Munkin saw the light, married a Rabbi Shneour from Baltimore, and began publishing anti-Zionist advertisements in the papers. During the Second World War, when your poor uncle Efrayim was wounded with the British commandoes, she was widowed, leased a suite in a Miami hotel, and ran her brother's casinos from there. In the files of the FBI she's known as "the Red Queen" to this day.

'And now,' he yelled, 'she's buried in your ground. In the earth of this Valley. A pioneer. A builder. A founding mother.'

'God rest her soul,' said Busquilla. He went over to the stone, politely removed Meshulam's foot, took a flannel rag from his pocket, and wiped the 'a' in 'Rosa'.

'You shut up, Busquilla,' said Meshulam, turning white. 'Shits like you should snap to attention when the founders are being discussed.'

'The deceased paid one hundred thousand dollars,' said Busquilla, to whom such slights meant nothing.

'Mafia money,' sneered Meshulam.

'Meshulam, what do you want from me?' I said. 'She came with the Second Aliyah.'

'And Shulamit?' screamed Meshulam. 'Did she come with the Second Aliyah too?'

'Don't be a wise guy,' I shot back angrily. 'Shulamit is a private family matter.'

When Rosa Munkin's letter arrived from America, Grandfather and Shulamit, his old love who came from Russia half a century after him – 'the Crimean whore,' as Fanya Liberson called her – were the only people buried in the orchard. Busquilla, who was the village postman at the time, came galloping up on Zis, the post office donkey, shouting, 'An aerogram! An aerogram! A letter from America!'

I was watering the year-round Burbank roses I had planted by Grandfather's and Shulamit's graves.

Luther Burbank had also left home because of a tragic love affair. And though Grandfather often told me about Burbank's fruit trees, prickleless prickly pears, and light-skinned potatoes, it was to my uncle Avraham's twin sons Uri and Yosi that he read the passage about Burbank's unrequited love, which made me so jealous that I almost burst into tears.

I slammed the door of the cabin and went outside, where through the window I heard Grandfather continue to read as if oblivious to my torment: ' "The truth is that I was very deeply fond of a beautiful young lady who seemed to me, I remember, less ardent than I was. A trifling disagreement, two positive natures, probably hasty words – and I determined that my heart was broken. To be frank, I think I gave that affair to many as my reason for coming West." '

'Don't shout,' I scolded Busquilla. 'This is one place where I won't have any shouting.'

He handed me the envelope and stood waiting by my side.

Busquilla arrived in the village in the early fifties, when Grandfather was still alive and I was still his child. Walking into the village co-op, he stood by the till where Shlomo Levin was seated. Busquilla, who was wearing loafers and a funny blue beret on his head, glanced down at the counter while pleasureably slurping a bottle of grapefruit juice. Levin was mumbling numbers as he added up a customer's bill.

'Two pounds fifty-four,' said Busquilla over Levin's shoulder before the storekeeper's pencil had finished the first column of numbers.

Levin's personal history had made him highly sensitive to *kibitzers*, people who advised you without being asked. There was nothing he liked less than feeling he was under surveillance, and turning around, he gave the uninvited guest an angry stare. The man, he saw at once, belonged to the transit camp for new immigrants that had been hastily erected on the hill beyond the eucalyptus woods, where it aroused the village's scorn and compassion. The villagers volunteered to help the newcomers, gave them surplus farm produce, and showed them how to use their work tools, but once back in the village they regaled each other with tales about the little men in blue berets who did nothing but drink, play cards, and shoot craps all day while 'longing for their caves in Morocco and wiping their rear ends with stones'.

The affront was so great that Levin sat there open-mouthed. He said nothing, however, and turned to the next customer.

'One pound seventeen,' announced Busquilla before Levin had even drawn a line beneath the numbers he had written down.

Shlomo Levin, who had managed the village store for decades, rose, doffed his cap, and demanded to know to whom he was speaking.

'Busquilla, Mordecai,' said the amazing newcomer. Sucking up the last of his juice, he added, 'Newly arrived from Morocco and looking for work.'

'So I see,' said Shlomo Levin.

In Morocco Busquilla had taught arithmetic and written letters in three languages for the courts and government offices. Now he was seeking a job as a book-keeper, a teacher, or a worker in the poultry incubator.

'I have a soft spot for baby chicks, children, and money,' he explained.

Though Levin was taken aback, he told Liberson, who was then the village treasurer, about the new immigrant.

'The man's got cheek, but he knows his arithmetic,' he said.

Busquilla's request was received sympathetically, although his weakness for money was held against him by most of the Committee members. 'Not to mention the beret,' said Uri. 'No one with any principles would ever wear anything but a worker's cap.'

'We discussed the matter in terms of our values, the overall needs of the new immigrants, and Busquilla's areas of competence,' Eliezer Liberson told me, 'and decided to try him out at onion picking.'

After two years, in the course of which Busquilla was indentured to the earth in such menial jobs as spraying insecticide, thinning corn, hoeing weeds, and picking fruit, the village postman heard the hyena laughing in the fields, lost his mind, bought a black crayon, and appointed himself censor of outgoing mail. The Committee fired him and gave his job and donkey to Busquilla. Busquilla planted Moroccan herbs around the post office, brewed spicy tea that had a maddening aroma, and won general approval by introducing home mail pick-up, thus saving the inhabitants the bother of betaking themselves to the village centre.

I opened the envelope. Since Shulamit's arrival from Russia, there had been no letters from abroad.

'What's in it, Baruch?' asked Busquilla discreetly.

'It's private,' I told him.

He backed off a few steps and leaned against Shulamit's gravestone, waiting to be asked to translate the letter.

'It's from some old lady in America,' he informed me after a glance at it. 'Her name is Rosa Munkin. She's from your grandfather's hometown. She was here many years ago, worked with him in Rishon-le-Tsiyyon and Rehovot, and thought the world of him. Someone wrote to her that you buried him at home, and she wants to be buried here too when she dies, right next to him.'

He handed me back the envelope. 'There's more in it,' he said.

Inside was a cheque made out to me for ten thousand dollars.

'This is just the down payment,' Busquilla said. 'She's a very sick woman and won't live much longer. Her lawyer will bring the rest of the money with her.'

'What am I supposed to do with this?' I asked, confused. 'It isn't even real money.'

'You'll need help, Baruch,' said Busquilla softly. 'We're talking big money. We're talking foreigners. We're talking English. We're talking lawyers and the Committee and income tax. You'll never manage it by yourself.'

With ten thousand dollars, I thought, I could plant the most fabulous trees around Grandfather's grave, Judas trees, flame trees, white oleanders. I could lay a path of red gravel from Grandfather to Shulamit. I could go looking for my lost uncle Efrayim or pay to have old Zeitser's stomach complaints taken care of.

'Don't breathe a word of this to anyone, Baruch,' said Busquilla. 'Not a soul. Not even your cousin Uri.'

That evening Busquilla came to the cabin with a black type-writer and wrote a letter for me in English. Rosa Munkin answered it, and three months later, in the middle of the night, she arrived personally in a shiny coffin, chaperoned by a lawyer with a headful of hair, a slick suit, and a smell of aftershave lotion such as had never perfumed the air of our village before. Vile and elegant, he stood watching me dig the grave.

'Just look at him,' Busquilla whispered. 'I know the type. This isn't the first corpse he's buried in the middle of the night.'

The lawyer sat in the dark on Grandfather's grave, dangled his polished shoes, and chewed on a blade of straw while disgustedly sniffing the odours of the village that came wafting on the warm night air from the cowsheds and chicken coops.

We lowered Rosa Munkin into the soil of the Valley. The American took a slip of paper and a skullcap from his pocket, recited a brief prayer in an incomprehensible Hebrew, instructed me to make a square concrete base for the headstone, and reached for a black attaché case in the back of his huge estate car. Busquilla counted the banknotes with a quick, moistened finger and made out a receipt.

A few days later the lawyer returned with a fancy stone of polished pink marble. To this day, among the grey and white stones chiselled out of local rock, Rosa Munkin's grave resembles a big box of candy.

I stashed the money away in the cowshed. Zeister was asleep

there, covered by the old army blanket that had been in his possession since the Great War, dead to the world. Then I returned with Busquilla to the cabin, where we sat at Grandfather's table drinking tea and eating bread with olives.

'I'm sure you'll want to tell your uncle Avraham and Pinness,' he advised me. 'Don't do it just yet, though. Wait a little while.'

The next day Busquilla quit his job at the post office and put himself at my disposal.

'I'll manage the business, and you can pay me what you think I'm worth,' he said.

That was the beginning of Grandfather's vengeance, which was carried out with the prophetic exactitude of a good planter, filled my sacks with money, and wreaked havoc on the most sensitive nerve centres of the village.

'They drove my son Efrayim from here,' he repeated to me and Pinness one last time before his death. 'But I'll get them where it hurts the most: in the earth.'

We didn't know then what he was talking about.

The Committee considered several candidates to fill Busquilla's position at the post office and finally settled on Zis. The donkey already knew every house in the village, and now that it was riderless, could carry packages too. Zis was the grandson of Katchke, a charter member of the village who had hauled water from the spring every day until he was murdered by a snake.

Zis, however, did not even last two years. 'The old-timers discovered that he was licking the stamps off the envelopes,' said my sardonic cousin Uri.

The Committee appealed to Busquilla to return to his old job, but by then he had a business card that said 'Manager, Pioneer Home' in Hebrew and in English, plus 'a herd of one hundred corpses', as old Liberson sarcastically put it until the death of his wife Fanya, his first and only love, who became the hundred and first.

# 4

The Mirkin farm was one of the most successful in the village.
So everyone said enthusiastically whenever Grandfather's fruit
trees broke into stormy bloom; so they said when my uncle
Avraham's cows gushed floods of milk; so they said, upset and
envious, when the cowshed filled with dusty insect moults and
bulging sacks of money while the orchard went to ruin and was
sown with bones and graves.

The graves ran in rows on either side of red and white gravel
paths. Scattered among them were green benches, flowering
shrubs, trees, and shady corners for meditation, and in the
middle was Grandfather's white gravestone. The whole village
shook its head at the sad fate of earth that was meant to bring
forth fruit and fodder but had become a great field of revenge.

'It's really quite simple,' I told myself, wandering through the
large rooms of my house. 'Why keep picking at it, prying and
looking for answers?'

Wasn't that why Grandfather had raised me to be what I was?
He had made me as big and strong as an ox and as faithful and
savage as a sheepdog, thick-skinned and thick-headed. And now
he lies in his grave, surrounded by dead friends and tickled pink
by the village's conniptions.

'Leave him alone. The child is nothing but a bag of yarns and
tall tales,' said Pinness when I announced that I had no intention
of appearing before the Committee for a hearing.

I was no longer a child. I was a rich young giant, burdened
with my money and my bulk. Pinness, however, had a way of
extending his pupils' childhoods to all ages, continuing to pat
them on heads that had long since grown bald or grey. 'Who
knows how many memories were crammed into the boy's big
body until it just burst and spilled its bile?' he asked rhetorically.

If Grandfather had been alive, he would have dismissed such a remark by saying that although Pinness knew many fine parables, 'he sometimes forgets what they're about'.

When asked to abandon the mortuary business, I myself always replied, 'I'm only doing what Grandfather wanted.' I sent Busquilla and his hired lawyer to the Committee hearing because they were outsiders, as smooth as they were crude. The fallen leaves of stories had not covered them, and the soles of their shoes kept the Valley's fine dirt off their feet. I pictured the scrape of spartan chairs in the Committee room, the broken-nailed hands drumming like hooves on the table. Let the two of them face those stalwart eyes for me, those rough fingers jabbing the air.

I was only Grandfather's little child, doing what he wanted. I had nothing more to say.

In Odessa Grandfather and his brother Yosef boarded the *Ephratos*, a small, filthy ship 'full of bad people' that plied the Mediterranean and Black seas. Like two sides of the same coin, Ya'akov and Yosef Mirkin saw different halves of the world. 'My brother was excited, tempestuous. He paced back and forth in the prow of the ship, looking straight ahead.'

Yosef nurtured dreams of white donkeys, Hebrew power, and Jewish homesteads in the mountains of Gilead. Grandfather thought of Shulamit, who had stayed behind after threshing his flesh with the flails of deceit and jealousy, and of Palestine, which was for him but a refuge from crimes of passion, a land beyond the borders of memory where he and his wounds might grow scar tissue.

He sat in the stern of the ship and gazed at the water, his bare heart unravelling behind him in the foam. 'Can't you see? Our warm hearts come apart like balls of twine,' he wrote in a note long years later.

During their days at sea, when all they ate was bread and dried figs, Ya'akov and Yosef Mirkin vomited incessantly.

'We arrived in this country and headed north. By summer Yosef and I were on the shores of the Sea of Galilee.' Grandfather's hand travelled back and forth, shovelling mashed potatoes mixed with homemade yoghurt and salty fried onions into my mouth. 'The first night we found work guarding the fields, and at dawn we sat down to see how the sun rose in the Promised Land. It came up at half past four. By quarter past five it was trying to kill us. Yosef hung his head and started to cry. That wasn't how he had imagined the day of redemption.'

Now his hands were busy with the salad. 'We were three friends. Mandolin Tsirkin, Eliezer Liberson, and me. My brother Yosef fell ill, couldn't take any more, and ran away to America.'

Hot, weak, and irritable, Grandfather oscillated between attacks of malaria and spasms of anger and longing.

Yosef made it big in California. 'When we were still walking around wrapped in burlap in winter, our socks stuffed with newspapers to keep out the cold, he was selling suits to bourgeois Americans.' When the village was hooked up to electricity a few months before Grandmother Feyge died and Yosef sent a money order so they could buy a refrigerator, Grandfather threw the letter into the slops ditch by the cowshed and told Grandmother that he would never touch 'the dollars of a capitalist traitor'. Yosef then went to Santa Rosa, Luther Burbank's small and beloved farm that attracted sentimental hordes of visitors, insects, and fan mail, and sent Grandfather a signed photograph of the great planter. I saw him in the trunk beneath Grandfather's bed with his straw hat, polka dot tie, and fleshy earlobes. 'But even a gesture like that couldn't reconcile Mirkin.'

Fanya Liberson was Grandmother's best friend.

'Feyge, who was already sick and weak, short of breath and love, came to me in tears,' she said after I had pestered her for hours, following her expectantly about. 'But not even we could convince your grandfather. He made her go on carrying those big blocks of ice for the icebox.'

'And your friend Mirkin was her biggest ice block of all,' Fanya said another time to her husband. Grandmother Feyge's sufferings and death still haunted her and made her furious anew each time she thought of them.

I couldn't hear Eliezer Liberson's murmured answer. Crouched by their house, my face pressed to the wet slats of the blinds, I saw only his lips as they moved, and her beautiful, bright old head laid across his chest.

Grandfather never forgave his brother and never saw him again. It was only after his death that I had Yosef exhumed and his bones brought from California to our Valley. His two sons, joint owners of the Mirkin & Mirkin Textile Company of Los Angeles, sent me a cheque for ninety thousand dollars.

'Your father was a capitalist traitor,' Busquilla wrote to them on the official stationery of Pioneer Home, 'but we are still giving you a ten per cent discount because he was a member of the family.'

The dead arrived in hosed-down farm trucks, in carts hitched to tractors, in the bellies of airplanes, in wooden coffins and lead caskets.

Sometimes there were big funerals with huge crowds and reporters and sweating troops of VIPs and politicians. Busquilla greeted them with scraping, sinuous gestures that disgusted me. They watched me dig the grave, shrinking back from the shower of earth I sent flying, while urging Busquilla to make his worker hurry up.

Other bodies came unattended, accompanied only by a bill of lading and a note with the inscription requested for the gravestone. Some were interred by a single angry son or weeping daughter. Some arrived alive, crawling through the fields with their last breath to be buried in Pioneer Home.

'With my old comrades,' they said. 'Next to Mirkin,' they pleaded. 'In the earth of the Valley.'

Before burying them, I opened their coffins in the shed by Busquilla's office to have a look at them. I had to make sure that no one ineligible was smuggled in.

The 'capitalist traitors' who arrived from America were already slightly decomposed. Their carnal frivolity moulted, they stared at me with fishy, apologetic eyes rheumy with supplication. The old comrades from the Valley were very quiet, as if napping under a tree in the fields. Many of them I knew from their visits to Grandfather or Zeitser when I was a boy, in their hands a gnawed branch, an old letter, or a leaf attacked by aphids that they had come to consult about. Others I knew only from stories, from answers to questions I had asked, and from what I had had to imagine myself.

Grandfather brought me to his cabin wrapped in a blanket when I was two years old. He washed the soot off me and picked the slivers of glass and wood from my skin. He raised me, fed me, and taught me the secrets of trees and fruit.

And told me stories. As I ate. As I weeded. As I pruned the wild suckers of the pomegranate trees. As I slept.

'My son Efrayim had a little calf called Jean Valjean. Efrayim got up every morning, took Jean Valjean out for a walk on his back, and returned home at noon. He did that each day. "Efrayim," I said to him, "that's no way to raise a calf. It will get so used to it that it will never want to use its own legs." But Efrayim didn't listen. Jean Valjean grew bigger and bigger until he became a huge bull. And even then Efrayim insisted on carrying him everywhere . . . That was my son Efrayim for you.'

'Where is Efrayim?'

'No one knows, my child.'

Though there were never tears in his eyes, the corners of his mouth sometimes trembled imperceptibly. Often, when the fruit trees were in blossom, or on an exceptionally fine day in the Valley, he told me about my uncle Efrayim's handsome looks.

'When he was still a little boy, the birds used to flock to his window to watch him wake up.

'Now I'll tell you about your mother. Ah-h-h . . . open your mouth, Baruch. She was an extraordinary young woman. Once, when she was a little girl, she was sitting on the pavement outside our cabin polishing the family's shoes: mine, and Grandmother Feyge's, and Uncle Avraham's, and Uncle Efrayim's, who still lived at home. Just then . . . open your mouth, my child . . . just then she saw a snake, a big viper, crawling slowly up the pavement, coming closer and closer.'

'And then?'

'And then . . . one more bite. What happened then?'

'What?'

'Did your mother run away?'

I knew the story by heart.

'No!'

'Did she cry?'

'No!'

'Did she faint?'

'No!'

'Well now, Baruch, my child, finish what's in your mouth. Swallow. Your mother didn't faint. What did she do? What did your mother do?'

'She sat there without moving.'

'And the viper came slowly, slowly crawling up the pavement, puffing and hissing, *psss*, *psss*, *psss*, until it was right next to your mother's bare foot. And then . . . she took the big shoe brush and . . .'

'Wham!'

'Right on the head of the snake.'

'Where is my mother?'

'You're with Grandfather now.'

'And the snake?'

'The snake is dead.'

'And my father?'

Grandfather rose and patted me on the head.

'You'll be as tall as your mother and as strong as your father.'

He showed me the crumbling flowers that my mother had dried as Pinness's pupil. He told me about a great river, 'a hundred times wider than our little wadi', about 'Gypsy thieves', about the poor German Templars who had tried settling the Valley before us until every one of their children, 'all yellow and shaking like baby chicks', died of malaria.

His fingers, used to binding grafts with raffia, hoeing weeds, and feeling fruit, undid my stained bib gently. He bent down to pick me up, his moustache springing against my neck as he tickled me with his breath.

'My child.'

'Where did Grandmother Feyge come from?'

Grandmother Feyge came from the same faraway land. She

was much younger than Grandfather, who was already an old farmhand when she arrived, inured to illness and able to digest whatever local slop was put before him. All the time, though, he thought of Shulamit, who had made his life wretched and now sent him letters from Russia. Twice a year a blue envelope arrived from her – via the Turkish mail, on winds that blew from the north, in the bills of the pelicans who came down to rest 'on their way to hottest Africa'.

# 5

Grandfather met Grandmother in Palestine when he, Eliezer Liberson, and Mandolin Tsirkin were working in Zichron Ya'akov, a town of private farmers supported by the philan-thropical Baron Edmond de Rothschild.

While the unruly trio sang Ukrainian songs 'to get the goat of the Baron's parasites', Feyge and her brother Shlomo Levin sat off to one side, their empty stomachs faint with hunger. Together they had come to Palestine and been cast by Arab stevedores onto a filthy wharf, from which they picked themselves up and wandered off in search of work, stricken by hunger, the sun, and dysentery. Their delicate mien discouraged employers, and when Shlomo Levin found work in a vineyard by removing the glasses that made him look too intellectual, his weak eyes could not tell the difference between a three- and four-bud cut, which made him ruin a whole row of grapevines and got him sacked on the spot.

They ate the potluck of charity: lentils in heartburn oil, Egyptian onions, Grade D oranges, brown strips of *kamardin*.

*Kamardin* was the poor man's candy, apricots boiled to a pulp and dried into leather. Each time I mouthed the word I could feel the sticky sweetness of its syllables. Shlomo Levin once told me how he loathed it.

'But it was cheap,' he said. 'And I and your grandmother, my poor sister, had no money.

'The poor need sweets because they're the taste of consolation,' he explained, still angered by the memory of how the boys of the village had stolen chocolate from his store. 'It's not as if they couldn't have afforded to pay for it, those big heroes!'

In Rehovot Feyge found temporary work as a seamstress. One day, as she was sitting on an empty orange crate patching clothes, several figures on horseback stopped in front of her. A thin, erect woman looked down from the saddle with lordly severity.

'Why are you doing ghetto work?' she scolded.

Feyge threw down her needle and thread, burst into tears, and ran off. Shlomo hurried after her.

'Do you know who that was?' he asked. 'That was Rachel Yana'it, the workers' leader.'

Ten years later, when Grandmother bought her first hen in the nearby Cherkessian village, she called her Rachel Yana'it and liked nothing better than to scold her for the tiny eggs she laid.

Feyge's hunger pangs flowed in her veins. She could feel them circulate through her heart, pumped all over her body. That day in Zichron Ya'akov, she and her brother were cleaning vats in the winery, and the fermentation vapours so tortured her empty belly that she felt she was going to faint. When the three young men working next to them stopped their singing and produced from their knapsacks pitta bread, olives, some slices of cheese, and a bottle of brandy stolen from the storeroom, her eyes clouded mistily over. They rubbed their hands and dug in. After a while Mandolin Tsirkin felt Feyge staring at the crumbs on his lips.

Tsirkin could read the hunger in anyone's eyes. With a tip of the neck of his mandolin, he invited her to partake.

'She looked like a hunted bird. I smiled at her with my eyes the way you smile at a child.'

Feyge let go of her brother's sleeve and joined them.

'She did eat of their own meat, and drank of their own cup,' quoted Pinness over Grandmother's grave.

Shlomo Levin didn't like the noisy threesome and was afraid of them. 'They ate and drank like Arab coolies and sang like Russian hooligans,' he told me in the office of the co-op. 'At a time when all of us were torn by a thousand loyalties and conflicts, nothing fazed them at all.'

He didn't look up at me. We sat by ourselves in his office, the sun glinting off the myriad particles of dust that danced outside the window. Levin was cutting carbon paper for the co-op's receipt books with his thumbnail. Though I was too young to understand everything he said, I didn't interrupt him with questions. Like the desert flowers in Pinness's collection, Levin opened up once every few years, and it would have been a great mistake to stop him.

'She fell for them at once,' he whispered, his blue fingers trembling. 'Like a dumb moth for the flame that kills it.'

Levin was shocked to see them tear off pieces of bread and cheese with their dirty fingers and put them in his sister's dry mouth. Though he tried to keep her away from them, that same night, when Liberson, Mirkin, and Mandolin Tsirkin were high from finishing their bottle of brandy, they founded the Feyge Levin Workingman's Circle 'in order to cheer your grandmother up'. They even voted a budget, wrote a constitution, and composed a preamble to it.

'The historians never took the Feyge Levin Workingman's Circle seriously,' said Meshulam Tsirkin to me. 'Perhaps it suffered from its name. What serious scholar would write a dissertation on an organisation with a name like that?' he grinned. 'Still, it was a living legend among the pioneers. It was the first true commune in this country, because it was the first to grant full equality to women. And though its by-laws were highly idiosyncratic, you'll find several important breakthroughs in them.'

Underneath Grandfather's bed in the cabin was a large wooden trunk. I shut the curtains and opened it. The documents lay beneath a white embroidered blouse, a Russian worker's cap, and a yellowing mosquito net. Her picture, too.

Grandmother smiled at me. She had two black braids and little hands, and looked as though she were about to come skipping right out of the photograph. Wheeling around, I saw Grandfather behind me, his pale face looking stern. He knelt by my side, prised my fingers from the picture one by one, returned it to the trunk, and took out an envelope with different photographs.

'This is Rilov, the famous Watchman,' he said in a mocking tone I knew well. Grandfather had never liked the members of the Watchmen's Society. 'Underneath that Arab cloak he's got two Mauser pistols and a French field cannon. Behind him is that good-for-nothing Rosa Munkin, and the two men lying down in front of him are Pinness and Bodenkin.'

He began to pace the room.

'In all our old photographs,' he said, 'you'll always find one row of us standing, another sitting, and two of us lying in front of them, propped on their elbows with their heads touching. One of those standing and one of those lying down always left the country in the end. One of those sitting always died young.'

He bent down, pulled an old sheet of paper from the trunk, and burst into laughter.

'Here,' he said. 'This is the constitution of the Feyge Levin Workingman's Circle.'

He stood up and began reading with a flourish.

'"Article One. The Feyge Levin Workingman's Circle will avoid the seductive and vain glamour of all cities.

'"Article Two. Comrade Levin will cook. Comrade Tsirkin will wash the dishes. Comrade Mirkin will look for work. Comrade Liberson will do the laundry and the talking.

'"Article Three. Comrades Tsirkin, Liberson, and Mirkin will make no dishonourable advances toward Comrade Levin.

'"Article Four. Comrade Levin will make no attempt . . ."'

The door of the cabin swung open and Meshulam Tsirkin barged inside, wagging his head energetically.

'Give that to me!' he shouted. 'Give it to me, Mirkin, I beg of you! I must have that document for the archives.'

'Why don't you go help your old man, he's bringing in the hay today,' said Grandfather. 'Make it quick, before I set Baruch on you.'

'Whatever you say about him,' said Meshulam Tsirkin after Grandfather's death, 'Mirkin was one of the revered figures of the Movement. It's no wonder that so many wasters are willing to pay a fortune to be buried next to him. That's a fine last will and testament he's left you!'

As soon as they signed the protocol, the three men turned to Feyge with deep ceremonial bows and asked her to join too. 'What about your brother?' asked Liberson once she had added her signature. Levin, however, pointed out gloomily that he hadn't yet made up his mind 'where my political sympathies lie'.

'In that case,' said Grandfather, 'since you have so much trouble making up your mind, you're the man we'll send to the next Zionist congress to deliver a speech on the subject.'

'You can always join the Hole Counters' Local,' said Mandolin Tsirkin. Until his dying day, 'hole counter' was the most savage term of abuse in his vocabulary.

Shlomo Levin rose disgustedly and went off to sleep in the workers' hostel, but realising the next morning that he was liable to be left all alone, he followed the Workingman's Circle southward to the vineyards of Judea.

'There were no roads or cars, and we didn't even own a horse,' said Grandfather. 'We walked the whole way and let the frogs guide us through the swamps.'

Although they seemed to him like a three-headed monster, Levin tagged after them for several days. Tsirkin played the mandolin until its notes 'nearly bore a hole in my skull'. Mirkin held them up for hours at a time to observe the slow dance of the stamen of the jujube tree. Liberson was the worst of them all. At night he lay croaking in low, lazy tones, keeping it up until he was covered with toads that converged on him from all directions. 'They're excellent sources of information,' he confided.

'They're nothing but a bunch of clowns,' said Levin to Feyge. 'They don't take a single thing seriously.'

Whenever he told me about his dead sister, he had to keep removing his glasses to defog their thick lenses.

'Our father made me promise to look after you.' Many times in his life he must have thought and uttered the words he declaimed for me now. 'I want you to leave them and come with me.'

'I'm seventeen years old, Shlomo,' answered Feyge, 'and I've found the man I'm going to live my life with.'

'Who?' asked Levin with a suspicious look at the three ragged young men weeding grapevines with dizzying speed.

'I haven't decided yet,' she said. 'But we can't put it off much longer. It will be one of those three.'

'They're hooligans. They'll make you cook for them, darn their socks, do their washing.'

'We have a constitution,' said Feyge.

'They'll turn you into their charwoman. You won't be the first girl who came here as a pioneer and ended up buried in the communal kitchen.'

'But they'll keep me laughing,' said Grandmother Feyge. 'And I'll get to know the land through them.'

'And no one can say,' said Shlomo Levin with a catch in his throat, 'no one can say that Ya'akov Mirkin did not help her get to know the land.'

By now, long years after her death, he had forgiven Grandfather, even helping him with the farm work and playing draughts with him. Twice a year, though, on the anniversary of his arrival from Russia and on that of his sister's death, he visited her grave 'so that I can have a quiet place for an hour or two to hate all the big shots and smart alecks'.

He followed them to the colonies of Judea, to the experimental farms, to the Jordan and the Yavne'el valleys. Grandfather told me how they had danced, hungered, drained swamps, quarried rock, ploughed fields, and hiked together through the Galilee and the Golan.

'We had no Busquilla or Zis to bring us mail in those days. Do you know how we got letters from Russia?'

'How?'

'Liberson had some friends who were pelicans. They brought them.'

I opened an incredulous mouth, into which Grandfather stuck a hard toothbrush smeared with acrid paste and began to scrub my gums.

'Have you ever seen the bill of a pelican?'

'Ah?' I gargled.

'It comes with a sack. Now rinse your mouth. The pelicans put the mail there, and on their way to Africa they stopped to bring us letters and regards.'

Pinness had no use for such stories. 'This Valley and the coastal plain aren't even on the pelicans' migration route,' he said to Grandfather. 'Why fill the boy's head with such nonsense?'

But Grandfather, Liberson, and Tsirkin didn't obey Pinness's laws of nature. Mounted on hoes, they flew over poisonous swamps and blazed trails through a rank cover of rushes and crabgrass while the light, fragrant cloud of Feyge's dress draped their faces with thin veils of devotion. I saw them airborne like groundsel seeds, white splotches against the drab landscape. Below them ran Levin, shouting at Feyge to come down.

'Not one of them dared lay a hand on your grandmother,' Pinness told me. 'They just romanced her with their pranks and silly jokes, making her laugh until their sweet blood built up her resistance against malaria and depression.'

They slung stones like shepherd boys, sang in Russian to the waterfowl that arrived each autumn from the delta of the Don, and bathed but twice a month. All night they danced barefoot, and with the break of dawn they walked across the country. 'They could work a whole week on no more food than five oranges,' I told my cousin Uri.

But my uncle Avraham's twins Yosi and Uri were not impressed by these tales.

'That's nothing,' said Uri. 'They forgot to tell you how Liberson streaked naked across the Sea of Galilee in Feyge's honour, how Tsirkin played the mandolin for her all night on the shore, and how three giant Saint Peter's fish jumped out of the water in the morning and landed bewitched at her feet, hopping on their spiny fins while Grandfather skimmed pebbles across the water to the other side of the lake.'

To be on the safe side, I asked Meshulam for his opinion. He knew of no source, he replied, 'that could authenticate the more fantastic stories about the Workingman's Circle.'

Meshulam had no sense of perspective. Pinness explained

to me that this happened to people who remembered other people's memories. In his unhierarchical, pigeonholing brain Eliezer Liberson's walking on water had the same status as land acquisitions in the Jordan Valley. And yet with my own eyes I had seen old man Liberson floating at night in the village swimming pool, gasping and gurgling to show his wife Fanya that he was still as young as ever, while if Tsirkin grew the tallest, juiciest penicillaria in the village, it was only because he strolled through his green fields at night, his white head gleaming in the darkness, serenading the tender sprouts with his mandolin. I was sceptical only about Grandfather, because he had never stopped loving Shulamit, the Crimean whore who betrayed him, cheated on him, 'went to bed with every officer in the Czar's army', and stayed behind in Russia all those years.

'But he married Grandmother Feyge,' said Uri, whose long, heifer-like eyelashes danced up and down whenever the subject was women or love.

I already loved Uri then, when we were children. We were sitting in a big field of clover waiting for Avraham and Yosi, who were out cutting alfalfa for the cows on a creaky horse-drawn reaper. In the nearby orchard Grandfather and Zeitser were burning weeds.

'That has nothing to do with it,' I said. I knew he had only married her because a plenary session of the Workingman's Circle had decided he should. 'Grandfather has a girlfriend in Russia, and someday she's going to come.'

'No, she won't,' said Uri. 'She's too old and too busy sleeping with retired Red Army generals.'

Grandmother Feyge had been dead a long time then, and I, who had lived with Grandfather since I was two, saw at night how he opened the box with the blue envelopes that came from afar, from the country of the wicked Michurin, the filthy *muzhiks*, and the infamous Shulamit, and sat slowly writing answers that were not always mailed, though he never crossed out a word of them. One morning when he went to the orchard, I found an unfinished letter on the floor among the night's harvest of notes.

I couldn't understand a thing. Not only wasn't it in Hebrew, it wasn't even in the foreign letters that appeared on the green glass of our big radio. I carefully copied a few words out on a piece of paper and took it with me to school.

During recess I went to see Pinness, who was having tea with the teachers.

'Ya'akov,' I asked him, 'did you ever see writing like this?'

Pinness looked at the paper, blanched, reddened, led me out of the teachers' room by the hand and tore what I had given him into shreds. 'You shouldn't have done that, Baruch. Don't ever go poking through your grandfather's papers again.'

I never cheated on Grandfather again. I never looked at his papers again either, until he was dead.

# 6

I remember Grandmother Feyge's brother walking down the streets of the village, his head and glasses glinting in the sun, his shoulders stooped, old crumbs of apricot leather yellowing between his teeth. Though public servants like Levin were not highly regarded by the farmers, he was the person they turned to whenever anyone was needed to do an audit or arbitrate a dispute, because he was as honest as the day was long and a great stickler for the facts.

One afternoon as he sat with his Yemenite wife Rachel under the white mulberry tree in their yard, tearing off little pieces of pitta bread and cheese with his thin blue fingers and placing them in her mouth, I eavesdropped on their conversation, scrunching myself up in a bush as best I could.

'Have some more,' he said, preparing another morsel.

'I don't need to be hand-fed,' protested Rachel, though she could not keep from laughing. 'I'm an old woman, not a baby.'

'My baby,' I heard Shlomo Levin sigh. 'My baby sister.'

Sometimes when the old-timers reminisced about Grandmother, they would let drop a few words about her brother, so that little by little I put together a picture of him, as I did of others whom I buried. Rilov the Watchman, for instance, was the object of my investigations for years – and a dangerous one too, since his grandson and I, and my father and his son, had a running feud between us. Worse yet, he spent most of his time in the septic tank of his cowshed, where he kept the village arms cache and any intruder was liable to be shot. 'If you value dying in your own bed, stay out of here,' he would say, giving you his famous four-cornered stare, which was composed of two shotgun barrels and two slanty eyes.

I never talked to Rilov in my life, but Levin was more approachable. He liked me and regarded me with melancholy amusement, baffled that a Goliath like myself had been born into a family like his. 'I only wish I was as strong and innocent as you,' he would say to me with a smile.

Levin stayed with the Workingman's Circle for several weeks and then decided to go off on his own. Not that Grandfather, Mandolin Tsirkin, and Liberson were unkind to him, but one look from them when he massaged his aching hands or wielded his hoe at a bad angle was enough to bring tears to his eyes and fill him with despair. He didn't understand their jokes and never managed to learn their songs, since each evening they invented new ones.

Their bestial habits, such as scratching their toes while they ate, picking their teeth with blades of straw, and conversing with mules and donkeys, depressed and frightened him. Even Feyge, so it seemed to him, no longer held him in esteem.

'Our father sent me to look after her, and there I was, a pathetic farmhand and a fifth wheel of an elder brother.'

And yet the three of them shared their food with him, found him and Feyge work with the farmers of the Jewish colonies, and even rescued them once from some Arab camel drivers who attacked them near Petach Tikvah and tried to steal their packs.

'You run ahead with Feyge,' shouted Tsirkin, 'and keep an eye on my mandolin!'

Shlomo and Grandmother hid behind a rise and watched

in astonishment as the 'three hooligans' wrestled with their attackers and drove them off. Liberson rejoined them with a split lip, triumphantly waving his Webley revolver, and Feyge cleaned the wound and kissed it tenderly to the gleeful cries of his companions.

Afterwards Levin chided her for her free ways.

'I love them,' she answered in the darkness.

He lay awake all night and announced with gloomy formality in the morning that he intended to leave them.

'We felt pretty awful when we first came to this country too,' said Tsirkin. 'In another month you'll feel better.'

But Levin decided that it was time to go his separate way, wherever that might lead him.

Liberson and Grandfather bought him a train ticket to Jerusalem and gave him a few Turkish coins. Feyge cried when her brother boarded the train.

He sat in the rickety carriage feeling low, his hands in his pockets for warmth, his knees no doubt pressed together at the same touchingly timid Levinesque angle they would later form when he sat behind his store counter. On the opposite bench a group of religious Jews and their wives regarded him with distaste while telling stories about their rabbi, who had flown on a Hasidic fur hat from the port in Jaffa straight to the Wailing Wall. Next to him sat a hunched merchant who whispered numbers to himself all the way to Jerusalem as if hoping they might safely conduct him to the terra firma of sanity.

Levin, who had barely freed himself from the oppressive presence of pelican postmen and froggy guides, suddenly realised that the country must be exuding maddening vapours that infected whoever lived in it regardless of age, tribe, or sect.

Looking out at the arid landscape, he nibbled at a slice of bread Feyge had put in his pack. Flakes of soot and bits of ash from the locomotive flew through the open window into his mouth, tasting like bitter groats. The desolation of the countryside depressed him. The grey valleys, spiny thickets, and ruined terraces of the hillsides seemed dead and pitiful compared with the vast green expanses that he remembered from the riverbanks of his childhood.

When the train swung around the last mountain curve and entered Jerusalem, Grandmother's brother took his pack, left the station, walked past the silenced windmill of Moses Montefiore, descended to the pool in front of the old walled city where cattle were drinking from the faecal waters, and passed through a gate in the wall. The filth and shabbiness of the city inspired fear and revulsion. An insipid date drink that he bought from an Arab boy only made everything grimmer. Toward evening he spied two pioneers like himself, followed in the wake of their Russian speech, and found shelter for the night. His mood, though, did not improve.

'The Jews here turn up their noses at us, and the Arabs have already twice assaulted me,' he wrote to his sister. 'This city, with its stones and poverty, will be the ruin of me. All one sees is vanished glory and dead ashes. The stones alone are at home here. This is no place for living men.'

For a while he tried to learn stonemasonry. The Arab masons amazed him with their sharp eye, which could peel the surface away from each stone and reveal its inner nature. 'They even had a word for it, *mesamsam*. You might have thought they were cutting dough instead of rock.' But Levin's fingers ached and swelled long hours after laying down his chisel, and he decided to go to Jaffa. 'It was a softer city,' he told me, 'not as stony.'

Lacking the money for a train ticket, he joined two youths and a young girl from Minsk who were going to Jaffa on foot. Oddly, this tiring journey, which took two whole days, was a pleasant experience despite the mountainous route that led them through thornbushes, over boulders, and past barking dogs 'to avoid the highwaymen of Abu Ghosh'.

Unfamiliar black birds chirruped all around, pointing their orange beaks in the air. Grey lizards, 'the lords of the wilderness', amused him with their prayers. The young men he was with were friendly, helped him carry his things, and even gave him good advice. The taller of the two, whose name was Hayyim Margulis, told him to wear a woollen belt around his waist even in the hottest weather and informed him that he intended to become a beekeeper in order 'to bring forth honey from the rock'.

'But bees are more than just honey,' said Margulis gaily. 'Without them we can never make the wilderness blossom. Without bees there is no fruit, no clover, no vegetables, nothing. The flies and wasps of this country aren't to be trusted.' During one of their rest stops Margulis showed him how to find wild bee hives. 'It's an old Cossack trick,' he explained, taking out a little box and striding over to a flowering thyme plant whose bright blossoms buzzed with 'savage bees'.

'That one is good and sozzled,' he whispered, pointing at a bee couched luxuriously in a flower. Stealthily stalking it with the box, he shut the lid on it, then did the same with several other bees.

'They always fly straight back to the hive,' he explained, freeing one of the bees and running after it with upturned face, tripping over stones and clods of earth. Levin followed closely behind him. When they lost sight of the little creature after a few dozen yards, Margulis freed a second bee and kept on running.

The sixth bee brought them to its home, which was hidden in the notched trunk of a carob tree. Levin stood a safe distance away, marvelling when Margulis rubbed his hands and face with wildflower petals and walked straight up to the hive, letting the bees land on his bare skin and crawl all over it. He scooped some honey into his hands and returned to the girl from Minsk, who licked it off his outstretched, dripping fingers as if she had been doing it all her life.

'Sweet Margulis,' she laughed. Her name was Tonya, and she didn't take her eyes off him for a second.

They saw caravans of camels, 'Turkish trains', as Margulis called them. Levin tingled with pleasure. Hayyim Margulis was the first person in Palestine not to humiliate him, and Levin felt the beginnings of a great liking for this fragrant young man, whom he already dared affectionately call 'Hayyim'ke' in the privacy of his thoughts. Perhaps, he imagined happily, he would be asked to join Margulis for good. Together, he daydreamed, the two of them would possess land and Tonya, together plough the earth and build a home. For a fleeting moment the future seemed to beckon from beneath a warm canopy of hope. It was all so sudden that he could feel the back of his neck go limp from sheer bliss. But no sooner had they reached Jaffa than Margulis took Tonya by the arm and disappeared with her and their friend behind the Park Hotel, waving goodbye. Sadly, Levin watched them depart. For several hours, until he was chased off by a waiter, he sat on a bench in the garden of the hotel, looking at the spire of the Lutheran church and the flame trees glowing red all around him. When night came, he bedded down on the dunes north of Jaffa. Cold lizards crawled over his belly, and the snouts of jackals sniffed his legs. He didn't sleep a wink, and when morning came he went to look for construction work in Tel Aviv.

'The girls here,' he wrote to his sister, who was then digging irrigation holes in orange groves near Hadera, 'are callous and crass and pay no mind to a young man like me who cannot serenade them or sweeten their lives with honey. They want strong fellows who sing while they work, and I, weak and afflicted as I am, am not well liked by them. How I long for a soft, pure hand, for the fragrance of a muslin dress, for a cup of coffee with little cakes on a white table by a green riverbank.'

Levin dug foundations and pushed wooden wheelbarrows through the sand until he felt his back would break.

'My poor hands are all blistered, and every blister has burst. My skin is peeling and full of bloody cuts. And each day's work is followed by a sleepless night. My back and sides ache, and each thought is more worrisome than the last. Will my powers hold out? Have I the mental and physical fortitude to pass the test? I would be happiest going back to Russia or away to America,' he wrote to Feyge, who was then singing away as she crushed stones into gravel near Tiberias.

Levin showed me Grandmother's answer. 'There are other women working here, and they indeed launder and cook for the men as you feared would be my lot. But how happy your little sister is! *She* is a real worker. Tsirkin, Mirkin, and Liberson – I call them by their last names, and they in turn call me Levin and salute me like an officer – all lend a hand in keeping up our tent. Tsirkin, when the spirit moves him, is a most wonderful cook. Give him a cabbage, a lemon, some garlic, and some sugar, and he will make an unparalleled borscht. From a pumpkin, some flour, and two eggs he whipped up enough food for a week. Yesterday was Mirkin's turn to do the laundry. Would you believe that a grown man washed your sister's underthings?'

Levin was so overcome with envy and abhorrence that he made a note of his feelings in his diary, thus condemning them to immortality.

'Do you remember that song I used to sing back home? Yesterday I taught it to the boys. Tsirkin played it for us, and we sang all night long until the sun rose and a new day of work began.'

Levin stuck his pencil behind one ear, rose, stepped out from behind the desk in his office, and began to dance slowly, describing a pained, graceful circle around his torment while singing in a high voice:

> I shall plough, and I shall sow, and I shall rejoice—
> Only when I am in Israel's land.
> You may dress me in plain cloth and call me 'Jew'—
> Only when I am in Israel's land.
> I shall eat dry bread and bow to no man—
> Only when I am in Israel's land.

He sank back into his chair. 'Israel's land,' he said. 'You can't throw a stone in this country without hitting some holy place or madman.'

All around him were the first houses of Tel Aviv, with their Jewish workers, Arab coachmen, and new inhabitants.

'Suddenly I realised that no one was ever born in this country. Those who didn't fall from the sky popped up from under the earth.'

He began carefully peeling more letters from the rustling bundle in his drawer. Elegantly anxious, Grandmother's large, round handwriting angled charmingly forward.

'I rose from my sickbed,' she wrote her brother, 'and toward

evening we went for a swim in the Sea of Galilee. The boys carried
on like naked babies in the water, and I waded in wrapped in a
sheet I threw back on shore once I was neck-deep. Then the three
of them had a contest. Liberson said he would walk on water
like Jesus and nearly drowned, Mirkin proved quite an artist at
skimming stones over the waves, and Tsirkin played to the fish
for our supper. In fact, though, I have eaten nothing but figs for
the past three days.'

Levin, who had never seen his sister in the nude, was stricken
with anger and shame. His short lunch break was already over.
Up and down the dusty street walked young men like himself
in tattered work clothes, sweaty, faded young women with
hunger and disease glittering in their eyes, and fine gentle-
men in white jackets and fancy shoes that never sank into
the sand. One of them gave Levin a rude look, and he rose
from the limestone ledge he was seated on and went back
to work.

'All afternoon I dreamed of returning at night to the sycamore tree on the dune, where I could sit in the dark with my
thoughts.'

That evening, however, when he climbed the sand dune and
came to the tree, beneath which he sought only to collapse until
he regained his strength, he found a young couple 'rutting like
pigs'. One look from them was enough to send the despairing
Levin running to the shore.

The next day he went to a bank in Jaffa and asked for a job.
He was in luck. Because he boasted a good hand, knew some
book-keeping, and had a nice, trustworthy smile, he was given
a trial as an assistant clerk, and a year later he was already a
cashier with a white jacket and a straw hat on his head. The
sores on his hands healed, his skin grew soft and smooth again,
and at night he strolled along the beach in a pair of moccasins,
listening to the whispers and songs of the pioneers on the dunes
and smelling the spicy tea they brewed in tin cans. His heart
leaped inside him.

Just then, however, when Fortune, or so it seemed from his
account, had begun to smile on him, a war broke out. Along with

everyone else in Tel Aviv, Grandmother's brother was banished from the city.

'During the war,' said Grandfather, 'we were given a forged *vasika*.'

I wrote down the word *vasika*. I never asked what anything meant, because explanations would only have snarled the threads of the story. *Vasika, kulaks, sukra, Ottomanisation* – the only reason I remember such words to this day is that I still don't know what they mean. Just like Levin and *mesamsam*.

'We lived on olives and onions and almost starved to death,' said Grandfather.

Every autumn he picked and cured a barrel of olives. I sat next to him on the concrete path, watching him peel garlic, slice lemon, and rinse stems of dill, his hands giving off a good green-and-white-striped smell. Each time he tapped his knife handle against a clove of garlic, the pure white tooth slid out of its skin with one quick tug. He showed me how much water and salt to fill the barrel with.

'Go and bring a fresh egg from the chicken coop, my child, and I'll show you a nice trick.'

He put the egg in the salt water, and when it was suspended halfway to the top, neither floating upward to the surface nor sinking down to the bottom but hanging by an invisible thread of confidence and faith, we knew that the salt was just right. The levitating egg seemed no less magical to me than the grafted fruit trees in our garden or Eliezer Liberson's walking on water.

Levin found a haven during the war in a refugee camp in Petach Tikvah. Either he had erased all memory of those hard times or else he didn't want to talk about them. He only remembered a single night, on which great swarms of locusts landed in the fields and devoured everything in sight with a ceaseless, menacing, yet barely audible crunch.

'When we rose in the morning, the trees were all white and dead, stripped clean of their bark.' The locusts' beating wings and masticating mandibles filled his brain like a hail of tormenting grit.

When the boom of the British field guns approached from the

south, Levin returned to Tel Aviv, walking slowly down sandy red streets that turned to yellow as they ran into the evening. Merchants were busy removing the boards they had nailed to their shop fronts. The smiles of the Australian soldiers strolling through town inspired them with new hope.

Levin did not return to the bank. He found a job in a stationery shop, where he learned the art of fixing fountain pens. Reverently he took apart the writing instruments of famous men like Brenner, Ziskind, and Ettinger, rinsing their parts in a solution made from sycamore galls that he himself had picked, honing their nibs, and overhauling their wells. 'Our political future lies in your hands,' said the shop owner with a smile as he watched Levin inspect Arthur Ruppin's black Waterman, and Levin felt a wave of contentment. The owner liked him and even introduced him to young ladies, the daughters of his friends. If only Levin hadn't missed the smells of straw, smoke, and dusty feet. He wanted to wrap himself in a blanket of stars and grass, to sleep on threshing floors and sand dunes. In the end he persuaded his boss to let him double as a travelling salesman, and once a week he set forth on a donkey to peddle his wares to the nearby Jewish colonies.

'I loved those trips.' His lungs grew used to the dust, and the patient plod of the donkey gave him a sense of well-being. His route wound between fragrant walls of orange and lemon groves and hedgerows of thorny acacia bushes that glowed with little yellow fireballs, passed the barred iron gate of the Mikveh Israel Agricultural School, and turned into the vineyards of Rishon le-Tsiyyon. The sea of flowers through which he rode seemed continually to part before him. The songs of pioneers travelled through the air. Spying a group of them sitting down to eat, he would bashfully rein in his mount and stand watching from a distance until he was invited to join in. He ate heartily of the Grade D oranges and the bread dipped in cooking oil that still gave him heartburn, and chipped in with a contribution of his own, the sweet rolls and Arab cakes that he bought in Jaffa expressly for this purpose.

'And *kamardin* too?' I asked.

He gave me a mournful smile of surprise. 'No,' he said. 'By then I was a little better off.'

'Sweet Levin,' a pretty blonde pioneer with a peeling nose once called him, laughing as she kissed his cheek after he had summoned up the courage to place a sticky crumb of cake in her beaked mouth.

'My heart skipped a beat.' At night he dreamed of her and of the farmhouse he would build for her and their children. There would be rows of sprouting vegetables, diligent hens, a cow, and no end of work. 'Even now I read farm journals the way women read cookery books,' he told me with a bitter laugh. 'Every time I travelled that way I looked for her blue kerchief among the trees and grapevines.' By the time he felt bold enough to ask about her a month later, he was told that she had died of typhoid fever. Once again he was plunged into deep gloom.

'I never even knew her name until she was dead,' he wrote to his sister, who had learned by then to plough with a team of oxen.

'It was my first furrow in the Land of Israel,' she wrote. 'At first I couldn't manage to steer and press down on the plough at the same time. Liberson had to take the reins from me. Now, though, I can plough straight as an arrow.'

She came down with malaria too. 'But their sweet blood is curing me,' she wrote to her brother.

Shlomo Levin made his rounds with pens, inkwells, stationery, nibs, commercial forms, and pencils in the saddlebags of his donkey. Though twice he was robbed and asaulted, he proved to be a first-rate salesman and was taken in as a partner in the firm.

That year the first Jewish settlers pitched their tents in the Valley of Jezreel. The Feyge Levin Workingman's Circle decided that 'Comrade Mirkin and Comrade Levin should enter the state of matrimony'. Together with the beekeeper Hayyim Margulis and his sweetheart Tonya from Minsk, who was later to fall in love with Rilov, the future pedagogue Ya'akov Pinness, and his pregnant wife Leah, who would die that same year, they formed the first group to scour the Valley for purchasable farmland, 'to search out the country', as Pinness put it biblically. Thus they became the founding fathers of the village.

'We had a donkey called Katchke. By day he hauled water from the spring, and by night, while we slept, he put on a frock coat, polished his hooves and glasses, spread his ears wide, and flew off to London.

'Just as the King of England was sitting down to breakfast, Katchke knocked with one hoof on the door of the palace. The King invited him in and offered him a soft-boiled egg in a cup and the softest white bread you could imagine. As soon as Katchke began to tell him about our village, the King ordered his servants to cancel his other appointments for the day.

'"But Boris the King of Bulgaria is waiting in the royal office, Your Majesty."

'"Let him wait," replied the King of England.

'"The Queen of Belgium is in the garden."

'"She can stay there," said the King. "Today I plan to talk with Katchke, a Hebrew donkey from the Land of Israel."'

# 7

'Grandmother Feyge,' said Uri, dreamy-eyed, 'walked through a field of jonquils in a dress without panties, just like a Ukrainian peasant. She got pregnant from the pollen. That's why to this day my father cries and sneezes when the jonquils flower down by the spring.'

The Committee counted the months and concluded that Grandmother would give birth around Shavuot, the holiday of first fruits. 'And what better first fruit could there be than the first child of the village?'

'Tsirkin and Liberson were thrilled by Grandmother's pregnancy,' said Grandfather in a tone that made it seem perfectly normal. The two of them went on dangerous expeditions to bring her lemons from across the Jordan, caper buds from the mountains of Samaria, and partridge chicks from the Carmel. Two devoted women comrades were sent from a settlement in the Jordan Valley to wait on her during her difficult last months. They read to her aloud from selected works of fiction 'and the writings of Movement theoreticians'.

'As ridiculous as it may seem, the myth of the firstborn child retains its power,' said Meshulam Tsirkin, who never forgave his father Mandolin and his mother Pesya for finishing second. 'Your grandmother Feyge carried the child of the whole village in her womb.'

Feyge strolled radiantly among the tents along the muddy paths of the village, her voice grown so opulent that it charmed man and beast alike.

'Mirkin too, who only loved her in partnership with Eliezer Liberson and Mandolin Tsirkin and never forgot his Crimean love even on the day he brought Feyge to his tent, looked at her moonily then,' said Pinness.

'He rubbed her belly with green olive oil,' declared Uri, adding an embellishment of his own.

When it was time for Feyge's accouchement, she was rushed by cart to the railway station, which was several miles away. The entourage had hardly left the village, however, when it saw the train come around the blue bend of the mountain and roll into the station.

The story of my uncle Avraham's birth was one of the most famous in the Valley. On the village's fiftieth anniversary it was even dramatised by a director from Tel Aviv, who astounded the locals with his purple pants and his loud efforts to bed every young girl in sight.

Mandolin Tsirkin and Rilov the Watchman 'jumped on their horses, galloped off like two Cossack lightning bolts', and caught up with the train. Over the protests of the engineer, who brandished a coal shovel, Rilov leapt from his horse into the locomotive, subdued the man with an angry glare and a stiff prod to the chest, and yanked the brake handle.

'We're not just anyone, we're Committee!' he told the engineer and his sooty assistant, who lay shivering on a pile of coal, stunned by this pronouncement and the sudden stop of the train.

'On your feet and shake a leg if you want to die in your own bed, you dead jackal, you!' shouted Rilov. 'Full steam ahead!'

The train started out with a groan, leaving behind a great wake of sparks, columns of smoke, two saddled horses, and Grandmother Feyge and her forgotten entourage, which ran shouting toward the tracks. There was no choice but to give birth in the fields.

My uncle Avraham was delivered an hour later, Grandmother and Grandfather's firstborn son and the first child of the village. 'He was born in our field, on our earth, beneath our sun, in the exact place where Margulis's main irrigation tap now stands.'

That day the cicadas kept up a steady roar in the fields. The pioneers sat up singing all night, and in the morning Rilov and Tsirkin reappeared, having run all the way back. Rilov did not even apologise. After sipping some water, he demanded a general meeting to decide what the child should be called. 'He's already been given a name by his mother,' he was told. 'It's Avraham, after her father.' Eliezer Liberson muttered something about 'comrades taking impermissible liberties' and even wrote in the village newsletter that 'the child is as much ours as hers', but there was nothing he could do about it.

Knowing that the birth of a first child afflicts all men with a sense of their own mortality, Fanya Liberson, who had been shanghaied from her kibbutz several weeks previously, made Grandfather leave Grandmother's tent.

'Fanya and my poor wife Leah moved in with her. The two of them embroidered nappies for little Avraham and wove him a cradle of reeds they had cut by the spring.'

A week later the circumciser arrived from the city beyond the blue mountain. The villagers dressed in white, cut their hair and nails, and sat in a semicircle in front of Mirkin's tent. A great cheer went up as Grandfather stepped outside holding his son high in the air. 'Your uncle Avraham was truly our first fruit, because he was born before the fruits of the trees had set.' To this day, on the holiday of Shavuot, the feast of first fruits, all that year's children are held high in front of everyone to commemorate the occasion.

The whole village was dazzled by the beauty and fairness of the new baby, who 'smiled with a mouth so bright that you could have sworn he had already cut his teeth. He was like a big jonquil swaddled in its calyx.' Avraham was born without the two deep creases that now furrow his brow, and with a friendly expression on his face, which was as fresh and smooth as the peel of a large apple.

'We formed a circle immediately,' said Pinness. 'Each arm found a shoulder or waist and the dance began.' Everyone felt that it was a moment of grace for the village, which now had 'someone to carry the torch forward in the great relay race of the generations' and need not fear extinction with the death of its founders.

Pinness smiled softly, the pleasure of the memory etched in every line of his face. 'The child bound us forever,' he said, the words dropping from his mouth like the fruit of the wild plum tree on Margulis's land – sweet, small, and precise.

'We passed him around from hand to hand and let everyone hold him in their arms. For a sweet, awesome moment each of us felt the promise of his delicious flesh and inhaled his good smell. One by one, as if he were a ritual object, we took him and gave him our blessing, some out loud and some deep in their hearts. Each of us had a part in him.'

'Someday I'll show you the protocol of the circumcision,' promised Meshulam. 'Liberson's wish for the baby was that he should grow up to plough the first furrow in the Negev desert. Rilov's was that he redeem the mountains of Gilead and the Bashan. My father promised to teach him the mandolin. They imagined him sowing and ploughing, bringing faraway Jews from the Urals and the deserts of Arabia to this country, and developing new, sturdier strains of wheat. And what did he turn out to be? Your uncle Avraham.'

Still, it was a fine hour, one whose bounty helped see the villagers through many long weeks of hardship and privation. They all felt quiet and content – all except Shlomo Levin, my grandmother's brother, who came by train from Tel Aviv. Afraid to appear in his citified white jacket, he wore a grey cap with a protective visor and a rough work shirt that made him break out in a rash.

Levin walked from the railway station through the fields, overwhelmed by the deep smell of the heavy earth that purred beneath his feet. And though Feyge threw her thin, tired arms around him, and Tonya and Margulis, who remembered him from their hike to Jaffa, smiled at him like old friends, he felt like an outsider among the excited pioneers who hugged him and plied him with drink. He even managed 'to hold the baby wrong', so that it bit his wrist with its sharp little teeth.

Then everyone went in search of the circumciser, who had gone out for a stroll to smell the good earth and murmur ecstatic prayers to himself. He took Avraham in his arms, clicked an appreciative tongue at the sight of his well-formed member, and relieved it of its foreskin. There was a profound hush. Even Liberson, who claimed that circumcision was a pagan custom, felt that it was no time for argument. And when the loud yelp of their firstborn son sounded over the fields, the pioneers burst into unashamed tears.

# 8

Efrayim, my lost uncle, was Grandfather's favourite child. He was a handsome boy, quick on his feet, and Grandfather never tired of telling me how he went off to war, how he carried his calf around on his shoulders, and how he vanished from the village. Efrayim was born a year after Avraham and a year before my mother Esther. 'The sight of all those children running about the village and helping out with the chores was a tonic for us all.'

Margulis's Tonya had a daughter too, but the child's father was Rilov. From the day of her arrival in the village Tonya had been swept off her feet by Rilov's fierce masculine charms. The only bed she wished to die in was his, and she was maddened with passion when he asked her to smuggle rifle bullets in her brassiere. He took her down with him to the arms cache in the septic tank, their shadows jiggling to the light of an oil lamp as his fingers drew the ammunition from her breasts. Once having counted out the cartridges, however, he helped her put her clothes back on. She could feel her heart in her throat as he tightened and tied the pink laces on her back. Smiling with visionary eyes, Rilov told her how he dreamed at night of Pesya Tsirkin. 'She has everything I need,' he explained. 'An automobile, the right connections, and a big bra.' Tonya was hurt but undeterred.

Rilov soon saw that she could be counted on to keep a secret. At night she went with him to meet Arab informers in the wadis, to stow hand grenades in hideaways, and to eliminate Jewish collaborators with the British. Covered with white flakes of explosive, they embraced on crates of concussion grenades, and when Rilov, whose stock of imagery was limited, called Tonya his Schwarzlose after his favourite machine gun, she no longer felt put out.

They were married secretly, surrounded by a wall of Watchmen whose wedding gifts included a Tatar saddle, a thoroughbred horse that twitched its hide all through the ceremony, and a whining, handcuffed rabbi from Tiberias who officiated with a black blindfold covering his eyes. A year later Tonya gave birth to a daughter without ever knowing she had been pregnant, because Rilov had dismissed her morning sickness with a wave of his hand, declaring that nausea and vomiting were a common reaction to repeated contact with gelignite.

Sweet Margulis came to visit the Rilovs, as good-natured as always. Free of such follies as jealousy, grudge-bearing, and vengefulness, he arrived with a large jar of honey in his left hand and his new girlfriend Riva Beilin in his right. Riva was a pioneer from the Workers' Brigade whom he had met on the train to Tiberias. Tonya, still aching all over from the birth, felt a rough edge of anger in her veins as she looked at her former lover and his new partner. That week she had had her first quarrel with her husband, who, true to the conspiratorial tradition he was trained in, had insisted on keeping the birth of their daughter a secret as well. This time Tonya was wounded to the point of hatred and tears.

Daniel, the son of Fanya and Eliezer Liberson, was the same age as my mother Esther. He was enamoured of her from the moment they were first laid beneath one blanket in a field, at the age of three weeks.

Grandfather, Liberson, Grandmother, and Fanya had gone to the orchard with their babies so that Grandfather could give them all a lesson in cup shaping young pear trees. The pruning shears clicked away in his hands while he scoffed at the theories of the Soviet agronomist Michurin, who claimed that the seeds of a grafted tree contained the genetic traits of both the scion and the rootstock.

Weak and pale, Feyge lay down on the ground, propped her head on Fanya's thigh, and watched the babies to make sure no insects bit them. Just then Daniel raised his bald head, forcefully rocked it back and forth, and turned himself over to face Esther. He was only three weeks old, and his mother couldn't believe her eyes. It never occurred to her that her son was seeking the company of her friend's daughter. Grandmother, though, understood it at once. Her husband, she thought, could say what he pleased, but Michurin was not to be gainsaid.

That same evening Daniel began to crawl, and when Grandmother Feyge made ready to go home with Esther, he startled everyone by following them to the door like an obstinate little lizard and wailing inconsolably. Several sleepless weeks went by before his parents realised that he was not crying from hunger or teething pains but because he wanted Mirkin's daughter. 'You'd better believe it,' said Uri. 'You'd cry too if you had a hard-on two weeks after your circumcision.'

Apologetic for waking them, Fanya would bring her son, blue in the face from bawling, to Grandfather and Grandmother's in the middle of the night. Before Daniel could walk he had learned to shinny like a monkey up his beloved's crib, where, clinging to Esther hand and foot like a cicada to a juicy branch, he calmed down at once and fell asleep.

He spent whole days at Grandmother's. If Esther was taken away from him for a bath or a nap, he burst into howls that could be heard on the other side of the blue mountain. At the age of seven months he was walking and running so as to be able to follow his darling, whose name he learned before 'Papa' and 'Mama'.

Grandmother Feyge regarded the two children fondly. She had always believed that every person in the world had a true love.

'It's just that someone usually sees to it that they're born at opposite ends of the earth,' she said to Fanya. 'They cry their way through life without knowing why. It was the fate of my daughter and your son to be born in the same village.'

'Like Adam and Eve in the Garden of Eden,' declared Ya'akov Pinness, the heartbroken young widower, who was so moved by the infant love of Daniel Liberson and Esther Mirkin that he couldn't wait to have them in his class.

'The real moral of the story of the Garden of Eden,' observed Pinness to the members of the village's loyal and argumentative Bible club, 'is not ethical but erotic. They were the world's only couple.'

Eliezer Liberson rose to his feet. 'What impresses me,' he said, 'is less Adam's being alone with his Creator than his being alone with Eve.'

The club members smiled and nodded. Liberson was equally renowned in the Valley for his atheism and his love of Fanya. Pinness was overjoyed. As always, the Bible interested him for its human situations and natural history. He had only disdain for the scholars, preachers, and politicians who found all kinds of messages in it.

'The only things that haven't changed since the days of the Bible are the heart of man and the soil of this land, and both are equally long-suffering,' he said.

Holding their oil lanterns, the club members left the teacher's tent and sloshed through the terrible mud. 'Every paradise has its snake,' said Grandmother to Fanya. 'Sooner or later it comes slithering out of the grass.'

'And hers lives in Russia,' murmured Fanya Liberson. 'The

fruit of the Tree of Knowledge arrives from there in blue envelopes.'

Her eyes sparkling with happiness, Feyge looked at little Daniel lying on his back sucking his beloved's fingers. 'He'll never look at another woman,' she said.

She died when Daniel and Esther were still babies, and didn't live to see my mother jilt her first love. Her photograph, an enlargement of the one in Grandfather's trunk, stood for years on Fanya's kitchen cupboard: the same black braids, the same clenched little fists, the same embroidered white linen blouse, the same eyes seeming to drift off to either side of the camera. From early on I knew that this was the look of a woman 'short of love'.

'To my friend Fanya,' the inscription on the photograph said.

In those days the village was little more than two rows of white tents barely visible through a miasmic veil of swamp gas and mosquito wings. A few lean-tos had gone up, there was a large trough for the cattle, and the chickens ran loose pecking at the dirt.

Eventually Grandfather planted some trees several hundred yards from his tent: a pomegranate, an olive, a fig and two rows of chasselas grapes. On them he nailed signs with such verses as 'And the vine shall give her fruit', 'Thou shalt have olives throughout thy coasts', 'Whoso keepeth the fig tree shall eat the fruit thereof' and 'The pomegranates put forth their bud'.

The pomegranate aged quickly: tears of yellow sap studded its sickly trunk, and only rarely did it yield some paltry fruit. After it had been unsuccessfully injected with various remedies and pesticides, Pinness pronounced it 'fatally infected with the moth of Doubt'. The first grapevines died of phylloxera rot, which caused Grandfather to graft the next vines on California stock despite his mixed feelings about that state, the home of his brother Yosef and Luther Burbank.

To this day, however, surrounded by gravestones, lawns and ornamentals, the fig and the olive still bear in abundance. So wildly vigorous did the fig become at Grandfather's magic hands, in fact, that its branches ooze puddles of sharp, viscous syrup all over the ground, while the olive's fine greenish drupes are speckled with yellow spots of oil.

Grandfather had a sixth sense for growing trees. Planters from all over the country consulted him and sent him infected leaves and pest eggs. The trees in his backyard made even the experts marvel. Every year pilgrimages of songbirds and agronomists arrived in our village to see and taste Mirkin's fruit. I myself remember visitors coming especially to watch Grandfather harvest olives in autumn.

'Come here, my child,' he said, teaching me to wrap my arms around the olive tree as he did. He didn't beat the branches with a stick as was the custom, but hugged the trunk with his face pressed against it while swaying with it gently. At first nothing happened. After a few minutes, however, I could feel the robust tree sigh and shudder, and soon, to the excited gasps of the crowd, a quiet downpour of fruit rained on my head and shoulders. I can still recall the faint drumming of those olives on my skin.

Grandfather planted the avenue of casuarinas when Avraham was born. 'That firstborn disappointment and vain hope,' as he was called by Meshulam Tsirkin, who was a year younger and had his own theory about why Grandfather had planted non-fruiting trees upon the birth of his first son.

When Grandmother Feyge gave birth to her second child, my uncle Efrayim, Grandfather was so happy that he grafted onto a single sour orange stock branches of orange, grapefruit, lemon, and tangerine. 'My quadratic equation', he called it, and once the wondrous citrus began yielding its various fruits, he went on filling the village with his mad experiments, which soon began to cross-pollinate each other. Muscat grapes rotted high on the unpickable branches of cypresses, and Iraqi dates turned yellow on plum trees. Eventually Grandfather grew alarmed by this unrestrained outburst of Michurinism, but the trees kept going strong.

The following year Grandmother had Esther, my mother and her last child, after whom her body ceased from fruitfulness and began preparing itself for death. Although these events took place but a few dozen years ago, they are already wrapped in the fibrous shrouds of time, embalmed in the black wax of mystery, as if they came straight out of Pinness's Bible lessons, in which Deborah's palm and Abraham's tamarisk still burgeoned prolifically, planted by the rivers of stories – nomadic tales of earth and tents, of legendary wells, trees, and wombs.

Grandmother lived long enough to move from her tent to the cabin I later shared with Grandfather. She scrubbed the wooden floor, in which faint depressions recall her knees to this day, until it gleamed. When a glass window was installed, she sewed bright curtains for it out of pieces of old cloth. Outside, by the fig tree, she built an earthen oven that stored the good smells of baked pumpkin and bread. Two half-breed Damascene cows stood tied in the shed, and little Avraham took them out at dusk to graze on the front of our land: Rachel Yana'it was joined by more colourful Cherkessian hens who pecked alongside her in the yard. When chicks hatched they were put in a wooden box warmed by an oil lamp, and soon they tempted the old wildcat to leave his home in the blue mountain and take up residence by the spring in our fields.

'They cooked in outdoor ovens, picked purslane for the chickens, went barefoot, and fetched water in tin cans,' said Yosi, Uri's twin brother. 'In short, they were your typical Arab village.'

On the land where Pioneer Home now stands, Grandfather planted his big orchard. He dug irrigation ditches between the rows of trees, which he watered at night so as not to pester them in the heat of day. When he grew sleepy, he placed his hose at the top end of a ditch and lay down to nap at the bottom. Awakened by the slow-flowing water when it reached him, he rose, moved the hose to the next ditch, and went back to sleep. This system of his was the butt of many jokes in the village. 'He only does it to avoid sleeping at home,' Fanya protested to Liberson. There were farmers who voiced the fear that if Mirkin ever forgot to wake up, the orchard would be flooded and the swamp would return to the Valley.

Grandfather paid them no mind. Shaking from happiness and

cold, he came home each morning vaporous with wet earth. At his hands the orchard was already bearing large fruit in its second year.

That same year Zeitser came for a visit from his commune in the Jordan Valley. He was an old friend of Grandfather's. Though he never complained about it, 'you could see that life in the commune didn't suit him'. Grandfather asked him to stay on in the village, and Zeitser agreed on the condition that their friendship did not result in special treatment. He considered himself a simple farmhand and wanted to be nothing else. So modest were his needs that he did not even care to sleep indoors.

'Why does he live in the cowshed?' I asked Grandfather. 'Why does old Zeitser live with the cows?'

'Zeitser is as stubborn as a mule,' smiled Grandfather. 'He's used to it and he likes it.'

He was a strict vegetarian. On the rare occasions when he accepted a piece of cake from Grandmother, who was very fond of him, he suffered pangs of remorse and indigestion.

Zeitser remained with us until his horrible death. His chief speciality, which was ploughing in a ruler-straight line, aroused great admiration. No work was too hard for him, and only on Saturdays did he take off for long walks 'to smell the flowers and think'.

'Take me with you,' I called, running after him on bare feet. 'Take me with you, Zeitser.' I knew that long ago, when Grandmother died, Zeitser had taken care of my uncle Avraham, playing with him and carrying him around piggyback. He never played with me or my cousins, though. He had grown old, his body mortified by its own arduous reckonings, so that all he ever carried on his back any more were his own memories and conclusions.

'Don't bother him, Baruch,' said Grandfather. 'It's his day off. Everyone deserves to be alone now and then.'

Zeitser's stocky body would disappear gradually into the distance. First it would be hidden by the orchard, then it would reappear as a flyspeck on the far-off yellow stubble, and finally it would vanish for good against the mountainside.

'Those were hard, beautiful times,' Pinness told me in the kitchen of his little home. 'We went barefoot and dressed in rags like the Gibeonites, but our hearts were overflowing.'

In summer they threshed the grain together. Eighteen farmers operated the big thresher and screamed at each other like madmen each time the drum was caught. The women brought biscuits and homemade wine to the threshing floor, and at night the huge bales of hay drew lovers, snakes, and choral groups.

'Nothing looks better on a woman than a few wisps of hay,' Uri commented.

'Every radish that reddened in the vegetable gardens, every baby and calf, were a new promise and hope,' Pinness told us during our history lesson in school. 'The fat content of the milk reached four per cent, and our new oil incubator could house three hundred and sixty eggs at a time.' Rilov began to disappear for long periods. Everyone thought he was off buying arms and spying in Syria, until one day they found out that the huge septic tank by his cowshed was a sophisticated arms cache into which he descended to prepare for the worst, coming up for air at odd intervals.

The Feyge Levin Workingman's Circle was no longer in existence. It had vanished in a cloud. 'You couldn't exactly call it a factional split,' said Meshulam. 'Maybe they disbanded, or maybe they just drifted apart. They never talk about it. I think it must have happened after Avraham was born.

'The roots, though,' he guessed, 'went deeper. They had to do with some secret among the three men.'

Every Saturday Mandolin Tsirkin came to visit Grandfather and eat olives and herring with him. Sometimes he brought little Meshulam along to play with Avraham. Tsirkin and his son always looked unwashed and neglected. Meshulam, bright streaks of hardened snot on his cheeks, stared wonderingly at the glass plates on the table, while Mandolin gave Grandmother a look that I only understood years later, when motionless in bed I listened to the two old men have an unusually harsh conversation. Not even the tea and olives could overcome their anger.

'We trusted you with her,' growled Mandolin Tsirkin.

'I don't want to discuss it,' retorted Grandfather.

'Well, I do!' Tsirkin said.

Silence. Olives. A carefully nibbled sugar cube.

'If the two of you loved her so much,' Grandfather burst out, 'what made you think up that nutty lottery?'

'No one forced you to take part in it,' hissed Tsirkin.

'I'm not blaming just you.'

'We wanted to heal you,' whispered Tsirkin. 'To cure you of Shulamit.'

'Feyge Levin,' declaimed Grandfather with wicked fanfare. 'Devoted in her silence, indivisible in her love: the innocent, the poor sacrificial lamb!'

Liberson dropped in sometimes too, though since his marriage his visits were rare. He felt Grandfather's changed attitude toward him, and besides, 'he wanted to spend every spare minute making out with Fanya'.

Everyone sensed the subtle resentment blowing from Ya'akov Mirkin toward his friends. Grandfather was too much of a gentleman to hurt anyone on purpose, but with resolute tact he refused to sit down and swap memories or discuss his life with Feyge.

'When you were a boy of four, some people came from the radio to make a programme about them. Your grandfather refused to take part in it.'

'The Feyge Levin Workingman's Circle,' said Grandfather, pushing away the microphone, 'is a private matter. If Liberson and Tsirkin want to tell you how they danced and made the wilderness bloom, let them go right ahead.'

But once a year, on the anniversary of the founding of the village, the Workingman's Circle held a reunion. People came walking from all over the Valley, converging from the reaped fields like black dots. Seated on the ground, they watched the three men and the woman mount a platform of baled hay and stand facing them. A great tarpaulin of silence descended on the crowd. Tsirkin played the mandolin, Liberson and Mirkin sang along with him, and Feyge, frail and sickly, drummed laughingly on a pot.

She was nearing the end. Fanya Liberson was her best friend, and she bared her heart to her.

'Twice a year those disgusting birds come bringing a blue envelope.'

'Every six months a letter arrived,' said Fanya Liberson, massaging her husband's back. 'And every six months she died all over again.'

Through the foggy windowpane, I could see her hands move. Though they already had liver spots, their anger and tenderness were still a young woman's.

Liberson murmured something.

'Your Workingman's Circle joke ended badly,' said Fanya.

Liberson wouldn't admit it. 'But one of us had to marry her. It was in the constitution.'

'Why didn't you?' Fanya asked.

'I didn't draw the lucky number,' smiled the old man, turning to gather his wife to him. 'And what would have happened to us if I did? You'd be stranded in the kibbutz vineyard to this day. Unless Mirkin had run off with you instead.'

'That's all I needed.'

'Grandmother spent three years being pregnant, milked the cows, hauled blocks of ice, cooked, sewed, cleaned, and loved Grandfather until her dying breath,' said my cousin Uri to me in an unexpected outbreak of emotion.

'Grandfather wasn't to blame,' I answered.

'He won't let anyone say a mean word about his wonderful grandfather,' hissed my aunt Rivka, Avraham's wife. 'It's no wonder he's the way he is. He's spent his whole life with addled old men who told him nonsense. He had his grandfather for a mother, that pest Pinness for a friend, and Zeitser to pass the afternoons with. Not that that senile old coot ever said a word to him. Why, he's never even had a girlfriend. And he won't ever have one, either.'

Her squat, heavy body turned to face me. 'They should have sent you to an orphanage,' she yelled.

I was a sad and angry seventeen-year-old at the time. My loneliness, the stiffening flesh of my adolescent body, the deviousness of my mind, which still followed every twist and turn of my childhood – all filled me with resentment, with a black, gritty, stinging bile. Shulamit had just arrived in Israel, and Grandfather had left me and gone off to live with her in an old folk's home. Every other day I went on foot to visit him, bringing him a can of fresh milk.

When I returned home with the empty can in my hand, I went as usual to see Pinness. My old teacher dragged a little table out to the garden. He was raising balloon spiders for observation in the bushes, where dozens of them hid in their leafy domiciles, ready to swoop down on the prey caught in their nets. Though Pinness was old, he could still trap a fly in flight with one hand and cast it into a web.

'All those years your grandfather went on loving Shulamit, until she finally arrived, and all those years I thought of my dead Leah. We were made of different stuff from you. The patience of an entire people, two thousand years of it, had built up in our bodies until our blood ran hot.'

He sighed. 'I envy you. We had our romances too. We danced shirtless in the vineyards, young men and young maidens, and made love on the threshing floors. But who among us could shout in public, "I'm screwing so-and-so's daughter, and so-and-so's granddaughter, and so-and-so's wife"? Who hath sent out the wild ass free, and who hath loosed his bands?" '

'Is he still at it?'

'Once every few months, the scum. Afterwards I can't sleep for a week. The first time I wanted to climb up after him and throttle him. Now I just want to know who it is. To look him in the eyes and understand.'

As I sipped my tea I put an olive in my mouth. Pinness patted me affectionately.

'Just like your grandfather, eh? He's a man worth modelling yourself on. Ya'akov Mirkin is one of a kind. Even here in the village there's no one else like him. He never went to congresses or lobbied in Jerusalem or galloped off on a horse with a bandolier of bullets and a black *Keffiyeh*, Arabic scarf, on his head, but everyone looked up to him. When Mirkin touched a fruit tree, there was an idea behind the act that we all understood. You were privileged to be raised by such a man. How is he?'

'He's living with her there. He spends a lot of time standing on the terrace.'

'Doing what?'

'Looking. Waiting.'

'Still waiting?'

'For Efrayim, I suppose. And Jean Valjean. Maybe for Shifris too.'

# 9

To this day I haven't managed to transfer Grandmother's body from the village cemetery to mine. I offered the village a fortune for it. I thought of robbing her grave. Even Pinness, who was dead set against Pioneer Home, filed a request with the Committee on my behalf and wrote in the village newsletter about it.

Fanya Liberson was furious. That evening she burst through the green gate that led to the teacher's garden and stuck her lovely old head through the patch of light in his window.

'Won't you ever let her rest in peace?' she shouted, returning home without waiting for an answer. I followed her as quietly as I could, skipping from shadow to shadow.

'Mirkin killed her, and now that undertaker of a grandson of his is trampling on her memory. What does he want? To make his grandfather a happy man with his wife on one side of him and his Crimean whore on the other?'

I huddled outside the Liberson house, trying to make my big body smaller. It was difficult to hear the rest of their conversation. A wind was blowing, and Fanya's lips were pressed against her husband's wrinkled neck.

Avraham, who was five years old when his mother died, still remembers her, her funeral, and her fingers on his wrist. Yet though the veils of orphanhood flit over his face and graze its terrible creases, he never mentions her.

'Avraham, our first son, is now our first orphan,' said Pinness over the open grave.

The huge cypresses in the village cemetery were tender saplings then. There were only ten graves at the time: six pioneers whose bodies or souls had given out; the old mother of Margulis the beekeeper, who arrived from Russia with a hive of choice Caucasian bees and died of happiness three days later; two children dead from the cold in their tents; and Tonya Rilov's secret daughter, who slipped out of her cabin at the age of one year, crawled across the yard, and was trampled by a cow. 'The poor thing didn't die in her own bed either,' said Pinness in one of the few cruel remarks I ever heard him make.

'It was then,' he added, 'that I first understood that we had founded two settlements, the village and the cemetery, and that both would keep on growing.'

A flock of sheep was grazing nearby. The tinkle of their bells, the daubs of colour on their wool, and the whistles of the shepherds drifted toward the mourners. In the crisp, still air they were small, clear, and precise. From the village came the melancholy cries of Daniel Liberson, who, left alone at home, had gone looking for Esther and had tripped and fallen in the hayloft. Shlomo Levin wept by his sister's grave.

Tsirkin and Liberson stood by Grandfather, their hands protectively on his shoulders, half touching, half shielding him. The Workingman's Circle was silent. It was a spring day, and flocks of pelicans glided over the village, flying low as they screeched their way north. Fanya stood apart from her husband and his friends, cursing and crying. 'You can go and tell that bitch that Feyge is dead,' she whispered, her face turned toward the sky.

I tried to picture Shlomo Levin receiving the telegram from Grandfather, dropping his fountain pen, and passing out on the floor of his stationery shop.

'No,' he said to me when I asked him if that was how it was. 'I just looked at the telegram and thought to myself, "The hooligans, the hooligans, the hooligans!" That's all I thought. Hooligans. Over and over.'

He had sat there in a chair, imagining the lash of his father's belt on his body. 'I was holding a fountain pen that I was fixing, and the broken well dripped ink on my trousers.' He shut the shop, wrote a letter to his family in Russia, and took the train to Haifa. Outside the station he was spotted by Rilov, who was transporting a cart full of cement sacks and hidden shotgun parts to the village.

'Don't I know you from somewhere?' Rilov asked suspiciously.

'"I'm Mirkin's brother-in-law," I said to him.'

'Hop aboard.'

'What exactly happened?' asked Levin. He sat by Rilov's side, feeling the sinewy thigh with its metallic bulge against his own frightened body. But all Rilov said was, 'She was ill.' His rough hands, the low, muscular brow behind which he was knitting plans for the establishment of military communes in Transjordan, and the unintelligible language in which he talked to his two mules reminded Levin of his first days in the country. It took an hour's silent deliberation for Rilov to decide to reveal another fact. 'There was something wrong with her,' he said. 'She wasted ammunition. Twice in the last month she went outside and started shooting at birds in the sky.'

Levin's hatred and fear of Tsirkin, Mirkin, and Liberson turned to pity when he saw my grandfather carrying Efrayim on one arm and Esther on the other with little Avraham clinging to his legs. Levin hugged his brother-in-law and cried uncontrollably for his dead little sister and his own directionless life. Everyone remembered him from Avraham's circumcision, and Hayyim Margulis patted him on the back.

'I have a new queen bee,' he whispered. 'Her name is Riva.'

Levin said nothing.

'Why don't you come over later for a bite of pollen, the sweet flour of spring,' said Margulis. 'You'll see how much better it makes you feel.'

After the funeral Levin stepped up to Grandfather.

'Ya'akov,' he said bravely, 'I'll stay with you for the week of mourning.'

And he did, cleaning, cooking, bathing Avraham, and changing Efrayim's and Esther's nappies. As he hoed the bindweed that had infested Feyge's vegetable garden, he felt for the first time since his arrival in Palestine that he was actually doing some good and that the sun wasn't roasting him alive. The black earth of the Valley stuck to his hands, and the scent of the mignonette and wild dill that he weeded among the tomato plants made him a happy man. Fanya Liberson, who was helping out at Grandfather's too, was impressed.

'He's an unusual man,' she told her husband. 'I know that you and your friends could never stand him, but he is a dear fellow.'

When the week was up Levin went back to the stationery shop, but he took no interest in the customers. 'I sat there making up my mind.' When he returned to the village a month later to visit his sister's grave, he asked the Committee for a position. As he was a good bookkeeper with business experience, the farmers were happy to have him.

Levin sold his share in the stationery business, was given a cabin and a plot of land, and began managing the village co-op while continuing to help Grandfather.

'Whenever he had a free moment, Shlomo came over. He bathed the children, made them supper, and brought them little presents.'

When he tried his hand at farm work, however, he ran up against Zeitser. The two couldn't abide each other from the start. Though Zeitser did not actively oppose Levin's presence, he never made any effort to help him. 'He looked right through me as if I wasn't there.'

Levin had a delicate constitution, and when he tried to join the threshing crew that summer he breathed chaff into his lungs and went around coughing for years. From then on he just worked in the yard. 'They gave him all the women's jobs,' said my cousin Yosi when we were discussing the family one day. Levin fed the chickens, collected eggs, shook out and folded the empty fodder sacks, and washed the milk cans. He also concocted excellent jam from Grandfather's fruit, and gradually they became friends. His senses, which had become as sharp as a rabbit's from years of timidity and failure, told him that Grandfather no longer felt the same about his two old friends. It gladdened him to see that Grandfather preferred his own quiet company to postmortem arguments with Mandolin Tsirkin and Eliezer Liberson.

'Your grandfather, who was guilt-stricken after his wife's death, developed a liking for his brother-in-law, whose good humour and tactfulness he appreciated. We weren't living in the old days any more. We had the ground beneath our feet, each man under his vine. We knew what home and family were. We danced less. We sang less. We hated less.'

On winter evenings the dead woman's husband and brother sat playing draughts. Zeitser stood behind Grandfather, kibitzing into his ear. 'It didn't help, though,' Grandfather told me. 'I always lost. It helped Levin to feel at home.'

Grandfather taught him grafting cuts, proper pruning, and the right way to probe an infected tree for the most feared pest of all, the tiger moth, which had decimated whole orchards of apples throughout the Valley. The trees, however, shrank from Levin's touch. When he notched the bark of a Santa Rosa plum tree, it lost all its leaves overnight.

'We have to find him a wife,' said the villagers, mentally listing all the widows and unmarried pioneeresses they knew of.

But Levin surprised them all. After a secret correspondence with some matchmakers, he drove off one day to Tiberias in the cart of the itinerant barber who cut the Valley's hair, and returned with Rachel, a Yemenite many years younger than himself. She had a great many bracelets and teeth, and hundreds of relatives who came on donkeys for the wedding celebration and camped out in the fields in tents made of reed mats. Rachel spoke with an incomprehensible accent and walked with inaudible steps, but the most wondrous thing about her was her habit of roasting grasshoppers on a sheet of red-hot tin and eating their big, crispy bodies. Levin couldn't take his eyes off her and blessed his lucky stars for shining on him at last, for the first time since his arrival in the country.

'Rachel,' he said, 'is my revenge on the locusts whose wings darkened my blue sky.'

After Levin's death Rachel came to me and said, 'I know he would have wanted to be buried in your cemetery. He was a bit of a pioneer himself. He came with the Second Aliyah. So do it, even if it means that I won't be buried next to him.'

Efrayim, my vanished uncle, was five years old when Levin married Rachel. He was fascinated by her many bangles, her quiet brown face, and her noiseless walk. The night of her wedding he clung to his new aunt's legs and refused to let her go home despite the laughter of the village. When he grew older Rachel taught him to bake bread on a hot tin, to pray to God, and to walk as silently as a cat on sand, an art that was to give more than one farmer a fright and cause the premature death of many a German and Italian soldier.

Efrayim and his Charolais bull Jean Valjean disappeared from home when I was two. Although I don't remember him, I still envy him his silent walk. My own big bulk always made so much noise that time and again I was caught skulking outside people's houses as I eavesdropped. Slowly, impaled on the pitchforks of their angry glances, I would rise and walk away without a word. And yet no one ever did a thing to me. I was a parentless boy, 'Mirkin's orphan', Grandfather's child.

'Take a deep breath, raise your knee high, let your breath out, and bring your foot down flat,' Rachel said to Efrayim. They were walking over autumn thistles, which are the noisiest thing you can step on. By the time he was eight my uncle could cross a corn field or creep through a bed of thorns without a sound. He had also begun to speak in thick Yemenite gutturals, which Pinness made great efforts to eradicate.

My mother Esther was a baby then. Fanya Liberson and Shlomo Levin helped Grandfather raise her. Zeitser imitated birds and animals for her, Pinness read her Tolstoy's 'Fi-Li-Pok', in Russian, and Tsirkin played her lullabies. Even Rilov entertained her by cracking his famous bullwhip, which exploded

sharply in the air. So deftly did he wield it that he could pick an
apple by severing its stem with his quivering lash.

'You're scaring the trees, go back to your septic tank!' Grandfather would shout at him. But he permitted him to amuse his
daughter.

Esther and Daniel grew up. By now Esther too was aware of
Daniel's love for her. Lit by the glow of his eyes, smothered
by his kisses and caresses, she never took her hand from his.
Grandfather, Liberson, and Fanya basked in the sight of their
two children spending long days together, rambling through the
fields or chasing young chickens in the yard.

'Who are you going to marry?' Daniel would be asked.
Approaching Esther, he would put an arm around her waist
and lay his head on her shoulder.

But when Liberson began to joke about an engagement party
and a bride-price, Grandfather responded with a curt, wooden
silence. Fanya proved an unexpected ally.

'You're always trying to decide people's lives for them,' she
said.

When they went out to do the autumn ploughing and sowing,
they took the children with them to the fields. Avraham was
already able to hitch the mules to the cart, onto which they
loaded the plough, the seed sacks, and enough food and water
for themselves and the animals. Rather than return home for
lunch, they sat eating under the cart with several families from
the fields nearby. Esther and Daniel played in its shade and
embraced on the ground, and were allowed to sit on the seed
box during sowing as they grew older. My mother was quicker
and wilder than Daniel, who was talked into some mad prank by
her more than once. One day they were pulled half dead from the
cows' drinking trough, into which they had fallen while playing,
their hair green and sticky from algae and spittle. Another time
they disappeared for half a day, only to be found crying on top
of the newly built water tower.

'There was just one real problem with your mother – she was a
total carnivore.' When she was six months old, her mother Feyge
threw her a chicken bone to suck on because she was teething.

From then on Esther was mad about the taste of meat and never wanted to eat anything else.

Grandmother Feyge left behind a little orphan who would not touch fruit, cheese, or eggs. Only meat. Three times a day.

When Esther was two and a half, Levin once left a plate of raw chopped meat and parsley on the sink. 'Your mother spooned it all up and was so angry when it was gone that she smashed the dish. All Sonya the nurse's theories about proper vitamins, healthy minerals, and the link between meat diets and bloodlust came to grief in the case of that child, who grew up to be a tall, beautiful girl. She shot up like a blood-watered tomato, with marvellous skin, a hearty laugh, and a wonderful temperament.'

# 10

Even before deciding to banish Tonya, Margulis the beekeeper knew that something was wrong. Her voice and smell had changed, her skin had lost its smoothness, and her speech had grown brusque. Most nights she disappeared, and when she stayed home she no longer talked in her sleep.

Margulis had a kind heart. Witch-hunts and investigations were not his style. But when he found a bundle of foul-smelling dynamite fingers in a cask of his beeswax, he quietly showed Tonya out.

'What a difference between my fingers and his!' he said sadly.

For a while he lived in gloomy solitude, busying himself with apiarian innovations. Margulis was the only beekeeper in the country to pasture his bees in the fields, where he trained them to land on specific flowers. This technique, which he had learned from the writings of the Russian beekeeper Khlimenko, who was a great partisan of Michurin, enabled him to produce new flavours of honey while pollinating only those plants he wished to. And yet while adopting the Communists' methods, he rejected the theory behind them, to wit, the claim that the acquired knowledge of insects, like the traits of grafted fruit trees and the beliefs of revolutionaries, could be passed on genetically, thus making possible the propagation of new breeds of bees that would be attracted by some flowers and not others.

'Red ones, obviously,' sneered Grandfather.

'They're wrong,' said Margulis. 'How can anything learned by a worker bee be passed on genetically? It's the queen bee that reproduces, and since she never leaves the hive, she never learns a thing.'

Grandfather was thrilled to find out from Margulis that each generation of worker bees needed to be re-educated. It was a bad day for Michurin in the Valley.

'What did Lenin know about bees?' he scoffed. 'Since when do Communists model themselves on monarchical societies?'

The two pioneers sat on the ground, their laughter breezing past young pear trees and tickling the funny bones of bees wallowing in the innards of flowers.

'In their admiration for the worker bees, the Stakhanovites of the hive,' said Margulis, 'the Communists completely forgot that it's the proletariat's mission to depose the Czarina and make a revolution.'

'Once,' Grandfather told me, 'Hayyim Margulis led his winged proletariat all the way to the railway tracks to show them the wild orchids and purple clover growing along the embankments.'

As the train crawled by, Margulis caught sight of Riva Beilin's profile through the window. Followed by a great cloud of bees, he jumped onto the train, still holding an earthenware beehive. The horrified passengers moved away from him, vacating the place beside Riva.

'There's nothing to be afraid of,' he told her. 'They don't bite.'

Riva Beilin came from a very rich family in Kiev. Dressed in expensive clothing that aroused the ridicule of her astonished comrades, she was grudgingly seen off to Palestine by her parents, who were sugar manufacturers and grain merchants. Now, as she looked suspiciously at Margulis, whose boots were covered with mud, he dipped a bare, practised hand into his hive, withdrew a honey-drenched finger, and extended it toward her mouth.

Though Riva was dumbfounded, the blue innocence of Margulis's eyes overcame her objections. Hesitantly gripping his wrist, she licked the honey off his finger. At once her eyes lit up and a smile spread over her lips. It was her first taste of Margulis's fingers and of the wildflower honey of the Valley. Sweetly and merrily, Margulis jumped out to rejoin his bees, but in the months that followed he travelled by train twice a week to meet his new love.

Every Saturday Margulis brought Grandfather a mysterious jar in which he had prepared a special concoction for the firstborn son of the village. Avraham's development was followed with patient expectancy by everyone. His height, weight, first words, and clever sayings were regularly published in the village news-letter. He was hugged and petted by all hands. The farmers brought him fresh vegetables and milk from their best cows, and their wives sewed clothes for him, but Grandfather could not be made to understand that his first son was communal property.

'It started when Feyge was still alive. Neighbours would arrive with visitors at ten o'clock at night to see the first child of the village. They insisted that Mirkin wake him up.'

Meshulam read me 'an original document' about Zakkai Ackerman, the first child born on the neighbouring kibbutz. 'He was considered a public possession. Everyone felt free to wake him up and bring him to the dining hall, even in the middle of the night. More than one long winter evening was spent by the kibbutzniks sitting around tables admiring the infant.'

'Leave the boy alone,' Grandfather scolded the stream of curiosity-seekers who came looking for Avraham, lifting the canvas tent flap at all hours and even crawling inside to see if there was any truth to the rumours that the baby shone in the dark.

Grandfather was incensed. 'We don't live in the old days any more,' he exclaimed, and taking Avraham, a shepherd's club, and a mosquito net, he went off to sleep in the thicket by the spring with a cry of 'The child isn't yours!' No one dared follow him. The area around the spring had once been inhabited by German settlers, every one of whom died of malaria, and the reedy death shrieks of their blond children could still be heard there, haunting the rushes and elecampane. This put an end to the harassment, though whoever looked southward from the watchtower that night saw a golden glimmer beaming through the dark patches of the blackberry bushes like the light of some great firefly. A few years later Grandmother died, and no one dared bother the orphan any more. Avraham's only memory of that night by the spring was a lifelong allergy to jonquils and swamp flowers.

And yet inwardly, there was no one who didn't worry and brood about him. Zakkai Ackerman, the firstborn son of the kibbutz across the wadi, had already raised a row of cucumbers that averaged eighteen inches and planted a medlar tree whose fruit was the size of a Grand Alexander apple. The first child of Kfar Avishai had made his debut at a Movement conference with 'an astounding oration' that unerringly prophesied the factional split in the Workers' Brigade, 'though he was only three and a half years old'. The first child of Bet Eliyahu was all of six when he began investigating the coccidiosis infection then ravaging the chicken coops, and soon after he was asked to join Professor Adler's research team, which had already developed a remedy for the epidemic of miscarriages introduced into our herds in the late 1920s by imported Dutch cows, and had received a decoration from the British High Commissioner and a parchment certificate from the Movement. Avraham Mirkin alone was a late bloomer who kept the village in suspense – or, to put it more bluntly, disappointed it.

'We would have taken it in our stride had he been an ordinary child, but everyone could see that your uncle did have something special about him.'

Avraham had the ability to calm a panicky animal with a single glance. During the gnat season he sometimes had to be called to the fields to treat a mule or farmer gone half out of their minds from the ceaseless buzzing. There were also other odd things about him that kept hopes for him alive, such as his habit of wandering around at night looking for no one knew what, a five-year-old boy who overturned stacks of cans, shook out piles of old sacks, lifted curtains, stared at sleeping calves, and scared the chickens in their coops as if in search of something.

Some thought it was because he was an orphan. 'He's looking for his mother,' they said. 'Poor Feyge.'

'And little wonder,' said Fanya years later. Held in her husband's embrace, ringed round by an inexhaustible reserve of Libersonian love, she had no inkling that someone was listening on the other side of the wall.

'And little wonder,' she said about my uncle. 'The child was born in a house without love.'

# 11

It was Pesya Tsirkin, naturally, who brought the American philanthropists for a visit, thus putting her oafish stamp on my family history.

Although Grandfather never said an unkind word about her, I was an expert at decoding the slightest tremor of every line and wrinkle in his face. He loathed her. And so for that matter did her husband.

Mandolin met Pesya at some conference where she gave an impassioned speech on the subject of mutual aid funds, bobbing her large breasts in time with her visionary ardour. Tsirkin, whose strong point was never the financial aspects of pioneering, was swept off his feet by pure lust. Trapping Pesya with his mandolin strings proved no problem, and when she became pregnant they were married – yet soon it dawned on her that life in the village lacked the emotional rewards of a career in the Movement, with its sense of mission, its joys of travel, and the polished intellects and shoes of its orators, bursars, and platform drafters.

For a while Pesya enjoyed stepping into the yard and calling 'Hssst, hssst' to the chickens, baking bread, and growing kohlrabi, Egyptian onions, and Wondermart tomatoes for home consumption. Before long, however, she found herself up to her neck in heavy soil and irritating poultry droppings. When Meshulam was two years old she took a trip to Tel Aviv, where, yielding to the exhortations of her comrades on the Central Committee, she returned to her old job.

Pesya Tsirkin quickly scaled the heights of public office and soon was in charge of budgets and bureaus herself. It did not take Mandolin many months to realise that the queasy feeling produced in him by his wife's visits was hatred pure and simple. After Pesya went to London on Movement business, she returned to the village cloaked in exotic perfumes that made the barnyard animals sneeze and stagger. Arriving home, she kissed little Meshulam, who was playing with some baby chicks on the floor, seized her husband by the hand with a strange expression, and tried to drag him off to the bedroom. Tsirkin, whose most ingrained beliefs were offended by the scent of her, slipped from her prurient grasp and found in her suitcase still more perfume, a pair of high-heeled shoes, and a black dress. A body search also uncovered a silk slip.

'You bought all this crap with Movement money,' he accused her, shaking with anger.

'Like hell I did,' laughed Pesya, opening her arms wide. 'I won the money in a casino I went to with Ettinger between sessions.'

The sight of her newly shaven armpits filled him with fear and indignation. Throwing the clothing and shoes into the barrel he used for burning dead chickens and poisoned mice, he doused them with the perfume to send the flames higher. That same Saturday he moved his bed out to the large mulberry tree in the yard and broke off relations with the woman who had brought such disgrace on the Movement, the village, and the Tsirkin family. Everyone knew that he slept in the yard whenever his wife came to visit, because he sat up half the night strumming away on his mandolin. His Sabbath clothes were stained with the black and purple blotches of ripe mulberries that fell on him in his sleep. Now and then he let out a shout that could be heard all over the village, for he was one of the first victims of the stealth of Efrayim, who took to sneaking up to his bed and poking prickly ears of wheat into his nostrils.

Forty years later Pesya was awarded the Labour Prize. The real reason that Comrade Tsirkin's whole life was 'devoted to her society and people', as it says on the parchment certificate hanging on the wall of Founder's Cabin, was her husband's unyielding abstinence. It was also the reason Meshulam remained an only child.

The guests Pesya brought were the Americans who had donated the money for buying the village lands, and who now wanted to see how they had helped make the wilderness blossom. The three Ford limousines they came in were the first American automobiles we had seen.

The wealthy Jews spent hours walking through the farmyards, smiling and taking pictures. 'Their clothes stank of sybaritism, and their smooth skins masked the hideous secrets of wealth. But what could we do? The money was theirs.'

One of them was accompanied by an attractive young woman. 'No one as beautiful as she had been seen in our village before. She was like the very heavens for purity, tall and striking, with grey eyes that crinkled like olives when she laughed. The spirit of gaiety lurked in the corners of her mouth.'

The visitors were shown the new refrigerator in the dairy, saw Avigdor Ya'akovi single-handedly yoke the breeding bull to a cart, and were taxied on it to the garden to pick fresh vegetables. They watched Ya'akov Mirkin graft vines onto the new grape stock they had brought him, and Rilov demonstrate the correct breathing for target shooting in the three standard positions, standing, kneeling, and lying.

It was then that Pesya announced her intention of showing them the village's firstborn son.

Grandfather objected. 'The child is not a display item,' he said.

Pesya stepped up to him with a smile, bobbing her breasts to heighten her persuasiveness.

'This isn't a London casino,' said Grandfather, who knew the truth behind Mandolin's stained Sabbath clothes. 'Keep your hands off the boy.'

Just then, though, Avraham came back from the fields on Zeitser's back. Grandfather turned to take him home, but something in the eyes of the village's firstborn son as they glanced at the assemblage made him freeze.

The philanthropists from America were agog at the sight of the earnest, motherless boy, whose radiant complexion brought home the full significance of the enterprise they were supporting. He smiled at them, and then, without being asked, knelt on the ground, dug a small hollow, placed a seed of corn in it, and covered it with earth. 'This symbolic act, which expressed the meaning of our lives so well, moved everyone greatly.' Two of the philanthropists immediately proposed bringing the boy back with them to America, where he would be sent to the best schools before returning to his homeland as an all-round Renaissance man. At this point, however, Pinness intervened to explain tactfully that a firstborn son's virility came from contact with his native soil, taken from which 'he will lose his strength like Samson and be like any other man'. And so the guests had to content themselves with asking the child to speak a few words to them about the Jewish people's return to their ancestral land, the village's ties to the earth, and so on and so forth.

Just then the young beauty approached. Seeing the firstborn son, she reached out unthinkingly to stroke his head. Avraham rose from the ground without a word and brushed the dirt from his hands and knees.

There was a sudden premonition of disaster in the air. Everyone who felt it realised at once that something terrible was about to take place.

The firstborn son turned his bold stare from the crowd of

guests to the beautiful lady and said to her:

And when a heavy dust falls from the ceiling
and the remembrance of my body strikes,
what will you say to appease the fire in your soul?
A blossom, warm and hard,
will bud in your flesh.
Your lover entrapped in the bonds of his words,
silent, at bay,
what will you say in your dream as his hand
like a creditor's soft palm descends on your skin?
The towering gourd of love above your head
refuses to wilt.
Then you will know the scorching east winds,
the sands' obstinate will.
Our backs we gave to the smiters,
your memory stifled and kept.
Ah, from the depths, the tenacious depths,
weeds of longing enwrap our heads.

So spoke Avraham, touching off a great uproar. 'What did he say?' asked the young lady in English, her perfect limbs ablaze. 'What did he say?' A reporter from the Movement newspaper who was travelling with the group took furious notes. Meshulam Tsirkin showed me the article he wrote: 'The village's first child, Avraham Mirkin, recited a poem of uncertain nature having no clear relevance to our national situation or goals.'

The comrades were in a state of shock. Fanya Liberson buried her cheek in her husband's neck with a movement that would become second nature and murmured that the thirst for love had passed from poor Feyge's tormented body to the child in her womb, driving him out of his mind.

'Now you see your fruit,' she whispered angrily. 'It wasn't blood and it wasn't sweet. It was poison. Never-clotting venom. And don't you dare tell me any jokes now.'

Pinness, who felt greatly sorry for Avraham and his father, tried to demonstrate that the child had merely 'linked together verses from the Book of Jonah by a process of free association', but Rilov snapped at him to shut his mouth if he wanted to die in his own bed.

Avraham alone paid the commotion no mind. He simply looked at the beautiful woman, who began to tremble, her flesh insidiously lanced by the child's stare. A strong oestrous smell known to every farmer cleaved the veils of her perfume, and the Dutch bull was heard to bellow dully as it charged the fence of its corral. The beautiful visitor laughed with an embarrassed stamp of her foot. Then, her hips and thighs stirring the air, she stepped up to Avraham, took a glittering coin from her purse, and waved it in front of his eyes.

'She gave him money,' said Grandfather to Pinness during one of their night-time talks. 'Money! That's what Pesya taught them to redeem land and souls with.'

The woman from abroad placed the coin in Avraham's shirt pocket, where it lay like a written anathema, and took a step back, waiting anxiously to see what would happen.

The firstborn son's face turned dark all at once. Two terrible furrows creased his brow from the bridge of the nose to the hairline, as though at the stroke of a pickaxe.

# 12

I lay on a bed of jonquils, staring up at the sky. Flocks of migrating storks soared overhead, circling like tiny water insects on a clear, transparent pond. Back in the Ukraine, two storks had nested in the chimney of Grandfather's house. 'I knew that they visited the Land of Israel each year and came back with a bellyful of the frogs of Canaan,' Grandfather told me. Were the grandchildren of those storks flying over me now?

Each spring and autumn Grandfather stepped out of his cabin and stared up at the storks and pelicans with his hand shading his eyes, full of the sorrow of great rivers, of vast fields of grain, of snowy steppes and forests of birch trees. 'Here I am among the blackberries,' he wrote, 'in the land of the grasshopper and the jackal, of the olive and the fig.'

I thought of Shifris. Was he still alive? Would he be able to find the paths that his comrades had long since built over? Where was he now? Killed by border guards and buried beneath snow or sand? Fallen like ashes from the sting of some electrified fence? Did he know that the swamps had already been drained and the wilderness made to bloom? That Grandfather had gone to live with Shulamit in the old age home?

Shifris would come, and I would let him have Grandfather's bed. He would cure olives, smoke in the kitchen at night, plant olive trees, pomegranates, vines, and figs. He would be a frail old man with a battered hat on his head, a rod of an almond tree in his hand, and a backpack containing mouldy bread, a canteen, olives, cheese, a Bible, and a couple of oranges. Sometimes he walked singing quietly, sometimes piping on a reed he had cut along the way. Slowly he crossed mountains and deserts and followed rocky coastlines, his lips dry and cracked, his shoes clouted like the Gibeonites'.

'We should make Shifris a little swamp to drain,' said my cousin Uri. 'And plant a bit of crabgrass so that he'll have something left to weed. And find him an old pioneeress with white braids to gallop over him at night on the threshing floor.' His eyes shone. He was a boy who hunted sensations, mocked memories, and cared only for love stories.

Like a small dot, Shifris would detach himself from the blue mountain and draw nearer, until he reached Grandfather's cabin and said, 'Go, my child. Go tell Mirkin that I'm here.' Weary from his long journey, he would fall on Grandfather's bed, wanting nothing but a glass of water. How light he would be, how thin and emaciated, as I carried him over the fields of the Valley to show to Grandfather!

I will go now to the spring to lie down in the thicket beside it. Coming back, I will pass through my family's fields, the same fields in which water buffalo once grazed, green rushes prospered, and the larvae of the anopheles mosquito multiplied in the execrable waters. Before they were dried and ploughed.

Before Grandfather grew his blossoming trees in them, and Avraham pastured his cows in their meadows, and I planted them with my ornamentals, my flowers, and my dead.

Unlike 'that boy of Tsirkin's', Mirkin's children helped their father with the farm chores. They were hard workers. Avraham had a great talent with the cows. At the age of twelve he conceived the idea of introducing artificial insemination, which was only impractical, the veterinarian explained to Grandfather, because there was no good semen available in the country. Scientifically, Avraham was often ahead of the scientists.

'Semen could be frozen,' he announced in the middle of lunch one day, the furrows in his forehead contracting in concentration. 'It could be frozen and brought to the cowshed instead of bringing the cows to the bull. We could get it from the best-bred bulls abroad. Think of all the time and work it would save.'

Ever since the episode of the 'American beauty', however, Avraham's ideas were received with suspicion. He was an introverted, unspontaneous child. Occasionally he would disappear for a day at a time, turning out to have been at the grave of his mother, whom he told all about himself.

Efrayim, having stealthily followed him, heard him talking to her.

'We have a raised floor for the chickens now, so that the manure drops down below. It's the best fertiliser there is.'

'Why don't you also tell her about the ice cream you're going to make from bulls' balls,' his brother called out behind his back.

Avraham spun around and went for him. Efrayim, quick and agile, dodged. Noiseless as a barn owl, he skimmed over the field, his bare feet kicking up little dust clouds. Avraham ran after him, sobbing all the way to the village, a distance of three miles. Now and then he bent to pick up a stone or clod and threw it at his brother.

At night Grandfather told the children stories from his childhood. He told them how his brother Yosef, the capitalist traitor, had been kidnapped by gypsies when he was three.

'The Czarist police found him in a sack in the Kharkov railway station. The gypsies had wanted to make an acrobat and a thief out of him. He was only with them for four days, but we had to teach him to talk again. He had forgotten all the words he knew, crawled around on all fours, and picked pockets.'

Grandfather told them how he had built a hothouse for myrtle bushes when he was ten. 'On the Feast of Tabernacles I sold myrtle branches to the Hasidim, every one of them ritually perfect. It was the first hothouse in Makarov. My father was very proud of me.'

'Tell us about our mother,' begged Avraham. Grandfather told them how Grandmother Feyge had thought of setting a male turkey on chicken eggs. The turkey was so big that it could sit on fifty eggs at a time. The problem was that it squashed all the eggs when it stood up. And so Grandmother gave it wine, and the drunk bird, its flushed wattles red as fire, sat happily smiling at the eggs and never stirred.

'All the women in the village switched to turkeys,' laughed Grandfather, 'even though Liberson wrote in the newsletter that "a Hebrew poultry run isn't a bar".'

I thought of those days with envy. They seemed to me a sort of dream, though Yosi said they had in fact been quite awful.

'They were three orphans and one father who had no idea how to run a farm,' he said. 'When everyone else was buying new double-bladed ploughs, Grandfather was busy hugging olive trees. They had no money for boots in the winter, they did all their milking by hand, and they shared their work animals with the neighbours, whom they were always quarrelling with. Today we have electric incubators, and soon we'll be inseminating the turkeys too.'

Yosi was proud of the new breeding coop he had built for his turkeys. It was an enclosed lightproof structure covered with tarpaper, in which the young females sat waiting to get good prices for their fertilised eggs. Blindly groping for their food, they were prevented by the darkness from thinking, hoping, or wanting sex. As soon as an order came in from the National Turkey Council, we hurried to bring them to the males. They staggered out warily on feeble legs, blinking the watery, sun-split lenses of their eyes. Five minutes in the sun was all it took to put them in heat. Kowtowing in the hot dirt with palsied wings, they summoned the males with shrill voices and the red flowers that pulsed beneath their tails.

'Stupid randy birds,' said Yosi. The turkey hens squatted in the middle of the yard and turned up their rumps, too much in heat to walk to the breeder. Yosi and Avraham had to kick them inside and strap canvas saddles on their backs to keep the heavy males from tearing their flesh when they mounted them.

'Just look at that,' Uri said to me. 'That's what falling in love is like. It lets in the light.'

The males squabbled near the impatient hens, pushing and shoving each other. As soon as one succeeded in doing his duty, his consort rose with smug languor, shook out her wings, and went off to her friends in a chatter of show-offy silence.

'She's running to tell them it was worth waiting for,' said Uri.

'The thought of spending two months in the dark just to be screwed by a turkey!' sneered Yosi.

But I was thinking of three children beneath Grandfather's sheltering wings, sitting down to a winter supper of potatoes cooked in their jackets, hard-boiled eggs, a bowl of homemade herring marinated in lemon juice and onion rings, and bright slices of radish. I was thinking of my dead mother; of her long braids and legs catching fire; and of Efrayim. To this day I sometimes whirl around suddenly, thinking he is behind me with his great Charolais bull on his shoulders, laughing at having startled me.

'No one understood how my son Efrayim could pick up a bull,' Grandfather told me with a smile.

No one understood and no one saw what was coming. Not even Pinness foretold the embryonic evil as it ripened. 'An orphan growing up with his grandfather is one big barrel of stories,' he said of me. I myself no longer know what I have heard and what I have seen myself. Was it Avraham who ran to his mother's grave, or was it me? Did I leave the village, or did Efrayim?

The large gravestones gleam brightly in Pioneer Home. 'Stones to stop the well of dreams with,' Pinness called them. At night I wander through the banker's big house, the bull of memory heavy on my shoulders.

# 13

'Your mother was a sentimental tomboy, a Tom Sawyer with a soul.'

Her carnivorousness, though, was more than Pinness could fathom.

'She was a good student. She knew the poetry of Tchernichovski and Lermontov by heart. And yet halfway through a lesson she would suddenly take a piece of meat from her schoolbag and tear into it with her teeth.'

Not only the teacher but the entire village watched the children hopefully. As healthy and quick as wild asses, they worked alongside their parents. The local air could not scorch their lungs, and their bodies soaked up the sun as if made of the local chalkstone.

'Mirkin's three orphans did all the jobs.' At dawn Avraham woke his brother and sister to help with the milking before going off to school. Before supper they found time to cut and load a cart of alfalfa and bring it to the yard, their pitchforks thrust into the rear of the tottering green bale on which Efrayim and my mother stood wrestling while Avraham, who practically speaking was already running the farm, taciturnly gripped the reins. The deep furrows of anger crawled like lizards up his forehead and disappeared into his bushy hair.

Shouting with merriment and anger, my wiry mother and her brother tumbled in each other's arms. Sometimes they fell off the cart and went on fighting by the roadside while their father watched them from the branches of his orchard.

'That girl is a greater menace to the chickens than the wildcat down by the spring,' said Grandfather to Zeitser. 'The way she eats meat, there soon won't be a hen left.'

My mother began climbing trees and roofs to catch starlings. She made Daniel Liberson come along on these safaris, and the love-stricken boy followed her through the fields, watching her remove birds from her traps. Because of her the migrating quail began overflying our fields, and vegetable gardens lost their rabbits. Calves froze with fright if she patted them on the back.

Once she clambered onto the roof of the village feed shed with Efrayim to ambush doves. A wooden plank broke beneath her. She skidded, grabbed hold of the rain gutter, and was left dangling by her arms twenty feet above the concrete pavement. Efrayim tried to pull her back up but couldn't manage.

'Hold tight,' he shouted. 'I'll run and get Daniel.'

He vanished while my mother gritted her teeth and held on to the gutter for dear life. Just then Benjamin Schnitzer, 'that idiot worker of Rilov's', passed by below.

'Benjamin!' the girl called down through clenched jaws.

Rilov's worker glanced up and looked down again in embarrassment, 'because,' as a bright-eyed Uri told me, 'your mother was wearing a flared dress and kicking her legs.' Benjamin had already been the butt of more than one practical joke in the village and suspected that this was another.

'Don't be so shy, Benjamin,' called my mother. 'It's all right, you can look.'

He was standing directly beneath her, and as he glanced up again he felt his throat constrict at the splendour of her thighs, which swung like warm clappers in the bell of her dress.

'Your father Benjamin arrived in this country in the thirties with a group of Jewish boys from Munich. He came to the village for agricultural training and was sent to work on Rilov's farm.'

He was a short, blond, powerful young man. In the album of the village war dead my father appears standing in smartly cuffed blue work trousers and a clean white undershirt beneath Rilov's date tree – the same tree whose fruit, according to Uri, exploded on contact with the ground. Blinking in the sun, his boyish, coarse-featured face stares out above rounded shoulders. The hands are thick and unshapely, like my own, and the arm, wrist, and palm look like a single two-by-four. He has a big, round barrel chest.

'You'll be as tall as your mother and as strong as your father,' I was always told. As I grew older, everyone was pleased to see the prophecy come true.

Benjamin held out his arms.

'You lets go, quick,' he said. His Hebrew was still rudimentary.

My mother hesitated.

'*Schnell, schnell,* quick, quick,' said Benjamin. 'I catch.'

The farmers of our village can guess a calf's weight at a glance, predict the winds from the colour of the moon, and tell you the nitrogen content of the soil by tasting an onion. My mother took a good look at Benjamin's calm eyes and solid shoulders, let go, and plummeted, her dress flying over her face and her stomach soaring up into her ribs. Eyes tightly shut, she felt herself cradled in his huge hands.

Benjamin grunted from the impact. My mother was tall and not at all light, and he had to go down on his knees to absorb the shock. Her terrified body struck his chest, her bare belly panting with fright against his cheeks, so close that I can still feel the warmth of it across all the yarns and years.

'You can let go of me now,' she smiled. She had got her breath back, but her nails still dug frantically into his shoulders and arms. 'You were great.'

My father was nonplussed. He had never before been so close to a female body.

'Thank you kindly, Benjamin,' she laughed, jumping from his arms and smoothing out her dress just as Efrayim and Daniel appeared carrying a tall fruit-picker's ladder.

'Hey, you German schmuck, what are you doing?' shouted Efrayim irately. Light and skinny fifteen-year-old though he was, he was on the verge of laying into Rilov's worker. Daniel stood there dumbstruck, pallid with envy, helplessness, and loss. His lips twitched.

'He saved my life,' said Esther. 'Rilov's stupid German saved my life.'

Once more my father heard her laugh and was brushed by a sweet breeze as my mother, Efrayim, and Daniel Liberson took off on the run around the corner.

My father was sixteen when he came to the village and went to live and work on Rilov's farm.

'He arrived from Germany right before the war,' it says in the village album. 'His entire family died in the gas chambers, and he met his death among us here. We will always remember the hardworking, thoughtful, cultured young man that he was. Who can forget him on his way to the dairy each evening, whistling symphonies and giving everyone a big hello while carrying four large milk cans on his shoulders?'

Rilov's stupid German carried the milk cans himself because he had trouble communicating with Rilov's mules. The four cans, weighing five and a half stone apiece, were chained to an iron yoke on his shoulders.

Rilov's mules arrived with the British army during World War I and decided to stay on.

'Apart from their annoying habit of cadging beer from every passer-by, they were excellent draught animals,' said Meshulam. In a box labelled 'Miscellanies' he kept the protocol of the Committee meeting at which Rilov requested a beer budget for them. It was his custom to read it aloud at village celebrations.

'"Comrade Rilov: Mules eat barley, and beer is liquid barley.

'"Comrade Liberson: Rilov is being sophistical.

'"Comrade Rilov: What about the turkeys who drank wine?

'"Comrade Tsirkin: No one wasted good wine on turkeys. It's just one of Mirkin's stories.

'"Comrade Rilov: After a little tipple, the mules work like the very devil.

'"Comrade Liberson: The request is rejected. We will not introduce alcohol into our work life.

'"Comrade Rilov: The Feyge Levin Workingman's Circle put away gallons of vodka.

'"Comrade Liberson: We thank Comrade Rilov for the comparison, but there were no mules in the Workingman's Circle, only jackasses.

'"Comrade Rilov: I'll brew my own beer, then.

'"Comrade Tsirkin: We did not come to the Land of Israel to treat our animals to champagne breakfasts."'

The audience would laugh and applaud, but everyone knew that Rilov had planted two rows of hops and that his mules could plough twice as much in a day as any other team. To this day the villagers remember the great steaming puddles they left behind. And yet even Zeitser, who was an expert on both mules and barley, declared that he was 'dead set against such decadence'.

Long years in armies, communes, and all kinds of rural settlements had made the two mules callous. Seeing a shy, innocent youth, they decided to have a bit of fun with him. They baulked when he tried to harness them, tangled the reins, pooped on the traces, and made each other laugh with hideous belches. My father, however, was an industrious young man, and while his hopeless awkwardness amused the villagers, his persistence and punctuality won their admiration. The story is still told about how he left Rilov unconscious in the slops ditch after Deborah, the vicious milk cow, had sent the Watchman sprawling with a kick to the head.

'But I cover him with a sack so he not catch cold,' apologised my father, who 'hated being late to the dairy', to Tonya.

In Germany he had studied at a technical school, and within a month of his arrival he had designed and built for Rilov's calves an automated watering system that was the talk of the Valley. He also scrubbed the cowshed with stiff brushes and Lysol and hooked it up to the phonograph in his cabin.

'Even Rilov's wife Tonya admitted that Mahler increased the cows' milk production,' Avraham once told me during one of our rare conversations.

'I was walking in the village one day when the strains of Beethoven drew me irresistibly to your father's cabin. I went over and peeked in the window. Your father was lying in bed listening to music, his hair a golden haystack on his forehead. He had a phonograph that his parents had sent him from Germany. They managed to get it to him before Hitler burned them.'

Pinness knocked and entered. Benjamin rose, clicked his heels, and bowed. Three things happened that day. My father's name was Hebraised from Benjamin Schnitzer to Binyamin Shenhar; he received his first private Hebrew lesson; and he lent Pinness two records.

'Your father was a hardworking, serious student. He never learned to speak Hebrew fluently, but his spelling was letter-perfect.'

There was in the village a merry band of youngsters known as 'the Gang'. These were the founders' children who had already reached adolescence.

'The whole village forgave their mischief because they were new Jews, children of the earth, suntanned and straight-backed,' said Pinness. 'At night they stole candy and coffee from the co-op and guns from the nearby British airfield. Sometimes Rilov sent them out to the fields with whips to chase off the Arab flocks that ate the young grain. Every year, at the ceremony of first fruits and newborn children, they put on a Wild East show, galloping past the audience while standing on their horses like Ukrainian bandits.'

After they had cleaned out all the chocolate in the co-op, Shlomo Levin came to Pinness to demand a tête-à-tête.

'The hooligans did it to get me,' he said. 'They look down on me because I'm not a farmer like their parents.'

'They did it because they felt like eating chocolate. The predilection for sweets is a biological universal,' Pinness said.

'They'd never dare steal from a farmer,' said Levin. 'If they can't afford chocolate, let them eat *kamardin*.'

'Just last week they pinched two jars of honey from Margulis's shed,' Pinness replied.

'That's exactly how I was treated when I came to this country,' continued Levin, deafened by anger. 'You people never had any appreciation of plain ordinary work. You were too busy acting in your great Theatre of Redemption and Rebirth. Every ploughing was a return to the earth, every chicken laid the first Jewish egg after two thousand years of exile. Ordinary potatoes, the same *kartoffelakh* you ate in Russia, became *tapuchei adamah*, "earth apples", to show how you were at one with Nature. You had your pictures taken with rifles and hoes, you talked to the toads and the mules, you dressed up as Arabs, you thought you could fly through the air.'

'That's what kept us going,' said Pinness.

Levin got to his feet, pale with hatred. 'I kept myself going too,' he said. 'I could have left and I didn't. I could have been a rich businessman in the city and I came here instead. You taught them to look down on me. And don't start in on that song and dance of yours – they're my saplings, they're my plant bed – because you're no more of a farmer than I am. We're both public servants. Both of us thought we were serving an idea, and now it turns out to have been just a bunch of *kulaks*. You can have them and their earth and their first fruits and their cows! Gordon and Brenner wrote with the fountain pens that I fixed.'

Pinness lost his temper. 'No one came here to do anyone a favour,' he said. He raised his voice. 'And no one deserves a medal for giving up a shop in the city. You came because you needed this earth as we all did. The feel of it, the smell of it, the promise of it. Needed it more than it needed you.'

Once Levin had left with an injured slam of the door, however, Pinness gathered the Gang and gave them a loud dressing-down.

'Our life in this village is more than just sweets. If all you want is bonbons and petit fours, you can pack your bags and go to the city.'

The Gang walked out shamefacedly and submitted to the pedagogical penance of building a big sandbox for the kinder-garten that the children still play in to this day.

My uncle Efrayim was one of them. He was a handsome, slender boy, as quick and unerring as a ferret, the biggest prankster and mocker of them all. One day the Gang decided to play a joke on Binyamin, whose slow, clumsy gait had caught their notice. Efrayim had hated and feared him ever since his rescue of my mother.

One Saturday while Binyamin was resting, the boys threw a young viper into his cabin and waited to see what would happen. When my father heard its slithering scales, he gave a cry and ran outside to gales of laughter. For a moment he stood facing them, his bright eyes slit against the afternoon sun with the fury of knowing he had been duped. Stepping up to Efrayim, who was then seventeen, he grabbed him by his broad leather belt and jerked him off the ground with one motion.

'Your uncle Efrayim squirmed and yelled and laughed, but your father, using only his left hand, carried him to the farmyard and threw him into the cow trough, Sabbath clothes and all.'

'Bravo!' shouted the Gang. In no time they had all trooped into Binyamin's cabin. Efrayim raised a heel tough as a horn and bashed in the snake's neck as it lay coiled beneath a chair. Then they made Binyamin sit down at the table and arm-wrestle with them one by one. Emerging unvanquished, he was declared a Gang member himself.

Slow, smiling, shy, and inarticulate, he met them every Friday. Before long they learned to use his technical talents and broke into Pesya Tsirkin's car, which had been given to her by the Movement. Told by them that it was needed to convey arms and important intelligence, Binyamin started it up without a key. Somehow, however, the group always managed to stop on its way at a cinema in the city.

Efrayim grew attached to Binyamin and forgot his old grudge at seeing his sister giggling breathlessly in his arms. Several times a week he went to listen to music in his cabin. In Binyamin's trunk was clothing from Germany that Efrayim found funny. Putting on a pair of leather Tyrolean shorts and a dark flannel suit jacket, he ran outside to make his friends laugh. At the bottom of the trunk he discovered a long muslin dress.

'What's this?' he asked, running his hand over the soft fabric. Nothing in the village could match it for sheer silkiness, not even the velvet noses of the colts or the petals of the apple blossoms. Suddenly, thinking of his mother, Efrayim felt tears in his eyes.

'For my wedding,' replied Binyamin. 'My mother for my wedding gave me it.'

He took a photograph from his wallet. 'Father, Mother, Hannah, Sarah,' he said, pointing. 'My mother gave me the dress.'

Binyamin's mother, a tall blonde woman, was seated on a chair, her two daughters, in identical dresses, beside her. Behind them stood his short, slender father with a clipped haircut and a military moustache.

Efrayim, who had no mother, and Binyamin, who soon would have no family at all, became fast friends.

'I can still hear their voices in my ears. My two pupils' voices, Efrayim's quick chatter and Binyamin's nasal bass. Your lost uncle. Your dead father.'

# 14

One day in late winter Tonya Rilov stole into Hayyim Margulis's bee patch. After the death of her daughter under the hooves of a cow, Tonya had given birth to a son named Dani. Rilov was a man of so few words that the boy did not begin to talk until he was five, and Tonya's hatred for her husband kept growing like a wall. Most of his time Rilov spent in the huge arms cache in his septic tank, where he had accumulated quantities of weapons that no one dared even guess at. No matter how hard he scrubbed himself with steel wool, his body still smelled of urea and dynamite. Tonya longed for the honeyed fingers of Margulis.

She hid among Ya'akovi's Japanese satsuma plum trees, observing her old love from a distance. In his cumbersome beekeeper's suit he looked like a jolly bear. He was moving his hives around among the trees while planning blossoming dates, new aromatic combinations, and the pasturing of his winged cows in the spring. Crouching low, Tonya followed him to his work shed and entered behind him. His heavy cloth-and-mesh mask kept him from noticing her.

Margulis took a hive down from a shelf, opened it and studied its honeycombs. Tonya could see how intense and happy he looked. Removing a honeycomb on which an excited throng of worker bees had clustered, he drove them off with his bare hand and beamingly laid on the table two bees that were embroiled in a battle. He separated them with two matchsticks, and when they flew at one another again, he parted them once more. Finally, when their strength began to flag, he put them in a special container with a glass divider to keep them apart. Stripping off his mask, he went to put it in its place and ran into a stiff embrace from Tonya, who was standing right behind him.

'Tonya!' breathed the startled Margulis. 'Are you crazy? In broad daylight? Your husband will murder me.' He pushed her firmly away, sat her down in a chair and served her honey.

'Why the spoon, Hayyim?' purred Tonya. 'Why not do it the old way?'

'You've just been a witness to my greatest secret,' said Margulis, ignoring her with a grin. 'The reconciliation of the queens.'

Tonya tried to switch the subject back to their own reconciliation, but Margulis just looked at her with his innocent blue eyes and went on talking.

'In every hive there's just one queen,' he lectured her. 'That's an inviolable law. It limits the number of new bees. And now, with spring blossoms on the way, I need as many workers as I can get.'

'You talk just like a capitalist,' smiled Tonya through her tears. But Margulis overlooked her humour and anguish alike.

'I wait for the new queens to hatch,' he continued, 'and when they attack each other, I keep patiently separating them with a stick, over and over, until they're tired of fighting and are willing to live and lay eggs together in one hive. That way I have twice as many workers and twice as much honey. You left me for him, Tonya, now sleep in the bed you've made.'

'But what's that got to do with it, Hayyim?' she murmured,

her lips softly closing over his name as she thought about his honeyed fingers. 'Why are you telling me all this about bees?'

Margulis, however, had returned to his fighting queens and was once more separating the murderous mothers with infinite patience, coaxing them with gentle words. Tonya left the shack and slipped back through Ya'akovi's orchard. Under a sky like flattened grey tin there was no sound but her own smothered sobs and the loathsome squish of her boots as they sucked in and out of the mud.

She was crossing the next plot of land, half hidden amid the first flowering fruit trees and some crowded rows of cabbage, when she spied Efrayim and Binyamin dancing a waltz among the Valencia oranges. At once she went home and told her husband.

Rilov hurried to Grandfather, less worried by the relations between the two boys then by the insidious appearance of bourgeois dances in the village. But the rumour began to circulate and people started to talk.

'He was only teaching me to dance,' explained Efrayim at the family table. 'I recited Pushkin for him and showed him how to harness Rilov's crazy mules, and he taught me to listen to music.'

'Isn't that the fellow who caught Esther when she fell off the roof?' asked Grandfather.

'I did not fall,' protested my mother. 'I jumped into his arms.'

'Why don't you bring that Romeo of yours home so we can meet him?' Grandfather said to Efrayim.

Rivka Peker, the saddler's daughter who was going out with Avraham, sounded a raspberry with her fat lips, and Avraham called Efrayim 'Strauss' and 'Matilda', for which he was rewarded by the discovery of a whole herring in his shirt pocket.

'I invited him for Friday night dinner,' announced Efrayim the following day. 'He eats whatever he's given.'

\*    \*    \*

Avraham began to sneeze a few minutes before Binyamin arrived, and everyone smiled with the realisation that the German must be bringing a bouquet of jonquils.

My mother was eighteen then. From childhood on she had been the motherless family's cook. She looked curiously at Rilov's dumb worker, who wielded his knife and fork skilfully but had dropped the flowers he picked for her in the wadi on the white socks she had worn in his honour. Her body still recalled his powerful hands and the hot breath of his mouth against her bare belly. Though they had passed each other often since the day she fell from the roof, he had stared down at the ground each time he saw her. The jingle of her legs in her dress made his mouth go so dry that he was afraid of not being able even to get out a hello.

Of course, Binyamin knew that Esther was the girlfriend of Daniel Liberson, the Valley volleyball star, her steady folkdance partner, and the son of Eliezer Liberson, who once a month assembled the young trainees in the village for a lecture on the principles and beliefs of the Movement.

He kept his eyes on his plate, swallowing his soup with a sound. Throughout the meal he seemed to be debating something, and right after dessert, as if having come to a decision that must not be frittered away, he asked Grandfather's permission 'to go for a walk with Esther'.

'The person to ask is the young lady,' said Grandfather, regarding Binyamin and his daughter. Whenever he saw a new couple he wondered when and how their love would go amiss.

They went out to the fields, Efrayim gliding after them like a polecat. For a long while he watched them walk in silence. At last Binyamin looked up at the sky and said in a strange, muffled voice, 'So many stars.'

'Lots,' said my mother, putting her hands on his shoulders. She was much taller than he was. 'Tell me, Binyamin,' she asked, 'is it true that where you come from people would rather eat sausage than meat?'

The following Thursday she asked Efrayim to sneak into the English base and steal some sausages from the canteen, because

Binyamin was coming again for dinner. 'And now, my child, finish your dinner too, and let's see you leave a clean plate.'

Grandfather sighed. 'That was the start of your parents' love affair,' he said. The love of the barefoot girl, 'Mirkin's wild she-goat', with her braids and long legs and brown eyes flecked with green and yellow, and the polite, awkward, inarticulate young man from Bavaria. My father's blond head reached his sweetheart's shoulders. His lumbering walk alongside her tall, merry skip amused the villagers no end. But there were also remarks about 'incompatibility', both 'physically speaking' and regarding the relationship of Mirkin's daughter 'with a young man who did not imbibe the values of the Movement with his mother's milk'.

There were also more practical considerations. Raising cows had taught the farmers that romance had its genetics, and the thought of crossbreeding Mirkin's daughter with Liberson's son tempted them greatly.

As for Daniel, having witnessed all his life the incessant pawing of his parents, who would rise from the table with an exchange of glances and disappear for passionate afternoon naps that kept the whole household awake and so frightened the animals that the hens began to lay less, he either could not or did not want to decipher the first signs of Esther's faltering love.

'Nothing worse could happen to a man,' said Uri one time when we were talking about my mother. 'He lost both his nerve and his head – and with them all his charm too.'

Daniel was condemned to the gauntlet run by rejected lovers. It was like having a limb amputated. Pitying glances followed him as he made his way toward our house, looking lost and crushed. At first he pleaded and wept. Then he grew quiet. At night he lay in the high grass across from Grandfather's cabin, peering through the stalks for a glimpse of his beloved's silhouette flitting across the lit window. After a few weeks Grandfather noticed that the grass had grown higher at a certain spot, as if from a leaky water tap. Going over to it one night, he found Daniel shedding noiseless tears.

'"You'll never get her back like this," I told him.'

Liberson and Tsirkin decided to have a talk with Mirkin but encountered an unexpected obstacle before they were out of the house. Standing in the doorway, Fanya announced that in matters of the heart the Feyge Levin Workingman's Circle had already made one decision too many.

'Once with Feyge was enough,' she informed her husband and his friend. 'Let the boys have it out between them, and let the girl make up her own mind. We're not Arabs or Orthodox Jews who marry off their children. And the days are also over when young ladies were given away according to your constitution and hearts broken to pieces by a comradely vote.'

Liberson was enraged. He did not consider Rilov's dumb worker fit competition for his son.

'What a waste of an immigration certificate,' he grumbled. Gently removing his wife from the doorway, he held her until Tsirkin was safely past. When they spoke to Grandfather, however, they heard the same refrain from him.

'I like your son very much,' Grandfather said to Liberson. 'But I have nothing against Binyamin either. He's a decent, hardworking, reliable boy, and I do believe that the girl loves him.'

Liberson and Tsirkin reminded him that Daniel had loved Esther from the age of three weeks, but Grandfather lost his temper and declared that he did not believe in such nonsense. 'Unlike certain other things we did,' he wrote in one of his notes, 'love has nothing to do with the staking of claims, the planting of flags, or the ploughing of furrows.'

# 15

When Eliezer Liberson was still a bachelor, before Daniel was born and Hagit was bought, he owned a big, thin Damascene cow with a long neck and long horns. His relations with the animal made the whole village laugh. She ate twice as much as other cows and gave almost no milk, which made Liberson hate her in a most unfarmerly way. 'The dregs of bovinity,' he called her. The cow, who had a tender and unforgiving heart behind her massive ribs, felt his animosity and repaid him in kind.

Once, when Liberson came home to his humble cabin from the fields, he found the cow sprawled on the floor, 'chewing on a bed sheet and an article by Borochov'. The table he ate, wrote, and read at, the only piece of furniture he owned, was smashed to smithereens. The cow took one look at his fury, realised that this time she had crossed the fine line between pest and menace, and ran alarmedly outside.

'And took the wall with her,' lamented Liberson. The next day he tied a rope around her neck and went off to sell her in the nearby kibbutz. Though the kibbutz's new barn worker had just returned from a course in Utrecht and was full of praise for Dutch cows, Liberson scared him to death with his stories of how such animals could not adjust to hot climates.

'They're spoiled,' he said. 'They're prone to parasites and depression.'

'It's not up to me,' said the barn worker. 'The kibbutz has to vote on it.'

'Of course,' said Liberson. General meetings were so much putty in his hands.

'Your Dutch cows need a mixture of local blood,' he told the packed dining hall. 'They'll supply the milk, and this wonderful animal of mine will provide the powers of endurance.'

The kibbutz members were entranced. 'Together we'll give the world its first Hebrew cow,' cried Liberson.

'And what now?' asked Tsirkin when Liberson came merrily back from the kibbutz and sat down to eat a bowl of lupin gruel with him. 'Those kibbutzniks will want their revenge. Are you going to leave your poultry and livestock unguarded each time you go out to your vegetable patch? You need a wife.'

Up to then, Liberson had been a conscientious bachelor. Now Tsirkin offered him Pesya with two cows thrown in for a dowry. Liberson, however, refused.

'That would have made three cows,' said Uri when the two of us heard the story, 'which is really too much for one bachelor.'

Since there wasn't a single available girl in the village, Tsirkin and Liberson decided to revive the old custom of bride snatching.

The two young men returned to the kibbutz. It was autumn, and several girls had been sent to the vineyard to pick the last grapes that were drying into raisins. Armed with a mandolin, a box of delicacies, and some kitchenware, they waited for them to arrive.

It took a great deal of pestering to get Fanya to tell me the rest. Her head nodded up and down as she spoke, her white hair a gorgeous sight.

'I heard someone playing an instrument at the other end of the vineyard and went to have a look. Behind the last row of vines stood two boys. One, whom I didn't know, was playing the mandolin, and the other was the nice young man who had just sold us a useless cow. He was cutting up vegetables for a salad and invited me to join them.'

'You'd better get out of here quick,' said Fanya to Liberson. 'The comrades have sworn to rope you to that cow's horns if they find you.'

Liberson just grinned, made a dressing for the salad, and started to slice bread and cheese. As he and Fanya sat eating, Tsirkin, a red gypsy bandanna around his neck, circled them 'like a cockerel' and played 'the sweetest, most seductive tunes'. Then Liberson told Fanya about himself, his farm, the Feyge Levin Workingman's Circle, and his trials and tribulations with the cow.

Fanya felt her heart skip a beat. In those days the Workingman's Circle was already shrouded in a thick cloud of mystery and adulation. Legends circulated among the women of the Valley about Feyge Levin, the first female pioneer to do the work of men and to be loved by three of them, who waited on her hand and foot, immunised her with their sweet blood, and washed her dirty clothes.

Modestly Liberson confessed that he indeed knew Feyge, had washed her clothes and cooked for her himself, and had even been bandaged and caressed by her hands. Showing Fanya the small scar on his bottom lip, he revealed to her that this was the exact spot where Feyge Levin had kissed him. When he saw that her face had grown soft and dreamy as expected, he made a secret sign to Tsirkin and began to hum the well-known lines, 'I shall plough, and I shall sow, and I shall rejoice / Only when I am in Israel's land.' Tsirkin played along, and Fanya could not resist the temptation to join in with her high, sweet voice.

Liberson was jubilant, so much so that he made the near fatal mistake of telling Fanya about the famous Hasidic court he had belonged to as a youth in the Ukraine. Though this titbit had worked well enough with the farmers' daughters in the colonies of Judea, Fanya was so allergic to anything involving prayers, religious ceremonies, or miracles that her exquisite face broke into a grimace when Liberson poured into her ears the names of renowned rabbis and preachers he had known.

Yet Liberson kept his wits about him. Like a falcon, the young man of the Workingman's Circle had the knack of reversing direction in mid-flight without losing altitude or speed. 'To tell you the truth, I'm a direct descendant of the Golem of Prague,' he said, earning a merry laugh from Fanya.

He knew all about love's link to laughter, which could inflame, incite, and liquefy a woman's flesh, and quickly struck again with a sharp jest about the kibbutz ideal of equality.

'Fanya, my angel,' he said, 'I took a peek at your mixed shower room the other day and saw with my own eyes that human beings are definitely not born equal.'

Fanya blushed and laughed again, her whole body rocking with pleasure. Quite unselfconsciously, she laid a hand on his knee. 'Make me laugh some more,' she said.

Now that he was confident that the pretty kibbutznik would be his, though he knew that years of courting and probation lay ahead of him, Liberson seized her hand and proposed to her. She came to our village straight from the vineyard.

'It's a lovely story, and Eliezer Liberson is a genius at such things, but that's not how it was,' said my cousin Uri heatedly. 'Tsirkin went to the vineyard by himself and played his mandolin among the grapevines. No woman could resist its music, and Fanya had to follow it. Tsirkin lured her past the grapes and into the high grass, and slid down the hill with Fanya hot on his heels. He led her a merry chase as far as the big oak tree, at which she arrived to see Liberson with a mandolin in his hands. Tsirkin was hiding quietly in the tree. It was only after the wedding that she discovered that Liberson couldn't play a note.'

'That same year,' said Meshulam, 'Ben-Gurion proclaimed that the kibbutz was a higher form of Zionism than the co-operative village, while Tabenkin stated that only the lust for lucre could make a person leave a commune. You don't have to be a great genius to understand the connection. My father and Eliezer Liberson's irresponsible action did nothing to improve relations between the two forms of agricultural settlement.'

Fanya's abduction led to a wave of hostility between the village and the kibbutz. Joint irrigation projects were cancelled. There were even incidents of stone throwing and fisticuffs in the wadi between us. In a comic issue of the village newsletter Fanya was referred to as 'fair Helen', and voices were heard to say that the redemption of the Valley should not be sacrificed on the altar of private concupiscence. And yet Eliezer and Fanya Liberson were the most loving couple ever seen on the soil of the Jewish homeland. Liberson never ceased wooing and amusing his wife, whose laughter and cries of surprise were heard all over the village. In those days, when the villagers lived in tents with nothing but a sheet of canvas to separate them from the world, everyone knew what was going on everywhere without having to creep up and eavesdrop beneath windows.

'First of all, get her to laugh,' said Liberson to his son. 'Women love that. They can't resist it.'

'Laughter,' said Mandolin, 'is the blast of the ram's horn that brings down the walls of Jericho. It is the open sesame to magic treasure caves, the first drops of autumn rain to fall on the parched earth.'

'Well said,' said Liberson with a startled look at his friend.

By then, though, Daniel was far removed from any possibility of laughter. His sense of humour, indeed, had been the first victim of his spurned love.

'Flowers! Song! Music!' declared Mandolin.

'Enough, Tsirkin,' Liberson said. He turned to his son. 'What does she like most?' he asked.

'Meat,' answered the sheepish Daniel.

Liberson and Tsirkin began to cook. Despite the general shortage of food in those days, Daniel began furtively visiting the Mirkin house at night with covered trays. The smell of roasted chicken, baked ribs of calf, and rare roast beef made the angry neighbours' mouths water. They complained about the waste, which was drawing cats and jackals from all over the Valley. And yet Esther, though she wolfed it all avidly and rewarded Daniel with happy hugs, did not cease her night-time walks with Binyamin.

My father made his sweetheart a huge hammock, which was nothing more than an old box mattress welded to iron chains and a railing. He hung it from two casuarinas behind the cabin, and the needles of the trees garnished her hair. The muffled sound of their laughter, Binyamin's quiet whistling, and Esther's low sighs when he took her in his smith's arms could all be heard from the cabin.

Tonya Rilov, whose rejection by Margulis had made her highly sensitive to public morality, scolded Grandfather for letting his daughter walk around holding hands with 'that new immigrant from Germany' and told him that the village children came to the orchard at night to peep at them.

That year Grandfather's orchard blossomed as never before. He asked Hayyim Margulis to place a few beehives among the trees, and the honey that resulted was nearly red and so sweet that it burned the tongue. All day long Grandfather circulated among his rows of fruit trees, whose dates of blossoming and parade of scents had been calculated from midwinter through spring, tottering drunkenly home from their lush fragrance. By now Avraham was in full charge of the cows, leaving Grandfather free to enjoy his private Eden, around which he planted thick hedges of cypress trees to shield it from the winter winds that came roaring down from the blue mountain.

The white blossoms of the almonds were the first to appear, the sweetness of their petals wafting through the air as if challenging the rain and the mud. Next the peach bloomed in a fierce pink, the tall, slender stamens of its flowers lighter than its rich, dark buds. Beside it glowed the delicate apricot, whose scent was like a woman's perfume. Soon the plums joined in, their little blossoms covering the branches with a velvety white. The apples flowered after Purim in reds and whites, their smell as full and juicy as their fruit. At Passover time came the quinces, from which Rachel and Shlomo Levin made jams and jellies, and the pears with their white flowers, winey-fumed and purple-funnelled. Finally, when the earth was hot from the ascendant sun that ruled the orchard, swelling its pregnant pistils, the orange trees brought Grandfather's scent fest to a close with a cloak of fragrance so heavy that it enveloped the whole village.

It was in this orchard, where the meadow browns flitted freely, the bees buzzed with loud gaiety, and the birds and buprestid beetles fell fainting from the treetops, that I buried Grandfather and his friends. But in those days Esther planted gillyflowers that opened overnight and led Binyamin to wet wallows of fallen petals. Before dawn she stole back to the cabin with her sandals in her hands, though the strong, familiar scent of wet earth, pears, and gillyflowers given off by her warm skin awakened Grandfather anyway.

'He was too happy for words. The smell of his daughter was as the smell of a field which the Lord hath blessed.'

'What a lovely story,' said Fanya Liberson. Her hair, I assume, was draped over her husband's chest, and her thigh lay across his stomach then too. 'As sorry as I feel for our poor Daniel, I'm glad for a change to see a man at Mirkin's who is crazy in love.'

For the first time, love reigned supreme at the Mirkin farm. With wild shrieks the two of them re-enacted their first encounter, Esther clambering up the bales in the hayloft and grabbing hold of the ridgepole while Binyamin stood below her, watching her kick her legs.

'I'm not letting go till you say *schnell, schnell,*' she would shout.

Avraham cleaned out the cowshed, his eyes darkly on the floor, the creases pulsing in his forehead.

One night, coming back from a stroll in the fields, I took off my shoes and tiptoed quietly up to Rivka and Avraham's window, where I heard my aunt discussing my mother.

'I remember her as though it were yesterday,' she rasped in her lizardy voice. 'Hanging from the roof of the hayloft. You never looked, but believe you me, she wasn't wearing any underpants.'

'I think my mother was jealous. My father never looked up her dress like that, and he never whistled any off-key operas for her either.'

# 16

In a nearby village there was an awful incident at the time. A farmer took his own life without anyone knowing why. 'He was buried with the secret of his death,' said our village newsletter. His body, covered with dead buds and the broken wings of satyr butterflies, was found in Grandfather's orchard with its skull blown off and its big toe on the trigger of an old five-round semi-automatic. It had been lying there for several days, the strong smell of the flowering fruit trees hiding the stench of the putrefying corpse until Grandfather's suspicions were aroused by the sight of swarms of green flies, which generally found blossoms repulsive.

The suicide left behind a widow, an only son aged eight, and the rifle, which was so rusted that Rilov had to cross it off his list of useable firearms in the Valley. The child was told that his father had gone on a long trip and would bring him presents when he returned, but the children in school told him what they heard at night when their parents were gathered at the kitchen table with their friends, whispering over tea after a day's work. The boy took to walking in his sleep, and came home every night before dawn with his feet scratched by thorns and stones.

'I hear my father calling,' he told everyone.

Pinness was furious. The children of the dead man's village attended our school. Every day they arrived in a cart pulled by a team of horses, their shoes wet from the dewy weeds by the roadside. 'How can a child be lied to like that?' he screamed in the teachers' room. 'How can anyone contaminate such a tender sprout?'

Though he realised at once that it was the work of the hyena, it was high spring and no one paid heed to his warnings. Man and beast wanted only to stretch out in the grass and take in the sun and warm earth. The cowsheds and rabbit hutches were full of the squeals of calves and babes. The young primiparous heifers came down with spring fever and ran wildly about with their tails sticking up, kicking the air. The deep winter mud was drying out, and the ground was no longer sticky and treacherous but soft and springy underfoot. The snorts of the wildcat cubs, scrapping playfully as they practised their murderous arts on carpets of grass and daisies, could be heard down by the spring. Hayyim Margulis's bees growled softly among the flowers as they transported their sweet cargo, while flocks of bee-eaters freshly returned from the tropics wreaked havoc among them. Male doves strutted atop the cowsheds, their bright, swollen crops and their sheeny breasts slicing the sunshine like prisms. Great flocks of pelicans passed overhead, bound northward for *there*, the land of wheat, wolves, and birches. On their way they flew low over Liberson's house and screamed mockingly at Fanya. The spring doubled its flow, and the last winter jonquils gave off such a powerful scent that Avraham broke out in long riffs of tears and sneezes.

Anxious and tense, Pinness took the children out to the fields for a look at the flowers.

'The month of Nisan is the month of our Movement,' he told

his pupils, his eyes combing his surroundings for the enemy. 'It's then that Nature lifts high her red flags in memory of our liberation from bondage in Egypt: the poppy, the anemone, the red buttercup, the pheasant's-eye, the mountain tulip, and the everlasting.'

'And then, as I was standing there listening to their laughter in the field, the green wall of young corn suddenly parted like a curtain, thrust aside by the shoulders of the hyena.'

Every spring the hornet queens emerged from their winter hideaways. Weak and frozen, they searched for a place to build their nests. Within a few weeks each had hatched a regiment of brigands. When summer came their black-and-yellow forms flashed through the air with a fierce, menacing rasp, raiding the grape clusters, descending on fruits and milk cans, biting men and animals, decimating beehives, and terrorising the whole village. The Committee paid the children a small bounty for every dead hornet, and every spring Pinness took them out to the field to trap the queens before they could establish a new generation of 'rapacious Midianites'.

'It isn't easy for me to ask you to kill a hornet queen,' he told them. 'It's not our way to kill living things. But the field mouse, the hornet, the viper, and all tree pests are our mortal enemies.'

The vipers emerged early that year, unwinding their thick bodies in the sun and waiting for a careless mouse, hoof, or bare foot. In the mornings we found their limp bodies hanging from the chicken wire that had trapped their broad heads at night while they were trying to steal eggs and baby chicks. Binyamin, who was scared to death of snakes, never went out to the fields without boots and a long hoe on his shoulder.

'My daughter just laughed at him, skipping barefoot through the clover no matter how he screamed at her to stop.'

'A big strong boy like you,' said Esther, 'and such a coward!'

They sat in a field overlooking the British air base.

'I steal a plane and fly to my old home,' said Binyamin.

'When my mother was still alive,' Esther revealed to him, 'we had a little donkey. Every night she spread her ears and flew off to Constantinople to meet the Turkish sultan.'

Esther lay on her back while Binyamin regarded her sceptically. He checked the lush grass, took off his shirt and boots, and lay down pleasurably beside her. Two minutes later Esther nudged him in the stomach and pointed to a large viper, as thick as a man's forearm, that was crawling slowly toward them. She could feel Binyamin stiffen and start to shake, every pore of his skin gushing sweat.

'Don't move,' she said. 'If I haven't eaten you, it won't either.'

But the viper kept coming toward them, sniffing the ground with its tongue. Esther pinned Binyamin down with her hand to keep him from moving. When the snake neared her foot, she picked up one of his heavy work boots and clubbed it on the neck. It lunged and writhed while she struck it again and again till its head was as flat as a wafer.

'What a stupid idiot you are!' she said to Binyamin. 'What a stupid fatso! Killing a snake is nothing. Efrayim once killed a viper with a shoe brush.'

Across the fields they saw Pinness and his children by the corn patch, far from the houses of the village. But they could not see the hyena, which was hidden up to its shoulders in the thick corn.

Pinness knew it would not attack. Hyenas rarely did, and even then only when they found a single weak, tender victim.

'But I recognised it,' he gasped. 'It made me feel murderous. I wanted to run at it, kill it, choke it. It recognised me too, though, and disappeared back into the thick foliage. The children never even saw it.'

He gathered the children around him, flapping his arms like a mother hen, and returned with them to the village, where he worriedly related his fears to the Committee head.

'The hyena must have been attracted by a carcass that somebody threw in the corn,' said the Committee head, who was reminded by Pinness's fears of 'some idiotic Arab superstition'. It couldn't possibly be the same beast that had bitten settlers and struck them down during their first years in the Valley, he argued. Pinness left more upset and worried than before.

He hurried to the teacher from the neighbouring village and urged him to set traps and post guards, but no one there had seen the hyena or even come across its tracks.

'Just as years later no one heard those obscenities in the middle of the night,' he said to me angrily.

The sleepwalker disappeared every night in search of his father. Without waking he loosed the ropes tying him to his bed and set out, vanishing under the noses of his pursuers as if he had dissolved into little flakes of darkness. Once the night watchmen saw his sleeping figure emerge from the shadows and cross right in front of the breeding horse, a splendid but violent stallion that had already trampled a calf and a hired hand to death. Not only did it do him no harm, it rubbed against the fence of its corral and whined as fearfully as an abandoned puppy.

'On the seventh night the hyena called again, and the blond little boy, thinking it was his father, was tricked into rising from his mother's bed and going out to the fields with his eyes shut, in nothing but a white nightshirt.'

Three days later the little body was found with a splintered neck bone, next to the jujube tree in the dry bed of the wadi. It was old Zeitser on one of his pensive walks who discovered it lying beneath the familiar, accursed green blanket of necrophiliac flies. He ran all over the Valley to tell the founders.

Pinness, who was not exactly 'a fire-breathing warrior', stood by the little coffin before the open grave, weeping and swearing revenge.

'It's no accident that it strikes at the smallest and weakest of us,' he said. 'The hyena is Doubt and Despair, the loss of faith and the sowing of confusion. But we shall be of good cheer and continue to build and plant, to sow and water, until the ploughman shall overtake the reaper and the treader of grapes him that soweth seed.'

The villages were in a state of panic. The broken neck and savaged chest of the little boy struck terror in all hearts. Children were no longer allowed out at night to turn off sprinklers or check that the barnyard gate was shut. And yet the springtime went its merry way.

'Before long the dead boy sank into the sediments of the Valley's painful memory. Along with the victims of malaria and of Arab bandits, the suicides and the fallers by the wayside, he too became a fable in our textbooks and a black-framed picture in the teachers' room. Each time I looked at his little face, I cursed the fates in my heart.'

The spring earth had dried out and cracked, the stalks of grain turned yellow, and our new Marshall thresher was brought to the fields. The harvest was a particularly good one that year, 'as if the earth had accepted our sacrifice'. Binyamin came to help out after finishing work at Rilov's, and my mother brought his meals to the field, poking fun at his sensitive skin that blistered in the sun, hissing like a snake behind his back, tripping him among the sheaves, and wrestling with him in the smothering dust of chaff that covered their faces and clothes.

The Mirkins were preparing for a double wedding – Binyamin and Esther's, Avraham and Rivka's. No one had the slightest inkling of the cunning ambushes of Time or the tubers of evil swelling in its furrows. My parents' death, Efrayim and Jean Valjean's disappearance, Zeitser's gruesome end, Pioneer Home – all these were not even the tiniest cloud on the horizon. In honour of the occasion Pinness and Tsirkin composed a short musical comedy on the history of threshing floors from the days of Ruth to the present. Some of the village women volunteered to make the food, and the Committee saw to the tables and tablecloths.

Two wedding canopies were set up between Mirkin's fig and olive trees. Grandmother and Grandfather's friends came from all over the country, embracing each other gaily and tramping over the pliant earth. Their fingers were arthritic from too much prying and milking, many were bald, and not a few carried reading glasses in their white shirt pockets.

'The shoulders,' said Eliezer Liberson, 'the shoulders that an entire people had leaned on were a bit stooped, but the eyes had a fiery glow.' Leading politicians came too. 'When the Feyge Levin Workingman's Circle married off a son and a daughter in one day, even the shirkers who preferred Zionist congresses to working knew they had better appear.'

Firstborn sons from all over the country came to Mirkin's double wedding. Posed in a group, they were a moving sight. Among them were military commanders, teachers, heads of villages and kibbutzim, inventors of agricultural machines, and philosophers – 'but all,' said Pinness, 'had the same clear eyes and proud bearing'.

My uncle stood solemnly beneath the canopy in blue trousers and a white shirt, a silent, searching groom who made everyone remember that Liberson once said of him, 'He's like an olive stone that lies in its husk for years before opening and sprouting.' The wedding guests scrutinised him, looking for the promise that had yet to be fulfilled. Rivka, the daughter of Tanchum Peker the saddler, stood by his side, frowning with envy at Esther's wedding dress. Her father, who had downed quantities of schnapps, walked among the guests in shiny boots redolent of leather, reminiscing about the wild officers' parties in his days in the Russian cavalry, the cooks and servant girls he had cornered in pantries among smoked meats and straw-cushioned bottles. Bowing his knees as though on horseback, he clucked to old steeds that he alone remembered, flushed with nostalgia and pride.

Under the second canopy Esther stood laughing. Now and then she spun around giddily, her Bavarian wedding dress flying up like a dish of white foam. Far away in the eucalyptus woods Daniel Liberson crawled among wet tree trunks, beside himself with anguish, his throat so dry from crying that all he could do was wheeze. The week before, when he had been awarded the contract to plough the village grain fields, which amounted to nearly a thousand acres, Tsirkin and Liberson had decided to launch an unprecedented last-minute offensive. Following their orders, Daniel took the D-4 and the disc harrow and ploughed the name of his beloved in a field of stubble. Half a mile high and half a mile wide, the word 'ESTHER' ran outlined in rich brown earth against a background of yellow straw. But since no one whose two feet were on the ground was elevated enough to see it, the desperate love note went unnoticed by everyone except some British pilots, 'and they couldn't read Hebrew'.

'And my father?'

'Binyamin smiled at the guests but didn't say much, because he missed his own father and mother.

'When the ceremony and the presentations were over, a space was cleared for the two couples to dance. Tsirkin struck up the mandolin, and your father and my son Efrayim stepped into the circle and danced a cheek-to-cheek waltz. Tonya Rilov had a fit, and the whole village split its sides with laughter.'

'And then?'

'Then, my child, a war broke out and Efrayim went off to it.'

# 17

Grandfather sensed the approaching disaster and took Efrayim to the orchard, hoping to divert him with new projects. Most pears and apples, he explained to him, just as he did years later to me, develop on special short branches that bear annual fruit and must never be pruned.

Next to these, Grandfather showed Efrayim, are tall, upright branches that grow more quickly but are less fruitful. Although all the experts agreed that these infertile shoots should be cut back, Grandfather showed Efrayim how you could bend them outward and back on themselves like a taut bow and tie their tips to their bases with twine. The village was astounded to see how much fruit these bound branches gave. 'He realised it during his first years in the country,' Pinness told me admiringly. 'Your grandfather discovered that not only men and horses but trees too can be harnessed and reined.'

Several years later, when an enthusiastic agricultural instructor appeared in the village to demonstrate the new 'Caldwell method' of branch bending developed in America, he was informed that we had been practising it for years without the fancy name. Moreover, Grandfather's method was still unique in its periodic freeing of the bound branches, which repaid such thoughtfulness by increasing their yield even more.

But Efrayim did not care about trees and was so overwrought that his skin began to quiver and twitch like a horse's hide. Every evening he went to Esther and Binyamin's cabin, on one wall of which hung a large map with pins and flags that were carefully moved about.

Men had already signed up and disappeared from the village. The first to go were our two smiths, the Goldman brothers. Since the day the village was founded they had shod its workhorses and tempered its pickaxes and ploughshares to make them strong. 'Like Jachin and Boaz, the two mighty pillars of the Temple, they stood over their hearth with their tongs in their left hands and their trusty hammers in their right, a red glow suffusing their chests.'

'One day when Zeitser and I came to the smithy,' Grandfather told me, 'the two brothers weren't there. The coals were cold and grey, the bellows silent, the smoke gone. Only their two big hammers were still floating in the air above the anvil.'

Next to go was Daniel Liberson, who stayed on in Europe after the war with a band of anti-Nazi avengers. Though his curt, angry letters to Esther never mentioned my father, the hatred expressed by his ardour for killing blond Germans blew like a chill wind through all his words and deeds.

At night Binyamin sat with Rilov and various strangers who arrived in the village disguised as fertiliser consultants or egg salesmen. Together they prepared arms caches and time fuses, used irrigation pipes to cast mortars, and agreed on a system of nocturnal voice signals 'that drove the owls and crickets of the Valley crazy'.

There was worry in the air. The war was far away, but there were times at night or in the quiet hours of the autumn afternoons when the villagers fell silent, gazing to the north and west as if they could see and hear what was happening. 'The blood of our distant brothers was calling and crying out to us.'

Efrayim begged Grandfather for permission to join the British army, but Grandfather wouldn't hear of it.

'A boy of your age can make his contribution right here. You're not going off to any war.'

'My handsome wanderer in foreign fields,' he wrote on a piece of paper torn from a notebook.

Efrayim went on working with his father. With a haunted expression on his thin, tense face he bound branches and kept his thoughts to himself. Pinness, who could predict the impending migrations of animals by their movements and expressions, warned Grandfather what lay ahead.

'I can't chain him down,' said Grandfather.

'Keep an eye on him,' Pinness urged.

'Did anyone ever manage to stop us?' asked Grandfather. 'Was your father glad to see you run away from home for this country?'

Over dinner he watched his son hungrily attack the vegetable salad. He looked at his strong, wiry arms and the green eyes that had lost their focus, and knew that deep down Efrayim had already spread his wings.

After the meal Efrayim jumped up from his chair and announced that he was going out to check the water taps.

'Goodbye, Efrayim,' said Grandfather.

'I'll be right back,' Efrayim said. And he was gone.

A week later his heavy Hercules bicycle was found chained to the fence of the British army base at Sarafand. By then he himself was aboard a naval vessel bound for Scotland. Though he wasn't seasick, his face was coated with skeins of foam. His noiseless feet were shod in stiff army boots, but even when he stamped on the vibrating iron deck, the sound was drowned out by the boom of the thrusting waves.

At night, listening to the sea pound and foam as it sprawls outside the windows of my white prison, I think about all the sounds that never stopped, though you had to concentrate to hear them: the wind in the casuarina trees, the ticking of the sprinklers, the burble of the spring, the cows chewing their cud, the scratchy slithers beneath the cabin floor. Pinness explained to me how Efrayim could walk so silently. 'He wasn't actually that silent. He just knew how to make his footsteps sound like one of the world's steady noises.'

'He was one of the few Palestinian Jews to serve with the British commandoes,' said Meshulam when Efrayim was already a memory that not everyone cared to believe in or carry the burden of. He began pulling papers and envelopes from an orange crate on which he had written 'Sons Who Served'.

'Fifty-three members of farming families signed up, among them two older men, thirty-eight boys born in the village, and thirteen girls. Four sons and two daughters of non-farming families joined too. Sixteen failed to return. I have the letters home of quite a few soldiers, but none of Efrayim's. Your family, for some reason, refused to let Founder's Cabin have them.'

When Meshulam said 'your family', he meant me. Grandfather was dead already, Yosi was in the army, and Uri was operating a tractor for an uncle of his in the Galilee, moving soil and firming sand. Avraham and Rivka were preparing to go to the Caribbean, where they had been offered the management of a large dairy farm, and the family farm was left in my hands, prospering nicely around Grandfather's gravestone.

'I don't want to be buried with them,' he told me, stating his will over and over. 'They drove Efrayim from the village. Bury me in my own earth.'

It took more than just a little nerve, I thought, for Meshulam to demand Efrayim's letters for his idiotic museum.

'I'll take my revenge where it hurts them the most,' said Grandfather in the words he repeated like a menacing slogan during the last years of his life. 'In the earth.'

And it was I who carried it out. The body of the old tree wizard poisoned the ground and stood the founders' vision on its head. The graves on Mirkin's land burned in the flesh of the village like open abscesses of mockery and chastisement. Spiders built their thick funnels in Avraham's modern milking stalls. Mossy lichen bruised the concrete walls, wiping out the last traces of bounty and blessing. Mud daubers constructed great colonies out of paper and mud in the chinks of the hayloft.

Neglect was everywhere, but the money kept pouring in. Sacks of it piled up in the old cowshed while my field of graves flowered. Pioneer Home made time stop like a great wedge thrust in the earth, shattering by-laws and ways of life, breaking the vegetative cycle, flouting the seasons of the year.

Two months after Efrayim's induction his letters began to arrive. They were short and uninteresting. Sometimes I reread them. Amphibious landings under live fire. Rock climbing. A boy from New Zealand who 'kept wanting to know about our breeds of milk cows' drowned during an exercise in fording rivers at a camp called Achnacarry near Inverness. I turned the strange syllables around in my mouth, seeking a taste of Efrayim's life there. Forced marches in full battle gear, a sapper's course in Oban. A snapshot of a night on the town, Efrayim in a Scottish kilt and a funny leopard-skin hat, a hairy sceptre in one hand. A letter of thanks to Rachel Levin for teaching him the art of silent walking.

'His Majesty's royal commandoes don't know the first thing about creeping up on anyone,' he wrote. 'They waddle like the porcupines in the rushes by our spring.'

He was caught, so I learned, poaching deer with a knife in the royal preserve at Van Kripsdale, sentenced to a week in the brig, and fined forty pounds. Later he received a Distinguished Service Cross for his part in the raid on Dieppe, when in hand-to-hand combat he wiped out a German gun crew that was inflicting casualties on Lord Lovat's commandoes. I read these letters out loud because I'm used to oral history. 'Dieppe,' I say to myself. 'Kripsdale. Lovat.' The foreign words make the air flow in unfamiliar ways through the cavities of my mouth and throat.

Time passed. The sun rose each morning on the foxholes of the soldiers in Russia, on Shulamit in the Crimea, on Shifris somewhere along his way, until it lit up our Valley, falling on

Grandmother Feyge's grave, on Grandfather's straw hat, on Avraham's cloven forehead, on my father and mother. Only then was it seen by Efrayim far to the west. Round and round it went for a whole month, until Grandfather received word that his son had been wounded in the battle of the el-Guettar Range in Tunisia.

For six long months after Efrayim's injury not a single letter arrived from him. Grandfather was beside himself with worry. One night he set out with Zeitser to climb to the top of the blue mountain, where you could see the sea.

Like a huge wall, the mountain screened us from the city, from the sea, from all vanity and seduction. Every year the village turned its eyes toward it and studied the clouds that formed among its ridges, filling and marshalling themselves before beginning their great journey over our fields. 'The clouds are the children of the mountain,' Grandfather told me when I was small. We were walking in the fields, waiting for the rain, my hand shading my eyes just like his. He crumbled some soil between his fingers and gazed straight ahead at the mountain.

'Once, when the rain clouds didn't come, we decided to go and see what had happened to them. The entire Circle was there – Tsirkin, Liberson, Grandmother Feyge, and myself. We spent a whole day climbing to the top over rocks and thorns, and a whole night looking for the Rain Cave, until we heard the clouds muttering and grumbling. A big rock was blocking the cave and keeping them from getting out. We began to tug at it, *raz dva, raz dva* – one two, one two – as hard as we could, pulling from one side while the clouds pushed from the other, and at last the rock rolled loose and out they burst. Tsirkin managed to hitch a ride on one of them and came down with the rain by his house.'

They stood looking into the distance until Zeitser coughed, catching a whiff of far-off smoke and explosives, and Grandfather, glimpsing the carmine flush of battlefields and hearing the screams that skipped like pebbles across the waves, buried his head in his knees.

They had already returned home when an English automobile drove into the village in the morning. The children ran

to tell Rilov that Major Stoves had arrived and that the septic
tank entrance should be camouflaged. Major Stoves was a tall,
limping Englishman who had been wounded in North Africa
and transferred to Palestine with his uniform and black walking
stick. He descended from the automobile, hobbled to the far
door, opened it, and saluted. Efrayim was home.

Wearing the soft yellow desert boots and winged-dagger
insignia of a commando, and his ribbons, decorations, and
sergeant's stripes, in his pocket a lifelong pension certificate
from His Majesty's government, Efrayim stepped out of the car
and smiled at the villagers gathered there.

The cry that went up at the sight of him was not soon
forgotten. Mouths opened wide, retching with horror and consternation. Men came running from the green fields, from the
leafing orchards, from the cowsheds and the chicken coops to
stand before Efrayim and howl. The veterinarian's wife, whom
he had slept with on and off, screamed for a full minute and
a half 'without stopping to catch her breath'. Children he had
taught to throw a knife and built kites for whimpered in high,
terrified voices. Ya'akov Pinness emerged from the school and
loped heavily toward his former pupil, then stopped in his tracks
as suddenly as if he had run into a wall. Shutting his eyes, he
bellowed like a slaughtered ox. The cows, the calves, the horses,
and the chickens made a hideous racket in their pens and runs.

A phosphorous mine planted by the Italian army, 'the Chicken
Corps', as Uri called it, had turned my uncle's handsome face
into a burned pudding of skin and flesh that glittered, 'How can
I describe the horror of it, my child, like a squashed pomegranate,
in every shade of red, purple, and yellow. You're lucky you don't
remember him.'

One of my uncle's eyes had been torn out, his nose was in the
wrong place, his lips were gone, and a crooked, wine-red gash
ran diagonally across his face from the forehead to the hollow
of the throat, disappearing in the collar of his shirt. His charred,
mangled skin hung loosely from his cheekbones. A single green
eye, sole testimony to the doctors' attempt to restore his human
visage, peered out from all that devastated tissue.

Efrayim, whose beauty had drawn curiosity-seekers from all over the Valley and made the startled birds swoop low overhead, had become a monster whom no one dared look at. The crowd pressed together in fear, 'a whole village standing and shrieking'.

My uncle's ghastly smile faded. He spun around as if wishing to vanish again. Major Stoves had already opened the door of the car with a muttered oath when the crowd suddenly parted to make way for Binyamin, who had elbowed his way through it like the solid blade of a ploughshare. Fighting to get to his brother-in-law's side, he looked at him without flinching, hugged him in his thick arms, and kissed the shiny, minced flesh that had once been a cheek.

My father's Hebrew had improved greatly. 'Welcome home, Efrayim,' he said, leading him away amid the silence that had collected like a puddle in the street.

For supper Efrayim asked for 'the house vegetable salad' and even told Esther how to make it. His voice was weak and throaty because his vocal cords were injured too.

'First cut the onion and salt it a bit, then the tomatoes, and salt them too. The green pepper and cucumber come last. Mix well, season with black pepper, lemon juice, and oil, mix again, and let it breathe for a while.'

For the past two years, he said, he had dreamed of our salad, which 'no one else in the world knows how to make'.

He shoved a heaped spoonful of it into his gullet and sighed with pleasure. As his horrid face made chewing motions and his flesh moved like a thousand crushed pellets, Avraham burst out crying and fled the table. But Binyamin remarked, 'He must have forgotten to shut the water tap in the alfalfa,' and went on talking with Efrayim about such subjects as the war, German submachine guns, a general named Rommel, commando training, and British military decorations.

'I couldn't speak,' said Grandfather. 'They had destroyed my beautiful boy. Before going to bed he said, "Goodnight, Father," and turned away at once to spare me from hugging or kissing him.'

'Every kiss not given him is a piece cut out of my heart,' I found written in one of Grandfather's notes.

All night Efrayim paced up and down in the yard, the silence of his feet keeping everyone awake. In the morning Binyamin arrived and sat down with him at the table, and the two sketched some plans on several large sheets of paper. Then Binyamin asked Zeitser to lend a hand. They took a cart through the fields to the English air base, where they were met by the lame Major Stoves, two lean, quiet Scottish commando officers who gave Efrayim an embrace, and an Indian quartermaster whose heart thumped loudly at the sight of the medals on my uncle's chest. When they returned to the village, followed by an army truck loaded with construction rods, sand, cement sacks, and gravel, the two Scotsmen, Binyamin, and Efrayim took off their shirts and began digging a foundation hole by the cowshed. Over it they built a brick room with windows and a door that faced away from the house, out toward the cowshed and the fields.

Binyamin hooked the hut up to water and electricity, built a wonderful wood-burning stove that heated the room and the boiler, and made brown wooden shutters with copper clasps in the shape of dwarves that turned green with the years and wept ugly stripes on the plaster.

'That's the shed I keep my tools and plant medicines in now.'

Efrayim moved into his new home and never left it.

'I circled the walls, which smelled of fresh, moist lime and plaster, waiting for my son to step out. Your mother put food in front of the door and pleaded with her brother to show himself. But he wouldn't.'

Pinness came, knocked on the door, and asked to see his old pupil.

'You screamed when you saw me,' rasped Efrayim from within, refusing to open the door.

'"I'm only human," I told him. "No one knew you were wounded so badly. Open up, Efrayim. Open up for an old teacher who would like to apologise."'

But Efrayim did not.

Grandfather and Pinness told me about it dozens of times, as if asking me to forgive them for Efrayim.

Binyamin came to visit him each evening. After a few weeks he advised him to start working in the cowshed at night.

'The cows are afraid of me too,' Efrayim said.

If he didn't put himself to work, said Binyamin, he would grab him by the belt again and throw him in the cow trough.

'But only at night,' said Efrayim, stepping out of his room.

'At half past nine I would see a strip of light as the door opened and the shadow of my son's legs slipped off to the cowshed. He shovelled the manure, rinsed the milk cans, and put feed in the stalls for the morning milking.'

His heart 'breaking into little pieces', Grandfather lay paralysed in the cabin, listening to the rumble of the manure cart on the metal ramp, the scraping of the shovel in the sewage ditch, and the lowing of the cows crowding together in the pen and glancing surreptitiously at his son with sad whispers.

After four nights of this, Ya'akov Mirkin rose from his bed and went to the cowshed. He stood outside in the darkness and called to his son.

'Don't come in, Father,' whispered Efrayim in a choked voice. 'Don't come into the cowshed.'

'I have to,' said Mirkin, stepping inside.

Efrayim managed to pull an empty feed sack over his head a second before he felt his father's hands on his shoulders. Mirkin kissed the coarse jute, grinding the last of the fodder between his teeth until it melted thickly in tears and saliva. Gently, he removed the sack from his son's head. Old Zeitser saw the two of them from his corner, where he pretended to be asleep.

'The next morning I went to Margulis, asked him for an old beekeeper's mask, and brought it to my son so that he could come and go among men.'

Efrayim's handsome looks became a forgotten shadow, a configuration that came to life only before the shut eyes of those who cared to remember. But the life of the villagers was harder without such beauty to contemplate.

'In a place so dependent on the laws of the earth and the weather, on the genetic quirks of animals and the acquired vagaries of men,' Pinness explained to me, 'Efrayim's radiance was like the cold of snow in the time of harvest, like rest for the weary, like a lake of water in the wilderness.' Only now did the villagers grasp what they had lost, which made their estrangement from him grow even greater.

Once a week my uncle ironed his khaki trousers and went to the military air base to chat with Major Stoves and the two laconic Scotsmen and drink beer with the British and Indian gunners stationed there. Sometimes he walked through the fields, waiting until he had left the orange grove to strip off his mask before the eyes of the startled bees who had followed him out of curiosity. Sometimes the base commander sent a car for him.

'Your son is spending too much time with the British,' said Rilov.

'The village threw Efrayim to the dogs. The British know how to honour their heroes,' snapped Grandfather.

'Those Indians are used to seeing monsters in India,' said Rivka.

Efrayim drank beer, ate sausages, and bought candy bars for the cows in the same canteen he had once stolen tins of bully beef from. My uncle Avraham complained mildly that the candy bars were giving the cows worms, but they loved Efrayim because of them. His friendship with the British, on the other hand, became a public bone of contention, especially since he angrily refused to help the village defence force. Though all of the old Gang was active in the Palmach, the underground Jewish army, Efrayim would not agree to give them lessons in demolition, sniping, topography, or any of the other things he had learned in the British army.

'Who does he think he is?' grumbled Rilov, who knew how well versed Efrayim was in all the techniques of guerrilla warfare.

'I would only frighten the poor boys,' said Efrayim.

One day when the war had ended and Uri, Yosi, and I were already in our mothers' wombs, a British army car drew up at our house. In it was Major Stoves, the two lean Scotsmen, and a red-haired sergeant with curly blond arms and the command insignia. Moving with the quiet efficiency of night fighters, they took a clinking case of beer and some tins of Players from their Land Rover, carried them to Efrayim's room, and spent the night with him there. In his report to the Committee Rilov mentioned that the commandoes hardly spoke, communicated by prearranged winks and grunts, and departed totally drunk, the sergeant shouting, 'You'll have the cow in two months.'

# 18

Like Grandfather, I too drink my tea while drawing sustenance from the bitter olive in my mouth and imbibing strength from the sugar cube between my fingers. Like him, I stand staring into the distance to see Efrayim and Jean Valjean return and Shifris finally arrive. From the rooftop of my large house I look out at the sea. White boats bob on the waves, combs bulge in the bathing suits of trim men, and burly women crouch on windsurfers, guiding their sails with distant hips while their short, stippled hair bristles in the breeze.

Once a great wave drove one of the surfers onto the rocks. I put down my binoculars, hurried to her, slung her over one shoulder and her surfboard with its sail over the other, and carried them to the safety of the sand, leaving her there in a prone position. Back on my roof again, I watched her get to her feet and look dazedly around, studying her bloodstains and my footprints on the sand.

So Grandfather stood atop the hayloft and on the terrace of the old folk's home, looking out over the Valley for his returning son.

The old folk's home is eleven miles from the village, a tall building that rises high above its surroundings. I went there every other day, taking a shortcut through the fields and furiously covering the distance in three hours with a pitcher of milk from the cowshed.

'Wait a minute, Baruch,' my uncle Avraham would say to me, 'I'll give you milk from a better cow.' While waiting, I carried heavy sacks of fodder, helped load the full milk cans, and slung timid calves into shipment pens.

My two cousins were busy with the cows: Yosi, as morose as his father, quick and efficient at work, his pet red falcon perched on his shoulder or hopping after him like a dog, and Uri, who had taken to disappearing at night and sleeping late in the morning.

'Some female of his must be in heat,' grumbled Avraham, slapping him fondly on the back.

Uri, said Grandfather, was like Efrayim, only dreamier and more delicate. The resemblance was strongest in their wiry bodies, gaunt cheeks, and breathtakingly good looks. You could see Grandfather turn his grandson this way and that with his eyes as though he were his lost son frozen in a drop of amber. 'Children. Strung pearls. Long necklaces of sperm,' he wrote in a note I found after he had moved to the old folk's home.

Before starting out, I wrapped the aluminium pitcher in jute and dipped it in water to keep the milk fresh. On my way I wet it again from the sprinklers I passed.

The air was cool and crisp when I set out, and dewdrops still hung from the leaves. The Valley was mantled by a sea of low-lying clouds, the mountain jutting above them like a blue isle. The rising sun, the same sun of the Land of Israel that had tried to murder Grandfather and his brother at 5.15 in the morning, was already stripping the fields of their white coverlet of mist, which dissolved like a seething blanket in the heat. Slowly the Valley threw off its soft bedclothes. The earth grew warm, drying out the damp soles of my feet. I always went barefoot, my sandals slung around my neck so that my heels could crush the earth beneath them. I can still feel the pleasure of that thin, hot soil between my toes, a grey flour ground by cart wheels and tough cattle hooves. Sometimes I walk along the sandy beach by my house, but its sharp, coarse granules are unlike the soft powder of the paths that took me to Grandfather.

Greenfinches jumped on the hedgerows along the path, and a pair of falcons tumbled in the air, sporting in high-pitched spirals. A yellow cloud of goldfinches swarmed anxiously over the thistles, their thick, short beaks sounding little squeaks of surprise.

'By their beaks ye shall know them. The goldfinch's is short and thick, well suited for cracking seeds, and the falcon's is curved and sharp, perfectly adapted to tearing meat.'

One morning Pinness took us to the edge of the eucalyptus woods, where the carcass of a cow had been dumped. Belly swollen, horns ploughing the earth, it had been dragged there chained to a tractor the evening before. 'He shall be buried with the burial of an ass, drawn and cast forth beyond the gates of Jerusalem,' quoted Pinness sadly, telling us to watch in silence. Several vultures were gathered around the dead body. I liked their familiar bald heads, fierce stares, and wrinkled throats. With their perfectly evolved beaks they disembowelled the dead cow, their featherless white necks in its gut.

Pinness told us how Darwin had studied the Galápagos Island chaffinches, 'a small, isolated community of birds equipped by evolution with a variety of beaks adapted to different kinds of food'. By splitting up into subspecies, each of which adjusted to new diets, the chaffinches ensured their survival. From here, via parable and analogy, it was but a short step to our teacher's exhortations on the advantages of multiculture farming. 'The orchard and the cowshed, the poultry run and the vegetable patch: thou shalt take hold of this and withdraw not thine hand from the other.'

Sometimes I would flush a mother lark from her hiding place, and she would run ahead of me and flop around in the stubble like a shrill, lame old woman, soiling her crest in the dirt while luring me away from her nest and camouflaged eggs. Green lizards ran quickly, leaving tiny cuneiform prints. Partridges took off with a loud applause of wings, and sometimes a mongoose scurried across the path, its long, wicked body wriggling like a snake. There were real snakes too.

'Though it eats baby chicks and eggs, the black snake is the farmer's friend, for it destroys the mice. Step aside and let it pass when you see it.'

The farmers who were out early in their fields knew me by my lumbering walk and the pitcher in my hand and said a friendly hello. Some even offered me a waggon ride. Carefully I crossed the wheat field of the nearby kibbutz, my muscles stiffening as a kibbutznik the age of my uncle Avraham stepped out from behind a tree with a small basket. Ages after Liberson's abduction of Fanya, the tension was still there. Future generations would never even know what had happened. The rivers of time, the dams of memory, and clashing politics and seasons had coloured Liberson's romantic prank in harsh, divisive hues. The bad blood between the kibbutz and the village kept growing, sending its tendrils out in all directions to fasten on trellises of hate. From time to time funds were fought over, stones were thrown, black eyes sprouted in angry faces, and shouts were fired back and forth across the wadi.

The man was alone. He approached me hesitantly with his eyes on the ground, as if expecting to find a cloven foot on me.

'Are you going to the old folk's home? You're Ya'akov Mirkin's grandson? My father used to tell me about him.'

Gently, bashfully, he held out the basket. 'I'd appreciate your taking this to Ze'ev Ackerman, room number five. He's a friend of your grandfather's.'

Everyone was a friend of Grandfather's. And I buried them all next to him. Ze'ev Ackerman, if my memory is not mistaken, is in row six, plot seventeen.

The straw basket held a cake and some enormous Japanese medlars that were as big as oranges. 'They're from our tree. You can eat one on your way. Only one, though.'

By 8.20 I was at the old folk's home, wiping my feet on the lawn before putting on my sandals.

'Mirkin's grandson is here,' said the old men sitting by the door as usual, desperately waiting for visitors. 'He brings his grandfather milk. He's a good boy.' They regarded me with fond glances. Some looked like Grandfather, as if they had been cast in the same mould. Others, city types, were a transparent grey, like the insect moults I collected in the fields, frail and timid like Shlomo Levin. Years of bad nutrition, 'ideological weakness', and 'estrangement from nature' had left their mark on them.

Originally the home had been built for our own old people alone, the village's and the kibbutz's. No sooner did they arrive than they held a general meeting at which they voted to throw the occupational therapists' beads and knitting needles in their faces and go to work in the flower garden. With rough, palsied hands they dug up the yellow roses and blue leadwort and sowed rows of beets, peppers, cabbages, and scallions. Then, singing lustily, they drained the gold-fish pond and diverted its water for irrigation.

'All that was missing was for one or two of them to commit suicide,' Grandfather said.

'No one knew what to do with us,' Liberson told me years later, when Fanya was dead and he himself had been brought to the home, blind and irritable. 'They weren't prepared for ageing pioneers. The sight of us mighty visionaries and men of action reduced to arteriosclerotic rheumatics sent them all into shock.'

I entered the dining hall, where Grandfather was waiting for me, and halted in front of him. Everyone looked at him enviously. He patted my stiff head of hair happily.

'Good morning, Shulamit,' I said to the woman seated beside him.

Grandfather's lady friend, a large, stooped, sickly-looking woman with white hair and reading glasses, smiled at me. I stared down at the ground.

Once when I came Grandfather was not in the dining hall. I crossed the garden to look in his window and saw Shulamit lying on the bed, her dress hiked up above her fallen stomach. Grandfather was kneeling on the rug, his bald head pecking at the flesh between her legs while she talked to him in the same crooning, spongy alphabet that Pinness had not wanted to translate. I left the milk by their door. Later Grandfather came looking for me on the lawn. His moustache had a scary swamp smell when he kissed my cheek.

Now I put the can on the table, removed the lid, and poured Grandfather a cup of milk. 'Straight from the cow,' I said, proudly looking around. Shoshanna, a housemother, wiped her red hands on her apron and clapped them together.

'That's wonderful, Mirkin. Drink, Mirkin. Isn't it good for you, Mirkin? There's nothing healthier than milk.'

'She thinks everyone over the age of sixty-five is senile,' grumbled Grandfather, polishing off the milk. Four cups of it, one after the other. Shulamit did not like milk.

Afterwards, watched by everyone, Grandfather and I went for a walk in the garden or chatted on the terrace. I had to tell him over and over what was happening at home, what was new in the orchard and the farmyard, what was the latest in the village.

'How's Pinness?'

'He heard that crank again.'

'Who was he screwing this time?'

'It's always someone else.'

'And Tsirkin?'

'Tsirkin had a big fight with Meshulam. He wanted him to burn some weeds in the yard, but Meshulam was too busy repairing the old binding machine.'

'That piece of junk?'

Meshulam had found the old Clayton binder next to the bullpen, its traces cracked and its wings broken, like the giant skeleton of some shattered bird. I stood up and started to mimic him. 'You do not throw out history just because it has no spare parts.'

Grandfather laughed. 'Meshulam will stuff his own father with his mandolin in his hand.'

When Grandfather moved to the old folk's home, Meshulam came to ask me for all his papers, letters, and personal belongings.

'Ya'akov Mirkin's memoirs can throw valuable light on the situation in this country at the beginning of World War One,' he declared.

'He didn't write any memoirs,' I said.

'Letters and notes are valuable too,' explained Meshulam importantly.

Grandfather laughed when I told him how I had grabbed Meshulam by his belt and collar and thrown him out of the window.

'Meshulam will cause some disaster yet,' he said as he saw me off. 'Don't forget to water the orchard and help in the cowshed. You don't have to wait for Avraham to ask you.'

After I left he would stand on the terrace for a long while, watching my figure disappear around the bend in the road. Once I waited there for half an hour and then ducked back and looked up. Grandfather was still at his post. Bent with work. Looking with longing. Waiting with vengeance. For his son Efrayim. For the blossoms in the orchard. For Shifris, the last pioneer, who would come walking slowly, making his way through sand and snow to the Land of Israel.

# 19

'I have a photo of him,' Meshulam informed me. Sometimes he would toady up to me, trying to get into my good books as we walked up and down among the graves.

He took it from his shirt pocket. Like all the old snapshots, its borders were cut in a wavy line. Efrayim looked like a beekeeper, his face invisible behind its mask. A slender young man in wide khaki trousers and crepe shoes. Neither beauty nor horror was immortalised here. Only quiet, still visible despite the years.

'I'll swap it for the constitution of the Feyge Levin Workingman's Circle,' offered Meshulam.

I pushed him away. 'Beat it before I beat you.'

I never liked Meshulam. When I was a boy he used to come to Grandfather to ask about his first years in the country.

'So tell me, Mirkin, did you meet Frumkin in Kinneret?'

'Yes.'

'In the pumphouse by the Jordan?'

'There too.'

'And you heard him call for a strike to make Berman resign?'

'Why make a big deal of it, Meshulam? Berman refused to let them have a horse and waggon to visit a sick friend in Tiberias, and when the friend died they were furious. He made life hard for them. Like the officials in Kfar Uriah and the other big farms.'

'Berkin wrote in *The Young Worker* that in Kfar Uriah there were four administrators, and that he had uncovered financial irregularities.'

'So?'

'Here, I'll tell you exactly what he wrote.' Meshulam shut his eyes and quoted from memory. '"Kfar Uriah has no less than four administrators, and what do they do? The first, who is the head administrator, lives in Petach Tikvah and comes to visit on a mule. As for the other three, one looks after the grain fields and one is in charge of planting trees."'

'Excuse me, Meshulam, but I have work to do.' Grandfather turned to go with a powerful shake of his shoulders. Meshulam ran after him to the yard.

'But don't you see, Mirkin? He says four administrators and then mentions one in Petach Tikvah, one in the grain fields, and one in the orchards. Where's the fourth? What happened to him? And Bilitskin only speaks of three. I'm looking for someone to put me right.'

'That's what's worrying you? The number of administrators in Kfar Uriah? Why don't you go and ask Zeitser?'

'You know very well that I can't get a word out of Zeitser.'

When he was ten years old Meshulam once spent a whole day following Zeitser around, pestering him with questions until he received a swift kick in the backside. He ran crying to his father, who told him that he would get a second kick if he didn't stop the nonsense.

None of the other founding fathers could stand Meshulam either.

'Get out of here!' shouted Liberson in despair. 'How am I supposed to remember how much money Hankin wanted from Abramson to buy the land at Ein Sheikha?'

After six hours in Meshulam's company, Liberson dropped the heavy bale of hay he was holding and wearily sat down on it. Eighty-year-old men do not like pedantic questions that point up their failures of memory.

'You don't have to remember,' said Meshulam. 'Just tell me.'

'Twelve francs a dunam.'

'You see, Liberson, when you want to, you remember,' Meshulam said. 'There's a little problem here, though, because Abramson, in his letter to Tyomkin at the end of the war, specifically speaks of fifteen francs a dunam. What happened to the rest of the money?'

I too ran out of patience.

'What's it to me?' I asked, throwing the snapshot to the ground. 'How do I even know it's Efrayim?'

The cow was a present from Efrayim's friends in the British army, who had scattered all over the globe after the war. She was a pregnant, pedigreed, highly valuable Charolais heifer. Most of the money for her purchase was donated by Efrayim's former squad leader, who had returned to his family diamond mine in Rhodesia. Two Scottish secret agents brought the money to an ex-Resistance fighter who was now a motorcycle repairman in Dijon, and he bought the cow from an old farming woman in the Charolais district and passed it on to them. From there it was led over back mountain passes to a Mediterranean port and taken to Palestine by the British navy in a grey frigate assigned to hunt down ships carrying illegal Jewish immigrants.

Efrayim put on his uniform and decorations and drove to the port in Haifa.

'He returned in a Bedford army truck with the lame officer, Major Stoves. The cow, still green from the voyage, was standing in a crate.'

The whole village came out to the main road to see her. She was the first Charolais cow in Palestine and had brought with her, in a flat walnut case with a green felt lining, her framed certificates from the French department of agriculture.

'We had never seen a cow like her before. She was broad and low-built, brimming with self-esteem and unadulterated genes of a purity unknown among men. When I saw her I understood for the first time why Jeremiah compares the glorious kingdom of Egypt to "a very fair heifer".'

Next to her, said Pinness, Ya'akovi's handsome heifer Modesty, that year's bronze medal finalist at the Haifa agricultural exhibit, looked like 'one of the shrivelled wine-bottles of the Gibeonites'.

'She had a tender smell of red meat that made my daughter Esther look at her so hungrily that everyone burst out laughing.'

A month and a half later Efrayim's heifer bore a magnificent Charolais calf. 'Nothing like it had ever been seen in these parts.' The birth was presided over by our animal doctor and the British district veterinarian, who was responsible for all the police dogs and horses in the area.

'She took it like a trouper,' they said, removing their rubber gloves and washing their hands of blood and excrement. The pedigreed cow had given birth without a peep in a private corner of the cowshed, unlike the mothers of our own mixed breed, who bellowed as though being led to the slaughter, encouraging all the other cows to come and watch.

Efrayim looked at the baby calf struggling to its feet and was beside himself with excitement. The animal's thick neck and square forehead, its stout legs and soft, bright curls, made him shiver with delight. When he knelt with his hand on its broad back and removed his mask, the calf stuck out a rough tongue, licked the charred flesh of his cheeks, and sought to nurse from his disfigured ears and nose. It still could not walk without stumbling. Its mother stood beside it, snorting in annoyance while burying the afterbirth with her hoof.

'That was the start of an unusual friendship,' I was told by Avraham, who was a great expert on cattle.

'Efrayim embraced the calf,' said Pinness, 'and then, overcome by a sudden, embarrassing urge, lifted it as the nursing father beareth a sucking child, walked out into the yard with it, and headed for the fields.'

'And so off went your uncle Efrayim with ninety sweet pounds on his shoulders. He had already decided to call his little Frenchman Jean Valjean.' Grandfather undid the bib around my neck, lifted me out of my highchair, placed me on his shoulders, and began to prance around the room with me. The Charolais calf laid its warm, kinky head in the hollow of its master's breast and grunted quietly. While Grandfather scrubbed my neck with his fingers, the maddened bleats of the cow looking for her baby sounded in the yard. Efrayim capered happily in the fields until an evening chill set in and he brought Jean Valjean back to his mother to be nursed.

The calf was the talk of the village. Two days later the British veterinarian returned for a check-up and swabbed Jean Valjean's navel with disinfectant. He and our own vet gave Efrayim some good advice on raising him.

Every day Efrayim took Jean Valjean out for walks in the yard and orchard, and every night, after cleaning out the cowshed, he came to check that he was safe and sound and that his straw mattress was dry. Only then did he lie down blissfully in bed, his one eye glittering in the dark. Binyamin teased him, calling him 'the Minotaur', but Efrayim did not mind. Having never seen him before he was wounded, he said, the calf accepted him as he was.

When Jean Valjean was a month old my uncle hoisted him onto his shoulders and went out in the street for the first time since his return.

'I'm taking him on a tour of our village,' he announced in his splintered voice.

A few astounded glances were sent his way, but Efrayim merely croaked from underneath his mask that he was showing the calf his future home. With self-conscious smiles the villagers followed after him, petting Jean Valjean and stroking his fine limbs. Several greeted Efrayim in a friendly fashion, causing new hope to spring in his heart. His relations with the village, he decided, were looking up – and so, when Hayyim Margulis came to ask for his help in hunting down Bulgakov, he was happy to agree.

Bulgakov was Riva Margulis's big pet cat, which had run wild and become the most dreaded killer in the area.

'Margulis's cat was the only animal I ever knew who killed for pleasure rather than from hunger,' said Pinness, who devoted a special nature lesson to him. 'It was the bad influence of human society on him.'

Having once been a pet, he explained to us, the animal had acquired human habits and forgotten 'the laws of the jungle'.

Bulgakov was a dazzlingly long-haired silver Persian who had jumped out of the city-bound bus that stopped every day in the village, and headed straight for the Margulises' as if he had lived there all his life. The splendid cat stepped inside and rubbed against Riva's calves until the two of them shut their eyes with pleasure. Riva Margulis had never seen such a beautiful creature. Bulgakov leaped onto the table, lapped up some milk, and surveyed the rows of jars there with a smile. Years later Riva still swore that he had read their labels aloud: 'Alfalfa Honey, Wildflower Honey, Pomelo Honey.'

The guest tapped a manicured claw on the Leek Honey to let Riva know that she should open it. When he was finished licking his whiskers and had curled up in her lap, she sat dreaming of her trousseau sent in a steamer trunk from Kiev, of its thick rugs confiscated by the Committee to be traded for Dutch cows and machine guns, and of the Limoges china and Steuben glass smashed in the wheat fields, where slivers of them still gleamed every autumn when the ploughshares turned up the earth.

The Persian cat arrived at the Margulises' exactly twenty years after the last cut-glass goblet had been shattered. 'It was the only cat in the Valley that wouldn't drink milk with a skin on it.' Riva was sure that it too was a gift from her parents and called it Bulgakov in honour of a young Russian cat lover she had once met at the writers' club in Kiev.

'I don't care if you smear me with a hiveful of honey,' she told her husband. 'This cat is mine, not the village's. It's not going to plough or pull carts or be milked by anyone.'

She tied wine-red ribbons around Bulgakov's neck and put out a wooden box of fine white sand for him. At lunchtime the handsome beast ate his first meal with the family.

The next day Riva Margulis took him to the village shop with her.

'You're making a big mistake, Riva,' said Fanya Liberson, who noticed the cat's crestfallen look at the sight of the poorly stocked shelves. 'That's no cat for a village like this. Either he'll suffer or we will.'

In answer Riva simply petted Bulgakov. His soft fur restored the smoothness to her blistered hands and turned her husband's dusty hayloft into a Ukrainian manor house festooned with golden ivy.

Margulis had nothing against it. 'Just make sure he keeps away from the hives,' he said. 'And he'd better not touch my Italian bees.'

Riva was a fiend for cleanliness, and Bulgakov was the only member of the Margulis household who was allowed to enter every room and sit on the antimacassars. As soon as the cat snuggled up on the sofa cover, every particle of dust disappeared and the air was filled with the subtle smell of berries in sour cream and the swish of serving girls' legs. Bulgakov shunned the hives, never climbed trees or hunted mice in the hayloft, and stood his ground when attacked by Rilov's dogs, studiously raising a large paw at the offender while baring his sharp claws one by one like a series of lightning bolts.

Three years passed in this fashion until, strolling through the fields one night with a lordly expression of boredom on his face, Bulgakov found himself in the thicket by the spring and soon met the wildcat, the eagle owl, and the mongoose. Although no one knew exactly what transpired there, his lifestyle underwent a drastic change. First he altered his meow to a hoarse, raucous screech; next he lost his good manners and became brusque, short-tempered, and violent. But though everyone noticed it, no one guessed what it would lead to. As always in our village, the warning signs were ignored. Had not the villagers already seen dogs run off to howl with the jackals, farmers' sons abscond for the city, calves elope with water buffalo? 'To say nothing,' added Uri, 'of the time one of Rilov's carrier pigeons flew away to nest in the cliffs with the wild rock doves and gave away all his military secrets.' No one suspected for a moment, however, that such would be the fate of Bulgakov, not even when he cropped his magnificent fur to an evil crewcut, grew tufts of savage black lynx hair on his ears, and finally ran away from home, leaving an amazed Margulis and a shocked Riva behind.

Riva went to look for him, scattering fried livers, beloved cream dishes, and piles of pure kitty sand in the fields – all in vain. Sometimes she saw him flit like a shadow among the fruit trees. Once she ran after him, begging him to come home. But Bulgakov merely bared his fangs at her and hissed. An overwhelming smell of rotten meat and digestive acids seeped from his gullet. Riva went home in tears and spent the night scrubbing door handles with lemon juice and brass polish.

His lust for murder caused Bulgakov to strew the chicken coops with hundreds of slit-necked, blood-spangled birds. Like all born-again evangelicals, he observed the commandments of his new life with uncompromising zealotry. So ferocious was he that the chickens, who generally made an insane racket at the slightest danger, were struck dumb when his handsome face appeared outside the wire fences of their homes. Ravaging whole coops of young Anconas, he wreaked the greatest havoc on his ex-masters. Try as they might to trap and ambush him, the farmers met with no success. They even brought a Druze hunter from the mountain, but when the devilish beast leaped on his neck and ripped his shirt and cap, the man turned pale and went home muttering prayers.

Desperately Margulis turned to Rilov, who summoned two old Watchmen from the Galilee. And yet their riding boots, old Arab cloaks, Mauser pistols, and secret passwords did not impress the cat at all. Slippery and clever, he knew the ways of men too well to be fooled by traps and poisoned meat. And he was as noiseless as a cloud.

'I'm sure he has the chickens so scared that they actually open the gate for him,' said Margulis to Grandfather and Efrayim.

Efrayim borrowed a rifle and a single cartridge from the British, waited for the sun to set, and took up a position amid the bales in Margulis's hayloft. I can picture his good eye peering through the wisps of hay. When Bulgakov appeared he crept out of his hiding place and stalked the cat quietly from the rear, smiling to himself behind his beekeeper's mask.

Margulis and Grandfather were hiding in the storage shed. 'We looked out of the window and saw the beast and the hunter go by like two apparitions.' Three green points, two low and one high, glowed in the dark. By the entrance to the brooding coop Efrayim called to the cat, 'Hands up!'

Bulgakov froze. 'Less from fright than from astonishment,' Grandfather explained. The hairy tufts bristled on his ears as he spun around to see who had bested him. But when Efrayim stripped the mask from his face, the cat dropped his jaw in horror. Into his open mouth flew the single bullet, the copper nose of which Efrayim had filed almost in two beforehand. The dumdum splintered in Bulgakov's skull, blowing his brains to wicked smithereens that went on squirming on the ground and walls.

'Now the two of us look the same,' said Efrayim to the mangled corpse, which was still twitching and secreting sticky poisons, and then he went back to his room.

# 20

Sometimes visitors from the village drop by: a hungry soldier on his way home from his base, or the village treasurer or a crop manager whose business has brought him to the metropolis on the coast. They walk through the large house in amazement, stepping out on the lawn to look at the female bathers on the beach. The younger ones shyly ask to borrow a swimming costume, which I don't happen to own, while the older ones find the panorama too much for them and stare down at the ground or into the nearest hedge, seeking the reassurance of familiar boundaries and limits.

I've had my fill of the sea. I don't even hear the sound of the surf any more unless I make an effort to listen. The waves too have lost their hypnotic effect on me. Close up, the sea is stripped of its intrinsic menace. Soft and lazy, it wallows fastidiously in the sun, and even in winter, when it turns grey and bitter and is pimpled by rain, there is something clownish about it. I don't swim in it and it doesn't scare me.

'How are you doing?' they ask.

'Just fine.'

I do my best to play the host. The not baseless rumours of my wealth have got around. Perhaps they expect me to serve prime beef and lamb chops, but I still wear the same old clothes and eat what I ate in the village. I just don't drink colostrum any more, because I'm big and strong enough as it is, exactly as Grandfather wanted me to be. At one end of the lawn I mixed eight cubic yards of soil from the village with the sand of the garden. Busquilla brought it in the black farm truck, and I grow a few tomato plants and some scallions, cucumbers, and peppers. My hens, which used to run loose, now lay their eggs in captivity because the neighbour's children threw stones at them and I was afraid I might retaliate too savagely.

'It's very nice,' say the guests, circulating through the rooms with the same careful steps they once took past the graves of Pioneer Home. Subdued and uncertain, they look for secrets and explanations.

I entertain them in the kitchen, where I make a salad, hard-boil some eggs, mash potatoes with yoghurt and fried onions, and slice a herring.

'What's going on in the village?'

They tell me about Rachel Levin, whom the years have not

touched; about the wife of Ya'akovi the Committee head, who started a drama society; about the arguments over who is supposed to sign for whose debts; about Margulis's son, who defied our co-operative marketing system and created mayhem at a general meeting by opening a private roadside stand for the produce of his bees.

'A lot of it has to do with you,' said Uzi, Rilov's grandson, who appeared suddenly one day, several months before he was killed in a war, as if he had quite forgotten jumping on my back and pulling my ears or his father Dani calling Efrayim nasty names. I don't blame him for it. I know now that there are people who don't remember like I do, and it no longer surprises me. Like Meshulam, after all, I used the memory lanes of others to train in.

'A lot of it has to do with you,' Uzi accused me. 'You ruined something basic in our life.'

'I did what Grandfather wanted,' I answered wearily.

Uzi gave me an annoyingly shrewd smile. 'You can tell an old pal like me the truth,' he said. 'Stop pretending to be so stupid. Everyone knows by now that you're smarter than they thought and a hell of a lot smarter than you look.'

One day I opened the door to find Daniel Liberson standing there.

'I happened to be in the neighbourhood,' he said sullenly.

'Come in,' I said.

Daniel was the first visitor who did not make a detour around the Chinese carpet in the living room. He trod over it in his work boots straight to the kitchen, opened the refrigerator door, and peered inside.

'Don't you have any cold water?'

Almost apologetically I showed him the little device in the door that spewed ice cubes.

He smiled. 'I can see there's been progress since your grandmother sat crying in our house because she couldn't have your uncle's refrigerator from America.'

I could easily picture him crawling in nappies toward my

mother's cot. He still had the same loving devotion in his face and the same murderous itch in his fingers.

He looked out of the window and took a deep breath.

'The air is so different here,' he said. 'Come, Baruch, let's take a walk on the beach.'

Daniel walked slowly, the intervals between his footprints as exact as if spaced by a ruler. I waved to the distant figure of David, the old man who rents out beach chairs.

'So what do you do all day?' Daniel asked.

'Nothing special.'

'Sometimes, on the anniversary of my father's or my mother's death, I visit your old place. Uri is doing a good job. He's a good farmer. Serious. He's changed a lot, your cousin. For the better.'

Daniel looks like neither of his parents. Eliezer Liberson had a head of curly hair until he died. Daniel is almost entirely bald, more rugged and quiet than his father.

'Sometimes, too, I go to visit your mother's grave on the hill.'

If that's what he wants to talk about, I thought, let him talk. I wouldn't stop him. I was bound and chained just like he was. The same ring of earth and memories led us both around by the nose.

'It doesn't upset me any more,' he continued. 'Today I think that I fell in love with her at the right age and that it broke off at the right age too.'

There was a sudden roar behind us. A boy and girl on a blue motorcycle were riding by the water's edge, spraying wet sand in a flare of golden limbs and toothy tyre marks.

'To this day, even when I have grown children with the woman I married, there are people who look at me with Esther in their eyes.'

I don't know Daniel's wife well. She's a small, sturdy, hardworking woman who reminds me of a donkey. He brought her to the village, nervous and excited, from an immigrants' settlement where he worked as an agricultural adviser. The news on her in the village is that 'for a Romanian, she's all right'.

'They still remember Esther and me when we were children. Meshulam says that our love was seen as an opportunity, a prophecy straight out of Pinness's Bible lessons. Liberson's son and Mirkin's daughter. And if it weren't for my mother and your grandfather, it would have come true.'

'How is Meshulam?'

He fumbled for words. 'You could have been my son,' he murmured. 'You would have been different then.'

'I would have been someone else,' I said.

'It was puppy love,' said Daniel. 'At the age of eight, when all the boys hate all the girls, Pinness put us next to each other in the school choir and I fell in love with her.'

'There are more versions of what happened in our Valley than there are people it happened to,' Meshulam once said to me.

'When we were about eight or nine years old she made me go to the mountain with her. "There are pheasants there," she said. "I want to catch some and pick flowers to dry." We roamed around all day, and when the sun went down she said, "Let's stay and sleep between the rocks." Nothing scared her. And yet, you know, even then she made me feel I was protecting her. A nine-year-old girl . . .

'We spent all night among the rocks, and it was then that she told me she could never marry me because I was too serious. Too loving and dependent. At the age of nine! All that meat made her think like a woman, even if she still looked like a little girl.'

'What happened?'

'Zeitser found us in the morning. The village was out looking for us all night. Rilov brought Bedouin shepherds down from the hills and horsemen from Tel Adashim, but the only one who ever managed to find lost children was Zeitser. He brought us home.'

'I meant what happened between the two of you.'

'What happened?' His voice rose to a bellow. Two fishermen who came to the beach every evening turned to stare at us. 'You want to know what happened? Are you making fun of me? You mean to tell me you don't know?'

I didn't answer. Comparing versions of old stories always left me disappointed.

'She chose your father instead of me because he was such a big, solid, dumb animal that he gave her the most marvellous feeling of masculine apathy.'

'He saved her life,' I shouted. 'When you and Efrayim went running for a ladder, he caught her in his arms.'

'What?' roared Daniel. 'That's what they told you? That he saved her life?'

I said nothing.

'They were a very interesting couple, your father and mother. Very interesting. The village is full of wild stories – that I courted her with pots of roast meat, that I ran shouting through the eucalyptus woods instead of coming to her wedding, that I ploughed her name in letters a mile wide . . .'

'You didn't?'

'Tell me,' said Daniel, turning toward me belligerently, 'do you think that at ploughing time, when you're racing to get the grain sown, anyone has time to make mile-wide letters? What the hell world do you live in, I'd like to know! Do you have any idea what's happening in the village? Do you have any idea what's happening in the country? Do you know that the Movement is in big trouble? That the young people are leaving and everyone is up to their necks in debt? That farmers are selling their cows and tearing out their orchards? Has anyone told you that men have been getting killed in wars, or do you think that the dead soldier's memorial gravestone is just one more fossil Pinness dug up from the earth?'

We walked on in silence. Slowly Daniel's breathing grew calmer and the tremor left his cheeks.

'The only one who ever helped me was your grandfather,' he said at last. 'I got over her the night he heard me howling like an idiot outside your cabin. He stepped outside with those bow legs of his and said, "You'll never get her that way." That's when I, the son of Eliezer Liberson, Daniel Liberson the athlete, the dancer, the romantic lover, picked myself up off the ground and thought, "But that's the only way to get her that I know of!"'

We fell silent again.

'I dug her out of me the way you dig out a weed. I left nothing in the ground and I burned all the pieces. She wasn't worth a minute of my love.'

'I don't know much about all that love stuff,' I murmured.

'That night on the mountain,' said Daniel, 'is the only memory I cherish. We were children. It's hard to believe, but we were little more than babies. There were wildcats around. The jackals came up to sniff our feet. She kept talking all night. I was so afraid that I kept hugging and kissing her. I could hear her talking through my mouth.'

My mother's vocal cords had made the air vibrate around her. The nine-year-old Daniel had had no idea that from then on his life would skid downhill on the terrible slope of disillusionment.

'What did you say?'

'Nothing,' I answered. 'Forget it.'

'I didn't mean to tell you all this,' Daniel said. 'I just happened to be passing by. I know you were very close to my parents as a boy. They loved you too. Up to a point, of course. Believe me, I never meant to tell you all this.'

'You didn't tell me that much,' I said. 'I already knew most of it anyway.'

'You always have to know better, haven't you?'

He regarded me curiously.

'When you were a boy, I used to watch you a lot. I'm sure you never noticed. Once Pinness asked me to come along on a class hike of yours. I never took my eyes off you. If anything happened to you, I was sure I would be blamed for it. You were a strange boy, always tagging after Pinness. You carried his chloroform bottles and butterfly nets, and you even moved your lips when he spoke.'

'Pinness was like a second grandfather,' I said.

'At their wedding and afterward everyone went around feeling sorry for me, as though I were some kind of charity case. You can't say our village has no principles. You help a comrade in distress even if he's young and stupid. The only one who thought it was funny was that goddess of love, my mother the field nymph.'

'You see,' he added after a brief pause, 'it only happened because my mother had this thing about your poor grandmother Feyge. That was the only reason.'

'All the loves and hates and feuds in our village are like a siphon,' he remarked as we walked back. 'You squeeze one end and all the crap comes out the other. In the end everything evens out and quietens down. It was me who paid the price of your grandfather's eternal love for that woman in Russia. Meshulam killed Hagit because Pesya Tsirkin wouldn't work on the farm. And your grandmother, poor Feyge Mirkin, paid for everyone. I still remember her, even though I was only a baby when she died. I do. My parents' only fights were over her.'

'Before coming to the village I saw your grandmother only a few times,' Fanya Liberson told me when I was a child, 'and always from a distance. The first time was near Migdal. The Workingman's Circle was camped on a hill above us, and the effect on our commune was electric. Everyone whispered and pointed. Feyge was wearing what Jewish farmhands in the Galilee wore in those days, a white blouse with red Arab shoes. You could almost see the strings tying them to her.'

Fanya smiled. 'I never ploughed or sowed or crushed stones. My commune was full of big idealists who talked a lot about equality and sharing and made the women work in the kitchen. The night before I had burned the lentils, and I'll never forget what I had to put up with. The men took the full plates, banged them on the table, passed them from hand to hand, and finally dumped them on the floor. I cried all night long. Among us women, Feyge Levin was a legend.'

When Fanya arrived in the village, she asked Liberson to introduce her to Feyge. 'I walked up to her bashfully and looked her in the eyes.' It was then that she noticed that Grandmother's eyes went off to either side. Without believing she was doing it, Fanya laid her hands on Feyge's temples. 'They were cold and damp. Her forehead always felt like frost.'

Grandmother brought her eyes into focus, and the two women became best friends. While Grandmother was having three children one after the other, Fanya had a stillbirth followed by Daniel, who was an only child.

'You should either have married all of them or none of them,' Fanya told Feyge. She knew that Ya'akov Mirkin's relations with his wife were affectionate but loveless.

'Ten years of being together had made them like three brothers and a sister,' Fanya said whenever people swapped tales or spun theories about the Workingman's Circle. She never forgave her husband and his two friends. From the day of Grandmother's death she went about in a perpetual rage.

'I saw her sitting and crying on a big black rock by the Sea of Galilee,' Fanya told Rachel Levin. 'It was evening, and the three of them were combing her hair. I'll never forget that scene.' The two old women were sitting in Rachel's spice garden, whose etheric smells enveloped me too as I crouched in its hedges.

Daniel smiled. 'Everyone knew you eavesdropped,' he said. 'Personally, I didn't give a damn.'

We were sitting on my rooftop. 'This is my observation post,' I told him as I set the table.

'I still remember your grandfather as a young man, and your grandmother, and Efrayim when he was a boy.'

'Your grandfather was the wisest person I ever knew,' said Daniel the next morning. 'The wisest and the wickedest.' He was in good spirits. Stepping out into my little garden, he picked a green pepper from a bush and ate it with relish.

'That,' he said, 'was a terrific pepper. No one grows vegetables in the village any more except for Rachel Levin. We buy them in the shop like city folk. They taste that way too.'

'I always wondered why people came from all over the world to be buried next to him,' I said.

'It became the fashion, I suppose. But he was certainly some-one everyone looked up to. Even my father felt like a worthless so-and-so beside him. To say nothing of Tsirkin . . .'

'You know,' he added, 'when I was a boy – and I hung around your cabin all the time, as you know – people came to him from all over to ask about their fruit trees. The whole country knew he had found the cure for gummosis in the orange groves.'

'I guess he was thought of as a saint,' he added a few minutes later. 'Mirkin underneath his palm tree. Saint Mirkin of the Green Thumb, with a halo of longing over his head.'

# 21

A great love bound Efrayim and Jean Valjean. Before a few weeks had gone by, in the course of which the calf gained several pounds a day, his appearance on Efrayim's shoulders was considered routine. Despite the burden, Efrayim felt as light and happy as if the calf were his own flesh and bone. By now 'the fat Frenchy', as the Charolais cow was called in the village, knew that her son would come home safely from his walks and had no qualms about Efrayim taking him. The calf too thought it a fine notion and waited for his master in the yard, skipping toward him with youthful coquetry and butting him playfully with his flanks and hard head as he begged to be taken out. According to my calculations, Jean Valjean must have weighed over twenty stone at the time. Though the calf did not seem heavy to Efrayim, his odd habit of carrying it around with him had its share of critics and opponents. No doubt there was grumbling among the livestock too, and certain villagers feared an insurrection among them.

Naturally, there were also jokers and spoilsports who poked fun at Efrayim and his lap calf. 'Before you know it our cows and donkeys will demand similar transportation,' wrote an anonymous contributor to the village newsletter.

Wickeder tongues wagged about 'les Misérables, Jean Valjean and his master Quasimodo'. Hearing such epithets, Grandfather turned white as a ghost and stayed that way. Esther and Binyamin hoped his colour would return with the spring, but he remained as pale as milk until his dying day. Beneath that white skin he had begun to hate with a cold and calculating passion that was already spinning threads of revenge. After a thorough investigation revealed that it was Rilov's son Dani who had come up with the label 'Quasimodo', Binyamin went over to him, laid a heavy hand on his shoulder, and said, 'You're not safe in your own bed either, because for my part you're kaput, got it?'

My unfortunate uncle, who had hoped that 'his love for Jean Valjean would win him friends again in the village', retired once more to the straits of his solitude. Silent and alone, as if thrusting aside unseen barriers, he strode along with the huge, magnificent calf on his back. Putting the streets of the village behind them, they tramped through the orange groves, orchards, and broad fields. Farmers avoided them when they saw them, and only the children still ran after them, begging to pet Jean Valjean.

Uncharacteristically, Grandfather went to his friends and demanded that his son be restored to society despite his disfigurement, lest he turn into a cattle-carrying madman. But Efrayim's hideous, masked visage and unconventional ways were too much for the frightened villagers.

'Our constitution made no provision for defaced children of charter members who went around with young bulls on their shoulders,' said Grandfather bitterly. 'And meanwhile Jean Valjean kept getting bigger and my poor son kept carrying him around.'

Upon reaching maturity, Jean Valjean weighed two hundred stone of ungovernable meat. The strength hidden in my uncle's body inspired awe and trepidation. But since Jean Valjean was the only bull of his kind in the entire country, the villagers were soon lining up outside Efrayim's door to seek a match for their heifers.

At first Efrayim turned them down indignantly. In the privacy of his thoughts, I imagine, the bull's surging masculinity disturbed his peace. In the privacy of my body, I can understand that well. Efrayim had been without a woman for a very long time. I daresay he may have preferred it that way, although I know nothing about such things. But Jean Valjean wanted a mate. Anyone could see that his virile powers needed an outlet, because often his pointed member crawled out of its sheath and groped in the air like a blind man's red cane.

At about that time a letter arrived from the Charolais district of France. I asked Busquilla, who shook with laughter, to translate it. The woman farmer who had sold her cow to the motorcycle repairman from Dijon was writing to inquire 'whether the bull has already become frisky', adding that 'each drop of his *crème* is worth its weight in gold'. Efrayim's English and Scottish friends were quick to point out too that the animal was no mere symbol of the fellowship of former fighting men but a practical expression of the wish to see an ex-comrade-in-arms make a go of it.

The farmers of the village were willing to pay handsomely for the enormous bull to frisk with their cows, and eager cattle raisers began turning up from neighbouring villages too. One glimpse of Jean Valjean was enough to take their breath away with the promise stored in his great bulk.

Thus Efrayim became a man of means. Rising each morning, he curried Jean Valjean's coat, washed his short horns and hooves until they gleamed in the sun, slapped his mighty hide, and rasped affectionately, 'Come on, you big brute, let's get to work.'

Jean Valjean shut his eyes, tucked in his stomach, and spread his stout legs wide, and Efrayim knelt and lifted him off the ground, gripping the huge forelegs in such a way that his horrid face was almost hidden by the panting, bright, mountainous belly of the bull. In their smooth pink sac, the two heavy testicles that were now his meal ticket bounced against his chest like exotic fruit.

By the time Jean Valjean and his master disappeared, the bull's lusty progeny were a common sight in all the cow pens of the village. Even today, on a visit, I sometimes spot a particularly bright-coloured calf, broad-headed heifer, or stout yearling with a great curly neck. Jean Valjean's *crème* still bubbles in our cowsheds, foaming like white cataracts of unmentionable rebuke.

Although the village children ran after my uncle and his bull in the hope of seeing it perform, Efrayim behaved with the utmost discretion. 'When he reached the cowshed of the heifer, he demanded that every man get out.' Unloading his burden in a corner, he checked to see that the floor was clean and dry so that the bull would not slip and break its shank bone and stretched a curtain of jute from wall to wall before leading Jean Valjean to the cow. Outside the shed you could hear Efrayim's soft rasp and the pounding of huge hooves, followed by the cow's loud moan as the great weight descended on her flanks, and the heavy breathing of the ejaculating bull.

Afterwards Efrayim would lift his mask a crack, poke out his still hidden head, bashfully announce, 'We're finished,' and wipe the bull's damp groin with a special disinfectant. Within a few months he had salted away enough money to build Jean Valjean a sumptuous private barn, buy himself a radio, a gramophone, and some records, and construct a large, suspicious-looking antenna on his roof. Afternoons he spent lying in bed listening to Scottish bagpipe music or Binyamin's records. Sometimes he had his British soldier friends over, closely watched by Rilov.

All this time Shlomo Levin continued to work on our farm. He was never anything but a rotten farmer, but his love of the soil persisted, and Grandfather was grateful to him for helping with the children and the housework when Feyge died. Now, however, Levin, reminding Grandfather that he had been 'practically the boy's mother', came out against 'Efrayim's shenanigans' and argued that only ordinary farm chores could help get him back to normal life. Grandfather responded bluntly.

'Anything that makes Efrayim happy is fine with me,' he said.

Meanwhile, Jean Valjean's fat French mother fell ill. Having never got used to the Land of Israel, she died one day from eating castor beans. Now her huge orphan's attachment to Efrayim grew even greater. Zeitser, who pitied the motherless bull and had a soft spot for it, as he did for anyone who stuck to one thing and did it well, got hold of Levin in the yard and told him curtly that 'farm animals are part of our national renaissance too'.

'If he's strong enough to carry a bull on his back,' retorted Levin, 'he's strong enough for other work. It's not good for him to lie in his room all day long living off fornication.'

But Efrayim's war injuries had in fact weakened him greatly. He had strength for Jean Valjean alone. Lesser burdens were too much for him. My father Binyamin, for example, could carry two fodder sacks on his back from the cart to the cowshed without even losing his breath, while Efrayim staggered under one. No one understood how he could lift a bull except Pinness, who claimed in the village newsletter that 'the case of Efrayim and Jean Valjean is not amenable to physical or biological analysis. The phenomenon is a psychological one of friendship, willingness, ecstasy, and great hope.

'Every man,' wrote Pinness, 'has a bull that he must lift. We are all flesh, seed, and a great bellow in the heart that will not rest until it is let out.'

# 22

One night I heard Rivka talking to Avraham.

'Are you sure that cow was really poisoned and not slaughtered by your sister for roast beef?'

I ran anxiously to Pinness's house. His door was never locked, and his old body, sprawled on its back with arms and legs outspread in childish trust, bespoke the faith and understanding inspired in him by all things.

'Rivka was a bad student,' he comforted me. He didn't even scold me for barging in and waking him. Since Grandfather's death I had adopted Pinness in his place, and he was now even more patient with me than usual.

'Don't you believe all those stories,' he said severely. 'There are even rumours that Efrayim was driven from the village because he passed secrets to the British. Major Stoves was a good friend of his, and there are people around here – I don't have to mention any names – who took a dim view of that.'

At the time there appeared in the village a consultant on chicken breeding who spent longer than was advisable in the vicinity of Rilov's yard. Several days later he was found in the eucalyptus woods with a dark, clotted red flower between his eyes and a page from the Bible pinned to his chest.

'That's nonsense,' said Pinness. 'Efrayim left because of your parents. He was very attached to them. Binyamin was like a brother to him. He loved him with all his heart.'

Others said that Efrayim ran away with a rubber woman who performed in the village with a man named Zeitouni, and still others that he had simply despaired of being able to 'rejoin society'.

'How long can a man go on keeping company with a bull?' asked Grandfather, who spoke of his son's fate with venomous anger.

'Don't bury me in their cemetery,' he instructed me again before his death. 'Those hyenas drove out my son. Bury me in my own earth.'

'What did they want from us?' asked Rivka. 'No one could bear to look at him. He was a monster, and a crazy one at that. What did they want from us?'

'I know Efrayim. He did it for revenge,' said Major Stoves, who spent a whole day ransacking the Rilov place with his men without ever suspecting that the arms were cached in the septic tank.

Rilov kept mum.

'He murdered my cat Bulgakov,' said Riva Margulis.

Since her cat's death she had made a bastion of her storage shed, stocking it with cleaning supplies, Lysol, detergents, and thousands of rags while talking constantly about the price she had paid for the Jewish people's return to its land.

Armed with brooms and rags, all the women of the village fought a daily battle against the dust from the cart wheels. Riva, however, was an exceptional advocate of cleanliness, and after

Bulgakov's death when the dirt drifting in through the windows stained even her purest memories, her obsession grew worse. To the three rooms in her house that were off limits she now added the bathroom, having discovered that drops of water from the shower left tiny white spots on the floor when they evaporated. 'Tile leprosy', she called it, sending her family to the laundry room or the cattle trough when anyone needed to wash.

The whole village saw that she was losing her sanity, but Margulis and his sons, nourished by the purest and most fragrant of all natural substances, were by nature equable and forgiving. Their lives with the bees had taught them to respect all hard workers, and they not only failed to reprimand the mad Riva but gave in to her every demand. Indeed, on the anniversary of Bulgakov's death Margulis bought his wife an American vacuum cleaner to assuage her grief and give her something new to live for.

When Riva opened the big cardboard carton with its strong smell of still remembered luxury, her heart skipped a beat from pure ecstasy. For the rest of the evening she almost forgave her husband for putting Efrayim up to killing Bulgakov. Her whole body throbbed to the powerful motor that sucked up the dirt and left clean pathways behind it, but when she opened the machine a blissful week later, she saw that the filth was now inside. Hurt and indignant, she realised that Margulis had tricked her. Far from getting rid of dirt, the vacuum cleaner simply transferred it to another, better-concealed place. 'Riva discovered the Law of the Conservation of Crap,' said Uri when he heard the story.

After scrubbing the vacuum cleaner inside and out, Riva wrapped its disassembled parts in clean, soft linen, locked them in the bathroom, and went to scream at her husband in his bee shed.

'Your machine just sweeps everything under the rug,' she yelled. 'I know that's your system. It's the way you do everything!'

One look at his wife was enough to convince Margulis that not even pure pollen could calm her.

'Don't come any closer,' he said. 'The bees might attack you.'

He himself could move among the hives without rippling the air. Through a curtain of angry worker bees prepared to defend him against all comers, he scrutinised his wife. Never before had he noticed the thick, flabby wattles that had developed on her knees from years of vigorous floor scrubbing, or the stubbiness of her fingers, which had shrunk to half their length from wielding too many rags dipped in ammonia.

'Leave me alone, Riva,' he said. 'You're not in your right mind.'

That night he went to Tonya's, waiting outside in the dark until he saw Rilov head for his septic tank with a flashlight and a machine gun. As soon as the little trapdoor with its disguise of earth and straw shut behind him, Margulis entered the house, his dripping hands staining the doorknobs with myrrh. Extending two sweet forthright fingers to Tonya, he told her that he was agreeable.

I don't remember Efrayim at all. Sometimes I try dredging my memory for a masked head leaning over my bed, its green eye protruding at me through the holes of a net. The mind-boggling picture of a man with a bull on his back is nowhere to be found in me either.

Nor do I remember my mother and father. I was two years old when the Mirkins were struck their double blow, the death of my parents and the disappearance of Efrayim with Jean Valjean. That's when Grandfather took me to live with him.

Voices, mostly women's, were heard to say in the village that an old widower was incapable of giving an infant 'the proper home environment', but Grandfather paid them no heed. He had raised children before, and now he simply added me to his mixture of olives, bereavement, and sugar cubes.

My loneliness and longing blur his image in my mind. Although sometimes I can conjure up a full portrait of him, pale and precise, mostly all I glimpse are scattered details that suddenly shine in a strong light, like a winter field when a sunburst pours through the clouds. A white arm resting by a glass of tea; the movement of a shoulder; a cheek and moustache leaning over me; the thin trunks of his legs, gnarled by work and years.

But I do remember a few things clearly and completely, even from my first year with him.

One is being weighed. Grandfather made sure to weigh me every month. I was still a baby when he began enriching my diet with various seeds and Margulis's royal bee jelly. As he dressed me each morning he gently pinched my thighs and shoulders to gauge the meat on them, happily noting my phenomenal growth. It was only years later that I understood that I was being checked against his plans for me.

The weigh-in was a ritual I loved dearly. Other babies were weighed in the village clinic, and later on, as they grew older, by the nurse in school, but I was weighed by Grandfather in the village feed shed. I remember myself in cotton shorts, proudly standing barefoot on the smooth, cool metal plate of the large scales while the powerful workers who carried the fodder sacks stood laughing around me. After adjusting the sliding weights in their grooves, Grandfather took out a battered notebook, contentedly jotted down some numbers, and patted me on the back of my neck. I shut my eyes as the grizzled skin of his palm grazed my flesh.

I remember him handing me a wooden hammer and sitting down by my side to crack olives for curing. The stinging juice squirted in my eye and I ran away crying for my mother.

I remember him washing me each night with a rough pad and a bar of laundry soap, scrubbing my elbows while describing swims in a big river, large geese, and a white-breasted heron in a clump of papyrus reeds, as lovely as a bright, beckoning woman.

I remember our breakfasts well. By the time I was three he would leave my food on the table and go to work. The same things always awaited when I awoke: two slices of bread with 'the hard part' (which was his name for the crust) removed for me, a wedge of my favourite farmer's cheese, some scallions, a sliced tomato sprinkled with rock salt, a hard-boiled egg, still warm, and a glass of milk mixed with colostrum from Avraham's cows.

I would sit down to eat slowly by myself, taking pleasure in the fresh tastes and smells coming from my plate and through the window, and in my small boy's independence. Then, wearing only my white nightshirt, I opened the screen door and skipped into the unsullied day that streamed outside. There was no one in sight. Barefoot, on soles that were already strong and tough, I crossed the black gravel to the kittens basking in the sun.

From all around came the soft bustle of the village, a dull cascade of purring engines and sprinklers, thumping hoes, rustling leaves, and the deep slurping of cattle. Even today I can hear it, like a curtain rising inside me to swaddle my ears. Looking around, I saw pigeons on a roof, ripening sunflowers, and Grandfather running toward me from the cowshed with Efrayim's sharp pitchfork in one hand and his open trousers clutched in the other. He had been peeing behind the manure pile when he suddenly saw the hyena slinking from the fields into our yard, tail curled between its haunches and mouth slobbering with hunger and cupidity.

'You were just sitting there teasing the kittens, throwing dust on them as they warmed themselves in the sun.'

As soon as the hyena appeared the kittens ran to hide beneath a pile of old cans while our watchdog Manya began to bark in terror. She was so frightened that she jumped onto the roof of the cowshed like a squirrel and lay there trembling on the tiles.

It was such a clear, bright day that I will always remember its bravery as being drenched in light. The hyena bared its teeth in a seductive smile, pointed its dry snout in my direction, and headed straight for me, its quivering butt so close to the ground that it stained the ground with its smells. I wasn't afraid of it, so I was told, because I was used to animals. Just then, however, it recoiled with a look of hardened cunning because it saw the old man running with trousers and pitchfork in his hands.

Grandfather's white face, tense and concentrated, floated toward me through the warm air. Still on the run, he drew back his arm and flung the pitchfork at the beast, missing his mark. The hyena, a sticky slaver of anger trickling from its mouth, looked from me to Grandfather, unsure whom to deal with first. Grandfather kept on running, sobbing and groaning under his breath, threw himself on the hyena, and wrapped his bony arms around its matted chest.

The hyena screeched and wheezed, squirming and thrashing its legs, its wet teeth scraping Grandfather's shoulder and ripping the sleeves of his grey cotton shirt to shreds. I remember the crack of snapping ribs in the clear air as Grandfather's white arms, used to hard work, opening letters, waving goodbyes, and grafting trees, crushed the animal's body. I didn't even bother to stand up. Cosy and confident, or maybe just curious, I watched the struggle go on until Grandfather rose from the ground, cursing in Russian through clenched teeth, with a large, spread-eagled carcass dangling from his hands.

'You ... you ... you ...' he kept moaning until the neighbours arrived and prised the corpse loose from his grip. 'No one is going to take another thing from me. No one is going to take another thing from me,' he said over and over as he hugged me and carried me home. For a few speechless minutes he said no more – and then, as the hyena's poison began to course through his veins, he uttered some ancient verses to a mournful chant, rocked strangely back and forth, and was rushed to the clinic.

The neighbours' son speared the dead hyena with the pitchfork, carried it to the manure pile behind the cowshed, doused it with oil from a yellow can, and set it on fire. The rancid smoke that rose from the corpse hung over the village for several days.

'What a lack of historical foresight,' Meshulam said to me years later. 'That hyena could have been in my museum.'

It was a great deed, the villagers agreed, and a small account of it appeared in the Movement newspaper under the headline 'Second Aliyah Man Saves Grandson's Life.' Once I was old enough to read, I would sit rummaging through Grandfather's drawers, reading the clipping until I knew it by heart.

'Ya'akov Mirkin, a Second Aliyah veteran and Valley of Jezreel pioneer, saved his little grandson Baruch Shenhar from the jaws of a marauding hyena by their house this week. Mirkin was working in the cowshed when he saw the dangerous beast, which had already attacked several residents of the Valley, approach his grandson, who was playing in the yard. With unhesitating courage he threw himself on it and choked it with his bare hands. Mirkin was bitten and taken to the clinic of the General Trade Union of the Workers of the Land of Israel Health Plan for a series of rabies shots. The little boy, Baruch Shenhar, age three, is the son of Esther and Binyamin Shenhar, who were killed last year when Arab raiders threw a bomb into their house.'

# 23

'But you did so pee,' I said to Grandfather years later, when I was older. I had asked about the story so often that I knew its every detail.

We were walking in the orchard. Grandfather was teaching me to notch the branches of the quince trees, which needed shaping because they had grown long and wild without forking properly.

'Now tell me, my child, where do you want this branch to fork?'

I looked at him disbelievingly. I didn't know that making branches fork was routine work in an orchard. Grandfather studied a straight branch, selected a developed bud on it, and made a crescent-shaped incision above it. The next time the tree leafed, each such bud would put out a side branch, and Grandfather would then prune the tree.

When he was a blind widower in the old folk's home, able to see only the shades of his love for Fanya, Eliezer Liberson once told me how Grandfather made his reputation as a planter.

'I can picture him right now with that sour orange stock of his,' he sighed with pleasure. 'It made a great impression. It wasn't every day that a little socialist from Russia showed up the orange growers of the colonies.'

I knew that Grandfather had quarrelled with the citrus growers after discovering that some of them were selling bud sticks 'irresponsibly' and compromising the quality of the Shamouti oranges.

'And then came the gummosis blight and wiped out whole orange groves,' Liberson told me. 'The trunks rotted, the leaves turned yellow, and the trees died. All the ointments and disinfectants and copper oxides and liming didn't help. Every time a hoe was used, it was sterilised as though in a hospital, but that didn't do any good either.'

Grandfather asked to be given an infected grove for experimental purposes, and the desperate growers, most of whom had their doubts about the young pioneers, decided to let him have what he wanted and put an orange grove, money, and workers at his disposal. Grandfather brought sturdy sour orange stock and planted it alongside the sick trees. When it was doing nicely, he peeled a strip from the trunk of each sour orange, cut a matching patch in the bark of each sick orange, tied the two trees together so that their exposed piths were in contact, and wrapped them in dry sacking for protection.

'The dying oranges recovered as if they had received a blood transfusion,' said Liberson.

'The pioneers made a big ideological fuss over it,' said Meshulam. 'It wasn't just a question of agronomy or botany for them. It was a symbol. The unspoiled new blood of the sour orange curing the rot in the decadent colonies – you can imagine how they went to town with it! You didn't know? Why, it was written up in all the newspapers.'

'Pioneers who pee don't make the newspapers,' joked Grandfather. But if with a child's peevishness I liked the truth better, which was that Grandfather had been urinating in the sewage ditch, not working in the yard, when he saw the hyena, that was because it made a difference. Anyone could understand that it was easier to throw down a pail of fodder or a bundle of hay than to stop peeing in midstream.

After the incident, I would sometimes go to the cowshed in the afternoon hours when Grandfather was napping in the cabin or under a tree in the orchard. Zeitser would be leaning wearily against a wall, perusing an old newspaper that Shlomo Levin had left lying in the yard; the cows would be drowsing in the cowshed; and even the exhausted flies would be resting on dusty piles of sacks in the corner or curled up in the fodder sweetly asleep on a piece of carob. Going behind the manure pile to pee, I would suddenly force myself to stop with a round, violent squeeze, grab a pitchfork, and run back with it to the yard. After many such practice sessions, I could do it without spilling a drop.

Grandfather returned from the clinic groaning from the painful injections. The first thing he did was summon Manya, our delinquent watchdog, and give her a dressing down. Hurt and disgraced, she slunk away, taking her food bowl with her, and was never seen again. Liberson, who was the village treasurer at the time and often went to Tel Aviv, claimed to have seen her there hanging around the boardwalk cafés and toadying up to the English. 'She was so embarrassed that she pretended not to know me,' he guffawed.

I pulled up an armchair for Grandfather to sit in. I was, so they say, a strong child even then. No one thought me particularly bright, but I was considered 'sturdy, responsible, and good-natured'. Grandfather sat down and told me a story of which all I remember today are the words I didn't understand – bacillus, anthrax, hydrophobia – and a vague something about a Ukrainian peasant boy who was bitten by a rabid wolf and brought to Paris to have his life saved.

'Yes, indeed, my child,' said Grandfather. 'Like Burbank, Louis Pasteur was the farmer's friend.'

Riva Margulis and Tonya Rilov came to visit, their faces furrowed with worry. When Grandfather looked at them in astonishment, because the two of them were never seen together, they explained that the Committee had recommended that Comrade Mirkin be given chicken soup as a restorative, and that they were volunteering to make it. Grandfather thanked them but said it wasn't necessary. He told me to bring the hatchet and the hook, and we went to catch a chicken ourselves.

At the far end of the cowshed we found Pinness measuring the teeth and skull of the charred hyena and jotting down the results in a notebook. Serene but excited, he hurried over to us when he saw us.

'I'm sure it's him,' he said. 'I'm absolutely certain.'

He began to cut the hyena's head off, inserting his knife deftly between the spines of the vertebrae and severing the large neck and shoulder tendons with practised strokes. A week later the animal's white, shiny skull was on display in the glass cabinet of the nature room. As was his custom, Piness did not remove the flesh with chemicals but simply buried the carcass with the eggs of the greenbottle fly. Within a few days the newly hatched maggots had picked the hyena's bones clean.

As soon as the anxious hens roving around by the hayloft saw Grandfather and me approach with the short hatchet and the long hook, they knew what we had come for. While Grandfather sharpened the hatchet, first honing it on a grindstone that spun around in a basin of water with a flurry of sparks and spray, then filing it down with a sickle, they ran around the yard beating their wings and screeching to one another. Grandfather, who was traditionally the family chicken killer though not much of a meat eater himself, brandished the hook, which was no more than a rusty reinforcing rod a yard and a half long and twisted at one end, swept our speckled hen Shoshanna off her feet with it, bent down with a grunt of pain because his stomach still hurt from the injections, and grabbed her by the throat.

The cows shut their horrified eyes. With a movement so lightning fast that it made me want to study it in slow motion to see how it was done, Grandfather laid Shoshanna's neck on the concrete partition of a feed stall and brought the sharpened hatchet down on her throat. Contorted beak opened wide, her combed head dropped on his black rubber boots as he flung her startled body over his shoulder in a parabola so perfect that he did not even bother to glance at the familiar curve.

The beheaded chicken, a flying fountain of blood, fell, writhed, and rose to its feet for its death dance. Grandfather moved away. He disapproved of the hypnotic way I stared at the hen doing her last little jitterbug. 'That's something you must have got from your mother,' he said.

Meanwhile Shoshanna ran back and forth, staggering and stumbling as the blood burbled from her headless throat and seeped into the ground with the ghastly yet attractive silence of a soul and body now suffering separate fates.

Even when her head and throat, with their vocal cords, memories, and pain centres, were lying on the straw by the feed stall, I feared that the hen might put herself back together and walk off. To be on the safe side, I picked up the bodiless head and threw it to the cats.

Shoshanna was beginning to slow down. Her friends went back to pecking by her side as though nothing had happened. The fiery little cockscomb in my trousers was dying too. When she finally collapsed, I went to take a good look at her last gasps. There was a brief spasm and a few more short jets of blood before some pink and black froth bubbled up with a curious wheeze from her slashed white gullet. Grandfather came, stamped on the puddle of blood to mix it well with the earth, and brought Shoshanna to Aunt Rivka to be plucked. The swarm of green flies spattered across the yard by her dance did not disappear for several hours.

That evening Fanya Liberson came to make the soup. Beautiful as always, she sat watching Grandfather eat Shoshanna and read him the village charter in her mellifluous voice.

'"Our goal is to create a community of workers that will live from its own labours without exploitation . . .

'"Our path is one of integrating reality with ideology . . .

'"The children of all members will receive equal and common educational opportunities . . .

'"The village's institutions will meet the spiritual and economic needs of every family . . ."'

'Mutual aid', 'self-sufficiency', 'the status of women', 'the return to the earth' – the comforting phrases sounded in Grandfather's room until his suffering features softened with sudden forgiveness. A bored smile played over the corners of his mouth, and he fell asleep like a baby. His face while he slept was like his face when he died, when I took his warm, soft, white body and buried it in the earth he had wished to be laid to rest in.

# 24

After Shulamit arrived and took Grandfather to the old folk's home, I went to Pinness when I wanted to hear stories. He lived by the water tower in a small house surrounded by an unusual garden of indigenous shrubs and wildflowers. In it he had planted dark corms of cyclamen and giant, colourful anemones; bulbs of oriental hyacinth brought from the hills above the Sea of Galilee; and wild lupin from the Carmel, with large poisonous seeds that produced splashes of bright royal purple. He had taken jonquils and veronicas from the swamp flora left by the spring, and his red buttercups were as shiny as if varnished by the village carpenter.

'If I had wanted rosebushes and chrysanthemums, I would have stayed in Russia,' he declared.

'The orchid is a marvellous wildflower that human beings have made an invalid,' he once said to me, scolding me for liking Peker the saddler's stories about being sent by a Russian officer to woo 'the general's beautiful daughter' with bouquets of orchids.

'Even Luther Burbank, who cultivated roses and chrysanthemums, swore never to touch the orchid. Its fate has been like that of the poor girls in China who have their feet bound in infancy.'

Each time I opened his green gate and walked up the flagstone path to his house, I again became 'Baruch from the fourth form' who was sent to the old teacher once a week for hitting another child.

'Why don't you go to Ya'akov to calm down a bit? Maybe he can make a human being out of you.'

He was the village's first teacher. He had taught my mother; he had taught my uncle Efrayim and my uncle Avraham; he had taught Uri, Yosi, and me. Pinness had taught everyone. Each time he started a group of five-year-olds on the alphabet you could feel a quiet sense of excitement throughout the village. People even gathered by the school fence to hear the laughter of the new pupils through the window. He never began with the letter *alef* but always with *heh*. 'The sound it makes, children, is "ha". Say it after me: ha ha ha ha ha!' For a year or two he played with them, took them for walks, and cast his spell over them, until they discovered that they were saddled with his bit firmly in their mouths and accepted his authority with a love and a longing that lasted the rest of their lives.

Of all the non-farmers in the village, Pinness alone was treated with full respect. Though the children sometimes made fun of him, he never ceased to awe them even when he was a retired ex-principal who would walk into a classroom without knocking, say, 'Don't let me bother you,' to the anxious teacher and excited pupils, and sit there watching the lesson with yearning and love.

No matter how many new teachers came to the village, Pinness never condemned them for their ignorance or wrong educational views.

'It's like tilting at windmills,' he would say, 'as when one doth hunt a partridge in the mountains.'

Students who got into trouble were sent to see him at home. Slowly the culprit would approach the hedge of arborvitae, open the green gate, walk up the flagstone path while being sprayed by the little sprinkler, and hesitantly open the never-locked door. Putting a friendly hand on the boy's damp neck, Pinness would lead him to the little kitchen, make him a cup of tea from an essence that was always in readiness, and talk to him. Sometimes it was about field drainage; sometimes about the parable of the vineyard in the Book of Isaiah, or bisexual flowers and their amazing strategies for avoiding self-pollination. Long after returning to the classroom with a cracker or a piece of candy in hand, the child would still feel the old teacher's warmth and the sweetness of the tea he had drunk.

In Pinness's younger days he would yoke a waggon to a team of mules and take twenty pupils at a time – 'Up you go, children, shake a leg there, my little flowers' – for a spring hike that lasted two weeks.

Old Zeitser, who was very critical, once expressed the desire to come along on one of Pinness's last spring hikes. Tired but excited, he returned smelling of campfire smoke and crushed wild garlic leaves to announce that 'you don't find teachers like that anymore'.

Pinness took us to Mount Gilboa to teach us David's lament for Saul and Jonathan, to En-Dor when we read Tchernichovski's poem about the witch from there whom King Saul consulted, and to the Jordan Valley when we studied the history of the Movement. He showed us the scent stations of the deer, the pollen trap of the bee orchid, and the sticky nets of the orb weaver in the rockrose. We, his little emissaries, gathered for him bits of ancient pottery from the old archaeological site, skink eggs from the fields, fossils from the limestone rocks of the hills. He sorted them, catalogued them, put them in boxes, and sent them to professors in Jerusalem and London. Beneath starry skies he took us out to the fields at night to see 'the heavenly bodies' and hear 'the plainsong of the toads'.

'Feyge died slowly,' he told me while serving tea and biscuits. He threw me a suspicious look, as if uncertain whether I understood. 'She was sick. She was overworked. Not everyone had the strength for those days. And she had given birth to several children in a row. Efrayim came right after Avraham, and your mother Esther a year after Efrayim. It was more than her body could take.'

I described the way I had seen Mandolin Tsirkin looking at Grandmother's photograph.

'All three of them loved your grandmother,' he sighed. 'They adored her and put her on a pedestal. They just didn't love her as a man loves a woman.'

'Fanya says they were like three brothers and a little sister.'

'They were like three brothers and a little brother,' said

Pinness. 'A little brother they were crazy about. Do you understand what I'm telling you?'

'Yes,' I said.

There's something about my big, dense body that makes
people think I'm slow-witted.

'I know how attached you are to your grandfather. He's really
an outstanding personality. And I know how hard it is for you
without him. But he loved another woman, and he waited for
her and fought against her all his life. That's something you must
realise by now.'

'Then why did he marry Grandmother?'

'My child,' Pinness laughed, 'it was the Workingman's Circle's
decision. Today that sounds like one of their practical jokes, but
back then such things were really voted on. When I was in the
commune in the Jordan Valley, there was once a meeting to
determine which women should get pregnant and when. That's
when I left with Leah and the twins in her womb. The kibbutz
next door had a huge debate about whether saying "good
morning" and "good evening" was a bourgeois custom or not.

'Maybe they were afraid she would end up with someone else.
Maybe they simply didn't think it through. She never understood
the relations that had formed among them either. Why, all four
of them used to swim naked together in the Sea of Galilee. Today
no one can understand that, not even they themselves, not even
that great scholar Meshulam Tsirkin. Knowest thou the time
when the wild goats of the rock bring forth? Hast thou entered
into the springs of the sea? Out of whose womb came the ice?
And the hoary frost of heaven, who hath gendered it?'

He patted the back of my neck. 'You're a strange lad,' he said.
'Yosi's a little *muzhik*, Uri reminds everyone of Efrayim, and
you're the old folk's boy, Mirkin's orphan. Come, my child, let
me put you to work. You can help me out in the garden.'

Efrayim disappeared with Zeitouni's troupe, carrying Jean Valjean
on his shoulders, as soon as the week of mourning for my parents
was over. The bomb thrown into their house had rolled beneath
my bed, where it lay hissing and smoking. The crack of the

window as it shattered woke my father, but precious seconds went by before he smelled the burning fuse, realised what had happened, and switched on the light. Raking me up in his arms blanket and all, he threw me through the window like a bundle. Then he threw himself on my mother, who twined her arms and legs around him and smiled in her sleep.

The villagers heard the explosion in the meeting house, where they were holding a general assembly. On the agenda was the replacement of several main irrigation pipes, an issue they were stormily debating. Together they burst from the building and ran toward the receding echoes of the blast, the crackle of burning walls, and the smell of roasted flesh.

By the time they passed Rilov's yard, all was quiet again. The cows had stopped screaming and gone back to chewing their cud. The smoke had dispersed. In distant Berlin I picture Daniel Liberson waking from a nightmare and wailing, 'I want to go home!' like a baby in a voice that could be heard far and near. He shat in his trousers, sucked his thumb, and crawled like a lizard over his bed until his buddies wrapped him in a sheet and rocked him back to sleep. In the morning two Scotsmen who knew many languages and roads arrived to escort him on the long way back to Palestine.

The leather pants from the Tyrol, the wedding dress, Efrayim's letters to Binyamin – all went up in flames. 'The only thing we could hear in the darkness was an infant's hurt sobs. We searched with our torches and found you crawling half naked in the grass, covered with large moths.'

I was two years old.

'We'll raise him with Yosi and Uri,' said Avraham.

But Grandfather wrapped me in a blanket and took me home with him. All night long he cleaned the soot and the charred powder of moth wings off me and tweezed little pieces of glass from my body. In the morning he dressed me and took me to stand with him by the coffins, which were already on display in the meeting house, draped in the flag and black bunting.

Rilov was there, dazed and overwhelmed by failure. 'At least they died in their bed,' was the best comfort he could offer Grandfather, who smiled wanly.

'Yes, Rilov, you're right. They did die in their bed,' he said, patting the Watchman on the shoulder where his skin was grooved by his rifle strap.

'That idiot,' Uri said to me. 'It runs in that whole family. What else can you expect from a man whose grandfather was the only Jew in Russia to rape Cossacks?'

'Mirkin is raising another orphan,' the villagers said. Shlomo and Rachel Levin came to make lunch and returned to offer their help. But Grandfather told them, 'Avraham will run the farm and I'll raise the child by myself.'

Jean Valjean rubbed up against the cypress trees that bordered the cemetery. Efrayim and Avraham shovelled earth onto my parents' graves. National eminences and leaders of the Movement came to give speeches. Grandfather held me in his arms while Tsirkin and Liberson stood like two snapshots on either side of him.

Afterwards the crowd broke into little groups that laid the usual flowers and pebbles on the graves.

'Come, Baruch,' said Grandfather to me. '*Schnell, schnell.*'

'You laughed because you knew those words from home.' He lifted me up and put me on his shoulders.

The village got over the tragedy. 'We were made of the toughest of cloths.' There wasn't a house without its dead, whether from malaria or from a bullet, from the kick of a wild mule or at the hands of the deceased himself. 'Or of the nation we served, or of the Movement and its dreams.'

'In the Diaspora too the Jewish people spills its blood,' wrote Liberson of my parents in the village newsletter. 'Yet there Jewish blood is as pointless in death as in life. Here there is meaning to both our lives and our deaths, because our Homeland and our Freedom call to us. May our determination be redoubled by our grief. We have chosen life, and we shall surely live.'

# 25

It was blind chance, said Pinness, concluding a conversation about the theory of evolution, that Zeitouni had returned to perform in the village right after my parents' death.

Like the obscene shouts from the top of the water tower, the recurrent visits of the hyena, the annual arrival of the Russian pelicans, and Shulamit's reunion with Grandfather – so the tawdry acrobat had come back to the fields of the village. Two tall, emaciated horses pulled a sorry-looking canvas-covered waggon trailing an old bear in a rusty cage. Juniper coals, pancake make-up, trompe l'oeil, and legerdemain emanated from the little caravan.

Zeitouni was a former Hasid from Tiberias who had lost his home and family in a flood. According to Rachel Levin, who knew him from then, he had shaved off his beard after the disaster, thrown his skullcap and prayer shawl into the torrents of brown water that had carried off everything dear to him, sold the Torah scrolls that were an ancient family heirloom, and begun to wander with his troupe between Damascus, Jerusalem, Hebron, and Beirut.

It was thus that he arrived in the Valley, so that his appearance among us and Efrayim's vanishing were all the fault of the flood. Grandfather, however, who believed neither in chance, omens, nor blind destiny, but only in flight and escape, was sure that Efrayim would have disappeared in any case and that the villagers and not Zeitouni were to blame.

'Bury me in my earth,' he wrote on a piece of paper. He knew that I collected all his notes. He had planned his revenge with a clear and calculating precision, marking weak points and baring soft underbellies.

At first Zeitouni made a living from petty theft and ordinary miracles of the kind known to him from his Hasidic life. He sold brass amulets to childless women, cured the pox by numerology, set piles of wet wood on fire with cunning incantations, and made rain by invoking the Tetragrammaton. But though such deeds aroused fervent hopes in various places up and down the Land of Israel, Zeitouni's pitiful wonders inspired only scorn and compassion in the Valley. 'We saw enough of that nonsense in the Hasidic courts of the Ukraine,' declared Eliezer Liberson to the nods of the other founding fathers.

At the end of his first appearance, which took place the year the village was founded, Zeitouni was received with less than overwhelming applause. When the troupe's performance was over he was approached by Mandolin Tsirkin, a merry young descendant of Hasidic rabbis himself on his mother's side and of leading Bolsheviks on his father's. Brandishing his hoe, Tsirkin proceeded to dig a deep ditch. The deeper he dug, the louder the earth growled, until finally, when the hoe struck the crust of the pent-up swamp, sharp blades of rushes popped up in a loathsome cloud of mosquitoes and lanced Zeitouni's delicate skin. Muscular leeches shinnied up his skinny calves and hung on there, while pale worms sought to drag him down into the depths. He stood screaming every prayer he knew until Rilov forced him to sing the old Valley favourite 'Friend of the Frog' and whisked him to safety with the tip of his whip.

'Sleight-of-hand and silly tricks, how low can you get,' commented Pinness. 'Here today and gone tomorrow. He's one big non-productive vagabondish bluff.'

Efrayim had spent such a quiet week by my parents' fresh graves on the hilltop that neither Feyge, Esther, Binyamin, nor any of the other dead noticed he was there. He did not even speak when Jean Valjean placidly cropped the juicy grass growing between the graves and lapped up the flowers on the gravestones with his long tongue. He drank from the cemetery sprinkler, ate the fruit of the big jujube tree on the next hill, and roasted partridges who never knew if what hit them was a wildcat, hawk, or polecat. At

night he watched the Little Owl bow and scrape on the cemetery
fence, regarding him with phosphorescent golden eyes.

On the seventh day, as my uncle rose to go home, Zeitouni's
entourage slipped out of the shadows of the eucalyptus woods,
crossed the track formerly used by the British ack-ack guns, and
pitched camp by the spring. It wasn't long before small fires
crackled beneath iron tureens and good smells of roast meat
and potage rose in wisps of smoke that drifted up Efrayim's
mangled nostrils.

The wandering players ate their meal while chatting in loud
tones that carried through the clear, translucent air. Among
them was a thin, top-hatted Assyrian magician who was also
the bear trainer, an Arab fortune-teller whose enormous buttocks
thumped together as she walked to the tinkle of the coins in her
brassiere, and a strong man who had split the logs for the fire
between his forefinger and thumb. Drawing the curtain on the
caravan, Zeitouni took from the rear a small wooden box the
size of a fruit crate, out of which wiggled a double-jointed
rubber woman who snaked softly like an adder on the ground.
Through the shimmering heat waves Efrayim's sharp eye saw
her brown-grey skin glitter as her boneless body, freed from its
bonds, coiled and slithered with soft susurrations.

According to Uri, Efrayim had seen such a woman once before,
during the war, in a port city of Algeria. Lowering themselves
by ropes from the roof and scaling the walls like spiders, his
commando unit had just captured the Foreign Legion fortress
commanding the harbour. After tossing grenades through all
the windows, they set out to clear the city of snipers.

Someone opened fire on them from one of the houses. The
men stormed inside, shot the sniper, and found themselves
surrounded by frightened girls dressed in see-through fabric and
coughing from the dust of bullet holes and smashed powder jars.
When the smoke of battle had cleared, the whores, convinced the
soldiers were American, asked for chewing gum. Captain Stoves,
Efrayim's platoon commander, borrowed a lipstick from one of
them and stepped outside. As he was scrawling 'Off Limits For

All Ranks' on the front door, he was shot in the left knee and forced to drag himself back inside.

Though the girls wore heavy silk veils over their faces, Uri related excitedly, their nipples could gauge the width of each commando's shoulders through their lace clothes. Pouring spicy perfumes on Captain Stoves's wound, they dressed it and laid him down on a soft divan to watch their act. Its principals were two tall Senegalese whose tribal morés allowed them to copulate only standing up, in such a manner that the male partner bumped his head against the arched alabaster ceiling upon climax; a young Hungarian with a velvet-lined oral cavity and fleshy flower petals fluttering in the depths of her throat; and an Anatolian shepherdess whose armpits, perfumed with tincture of nasturtium buds, sprouted long braids festooned with coloured ribbons, while her pubic hair – as could be seen by anyone giving it a gentle tug to make sure it wasn't a wig – fell in a dense, curly curtain from her navel to her knees. There was also a Communist from Cracow, a Jewess with thin eyebrows who demanded absolute silence in her boudoir so that she could concentrate on speaking from between her legs. 'Not that Efrayim understood a word, because he knew no Yiddish,' Uri rhapsodised. Each time he told the story, the marvels of the prostitutes grew greater.

They did their best to entertain the platoon, and 'Efrayim learned in a night whatever our veterinarian's wife still hadn't taught him.' Coloured fountains shot up merrily from the establishment's bidets, and trained pornithological jackdaws cawed in all the languages they knew to arouse the young lads and ladies. One bright talent performed the dance of the rubber woman, which ended with her applauding herself by clapping the soles of her feet behind her back. Zeitouni's rubber woman, Uri explained, reminded Efrayim of the little silver bells on the toes of this Algerian harlot, which had gone on tinkling in his ears when her dance was done, in a purple-canopied bed on the building's second storey.

Pinness saw them setting up camp by the spring and didn't know what to do. Normally one spoke to Rilov in such cases, but Pinness and Rilov weren't on speaking terms. In the end he ran to tell Margulis. Margulis told Tonya, who hurried outside and knocked on the iron door of the arms cache.

She was greeted by a flashlight and the twin barrels of a shotgun.

'What do you want?' demanded Rilov, grabbing his bullwhip, jumping on his horse, and galloping off to the fields as soon as he was told that Zeitouni had arrived.

Like all the founding fathers, Rilov knew Zeitouni and didn't like him.

'Care for a bite?' asked Zeitouni, reaching for a ladle and removing the cover from a pot as Rilov rode up.

'What do you want here, Zeitouni?' snapped Rilov, rearing his horse.

'We'll have something to eat, put on a show, and be on our way.'

'You'll have nothing to eat, put on no show, and be on your way!' Rilov corrected him, adding his usual threat about out-of-bed deaths.

Zeitouni smiled. 'This is our livelihood,' he said in a syrupy voice. 'And it's all the same to me where I die.'

'You're not dealing with just anyone!' Rilov threatened him. 'I'm Committee!'

Zeitouni, however, was made of sterner stuff than train engineers and argued unperturbedly back. Rilov's first thought was to call Mandolin Tsirkin to swamp the circus owner again. Despite appearances to the contrary, he was by no means an extremist and 'made do with reaching for his whip, which lay folded in his saddlebag'.

Just as the strong man, reading Rilov's mind, was about to desert the rock he had been sitting on and join the fray, men and women began arriving from the village in animated conversation, eager to have their minds taken off the oppressive atmosphere of mourning that had lain over them for a week. While Pinness ran after them, stumbling over the uneven ground as he shouted at them to come back, Zeitouni signalled his troupe to begin and shinnied up a large palm tree to direct it.

'But why did it matter to you?' I asked Pinness.

He still remembered all the pros and cons from the day of Efrayim's disappearance. 'Look here, Baruch,' he said, calm and affable, 'apart from the fact that we had just buried your parents, there were a few matters of principle involved. Men and woman seeking to strike roots in the earth after two thousand years of alienation from it didn't need to see a Jewish tightrope act; that fortune-teller might have foretold a future that didn't square with our own vision; and the fraudulence of the magician could have misled our youth into looking for easy solutions to our problems – solutions whose whiff of opportunism would only have heightened the doubts that were already undermining our resolve.'

His voice dropped to the Russian whisper. 'Besides which, we could never have allowed that queen of the cesspool – that rubber woman, that human chamber pot – to display her lewd obscenities. Who could have doubted for a moment that her unmentionable bumps and grinds would have a bad effect on our young farmers? Yea, for a whore is a deep ditch, and a strange woman is a narrow pit.'

We were sitting on the wooden bench by Grandfather's grave. Pioneer Home had already overrun all of Grandfather's land. Avraham and Rivka were abroad, Yosi was a career officer rising rapidly in the army, and Uri was driving tractors for his uncle in the Galilee.

The money piled up in the cowshed, and a good smell of flowers and well-nourished earth hung in the air. A few visitors circulated among the large gravestones, pleasantly crunching the gravel under their shoes: relatives of the deceased, high-school students writing sentimental essays, and hefty female youth group leaders waddling around inhaling the fragrance of the dappled shadows. A silvery shadow herself through the glimmering wings of the bees that swarmed about her, Tonya Rilov sat in her usual place on Margulis's grave. 'She's his true gravestone,' responded Uri with surprising pathos when I wrote and told him how old Tonya sat sucking and licking her fingers without cease on the grave of her beloved.

Busquilla strolled up and down the paths with two young

Americans, the sons of a cosmetics manufacturer from New York by the name of Abe Cederkin, a one-time member of the Jordan commune who had sent them to pick out his grave site. They were in a state of high emotion.

'Wonderful,' they kept saying. 'Marvellous.'

Busquilla thanked them for their compliments.

'Our father worked in Baron de Rothschild's winery for three weeks before his mother took sick and he had to leave Palestine,' they told Busquilla.

'A good pioneer had to think of his mama too,' Busquilla beamed. He showed them a few available sites on a map of the cemetery. 'The price varies according to the distance from Ya'akov Mirkin, may his memory sustain us,' he explained.

'Our father worked with Mirkin for four days in Petach Tikvah,' said the two.

'All Jews are brothers,' replied Busquilla. 'Who didn't work with Mirkin at one time or another?'

'Our father wants to know how Balalaika Tsirkin is doing,' said the older son.

'Mandolin,' Busquilla corrected him. 'Mandolin Tsirkin. Row five, plot seven, beneath that big olive over there. He was Mirkin's best friend.'

'So was our father,' said the American.

'We don't give discounts,' Busquilla declared. 'All that matters is that your father, may he live to a ripe old age, belonged to the Second Aliyah.'

'Naturally.'

'You'll give us a deposit now to reserve the place for you. The balance will be paid upon delivery. Of course, there's no rush. This way to the office, please.'

Pinness watched Busquilla's sales pitch with interest, then grunted and turned his back. He was a very old man. His eyesight was poor, and his cheeks and tongue moved incessantly, as if chewing an endless bowl of pabulum. He had put on a lot of weight too.

'Yea, I'm an old man and heavy,' he said of himself.

'In the end Zeitouni backed down,' he told me. 'He agreed

that only the bear and the strong man would perform.'

The show was subdued, professional, and rather disappointing.

'It's true that the bear could do arithmetic,' said Uri, who liked to embellish the story of Zeitouni, 'but any seven-year-old could have done as well.'

The strong man, on the other hand, aroused initial interest by braiding some thick nails together and smashing several bricks against his forehead. The farmers regarded him with curiosity, as if appraising a valuable work animal. Their excitement grew as he began to flex and ripple his muscles, which looked like large rats scrambling beneath his skin from his sloping shoulders to the two babyish hollows in the small of his back.

Just as he let out a mighty roar, however, all flushed and quivering with the pleasurable exertion of lifting his 'Apollo Weights', a pair of train wheels joined by their heavy axle, Efrayim came tripping down from my parents' graves to see the show with Jean Valjean on his back, a ton and a half of horns, hooves, *crème*, and meat.

The villagers grinned. The strong man stared at Efrayim and the bull as if delirious, began to sway dangerously, dropped his dumb-bells, and tumbled to the ground. Efrayim's green eye peered at him through the screen of his beekeeper's mask.

'That's fabulous,' shouted Zeitouni, hurrying over to Efrayim. 'Fantastic! And I love your hat too.' According to Pinness, he was quite out of breath 'from avarice and the prospect of settling old scores'.

Efrayim stepped aside with a yawning Jean Valjean on his shoulders to watch the mangy bear jump through a flaming hoop, whimpering with pain.

'How much do you want to appear?' asked Zeitouni.

A mutter of protest ran through the crowd. Efrayim turned himself and the bull around to face it.

'For them it's on the house,' he said, stripping off his mask.

There was not a peep from the audience.

'Good afternoon, folks,' Efrayim said.

'We all stared at the ground in shame and horror.'

My uncle turned back to Zeitouni and his troupe. Taking one look at him, the strong man began to vomit metal screws and slabs of concrete. The magician's doves shut their eyes. 'I see much fire and great pain!' screamed the fortune-teller.

'Shut up, you moron,' Zeitouni brayed at her.

'So, Zeitouni, how do you like my appearance?' asked Efrayim.

'I couldn't care less,' said Zeitouni. 'Man looketh on the outward show, but Zeitouni looketh on the heart. You'll make a fortune with me.'

'I don't need it,' Efrayim replied.

Zeitouni gave a barely perceptible eye signal to the rubber woman, who squirmed over to Efrayim like a serpent, wound her ankles around her neck, and rocked back and forth on her back like an upended turtle. Freeing one leg, she ran it all over herself. Her flat belly rippled. She laid one cheek on her mons, which bulged conspicuously.

Pinness coughed delicately. 'That's the word for the fatty tissue beneath the pubic hair,' he explained with the utmost patience. 'She was like the promise of every forbidden pleasure that the body secretly dreams of,' he said. 'A horrible, disgusting sight. An alley cat. A hyena.'

Since his return to the village, Efrayim had been without a woman. The wickeder gossips claimed that he got his thrills from Jean Valjean's copulations. As a young man, they recalled, he had sometimes slept with the veterinarian's wife, a coarse, oversexed woman who liked to watch her husband castrate colts and calves. Now he felt his stomach kink with a hot, phantasmal hate. Moist memories of purple canopies crawled up his loins. He swivelled his one eye from the rubber woman to Zeitouni.

'I'll be back to talk to you this evening,' he said. 'Wait for me here.'

And bounding Jean Valjean on his shoulders to get a better grip, he glided home as if floating on air in his soft desert boots.

'Seen from behind at a distance, the two of them looked like a giant boletus on a tiny stem,' Pinness said.

He rose from the bench with effort, took off his glasses, which were foggy despite the heat, and began wiping them with a corner of his blue shirt, making the same circular movement over and over.

'Who is that over there, Baruch? Isn't that Bodenkin?'

'Yes,' I said.

Yitzchak Bodenkin, one of the first settlers in the Jordan Valley, now a half-deaf old man with a mouth as limp and twisted as last year's blade of grass, was slowly weeding the row of zinnias by the gate.

'What is he doing here?'

'He came a week ago,' Busquilla explained. 'He ran away from the kibbutz isolation ward. He walked all the way, arrived half dead, and asked permission to stay until his other half dies too.'

'And that's where he sleeps at night? Out in the open like a dog?'

'Of course not,' I said indignantly. 'Weeding the flowers was his idea. He sleeps in the old cowshed.'

'In the cowshed?'

'I offered to put him up in the cabin, but he would rather be with Zeitser.'

'Like the elephant who comes home to die,' said Pinness.

He went over to say hello to Bodenkin. The old man didn't recognise him.

'Don't keep me from my work, boy,' he grumbled. 'After lunch I'll take you to the fair and buy you a lollipop.'

'He doesn't remember me,' Pinness said. 'We once worked together for a few days in a grapefruit grove near the pumphouse by the Jordan, painting tree trunks with your grandfather's black salve. There were rats there as big as cats who had gone mad from the heat and the loneliness. They climbed the citrus trees and ate their bark. The trees had terrible wounds in them.'

He sat down again, sad and tired.

'We never guessed what would happen,' he said. 'Rilov should have sent that troublemaker Zeitouni packing. He should have whipped the living daylights out of him, a whip for the horse and a rod for the fool's back.'

# 26

I never go down to the public beach below my house before evening. The swimmers and surfers are gone, and there is not a soul in sight. Half-eaten sandwiches, lost sandals, and the twiggy skeletons of grape clusters litter the sand. The slowly dissolving cries of children still hang in the air like dirty rags. Out at sea a sturdy grey coastguard vessel rocks rapaciously on the foam.

David, the old beach chair man, sees me coming and puts the kettle on the little gas burner in his cane hut. I always bring him something to eat, or else a bottle of spirits from the banker's cellars or a book from his library. David devours books in both French and Spanish.

'Just call me Da-*vid* and rhyme it with "read",' he introduces himself with a rusty laugh. His teeth are big and white. His body is burnt and shrivelled from the sun.

We drink spicy tea and chat lazily while the sand around us squirms with fine-pincered little yellow crabs.

'They're my beach cleaners,' says David.

The sand crabs scuttle out of their holes and run about, their arms raised in that most moving and primeval of human gestures that is both threat and plea. So Efrayim raised his hands to his face when he stepped out of the British automobile in the village. So Grandmother Feyge raised hers, searching the skies for pelicans and rain.

Other crabs, busy refurbishing their burrows, give themselves away by little flurries of wet sand. Their tawny colour makes them hard to see when they stand still, but I, who was taught to pick out a praying mantis on a dry branch, to open the camouflaged trapdoors of spiders, and to tell the caterpillar of the geometer moth from a bare twig, am able to spot them easily.

'You like those little things?' David asked, following my gaze. 'They're not kosher.'

'I do,' I said. 'I don't eat them. But I have an old aunt who eats grasshoppers.'

'There are grasshoppers in the desert that look just like pebbles until they move,' chuckled David.

'It takes patience,' I said.

Little insects hid in the silver whitlowwort, disguised as shiny dry leaves.

'It takes patience, Baruch,' said Pinness. We were crouched in ambush by a shrub. 'Some of those little white leaves swaying back and forth are insects that can mimic the motion of a leaf in a breeze. As soon as the breeze dies down, you'll see. The real leaves will stop moving while the silly insects go on.'

Human beings and insects, he explained to me, were polar opposites in their methods of adaptation. The former, poorly equipped and vulnerable, depended on their inventiveness and ability to learn, while the latter, rugged and prolific, were incapable of learning a thing. They were born with whatever they had. Even behaviour as complex as that of Margulis's bees, said Pinness, had nothing to do with learning or experience.

Grandfather watched us stand on two milk cans by a wall of the cowshed, examining the mud daubers' houses in a corner of the ceiling. Pinness took a blade of straw and poked a hole in the bottom of one of the little juglike structures, showing me how the wasp continued to work on her roof without bothering to repair her ruined floor.

'She's obeying inherited patterns of behaviour,' he said, immediately adding the question: 'Which is better, the small but precisely programmed intellect of the insect or the capacious and unconcentrated mind of man?'

'Take Rilov and his son,' he said to me another time. 'They were born total morons and that's all they'll ever be. No more than five per cent of the volume of their brains is even useable. But unlike all the scatterbrained geniuses, they utilise that five per cent with single-minded efficiency.'

I told David about the giant long-horned grasshopper that

Pinness brought from the Galilee. Pinness's eyes sparkled when he added it to his collection, fearsomely impaled on a pin.

'Just see how perfectly camouflaged it is, Baruch,' he said. 'It's green and looks like a long leaf when it stands perfectly still. When its prey approaches, it leaps on it and embraces it in a death hug, crushing it against the spines on its chest. So Joab took Amasa by the beard to kiss him while shedding his bowels on the ground with the sword in his other hand.'

'You had a good teacher,' said David.

'It even eats small birds, mice, and lizards,' I said, proud of my erudition.

David was incredulous. 'A grasshopper that eats mice?' he marvelled. 'The little devil!'

'Small snakes too.'

David proposed a toast to grasshoppers. Then, tactfully, he began to ask me about myself and my family.

'You're an odd one,' he said. 'If you live here, you must have money, but you're not like the others who have it.'

'I'm an off-duty farmer,' I answered. Off from the village. From my family. From the earth.

Later, when I return to the banker's house, I like to look at Grandfather's letters and notes and at the volume of Luther Burbank he left me.

'No man, in death, ever presented a countenance more beautiful, peaceful, or serene. He was like a child asleep . . .

'We laid Luther Burbank to rest under a cedar in the garden of the old farmhouse in which he lived for forty years and in the grounds of which he did most of his revolutionary and incalculably valuable work for his fellow man.

'He used to go there, often, where the drooping limbs of the great tree sweep down to touch the earth and to form about the stalwart, friendly trunk a little quiet house of coolness with the sweet balsam of the needles . . .

'That is why he was laid there for his long rest, . . . blanketed with flowers.'

In an old issue of *Field*, where I found some dried cyclamens

and crocuses left for my prying fingers by my mother, Grandfather had underlined in blue a eulogy for his hero written by a
certain A. Feldman. 'He was seventy-seven when he died in his
humble home in Santa Rosa among his plums, roses, grapevines,
and prickly pears.'

'Grapevines, prickly pears, thorns, and the narcotic henbane,'
wrote Grandfather in the brittle margin. These were the plants
that had welcomed him to Palestine.

'Blanketed with flowers', I repeated out loud to myself.
'Blanketed with flowers.' But though he too fled from the
woman he loved and planted good fruit-bearing trees, Burbank,
that happy, prolific, and contented man, never cultivated his
garden in the mud of Sisera, or was buried in the land promised
to his forefathers, or had a constitution or someone to avenge.

Zeitouni watched Efrayim grow smaller in the distance. Then,
having scented an easy windfall and a quick come-uppance, he
rubbed his hands and turned away.

'Move yourself,' he shouted at the strong man. 'Go and clean
out the big pot. Move, you bloody woman, you!'

The villagers rose uneasily and began to disperse. On Rilov's
insistence, Zeitouni and his troupe left the spring and spent the
night outside the borders of the village.

'Next morning we had a visit from Hussein, the old Bedouin
from the Mazarib tribe, who had gone out at the crack of dawn
to calm his dogs.'

Through the tatters of mist that still lay upon the fields,
Hussein had seen the caravan and its bear cage heading east,
followed by Efrayim with his soft, indefatigable, steady stride.
Jean Valjean squatted on his shoulders, still asleep. Though the
old Arab's first thought was that Efrayim was taking the bull
somewhere to mate, he felt uneasy all day. Deciding to inform
someone, he went to see his old friend Rilov that evening.

'Your bull man is gone,' he called, knocking on the door of
the secret arms cache. 'Your bull man is gone.'

But Rilov was not in, because he was out driving a small
truck over a secret back road to the village, taking the downhills

with the engine cut and the headlights off, towing a new Czech combine full of dynamite. Hussein knew, of course, that Tonya could be found draining the last lees of sweet passion with Margulis among the hives in the orchard, but loath to upset the bees, he went to the Committee office. A search party was sent out at once, but Efrayim, Jean Valjean, Zeitouni, and his troupe were nowhere in sight.

'I never saw my old pupil again,' said Pinness. 'And that was the last Mirkin saw of his son too.'

He wiped his glasses again. 'How could a bull that weighed a ton and a half, the only one of its kind in the country, and someone who looked, so help me, like Efrayim, have disappeared? How could it have happened?'

'Efrayim could have walked through a cave full of bats without being noticed,' I said to him. 'You yourself told me the story of Margulis's cat.'

Pinness began to walk up and down among the graves.

'When you first started this horrible business, I was dead set against it,' he said, his false teeth slobbering in his mouth. 'You may recall that I was even present at the Committee meeting you sent that crook of a lawyer to.'

I said nothing.

'Don't think I changed my mind because of the poppycock he talked there. A cemetery is a legitimate business . . . a branch of agriculture . . . a way of making a living from the earth . . . You should have been ashamed of yourselves! I was when I heard him. I was mortified. Who could have imagined that a grandson of Mirkin's would ever say such things!'

'And now?'

Pinness laughed. 'I'm a different man now. The dykes are down. As a matter of fact, I'm saving up my pennies for you to bury me.'

'What are you talking about, Ya'akov,' I exclaimed heatedly. 'How can you believe I'd take money from you?'

'You'll bury me for nothing, eh?' said Pinness.

Though I could tell from his face that I had said something wrong, I couldn't work out what it was.

'My child,' Pinness said, patting me on the cheek. 'My child.' Its skin smoothed by chalks and ethers, its grip shaped by flutes and pens, his soft hand brushed my face and curled around my neck. I shut my eyes.

'You can be proud of what you've done here, Baruch. Sometimes we do the right things for the wrong reasons. But I'll find myself a grave somewhere else.'

He walked slowly, his hand outstretched as though still on my head like Grandfather's. Like the music of Mandolin Tsirkin. The icy touch of Grandmother's forehead. The downy fuzz of the baby doves on the roof of the village feed shed.

Thirty-eight years old and weighing twenty stone, the owner of a seaside villa, I am still Pinness's pupil and Grandfather's child. I still wait for the feel of Grandfather's moustache on my neck, for his stories, for the sliced tomato with rock salt that he put on the table for my breakfast.

The thin, ticklish warmth of soil against my toes. The sweet blood that saves from malaria and depression. The poison that never loses its potency. Shifris will appear, ragged and mouldy, to the pied piping of the symphonies of Mahler. Storks on the chimney of the old house in Makarov, dreaming of the frogs of Zion.

The boom of the surf through the window of my big house. The rustle of money sacks. Two hundred and seventy four old men and women, one mandolin, and one old mule are buried in my graveyard. Pioneers, practising idealists, and capitalist traitors.

# 27

Uri and I could read at the age of five. Yosi refused to learn and sat silently beside us while Grandfather drew words for us on paper. Grandfather did not teach us each letter separately like Pinness but started with whole words. 'They'll learn to recognise the letters on their own,' he said. 'Single letters don't mean a thing. They only come alive when joined to others.'

In nursery we played in the sandpit Efrayim and his Gang built after the great chocolate robbery and rode on the old iron-wheeled Case tractor that was donated to us rather than to Founder's Cabin over Meshulam Tsirkin's objections.

Sometimes Levin came from his nearby shop with cold juice or fresh rolls for us. We took the rolls to the woods behind the meeting house where the wild garlic grew – a last remnant of the days when anopheles mosquitoes warred on us and the water buffalo stuck out its tongue at us – and ate them with the long, odorous leaves sandwiched in.

'Nature's bread spread,' our nursery teacher Ruth called the wild garlic. 'Now let's go and have Nature's bread spread.'

Wearing shorts, white cotton hats, and identical crude sandals that Bernstein the shoemaker stitched for us, we all trooped off singing to the woods. Every year before Passover Bernstein received us in his cabin. Placing weights in our hands to keep our excitable feet glued to the strips of leather he stood us on, he sketched our soles with a rough pencil that tickled our big toes.

'No talking, children,' he warned us through clenched teeth, because his mouth was full of nails. At least once a week we heard him screaming from pain in the bathroom behind the shoe shop.

'In the days before you were born, we didn't have such footwear. Avraham went around in sandals cut from old tyres, while your mother and Efrayim went barefoot.'

We walked to the woods in single file. Because I was the biggest, I was always at the end. Yosi kept straying out of line moodily, looking for round pebbles for his catapult, and Uri skipped along beneath Ruth's dress with nothing showing but his calves and feet, which resembled the hind legs of a bee inside a big, sweet flower. Ruth, a placid look on her broad face, called to mind a quadruped with two large, unshod forepaws and two little rear ones in sandals.

'There's more to that boy than meets the eye,' jested Pinness affectionately at the sight.

'I want you to stop it!' shouted Rivka at her son. 'You're the talk of the whole village. What kind of business is this?'

Not even a five-year-old, though, likes to be deprived of his pleasures.

'I like it,' said Uri.

'But no one walks that way,' Avraham butted in.

'You mind your own business,' said Rivka. 'We know all about the poems you recited when you were nine. The child is a chip off the old block.'

'Ruth lets me,' said Uri.

'I'd like to know what she'll be letting you do two years from now,' snapped Rivka.

'Ruth smells nice,' said Uri.

It was because of Uri that the Committee ordered Ruth to come to work in trousers. My cousin was reduced to coming to her after the ten o'clock break, taking off his shirt, slouching against her solid thighs, and asking her to 'make my back feel good'.

On the first day of school Grandfather took a half-day off from his trees to escort me, Yosi, and Uri to our classroom. Yosi stepped up to the front wall, regarded the big poster that Pinness had hung above the blackboard, and slowly read from it out loud.

'Not the soldier's sword, but the farmer's plough, conquers the land.'

Grandfather burst out laughing. 'You completely fooled us,' he said to Yosi, who was blushing with pleasure. 'All the time you sat there quietly understanding everything!'

Being a head taller than anyone else, I was placed in the last row. I put down my schoolbag, a leather briefcase from Germany that had belonged to my father Binyamin, and watched Pinness enter the classroom. This was not my first lesson with him. When I was five he once took me out to the orange grove to show me a roofed oval nest with a round entrance on one side.

'This is the nest of the graceful warbler,' he said. 'Its fledglings are gone already. You can stick your hand inside it.'

The inside of the nest was lined with soft, warm down and groundsel seeds.

'The warbler is our friend because it eats harmful insects,' said Pinness. 'It has a little body and a long tail.'

He took me home with him. From the hundreds of hollowed-out birds' eggs he kept in boxes, he produced a warbler's egg to show me. It was pale and tiny with red speckles at the ends. A few days later we dodged through thick undergrowth, listening to the male warbler's mating chirp and watching him balance with his tail. His long, sharp bill was indeed perfectly adapted to catching insects.

'Good morning, boys and girls. My name is Ya'akov.' Pinness's spectacles swept over the room and paused to smile at me and my briefcase, which had once been filled with classical records. It had been in his house the night of my parents' death and so had survived the fire. Before the start of the school year he brought it to me. 'Tomorrow you're starting school, Baruch. This is your father's briefcase. I kept it for you.'

Every year he came to the first-year classroom to greet the new pupils. Generally, he took advantage of the opportunity to tell a story. This time it was about the mighty Samson. The school walls shook when he roared like the mangled lion.

'Now tell me, children,' he asked when he had finished, 'what made Samson a hero?'

''Cause he killed the lion,' said Rilov's granddaughter Ya'el.

''Cause he knocked down the Philistines' house,' said Yosi.

'He wasn't afraid of bees. He took the honey with his hands,' said Margulis's grandson Micha.

'I never thought of that before,' Pinness commented excitedly.

After school he held a teachers' meeting.

'I have been young and now I am old,' he said. 'I've seen generations of children come and go, and still I am filled with wonder by their wisdom. This morning a boy in the first year told me that the heroism of Samson was more a matter of mental courage than of physical strength, as evidenced by the fact that he was not afraid to reach bare-handed into a wild beehive for its honey.'

He eyed the teachers one by one.

'You are the custodians of a rare treasure, of the tenderest, most beautiful saplings that this village has planted in its earth. You must water and fertilise and enrich them, but be careful how you prune them.'

That night, while I lay eavesdropping on them from my bed, Pinness told Grandfather about Margulis's grandson and his talk with the teachers.

'You see, Ya'akov,' said the teacher, 'Hayyim Margulis's little grandson sees his father and grandfather put on masks, gloves, and protective suits and smoke the bees from their hives. But Samson stepped up with no protection at all and took the honey as easily as bread from a baby. In that boy's eyes no deed could be more heroic.'

'That's marvellous,' said Grandfather. 'But ripping apart a lion bare-handed is a tall order for anyone, beekeeper's mask or not.'

I could hear his voice choke. He grimaced as though from pain.

'What's that got to do with it, Mirkin?' asked Pinness. 'What does it matter if the boy was right or not? What matters is the sweet freshness of these children's pure, innocent minds. You, as a planter, should be the first to realise how difficult it is to cultivate such a thing.'

'It's time you stopped making all those comparisons, Ya'akov,' said Grandfather. 'There's no connection whatsoever between planting and education. Or between human beings and animals. Or between a Capnodis caterpillar and the way a man thinks.'

After school I had lunch with Grandfather. Sometimes, though, if he had work to do or was feeling below par, I ate in Rachel Levin's house. Her thick, tight curls were already streaked with grey. All day long she went about in a green work smock.

I was fascinated by the bottoms of her feet gliding soundlessly across the floor.

'Would you like to learn to walk quietly?' she asked.

'Yes,' I said enthusiastically. I had heard stories about my uncle Efrayim and had already begun my own prowling.

'Come, I'll show you how it's done.'

She took me out to her garden. The Levins kept a few chickens and a rabbit hutch near their house, beside rows of vegetables and spices. Levin had tried growing vegetables on his own when he first came to the village, but he possessed a grey thumb that made plants wilt on the spot. He ate his sallow tomatoes and pallid peppers with relish and even tried convincing the experts that they were new varieties he had developed, yet it was only after his marriage, when Rachel took over the garden, that Levin, who had always dreamed of being a farmer, enjoyed the fruits of his land at last. Rachel Levin planted vegetables and flowers and brought boxes and cans of basil plants from her parents, and at night man and beast came to stand outside her fence and imbibe the good smell.

Rachel broke a few dry twigs from the hedge and scattered them over the path.

'Watch carefully, Baruch,' she said, stepping soundlessly over them. 'Now you do it.'

The twigs popped beneath my feet. Rachel laughed.

'At your age Efrayim was as quiet as a flannel cloth on a table. When you put down your foot, make sure it's soft and flat. And breathe from the stomach, not from the chest.'

She laid down some more twigs, but with the same results.

'You walk like an old cow,' she sighed. 'We'll have to wait for Efrayim to return.'

Levin came home for lunch. He didn't look like Grandmother's photograph at all. He was always pale and weak, and dragged his legs instead of walking quietly.

And yet, I thought, perhaps all the Levins were like that, which was why Grandmother had died young.

Sometimes Avraham invited me to eat with him. Because of Rivka, however, that was something I preferred not to do. Best of all I liked eating with Grandfather, even if all he could cook was baked potatoes. After lunch I stole over to the paved path beneath Avraham and Rivka's window to listen in on their table talk.

Uri, a curious and cynical thrill-seeker even then, had no trouble spoiling his parents' appetite.

'What did Grandmother die of?' he asked all of a sudden.

I could hear Avraham frown. 'She was ill.'

'What with?'

'Stop being a pest, Uri.'

'Nira Liberson says she wasn't ill.'

'Why don't you tell Liberson's granddaughters to mind their own business.'

It was quiet for a while. Then I heard Rivka say: 'She was killed by the grandfather you all adore. Didn't you know?'

I stood up and peeked over the windowsill. Rivka was angrily scrubbing the oilcloth on the table, her chest, stomach, and thighs wobbling beneath her dress like a herd of double chins. Flies kept landing on the jam stains left from breakfast. Avraham ate in silence. So did Yosi. Both used their bread to shovel food onto their forks.

'The salad needs more dressing,' said Yosi. He and his father liked to dip their bread in the salad dressing.

'Do you want a salad or a swamp?' Rivka asked.

'He's right,' said Avraham. 'We like dressing.'

'Yes, and you've both got fat sopping it up with bread.'

'But how could he have killed her?' asked Uri, who saw no future in discussing the salad.

'With blocks of ice and letters from Russia,' said Rivka.

'I don't think these are stories for nine-year-old boys,' said Avraham, the lines beginning to crawl in his forehead.

There was a sharp rap on the window. It was Yosi's falcon, beating its wings against the glass pane. Hurriedly I ducked and crawled away. Yosi had taken the red falcon from its nest when it was a fledgling covered with white fuzz, hissing and bristling angrily at the world. For three months, while it grew and got its wing feathers, he fed it mice and lizards that he caught. Hopping and stumbling about on its sharp talons, the bird followed its master around the yard as faithfully as a dog. When the time was ripe, Yosi took it up to the roof of the cowshed and tossed it in the air to teach it to fly. The falcon learned but did not fly away. It remained in our yard, trilling and calling for Yosi all the time. You couldn't leave a window open for a moment, because it would fly inside, tearing curtains and smashing vases in its delight. When all its fellow birds had already left for points south, it alone remained behind.

'Highly unusual,' said Pinness. 'It's highly unusual for a red falcon to winter in this country. Such loyalty!'

'Get that damn bird out of here!' screamed Rivka.

Uri began to giggle.

'You should be glad it comes to us and not to your father,' said Avraham.

Rivka's father, Tanchum Peker the saddler, had waxed enthusiastic when his grandson decided to raise a falcon. 'We'll make a hunting bird of him,' he said, his bald head glistening with anticipated excitement. Peker had once been one of the busiest men in the village, a stitcher and mender of harnesses, bridles, reins, and traces whose hames were famous in the Valley for never chafing an animal's neck. Grandfather once described to me how Peker had cut strips of leather into whips, running his knife along the large hides while grunting, tongue out with the effort. 'He had such a sure hand that the tip of the whip began to quiver as soon as it was free.' Peker's business declined when draught animals were replaced by tractors, but the odour of leather and saddle soap clung to his fingers and boots, and the wooden walls of his workshop continued to smell of it.

'A trained falcon like officers and noblemen used to have,' Peker dreamed.

As a young man he had served as a cavalry adjutant in Czar Nikolai's army.

'Those were the days,' he liked to say with a nostalgia that annoyed the founding fathers. 'Officers with swords and gold epaulettes, daughters of landed aristocrats, balls, hooped dresses, waltzes, sweet whisperings in the garden . . .'

Peker was fond of describing the annual ball of the provincial police inspector. 'They served enormous river fish, huge pike and perches. I was given my fill too, and then the dancing began.'

'And a yid like you, Peker, did you also dance and whisper in the garden?' Liberson asked scornfully. 'Or did you just lick the boots of those who did?'

'I danced,' answered Tanchum Peker proudly.

'With the major's livery boy or with the governor's mare?'

Peker did not reply. It was he who had stitched the saddles and girths for the horses of the Watchmen's Society, thus earning him the place in the pages of history that all the elders of the village hungered for. The index of *The Watchmen's Book* seemed to him a sufficiently honorable memorial to make any further acknowledgment from posterity quite unnecessary.

Grandfather couldn't stand him, because when the Workingman's Circle had worked as shepherds during World War One, the Watchmen had harassed them, stealing their flocks and spreading rumours that kept their employers from paying them. Hunger and hard work took their toll on the four and reduced them to a single pair of shoes, which they gave to Feyge. For hours on end Tsirkin sat playing his mandolin, gulping the strummed notes to appease his growling stomach. Feyge's skin was covered with boils. Haggard and sun-scorched, she forced herself to keep going, reaching out a weary hand to stroke the heads of her comrades.

'My boys,' she called them. 'My loves.'

Her boys wrapped their feet in rags. No longer did they float on air. Their skin grew tough and heavy, and hunger pinned them to the ground. Had they stood motionless, I could not have seen them, because they would have been as invisible as clods of earth. Every other day Tsirkin cooked a gluey porridge of corn and chickpeas in a tin stove he had built in a pit with a broken clay jug for a chimney.

Years later, when they no longer smelled of the smoke, Grandfather and his friends still bore the Watchmen a grudge. 'Those satraps who wanted to found a commune of Arab horses in the Galilee,' he called them.

\*     \*     \*

'A hunting falcon,' said Peker, taking the old awls and crooked needles from his toolbox and sitting himself down at his saddler's bench with its bulky wooden vices in the middle. Yosi, Uri, and I sat beside him, entranced by the wisdom of his fingers and the good smell of his work. The old man smeared some threads with wax, spat on the fingernail of a brown thumb, traced a line with it for his knife and stitched together several strips of thin, soft leather to make a blindfold for the bird. 'As long as you cover the falcon's eyes,' he explained, 'he just sits there as quiet as a baby.'

He cut an opening for the falcon's curved beak and then, from some thicker leather, stitched himself a large elbow-length glove. 'That's to guard my arm from being shredded by the falcon. Just look at those talons of his.'

By then the falcon had started hunting on his own. Yet whenever he heard Yosi's whistle he hurried back to land at his feet.

'The fact that he's already trained to return is excellent. Now we'll teach him to stand on my arm. Just wait and see, Yosi, in two weeks he will be bringing us rabbits for lunch.'

'The red falcon is too small a bird,' scoffed Pinness, dismissing the whole idea. 'The most he will bring you is a mouse. For hunting you need a peregrine falcon. Besides which, Yosi, falconry is a revolting sport practised by an exploitative and decadent social class that leads a life of parasitic luxury.'

'Why don't you tell your teacher to go back to hunting frogs at night,' snorted Peker the saddler when Yosi anxiously reported this conversation.

Yosi and his grandfather took the falcon out to the fields. Uri and I were told to walk a distance behind them so as not to get in the way. The falcon sat obediently on the old saddler's arm, his white talons gripping his glove and his chiselled head motionless inside the leather mask. Peker chose a suitable site, wet his finger to test the wind, removed the blindfold, and let the falcon take off. The splendid bird soared aloft, his brown-striped red belly gleaming in the clear air.

'A-a-a-ll right! Whistle for him now!'

Yosi stuck two fingers in his mouth and whistled. The falcon froze in midair, fanned his tail feathers, fluttered in place for a moment, and dived diagonally towards them with half-folded wings. The old saddler held his gloved arm out to the bird. With a flap the falcon spread its braking pinions, but the outstretched arm scared him off. Beating the air, he made for Peker's bald head.

'It was horrible,' Peker told the doctor who stitched up his skull. 'I thought I was done for.'

Unable to gain a foothold on the smooth surface, Yosi's falcon kept jabbing it with razor-sharp talons. His face streaming with blood, Peker passed out. The damn bird flew away in a fright, and we ran home to get help. No one was there except old Zeitser, who was working in the yard and came back to the field with us. Green flies covered Peker's head, from which the scalped skin was hanging free. We helped Zeitser hoist him onto his shoulders and carry him to the village clinic.

Within a few days, once it was clear that Tanchum Peker would recover, since he was already up and about with a huge turban of white gauze on his head, nicknames like 'Hawkeye', 'Nimrod the Hunter', and 'Sultan Abdulhamid' were being tried out on him. In the village newsletter Liberson wrote that while we were indeed building a new society that sought to return to nature, this did not mean 'exploiting the instincts of predatory birds for our own primitive needs'.

'The beast hunts for sustenance, man for perverted pleasure,' declared Pinness in school before reading us a few relevant passages from *The Jungle Book* of Rudyard Kipling, who was 'a wise man for a colonialist'.

I stood up and sent the rock I was holding crashing through the window. Slivers of glass fell on Avraham and Rivka's table.

'Grandfather did not kill her,' I said heavily.

'Like grandfather, like grandson,' mocked Rivka. 'Get him out of here before I murder him.'

'That's enough!' said Avraham.

'I suppose you'll ask your father to pay for the window!'

'I want you to calm down this minute.'

'Just wait till the old man dies,' Rivka snarled, 'and he starts brawling over the inheritance.'

'I said, enough!' shouted Avraham.

He rose, went outside, and came over to me.

'Don't worry about her, Baruch,' said my uncle Avraham. 'She's just worked up. You can stay here as long as you like. No one's kicking my own nephew out of my house.'

I looked at him. His short stride, his sloping shoulders, and his ploughed forehead formed an impenetrable grid that moved with him like the shell of a turtle. Sometimes he took the twins and me to the hayloft and encouraged us to wrestle on the bales of hay. I never knew whether or not he liked seeing me floor his two sons. Uri would leap on me from behind and break into helpless giggles as I lifted him in the air, while Yosi, humiliated, would run to his mother with hurt sobs.

Avraham took my hand in his. I liked the feel of it. Even then I understood dimly that certain members of our family shared the same portion of pain. As a boy, it was said in the village, Avraham had attacked a foreign woman who came to visit, screaming, kicking her legs, and biting her in the stomach until a slap from Rilov sent him sprawling. But my uncle was an excellent farmer who read volumes of professional literature and was often called to a neighbour's farmyard to help make a diagnosis. He kept careful tabs on all his cows, writing down the family tree of each beside a record of milk production, fat content, number of inseminations, calves, stillbirths, and cessations of lactation. This made for an unusually detailed farm log even without the section in which he entered the exact dates when his bereaved cows' sons were sent to the slaughterhouse.

My mother was dead, Efrayim was gone, and Avraham was the only one of Grandmother Feyge's children still at home. All those years he continued to visit his mother's grave regularly. Uri and I used to watch him riding Efrayim's heavy Hercules bicycle up to the cemetery on the hill.

'He's going to talk to Grandmother,' Uri said. 'He tells her what's new on the farm.

'Your mother's there too,' he added. I didn't answer him.

Never without trepidation, I myself went once a year with Grandfather to visit my parents' graves. Time in the village moved in loops of rain clouds and was measured by gestations, the length of furrows, and the mysterious, irreversible processes of decay, and I did not want to add memorial days to the list. Years later, when I had become an expert undertaker, I learned to hear the violent popping of death-bloated bellies in the earth. Then, though, I simply sat with Grandfather by my parents' headstones and walked with him to his wife's grave, which was always spotless and well kept. The concrete gutter at its foot was bright with yellow-white jonquils and purplish-green stalks of basil.

'My father planted the jonquils,' Uri said, 'to make it easier for him to cry.'

# 28

We were eleven when Pinness organised one of his last hikes.

'We'll do it like the good old days, in a horse-drawn cart,' he announced.

When he was younger he used to take his pupils as far as the Golan and the Horan on expeditions that lasted up to three weeks. They dried flowers, trapped insects, and slept at night in Jewish settlements, as well as in Arab villages that Rilov gave a clean bill of health. Angry parents complained that Pinness took their boys and girls away during the busiest times on the farm, but Pinness, at a special meeting convened to discuss the matter, retorted that 'education knows no slack seasons'.

'Have patience, friends,' he said. 'What the school sows now, you will reap in ten years' time.'

This time he had planned a mere three-day hike.

'I'm sorry, my children. Your parents will tell you about the great hikes of long ago, but my strength now is not what it was then. We'll go only so far as the Kishon River and ancient Beth-She'arim.'

Before it was light Grandfather brought me to Pinness's house.

'Take good care of my child, Ya'akov,' he said.

At the age of eleven I was as tall as Grandfather. Pinness laughed and said that no doubt I would take better care of him.

Daniel Liberson came along as our escort. He rode on horse-back, armed with a rifle and a whip. His glance seemed to flay me alive, searching my forehead for lost signs. When we reached the channel of the Kishon, we took our little pocket Bibles from our knapsacks and read in high, excited voices:

'The kings came and fought;
Then fought the kings of Canaan in Taanach by the waters
    of Megiddo;
They fought from heaven;
The stars in their courses fought against Sisera.
The river of Kishon swept them away,
That ancient river, the river Kishon.'

Pinness rocked back and forth to the ancient cadence and spoke scathingly of the elders of the city of Meroz, 'who avoided conscription by hiding at the town dump'. And he added, 'The Canaanites had nine hundred chariots. They thundered through the Valley while we hid among the oaks on Mount Tabor.' He traced great movements in the air, his voice growing passionate. 'And then it rained. And what do we get in our Valley when it rains?'

'Mud,' we shouted.

'How much mud?'

'Lots,' we shouted. 'Mud up to your boots.'

'Mud up to the cows' stomachs,' said my cousin Yosi in all seriousness.

'Then it came up to the horses' stomachs,' said Pinness, leading us step by step. 'The chariot wheels stuck in the mud, and down we came from the woods and smote them so hard that the land was quiet for forty years.

'Such quiet,' he repeated as though to himself, 'such quiet that it could only be measured in years.' But we were children and did not understand his mutterings.

The next day we travelled to ancient Beth-She'arim. On our way Pinness warned us that we were about to visit 'a terrible place'.

'Here the dead were brought from the Diaspora to be buried in the soil of our land,' he said to us as we stood in the large burial cave. His voice echoed in the chill gloom, his shadow flickering over the walls and running down the ancient sluices left by the quarriers' chisels. 'Rabbi Judah the Prince lived and died in this place, and after his burial here, it became an important necropolis.

'But we, children,' Pinness went on, 'returned to this land not to die but to live. In those days it was believed that being buried in the Land of Israel would purge you of sin and make you worthy of eternal life. We, however, do not believe in the resurrection of the dead and ritual atonement. Our atonement is the tilling of the soil rather than the quarrying of graves. Our resurrection is the ploughed furrow. Our sins will be purged by hard work. The accounting that we give will be in this world, not in the next.'

'Why fill their heads with all that nonsense?' Grandfather asked him during one of their night-time tea talks. Liberson, however, interrupted to say that Pinness was right, because the next world was the cunning invention of unscrupulous rabbis and priests who had failed to keep their promises in this one.

Ten years later in my own cemetery, which was populated largely by Diaspora Jews, Pinness reminded me of our hike to Beth-She'arim.

'What a pedagogical failure,' he said. 'I never would have dreamed that one of my own pupils would decide to ape what he saw there. I thought I was sounding a warning, but now I wonder whether I didn't plant the idea for this monstrosity in your mind then.

'Ninety per cent of the pioneers of the Second Aliyah left this land,' said Pinness. 'Now you're returning them to it.'

We were standing by Mandolin Tsirkin's grave. 'He's still playing away down there,' Pinness said. 'Still playing away.'

It was there, by the grave of Mandolin Tsirkin, that Pinness had his stroke. He had bent close to the earth in his fashion, keeping his ear to the ground, when suddenly he smiled weakly, his expression slowly changing to that of a man who has heard a secret burble in his head. At first I didn't realise what had happened, but as soon as I saw his body start to slump I threw down my hoe and hurried over. Too timid to grab him with both arms, I held out a hand for him to lean on, but he was unable to find it with his own. The same hand that had dissected tadpoles beneath the microscope and strummed the drumheads of crickets now groped feebly in the air like a blind proboscis.

He raised his head heavily, his lips grimacing as he tried to speak. All that came from his throat were some thick rasping sounds. As if sinking into quicksand, he fell slowly to the ground. His face went white, his breathing grew quick and shallow, and sweat trickled down his cheeks. I put him on my shoulder and ran to the clinic.

Doctor Munk, our repulsive village physician, called an ambulance, and I went along to the hospital.

'It's difficult to predict the outcome,' the doctor in the emergency room told me. 'We'll have to keep him here. You never know with these things.'

Pinness lay writhing in his bed like a huge maggot exposed to light. White, bulky, and damp, he squirmed on the sheets, ate incessantly, and kept trying to make himself talk. When I gave him a pen and paper, he made some squiggles in the far margin of the page and went on writing in the air. One leg could barely move, anhis eyes bulged and rolled in their sockets like overripe fruit.

His skin mildewed, thin grey webs of it clinging to the sponge when the nurse washed him in the morning. They grew back again at night, as if he wished to spin a cocoon around himself and awake, winged and well, in a familiar world of flowers and sunlight.

He had me very worried. He cackled like an animal, wet his bed, and now and then tried to get his hands to meet in midair. I sat up by his bedside for two nights and three days, all but going mad from the grinding of his jaws, which never stopped working away. Luckily, the village sent someone to relieve me and look after him until he recovered.

It took three weeks for his skin to return to normal and his speech to be restored. At first he found certain consonants difficult, but from the moment he started to talk again, the power of words lifted him out of the depths. It was a while before I realised that he was not using the past or future tense. That was a good sign, I tried telling the doctor, because it meant that the old man was fighting to regain a sense of the time he was living in. Gradually, more and more words reappeared with their grammar, gathered like ants on a fallen fruit, and bore him back into consciousness in a great, excited procession.

'Excellent,' said the doctor. 'He's much improved.'

Once he could speak again, Pinness recovered quickly. The doctor was surprised by his powers of recuperation. He never understood that a man like Pinness, a man of language and vision, could bypass his blocked synapses by speaking directly to the limbs of his body and making them obey his words. This was how he regained control of his leg, and eventually, of his fine motor co-ordination.

For three days he talked only to himself. Then, on the fourth, he turned to me and said perfectly clearly, 'My distant ancestors were the cavemen.'

I stared at him in amazement. Irritated by my slowness, he continued as if giving dictation: 'To seek to bind men to the earth is to turn them into blind moles and dumb cattle.'

It was then I first understood that although the old teacher might speak, walk, go home, and run around again with his butterfly nets, he would never really get well. The world of values he had constructed, the walls of faith and the reservoirs of hope, had crumbled into a feeble fretwork of foam when the dark blood haemorrhaged in his brain.

'Now everyone will think I'm crazy,' he began to wail a few days later as it dawned on him what had happened. I tried to calm him by pointing out that there wasn't a person in the village who was considered sane by anyone else. Sanity, in fact, meant no more to us than a majority vote on who was or was not in his right mind. To this day Efrayim is thought to have been a madman because of Jean Valjean, to say nothing of being an informer and a traitor. Plenty of Committee members thought Pinness was crazy even before his stroke because of the shouts he heard at night. Others believed Grandfather to be an old loony because he stopped picking the fruit in his orchard from the day of Efrayim's disappearance, letting it fall to the ground with the disdainful remark that he was growing the trees for their flowers. When Rilov discovered that Margulis was carrying on with Tonya, he decided that the beekeeper must be crazy, not to mention stupid. Margulis, for his part, thought Riva was insane and flung himself on Tonya Rilov's bony, forgotten body with all the fluttering passion of a moth, 'busily buzzing her' with his sweet virility as Uri put it. Tonya knew that she was not all there herself but preferred her madness to her husband's smell of rifle grease, gunpowder, and urea.

I too, in the days when I still lived in the village, was thought to be demented. My cemetery was the final proof, but even in kindergarten the other children kept away from me, and I never had a friend my age except Uri.

Grandfather and Pinness crammed me with stories and taught me about insects and trees, and Tsirkin played his mandolin for me and made me gape by pounding nails into boards with his bare hand, so tough was the skin of his palms. Whenever I shook his hand, there was a sound like the creaking of dry wood. 'Ever since one of them broke its sting on his hand, the scorpions in my father's cowshed have been scared stiff of him,' said Meshulam with a smile. And yet when Mandolin did the milking, his hands grew so soft that not a cow complained of their roughness.

And Liberson read me stories from books and once even played hide-and-seek with me.

'They did it for your grandmother,' said Pinness.

# 29

Eliezer Liberson didn't always have time for me. After turning his farm over to Daniel, he devoted himself to finding new and better ways of courting Fanya.

He never ceased amusing and surprising her with a *savoir faire* that, latent in him from the start, had developed remarkably from the moment it was pressed into use. Well aware that no loam was more mysterious and demanding than love's, he declared that it did not tolerate such commonplace methods as crop rotation and fallowing, which were intended for poor soils and unimaginative farmers. Periodically, the whole village heard the ripples of Fanya's laughter through the Libersons' windows. 'Liberson's done it again,' was always Uri's admiring comment.

None of us could resolve the contradiction between Liberson the stuffy ideologue, who bombarded meetings and the village newsletter with utopian avalanches of words, and the concealed Don Juan who would do anything for Fanya. He taught the jackdaws in his orchard to wolf-whistle at her and took her out to the fields on summer nights for erotic walks that sometimes had me as their secret companion. Years ago, Pinness once told me, when Fanya was working in the village packing house, Liberson prepared a cup of rich cocoa with sweet cream and sugar, filled his mouth with it, and went off to give his wife a custardy kiss. 'No one who stopped to talk to him on his way could understand why, for the first time in memory, he kept his mouth shut.'

On the occasion of their tenth wedding anniversary he overcame his proletarian principles, went off to town in his cart, and returned with some expensive scented soap that smelled of frivolity and rank heresy. Hitherto the women of the village had bathed and washed their hair with huge bars of smelly grey laundry soap. Though Fanya used the gift only on Fridays, the seductive fragrance of her skin made her self-conscious, led to disapproving whispers in the village, reminded several old-timers of Riva Margulis's infamous luxury trunk and Pesya Tsirkin's perfume, and tripled Liberson's passion for her.

Two months went by, and when the soap was almost gone Fanya discovered in it her husband's real present – 'a silly note' in a tiny tube he had had the tinsmith make specially. Liberson came running as soon as he heard her merry squeal in the laundry shack, which was where the showers were located in those days.

Subsequently, so it was said, he began leaving her notes wherever possible. Fanya found his little tubes in wheels of farmer cheese and in the feed stalls of the milk cows, heard them rattle in the oil cans of the brooder, and – for by now Liberson was a past master – even discovered one of them in the craw of a chicken she had slaughtered and was cleaning for dinner.

'As usual, Eliezer is overdoing it,' commented Pinness approvingly. 'If he keeps it up he'll make Fanya paranoid, though I must say his hiding places are far better chosen than that stinking arms cache of Rilov's.'

Tsirkin, on the other hand, still devoted himself to his farm, though he was thoroughly sick of his life, his worthless son, and 'that double-breasted politician' his wife.

Meshulam, having salvaged dozens of boxes of old papers from a kibbutz in the Valley, was busy cataloguing them in those years, while Pesya occasionally sallied forth from the Movement's headquarters in Tel Aviv to turn up in the village with foreign socialist leaders, agricultural experts from Burma, or some African minister in a gaudy skirt and baker's hat. She was also active in the immigrant camps, where she organised social and educational activities, and even had her picture in the paper bathing a baby from Morocco in a tin tub while smiling at its mother. 'Comrade Pesya Tsirkin Teaches New Immigrant Mother-Love' was the caption beneath her maternal breasts.

Behind his impeccable manners Grandfather went on nursing a keen, secretive grudge against his two old friends. Meanwhile, he raised me, pruned and cultivated his trees, wrote notes, and made plans. The same passage of time that filled me with stories and layered my bones with thick flesh put an end to the Feyge Levin Workingman's Circle, of which nothing was left but a monumental legend, a few torn snapshots, and some disembodied shadows.

I still thought of Tsirkin and Liberson as family, however. One day, finding no one in at the Libersons, I picked up the storybook he always read to me from. Although I was still a little boy and couldn't read, I knew enough to realise that the glossy white pages of the book were blank in their cloth binding. Liberson had made up every story I had heard from him: 'The Ant and the Grasshopper', 'The Stork and the Fox', even 'The Flower of the Golden Heart'!

Pinness burst out laughing when I told him.

'In general,' he said, 'we all either invent stories or retell those we've heard. And in particular, the tale of the Ant and the Grasshopper happens to be a lot of twaddle.'

One night I heard him talking with Grandfather in the kitchen.

'He should spend more time with boys his own age,' he said. 'It's no good for a small boy like him to be always with grown-ups.'

'He's my child,' answered Grandfather, sucking extra hard on the bitter olive in his mouth.

'Mirkin,' insisted Pinness, 'whether or not it's what you want, you're bringing Baruch up in an old ruined cloister. I see how he is in school. He doesn't play with marbles or a ball during break. He doesn't talk to anyone. All he does is crawl on the lawn. By himself.'

'He's looking for beetles, just like you,' said Grandfather.

Sometimes I glanced up to see myself encircled by a shouting, jeering crowd.

'The children surround him like a flock of songbirds that has cornered an owl. They screech and make fun of him.'

'It doesn't worry me,' Grandfather said. 'And I don't envy the child who provokes him.'

When I was six I broke two of Uzi Rilov's fingers. I was crouched by the white oleanders near the fence, looking for green hawkmoth caterpillars. Thick and shiny, they wriggled cumbersomely over the poisonous bushes, turning their necks to give me a frightening look when I touched them. I knew that their big blue mascara-ringed eyes were a bluff, because Pinness had told me that they weren't real and were only there to scare away predators.

Uzi Rilov landed on my back with a thump, grabbed me by the ears, and began to shake me back and forth. I got hold of his wrist and spun around to face him. At thirteen he was older and quicker than me. For his bar mitzvah his grandfather had given him a stallion and a revolver and sent him off without food to survive as best he could in the hills near the Cherkessian villages. But though I was only six, at six stone I was just as tall as he was and had been raised by Grandfather on colostrum and hate. Slowly I bent back two of his fingers until I heard them snap. Turning pale, he toppled to the ground and passed out. Two teachers carried him off while I bent back down for a look at the make-believe eyes of my caterpillars.

That evening Rilov came to the cabin to talk to Grandfather. With a contemptuous rattle of ice cubes between his teeth, Grandfather advised him to tell his grandson to pick on children his own age and keep away from little boys with a big punch.

That was the last time anyone tried that with me. But comic songs were sung about me during break, and Pinness, who had a knack of looking out the window of the teachers' room in the nick of time, would come and lead me away just as I was about to charge, his hand drawing out the stiff tension in my neck.

Two afternoons a week I went out to the fields with him, to 'the School of Nature'.

'Nature lets nothing go to waste,' he declared as we trod the rough path leading to the wadi. 'Everything is grist to its mill. Seize the one and withhold not thy hand from the other. There are worms that live in garlic peels. There are spiders that eat their mates. Cattle dung, rotten fruit, fabric, paper – it's all grist to the mill.'

He had his hands crossed behind him like a landowner inspecting his estate. On my back I carried a square army pack with his pincers, nets, empty matchboxes, and sealed bottles of chloroform. 'Your grandfather gave me this knapsack,' he said. 'It's an English wireless operator's pack that belonged to your uncle Efrayim.'

I asked if we could catch a praying mantis, an insect whose mincing gait and pious mien intrigued me. Just then, though, our path was busily crossed by an orange beetle with a black-spotted carapace, and I pointed it out to Pinness, who kept looking around while talking continually. He was thrilled to see it.

'Maybe we'll be in luck this time,' he said, ordering me not to lose sight of it.

The beetle proceeded in a straight line, its two clublike antennae moving ceaselessly. Clearly it had something on its mind.

'It has a wonderful sense of smell,' whispered Pinness, crawling after it on all fours.

A quarter of an hour later the beetle quickened its pace. Shortly we too smelled the faint scent of carrion.

The beetle disappeared beneath a bed of straw.

'Well now,' said Pinness, 'let's have a look.' Lifting the straw, he bared the dead body of a goldfinch. We sat down upwind to avoid the smell, and Pinness told me to watch carefully.

A second beetle appeared, making its way among the clods of earth. Without further ado, the two began mating by the corpse.

'Look how nature has a place for everyone, Baruch,' Pinness said. 'Some couples meet in fields full of flowers, others at the theatre – these two prefer the stench of death.'

Now the two beetles began to burrow beneath the goldfinch, excavating little pebbles and bits of earth as the dead bird sank into the hole. We sat watching for several hours until it was completely underground and covered with soil.

'Now,' Pinness said, 'Mother Beetle will lay her eggs in the carcass, chewing and softening its meat for her maggots. Some children grow up in palaces and others in corpses. May my lot always be with the salt of the earth!'

He took my hand and we went home.

When the doctors announced that Pinness could return to the village, Busquilla hired a taxi to bring him. I suggested to the old teacher that he spend a few weeks with me, but his only answer was, 'Home.'

His eyes welled with sorrow and exertion when we got there. He had aged greatly. The little blood clots had attacked him with surgical precision, severing the bonds of memory, destroying the walls he had built during his long years in the country, and causing his brain to send out unremitting signals of hunger.

'All the old boys are dead now,' said Pinness. 'From hard work and battling temptation. Levin alone is still alive. Levin alone, and I who live on with him. Two old dotards.'

He taught no more classes and rarely had pupils over to his house. He did not go out to the fields any more either. Sometimes he sat in his garden watching the ants and grasshoppers scurry across the lawn. A sand boa he released from its cage in the nature room lay limply coiled among the wild flowers. He had divided his zoological collection between me and the school, the arthropods, the bleached reptiles in their jars of formaldehyde, and the hollow birds' eggs remaining in the nature room. Alongside the more conventional systems of taxonomy, however, Pinness also classified all life into Helpful and Harmful, and his own private collection had two categories alone, Our Friends and Our Enemies.

'There are some borderline cases,' he admitted. 'Take the bee-eater. On the one hand, it kills wasps, but on the other, it eats Margulis's bees. The mongoose preys on both voles and baby chicks.'

'Whenever you see an insect, bird, mammal, or reptile, ask if it is friend or foe,' said Pinness to me on one of our first outings, when I was five years old.

'Someday I'll leave you this collection,' he informed me. 'You deserve it.'

He often consulted with Grandfather, who was an expert on tree pests, and together the two taught me to identify and eradicate them. Taking me to the orchard, they put their hands on my shoulders and pointed me at a pear tree.

'Watch carefully,' said Grandfather.

The two men, both in grey work shirts, one wearing a worker's cap and one a floppy-brimmed straw hat, looked down at me ceremoniously. I could feel their emotion, although I did not understand the cause of it.

'I don't see anything,' I said.

Grandfather knelt and showed me a round hole, about a quarter of an inch in diameter, in the trunk of the tree. Directly beneath it on the ground was a little pile of sawdust.

'Such a predator can eat a whole tree,' Pinness said.

Grandfather took out a long, thin piece of wire that was coiled like a spring at one end.

'The planter's fishing rod,' he said. Slowly but surely, he inserted it into the caterpillar's tunnel. A yard and a half of wire disappeared gradually up the tree as Grandfather sighed quietly, realising the extent of the damage.

'Damn you!' he swore when he felt the tip of the wire pierce the caterpillar. He gave it a twist, corkscrewing it into the grub's flesh, and gently began to retract it. The caterpillar let out an eerie squeal and a soft, repulsive whistle as its jaws and nails tore loose from the pith of the pear tree, scraping the sides of its wormhole on its reluctant journey to the sunlight.

'Aha!' exclaimed Grandfather, pulling out the last of the wire. Impaled on its tip was a soft, black-spotted, yellow-orange blob that squirmed and wriggled as Grandfather held it up to me. I felt a wave of nausea and hatred.

'Take a good look, my child,' said Grandfather. 'This is the enemy. The tiger moth.'

That was my first lesson in agriculture. Thenceforth I was sent to the orchard twice a week to look for the telltale sawdust at the base of the fruit trees.

I can still remember fishing my first caterpillar out of a Rennet apple tree. The feel of the monster writhing and gnashing its teeth inside the tree trunk ran along the steel wire into my fingers and up through my wrist to my spine.

'Don't be afraid, Baruch,' said Grandfather. 'You've got him where you want him.'

I dashed the grub to the ground and stamped on it with my foot.

When a tiger moth murdered one of Liberson's apricots, Pinness chopped down the dead tree and tunnelled in its trunk with a little axe until he found one of the caterpillars.

He cut off a section of tree trunk with the caterpillar in it. 'We'll add you to our collection,' he smiled, 'and burn the rest of your comrades at the stake.' We dragged the tree's carcass out of the orchard and set it on fire.

'So long, you scoundrels,' said Pinness as the screeches and death coughs rose from the burning branches.

He took me home with him. Removing the caterpillar with a pair of padded pincers, he wrapped it in blotting paper. 'Some larvae secrete a staining substance when they die,' he explained.

He put the still wriggling caterpillar in a test tube, added some petrol-soaked absorbent cotton, told me to have a seat, and gave me a biscuit and a lecture.

'This is the true test of every collector,' he said. 'Nothing is harder than preserving a caterpillar. It's so juicy that it decomposes easily, and there's no exoskeleton to keep its shape.'

When the caterpillar had been gassed to death, Pinness took it from the test tube, laid it on a glass slide, and made an incision near its anus with a sharp little surgical knife. 'I stole this knife from Sonya in the clinic,' he confided, his body shaking with suppressed mirth. Rolling a pencil down the grub's body until the intestines were squeezed out through the opening, he severed them and tossed them out the window.

'For the birds of the heavens and the beasts of the earth,' he intoned.

He took a small straw, inserted it into the caterpillar's hollow corpse, and blew gently, his eyes blinking behind his concentration-fogged glasses. As the caterpillar slowly expanded, Pinness rose carefully and bent over the table lamp, rotating the larva above the hot bulb while continuing to blow softly.

'A hot iron will do the job too, but not an open fire.'

Within a few minutes the caterpillar's skin was dry and hard.

'The purists coat it with clear varnish,' Pinness said, pouring a drop of diluted glue into the cut in the caterpillar's rear.

He took the section of the apricot tree, sawed it lengthwise to expose the tiger moth's tunnel, blew away the sawdust, and restored the now immortalised pest to its former residence. After writing down the date and site of its capture on a slip of paper, he opened a little box, took out a large, hairy adult moth with spotted wings, and placed it on the tree trunk still pierced by its pin.

'It's important to exhibit them in their natural habitat,' he declared with a sigh of contentment.

# 30

Towards the end of his life Levin grew cross and insufferable. Grandfather, the only man he had ever deferred to, was already dead, and in a moment of weakness I gave him the old work boots Grandfather had worn in the orchard. Levin sat on my bed, thrust his thin legs into them, stood up, and walked around as happily as a child with his first pair of grown-up shoes, shaking his head like a giddy colt each time he looked down at the battered toes.

'What did you give him Grandfather's boots for?' grumbled Yosi. 'Now he thinks he's somebody.'

Inspired by the boots, Levin began poking his nose into the running of the farm and grew careless with the co-op books. He also yelled at Rachel, went for long, booted walks in the fields, stopping to look at his reflection in every puddle, took to calling himself 'Sweet Levin', made his wife go around in a blue kerchief, and developed a grasshopper phobia.

Unable to control myself one night, I went to peek through the window of his house and saw him take out a black notebook and wave it angrily beneath Rachel's nose.

'All the sins of the Workingman's Circle,' he hissed. 'They're all written down here!'

'I wish you'd calm down,' said Rachel wearily. 'Tsirkin and Mirkin are dead. Poor Liberson is blind in an old folk's home. Who are you still out to get?'

'It was the way she laughed,' replied Levin. 'She went out with them every night, laughing. They purposely put funny words to Hasidic songs to make her laugh and insult me.'

Feyge's laughter, the stains of stolen chocolate, Zeitser's mocking glances – all left their mark on Levin's thin skin like the voracious teeth of locusts. He recalled how Liberson had pestered him a whole night over whether the Feyge Levin Workingman's Circle should play a more active role in the Chinese workers' movement. 'The FLWC is coming, O ye yellow masses,' the young pioneer called out into the darkness. Feyge burst into giggles and embraced him, pressing her body against his. Levin didn't sleep a wink that night, convinced that his sister could no longer tell reality from revolutionary fantasy.

In Petach Tikvah Mirkin smoked publicly on the Sabbath and started a row with the local religious farmers. In Jaffa Tsirkin told stupid anti-Hasidic jokes to two Hasidim they happened to meet. In Rishon-le-Tsiyyon Liberson was apprehended in the vineyards with his hands inside the blouse of the school principal's daughter. All three of them regularly dressed and undressed in Feyge's presence.

In a little black notebook Levin began to record secretly all the misdeeds of his sister's corrupters. One evening he produced it and read the list out loud to them.

'You forgot about the time Mirkin stole oranges in Jaffa,' said Liberson.

'I didn't forget a thing,' Levin told Rachel. 'They humiliated me and killed my sister, and they got off scot-free except for Mirkin. He's the only one who was punished.'

He began asking Meshulam about suicides in the early days

of the Second Aliyah. Every graveyard in the old villages and
kibbutzim had its pioneers who had taken their own lives, leaving
behind gravestones carved with guilt and remorse. Most of these
had been transferred to my keeping, and Levin walked up and
down among them, reading the inscriptions. 'Died at His Own
Hands', 'Overcome by His Suffering', 'Drank the Hemlock',
'Put an End to His Own Life'. Dreamly, he murmured the
awful words.

Now and then he ran screaming out of his house with a can of
green insect spray in his hand, Rachel hurrying after him. Though
she was younger than he was, his madness made his grey limbs
strong and spry. Once she found him lying in a field, waiting to
die from the spray can he had drained. But long years spent in the
store amid fumes of ammonia, DDT, parathion, and benzoic acid
had immunised him against all chemicals. Two hours of lying in
the sun was enough for him, and rising despairingly, he went
home with Rachel walking wordlessly by his side.

Even after Grandfather's death, Levin kept coming to look for
odd jobs in our farmyard. My uncle Avraham, who remembered
how his kind hands had fed, bathed, and clothed him as a little
orphan, put up with him and had him collect the old wires
scattered among the bales of hay. Not that they were worth
anything, but it was just as well not to have them getting into a
feed stall and killing a cow. Levin even made himself a little work
corner in the cowshed, where he sat for hours drawing coloured
charts of milk production and straightening old nails for re-use.
Now and then the blows of the hammer were accompanied by a
groan of pain that was taken up by a merry chorus of turkeys. 'I
think your uncle must have straightened more fingers than nails,'
I once heard Uri say to his father over lunch. Yosi complained
that the clouds of thick dust billowing up from the old fodder
sacks Levin kept shaking out and folding were giving the poultry
laryngitis. Stepping into the yard, he bawled him out rudely,
assisted by juicy imprecations from his mother Rivka standing
on her porch.

Enraged and humiliated, Levin went home to plot his revenge.
The mockery of the Workingman's Circle resounded again in his

mind. One day he surprised Avraham during his afternoon nap.

'Me you treat like an animal, but Zeitser you keep on!'

'Zeitser worked with my father back in the old days,' said Avraham. 'We won't throw him to the dogs just because he's become old and weak.'

'Zeitser is an extra mouth to feed,' snapped Levin. 'He's a sponger.'

'Zeitser,' replied Avraham, 'is the best mule in this village. He was always more than just a draught animal to my father and me. He's worked and sweated for us his whole life. A lot of two-legged pioneers never did half as much.'

'He may *have been* the best mule in this village,' said Levin, personally affronted by the reference to sweat, 'but I never heard of a mule getting a pension. Why don't you sell him to the Arab sausage factory or the glue works in Haifa bay? No one keeps an old mule in stock who can't pull a cart any more.'

'Don't force me to choose between the two of you,' said Avraham. 'Zeitser isn't stock and never was.'

Most of the mules in our village were English or Yugoslavian. Two were German, left behind at the end of World War One. Zeitser, I was told, was the only mule from Russia, whence he immigrated with a group of pioneers whose home was a place called Mogilev. They bought him the day they set out for Odessa. Seeing him on sale at a market, one of them joked loudly to his friends, 'I know that mule. He's a direct descendant of the mule of the Baal Shem Tov.'

'Unbelievers!' scolded the Hasid who was holding Zeitser's tether. 'Since when do mules have descendants?'

'Are you questioning the Baal Shem Tov's powers?' answered the pioneer to the laughter of his comrades. 'If the holy rabbi wished, even a mule could have sons.'

The Hasidim of Mogilev nearly came to blows with them, but the clink of roubles had a calming effect. The pioneers bought the mule, and Zeitser gratefully carried their belongings to the wharf. When they boarded the steamship *Kernilov* and saw how sad he looked, they chipped in for an extra ticket, 'hoisted him

on deck in a huge net that hung from a crane', and brought him
to the Land of Israel.

'They never regretted it for a minute. No job was too hard for
Zeitser.'

It was Meshulam Tsirkin who discovered that Zeitser had
worked in Sejera with Ben-Gurion. He read one of Ben-Gurion's
letters to me, a document he had got from the Movement archives
in a swap.

Sejera
April 2, 1908

Before the sun is up, at half past four, I rise and go to the
cowshed to feed my animals. I sift hay into the feedbox for
the oxen, sprinkle some vetches over it and mix them, and
then make myself tea for my breakfast. With the first rays of
the sun I take my herd, two teams of oxen, two cows, two
calves, and a donkey, to drink from the trough.

It was one of the few times I saw Meshulam laugh.

'A donkey!' he roared, slapping his knees and his stomach.
'A donkey! That donkey was Zeitser. But fat chance that some
socialist fresh off the boat from Russia would know the difference
between a donkey and a mule!'

Zeitser belonged to the Mogilev commune for several years.
Now and then he ran into Grandfather and his friends, and for a
while they even worked side by side. When his commune found a
piece of land to settle down on, however, he began to have second
thoughts. The main problem, as Grandfather put it, was that
'Zeitser's penchant for solitude and private initiative clashed with
the rigidly communal framework'. Zeitser hated meetings and
debates, and such questions as 'the status of pregnant comrades',
'the latest news from the workers' movement in Latvia', and
'improving the nutrition of field hands' did not concern him in
the least. Most of all he loathed the public confessionals in which
the commune members bared their hearts to each other.

One day, according to Uri, when a female communard who
was cleaning out the cowshed laid a soiled baby in his stall,
Zeitser decided that his notion of family life was incompatible

with that of the kibbutz. That same day he picked himself up and went to inspect a co-operative village.

'Zeitser was an unusually good worker,' Grandfather told me when I was a small boy. 'He always knew what field to go to and never had to be steered.'

Zeitser ploughed and cultivated our fields, uprooted dead trees, pulled loaded carts, and was as thrilled as the rest of us by each new sprout and can of milk. When his shoes needed adjustment or replacement, he went on his own to the Goldman brothers' smithy. He was the only draught animal in the village not to wear the leather blinkers Peker made against worldly temptations, because 'nothing ever tempted him but work'. Only once did he succumb, when he mistakenly ate some Jimsonweed flowers growing by the manure pile. He got high, walked around in circles for two days, made eyes at the young female calves, and behaved like any hot-blooded numbskull.

With the passage of time, his strength faltered. Grandfather, who was personally acquainted with the ravages of old age and could easily discern them in the mule's wasted body, tried easing up on his work, but Zeitser refused to acknowledge his decrepitude until one day he collapsed in the traces.

Generally, I remember what I am told better than what I have seen, but that day, like the day of my rescue from the hyena, sticks in my memory. Grandfather, Zeitser, and I had gone to fetch fodder and had loaded some twenty sacks of it on the cart. On the short uphill before the last bend Zeitser suddenly stopped with a queer, high-pitched snort, and the heavy cart began to roll backwards. Grandfather had never whipped Zeitser in his life, and now too he merely urged him on with shouts and slaps of the reins. Quivering all over, Zeitser managed to brake the slipping cart and braced himself to pull it up the hill, his haunches sinking nearly to the ground and his iron horseshoes striking sparks on the paved road. When his laboured panting turned to deep wheezes, Grandfather threw down the reins and climbed out of the cart. Anxious veins made an alarming wreath on his bald scalp as he tried to calm the mule and free him from his harness. Gathering his strength for one last mighty effort, however, Zeitser let out a huge fart, lost his balance, and collapsed. There was a loud crack from up front as the longpole snapped, leaving the traces hanging from the mule's neck. Grandfather quickly slipped off the hames and grabbed Zeitser's head in his hands. For a while they remained there, weeping soundlessly together.

Zeitser returned home without the cart, his head bowed with shame. I walked alongside him, not knowing what to say.

'He's a work animal,' Grandfather said. 'At least sit on his back so he'll feel he's doing something.'

I rode him home, feeling the twitching and damp breathing of his mortified hide in my thighs. Tsirkin's horses Michurin and Stalin brought the cart to our yard, and that evening Grandfather and Avraham decided to start putting Zeitser out to pasture. It was then that we bought our first oil-fuelled Ferguson, which Grandfather never learned to drive, leaving Zeitser only the milk cans to haul. A few years later, when the phlebitis in his forelegs and the strongyles parasites in his intestines had depleted his remaining strength and even the simplest words, like 'giddyup', escaped him, Grandfather tethered him to a long rope in the shade of the big fig tree. Beneath the tree Avraham set out both halves of a sawed barrel, one for water and one for barley, and now and then Grandfather took Zeitser for a leisurely walk, just the two of them, to meditate and smell the flowers.

Unlike most old men, who forget the present and remember the distant past, Pinness had forgotten his childhood and youth entirely.

'I know who I am and where I'm going, I just have no idea where I've come from,' he explained to me, to himself, and to everyone.

He looked at me sadly when I came to visit him in his garden. The day before he had attended Bodenkin's funeral in Pioneer Home, and now he was upset and mournful. All his life he had been a great believer in education, and he held himself partly to blame for my lapse. 'Did I go wrong on that hike to Beth-She'arim, or was it those carrion beetles?' But I knew that his anger was halfhearted, like his response to the nocturnal cries he still heard. He had stopped turning livid when telling me about them, cursing in Russian and waving his arms. Indeed, the look on his fat face was more one of baffled curiosity. The swamp of blood awash beneath his cranium could no longer be kept down.

'Well now, Baruch,' he smiled. 'It seems I've gone through some kind of mutation. I just don't have anyone to pass it on to.'

He was very old. Every week I brought him his clean laundry and changed his sheets and tablecloth.

'Why are you doing this for me?' he once asked me shrewdly. 'What are you plotting?'

'Neither of us has anyone else,' I answered. 'I have no grand-father, and you have no grandson.' Despite his sorrowful smile, I could see he was pleased by what I said.

He had few friends left in the village. Grandfather, Liberson, Fanya, and Tsirkin were all dead. Even Rilov. Every morning Tonya paid a brief visit to her husband's grave to make sure he hadn't found a secret escape hatch, and then, supported by an aluminium frame, pulled herself along the gravel paths to Margulis's tombstone, on which she sat senilely licking her fingers. I buried Margulis as per his request, perfectly embalmed like a Hittite monarch. His sons coated him with a black layer of bee glue and put him in a coffin filled to the top with honey and sealed with beeswax. In midsummer, when the white-hot earth turned so dry that it cracked, orange-coloured fumes rose from the grave, and Margulis's bees, maddened by so much sweetness and longing, buzzed around it with loud melancholy. Tonya never budged from there. 'Like Rizpah the daughter of Aiah by the corpses of her sons,' whispered Pinness admiringly. 'That's the difference between us and you,' he added. 'We did it with sacred devotion. You do it with obscenities from water towers.'

Meanwhile, Riva was at home, scrubbing the last sticky stains left behind on the floor by her husband and dreaming of lace tablecloths, lacquered Chinese furniture, angora cats, and vacuum cleaners.

'If Riva knew that Chinese lacquer is nothing but the secretion of certain aphids,' Pinness said, 'she wouldn't make such a fuss over it.'

His blood carved out new channels, shooting the gaps between nerve endings and the chasms of memory. 'It's as though I was born an eighteen-year-old on the day I arrived in this country,' he said. 'My father could have been the hotel owner in Jaffa. He's the first person I remember after birth.'

He had forgotten the names of his parents and sisters, his native landscape, the *yeshiva*, religious school, in Nemirov where he had studied before running off to the Land of Israel.

'Every bit of it has been wiped out.'

For the first time, he revealed his old hatred of Rilov in public. No one understood why, because Rilov himself was already dead. 'A he-man, a coachman, a flea-man,' he called the dead Watchman. 'A gentile's brain in a Jew's body.'

He piled his plate with more than it could hold and stuffed himself with huge mouthfuls, wolfing his food as if hungry jackals were waiting behind him to pirate it. Half-chewed, slobbery shreds tumbled out of his mouth and ran down his glistening chin. Little mounds piled up on the table around the rim of his plate.

'I put it away like Jean Valjean, eh? As the ox licketh up the grass of the field.'

He felt so fatigued upon finishing a meal that he fell into bed at once.

'Rest is vital for the digestion,' he announced. 'The body must not be asked to do more than one thing at a time. A time to mourn and a time to dance, a time to embrace and a time to refrain from embracing.'

I wasn't the only one in the village concerned for the childless old teacher. His food was delivered from the co-op to keep him from having to carry baskets. Rachel Levin brought him cooked meals, slipping into his house on her silken old soles and startling him with the sudden clink of cutlery as she set the table.

'I want fresh food, not meat from the fleshpots,' he told her biblically. 'Bring me of the fruit of your garden, a banquet of greens and quietness therewith.'

Once a week I brought him vegetables from the patch I kept near the cabin. It was alarming to watch him gulp them down. Busquilla came with pots of home cooking from the nearby town where he lived. In his old age Pinness had fallen in love with Mrs Busquilla's couscous. Though he didn't touch the meat, he ate the steamed vegetables and semolina ravenously, yellow morsels clinging to his bottom lip.

'Thou hast tempted me and I have succumbed,' he quoted to Busquilla. 'Your wife should have run the workers' kitchen in Petach Tikvah. No one would have dumped *her* food on the floor.'

'Enjoy it, Mr Pinness,' said Busquilla. He liked Pinness, was afraid of him, and sometimes furtively kissed his hand, dodging back to avoid a swat from the other hand, which could still be as quick as a jumping spider. Despite Busquilla's explanation that 'it's just a Moroccan custom', Pinness disapproved of such manners.

I offered to pay Busquilla for his wife's food.

'Shame on you, Baruch,' he said. 'Pinness is a saint, a holy man. We're nothing but his servants. You don't understand it because you can't read the signs. Do you think those white pigeons that are always on his roof are just a lot of birds? And what about that snake that guards the gate of his garden?

'God forgive me for even mentioning his death,' said Busquilla with a heavenward glance, 'but on that day light will flash from his grave, or perhaps water will flow from his gravestone. It's an honour to bring him food, because it's serving God.'

Uri scoffed at Busquilla's beliefs and called the old teacher 'Saint Pinness' behind his back.

'Let's go and visit the saint,' he would say to me. But our conversations with Pinness were monotonous. Once again we were his pupils, to be lectured on Shamgar the son of Anath who routed six hundred Philistines with an oxgoad or on the life cycle of the great titmouse. He even tried to give us homework.

Every few months he still heard the cry of the brazen fornicator from on high.

'I'm sure he does it on the water tower,' he told Uri and me through a mouthful of sweet peas. 'One difference between *Homo sapiens* and birds is that men don't copulate in the treetops.

'He's already, you should excuse the expression, screwed half the village,' he winked slyly. 'Married women too. Last night it was the wife of Yisra'eli's oldest grandson. I don't get it. Why, they were just married two months ago, and she seemed such a lovely young lady!'

It baffled him that no one else heard the cries. 'How can it be?' he asked. 'It's been going on for several years. There are night watchmen in the village who are supposed to keep their ears open. There are farmers who get up in the middle of the night to help a cow calve or prepare a shipment of turkeys. There are early-morning sprayers and the drivers of the milk lorry, which never leaves before midnight – why does no one hear it but me?'

He paused to consider. 'I'll bet it's poor Daniel Liberson. He never did get over it. Or maybe it's Efrayim, coming back at night to take revenge.'

Uri and I glanced at each other uncomfortably, wondering in what damaged lobe of his brain the old man was weaving such fantasies.

'I'll get to the bottom of it if it's the last thing I do,' declared Pinness. 'I'll climb the water tower and wait there for him.'

I smiled and did not try to talk him out of it. The old teacher, I felt sure, was too fat, sick, and weak ever to climb the ladder of the tower. With his usual scientific pedantry, however, Pinness was determined to solve the mystery. He sprawled for hours in his armchair, going through old notebooks in the hope of finding some childhood deviancy or telltale clue. He had kept a special journal of the best poems and cleverest remarks of his pupils, selections from which he sometimes sent to the village newspaper. These items invariably aroused the wrath of his ex-students, some of whom were already in their fifties or sixties.

Once the publication of a poem of Dani Rilov's had the whole village in stitches.

> Chick-chick-chickina
> Eats semolina.
> Poor little hen,
> She'll get old and then
> Off with her head
> And she's dead!

Forty years after the composition of this lyric the compassionate poet was a calf breeder whose best friends were brutal meat merchants and coarse butchers. But Pinness merely smiled when told that Dani Rilov was furious, and went on tending his many nests and keeping a kind eye on his fledglings. Meshulam, too, was enraged by this poem, which he considered a gross fabrication.

'Who had money in those days to feed his hens semolina?' he fumed. 'It's disgraceful how some people will rewrite history just for the sake of a rhyme!'

Pinness noticed that I was prowling around his house at night to protect him from the vengeance of the Rilov clan.

'Go to sleep, Baruch,' he said, stepping outside. 'I've already scattered my spore to the winds. Childless old teachers are indestructible. The seeds I planted won't sprout till after I die.'

In a second, more secret notebook he had jotted down over the years various comments on his pupils' families. Although he had always exhorted the schoolchildren to help their parents with chores, he knew that some of the farmers overworked them.

He told me about his first years as a teacher. The school had only a few students and was poorly and cheaply equipped. In summer the children sat on reed mats, and each morning he examined them 'as the shepherd surveyeth his flock', running his eyes over the classroom to see which of his pupils had been petted, fed, and kissed, and which had been dragged out of bed before dawn to do chores. More than once Riva Margulis's daughter, who was awakened at 5 a.m. every day to scrub the paving-stones outside the house, came late to school, since her mother kept turning back the hands of the clock until the strip of pavement gleamed. There were no milking machines then in the village, and some children came with fingers so stiff from milking that they couldn't write a word. Pinness made no comment when sleepy children shut their eyes and let their heads sink onto their chests, but everyone knew that he would have a private talk with the parents that evening.

'Every child was a world in itself. I never tired of observing them.'

He made a point of arriving in the classroom before his pupils to hang pictures and posters on the walls, and then he sat down to wait for them. Avraham once told me that the year of Scott and Amundsen's race to the South Pole, Pinness kept the children posted on their daily progress. When terrible mud covered the village in winter, he carried his little charges on his back or hitched himself to one of the legendary mud sleds and pulled them home, barking like an Antarctica-bound husky.

Avraham and Meshulam were in his first class, which had only seven pupils. While Avraham was quiet, neat, hardworking, and uncommunicative, Meshulam was lively, resentful, and argumentative. He was fascinated by Pinness's stories about the old pioneer days, but the nature lessons left him cold.

'Your uncle had no mother at home, and neither for that matter had Meshulam.' Pinness noticed that Meshulam did not bring a sandwich to school like the other children but only a plain slice of bread. He knew too that Tsirkin raised the boy on baked pumpkin and hard-boiled eggs, the only dishes he could prepare, which were sometimes supplemented by good-hearted neighbours who brought Meshulam hot meals or invited him to eat with them.

'Meshulam could have been our pride and joy,' he said. 'He had a good head and a steadfast character, but his childhood diverted him into a world in which torn clothes and baked pumpkin were lofty ideals instead of signs of neglect.'

He knew that Meshulam's laziness had turned the whole village against him. 'Still,' he said to me, 'I would have expected you to be more understanding of him.'

'Grandfather couldn't stand him either,' I said.

'Your grandfather couldn't stand anyone,' said Pinness. 'Except, sometimes, me, and that too for debatable reasons. You see the village and the whole world through your grandfather's eyes. You're still tied to him by the apery strings.'

He chuckled at his own pun and told me in a near whisper how Meshulam had celebrated his bar mitzvah. Since Pesya was never at home and Mandolin Tsirkin was always tired from the farm work, Meshulam had to prepare the party for his schoolmates on his own. Finding a few dried tortes left over from a visit by the Zionist leader Chaim Weizmann, he cut them into thin slices and brought them to the classroom early that morning. Pinness arrived at 6 a.m. to find the frantic boy wetting the desiccated cakes with tears and drops of sweet wine in the hope of bringing them back to life. Retreating silently, he went home and came back with a tray of crackers spread with jam.

'Your mother left these with me for your birthday,' he told Meshulam, who said nothing though he knew it was a lie.

All these things were recorded by Pinness in his notebook, which he referred to as his 'barn log'. There, in the old teacher's handsome hand, you could find whatever failed to appear on his pupils' report cards. His handwriting was so elegant, and his concern for penmanship so great, that all the children of the village learned to write exactly like him. In fact, they still do, which has led to the misattribution of anonymous love letters and the crediting of cheques to the wrong accounts. Once, when the poet Bialik came to visit, Pinness presented him with an album of poetry composed in his honour by the schoolchildren. The great writer was so struck by the sameness of the script that he joked that the teacher must have written everything himself. Pinness was too insulted to respond, but that very week he took his students to the foot of Mount Gilboa to study the verse of Bialik's rival Tchernichovski.

I watched him open his green gate and hobble up the street to Levin's house. Tonya and Riva were the last of the village's female founders, while he, Zeitser, and Shlomo Levin were the three surviving males.

'Zeitser was never much of a conversationalist, Rachel stuffs me with food, and Levin, who couldn't learn to farm a plot of land, now does nothing but cultivate plots all the time,' he said after returning one night to find me sitting by Grandfather's grave.

# 31

Every year Zeitser participated in two festive events. On the anniversary of the founding of the village he was invited by the culture committee to join the founding fathers on the stage, an honour reserved for him and Hagit alone among the animals, and on the holiday of Shavuot three neatly combed boys in white shirts came to take him to Meshulam's yard, where he was hitched with a great to-do to 'the first cart', which was then piled high with fruits, milk cans, garlanded sheaves of wheat, screaming infants, baby chicks, and calves. It was the only day of the year on which Zeitser agreed to doff his old Russian worker's cap with its specially made earholes and don a wreath of flowers that gave him a slightly Dionysiac appearance.

When an irate Shlomo Levin was reminded of all this, however, he raved and ranted even more, labelled Zeitser 'an old parasite', and related with loud shouts how he had left his newspaper in our cowshed the night before and had returned there to find Zeitser squatting hoofishly on his haunches against the fig tree, perusing by moonlight the paper spread out in his lap. His, Levin's, newspaper!

This argument raged not far from the mule himself, who was tethered to the fig tree beside his food and water, delicately being deloused by two devoted cattle egrets who had come especially from the Jordan Valley. The earth packed hard by his hooves described an exact circle around him. Dipping his big jaws into his barrel, Zeitser stood smacking his lips over a mouthful of the best barley. A thin smile flitted over his face, and he pricked up his ears through his battered cap as though listening. Levin, angrier than ever, stepped up to the mule's water barrel and kicked it over. Avraham lost his temper and chased his uncle from the yard.

The next day the old man returned to apologise and went back to work. Meanwhile Avraham, who was equally contrite, came to talk things over with me.

'We owe both Zeitser and Levin a great deal,' he said. 'Obviously we can't send Zeitser to the glue factory, but we mustn't hurt Uncle Shlomo's feelings either. He may be no great shakes as a farmer, but my father would never have managed without him.'

Yosi hated Levin, and Uri was for sausaging both him and Zeitser, which was why Avraham asked me to keep an eye open. Before long I discovered that old Levin, hoping the mule would die of thirst before anyone noticed, was secretly moving Zeitser's water out of reach.

Now and then, while weeding the gravestones, I waved to the old mule to let him know that I was keeping a protective eye on him. Zeitser never waved back. Since Grandfather's death he had lost the last of his old verve, and Levin's harassment made him nervous and irritable. The appearance of the store manager's thin shadow in the yard caused him to stiffen tensely, and though his big head remained hidden in his barrel of expensive barley, his rear end shifted back and forth in carefully calculated movements to ensure that he had a leg to kick with.

He had become a crusade for Levin. An excellent bookkeeper, Grandmother's brother came to Avraham one evening with 'an exact cost accounting' of every penny that had ever been spent on 'that pompous, freeloading ass of yours'.

It was a hot night, full of buzzing crickets. Through the open windows I could hear the whole angry debate. Levin read 'the mule sheet' out loud in a level, venomous voice. 'Eighteen pounds of ground barley per day, plus three and a half pounds of vetch hay, plus six pounds of straw.' He went on and on until Avraham told him to stop making a fool of himself.

Levin stalked out, slamming the door behind him. Stooped,

crushed, and swearing under his breath, he passed by the casuarina in which I was sitting, too injured to notice me.

He stayed away for a week, at the end of which his answer appeared in an article in the newsletter that spoke of 'a certain family that is maintaining a dissipated mule and feeding it royally in utter disregard of our Movement's commitment to economic productivity'.

For several weeks there was a boom in the readership of the newsletter, which generally contained little more than seasonal figures on rainfall and milk prices, indiscreet insemination notices, the morbid reflections of adolescent girls, and announcements of deaths, births, and weddings. Now its pages were flung open to the Zeitser–Levin debate.

Though Zeitser had his share of supporters, so did the store manager. Dani Rilov, whose intimate involvement with slaughtered cows had made him a budding satirist, wrote a humorous sketch about an imaginary society in which 'benighted and compassionate souls' filled the Jewish homeland with 'sanatoriums for ailing donkeys and old age homes for menopausal hens'. And yet, he concluded, 'in a family long noted for carrying livestock on its back', there was nothing surprising about Zeitser's costly maintenance.

Eventually, Eliezer Liberson himself was drawn into the dispute. Liberson, the last surviving member of the Feyge Levin Workingman's Circle, was then in the old folk's home, where he occupied the same room that had belonged to Grandfather and Shulamit. A blind old widower who was as good as dead in his own eyes and the village's, he sent me a message that he would welcome a speedy visit from me 'equipped with pencil and paper'.

We sat on the terrace. Liberson asked me about the village. He reminded me of Grandfather, except that there was more anger and yearning in his voice. He asked if I watered the flowers around his wife's grave and if I ever talked to his son.

'Not really,' I answered, apprehensively changing that to, 'I mean, I do water the flowers, but I don't really talk to Daniel.'

'Everything could have been so different,' said Liberson.

'Yes,' I said.

'Yes?! What's that supposed to mean?' exclaimed the old man fiercely. 'He doesn't even know what I'm talking about, and he says yes!'

I said nothing.

'Did you bring pencil and paper?' he asked.

'Yes.'

Crossly he dictated a few short, stern sentences for me to give the newsletter. Expressed in them was the opinion that 'although there may be an economic logic in the arguments of Comrade Shlomo Levin, whose dedicated labours in the co-op were greatly appreciated by us farmers, it is nevertheless unthinkable that the nonagricultural population should interfere in the productive life of the village to which our dear Zeitser belongs.'

'Excuse me for shouting at you, Baruch,' said the blind man as I departed. 'One day you'll see what I see. Forgive me, and come again soon.'

Neither Pinness nor Levin could sleep at night. Each lay planning and plotting in his bed.

Levin sought vengeance on the mule, because of whom Eliezer Liberson had humiliated him in public as he had never been humiliated before. Through his window I could see his stinging old wounds reopen and suppurate with shame. Once again the uncouth hooligans of the Workingman's Circle shot their mocking darts at him, mountains of sand and chocolate threatened to bury him, and hordes of locusts crawled over his bed, skinning him alive.

At that very moment, having gone to the refrigerator for some leftover couscous that he dribbled all over his pillow, Pinness was reflecting on the lascivious cries that pierced his tender eardrums and defiled all that was dear to him. Now that the blood soaking his brain had diluted his anger and swamped his thirst for vengeance, he merely desired to uncover the culprit.

He rose with difficulty, went out to the garden, crossed the street, and walked up and down beneath the large concrete columns of the water tower. It took him a while to get over the annoying hot and cold flashes in his body. Then, grabbing hold of the iron ladder, he began to climb to the top.

'It was only the second time in my life that I had done that,' he told me. 'Thirty years ago, when some high school students wanted to practise rope gliding, I climbed up there with Efrayim, Meshulam, Daniel Liberson, and Avraham. They all came down by rope except for me and Meshulam. We took the ladder again.'

He was afraid of being seen, and worse yet, of his own sick body failing him. 'Every ounce of logic I had left argued against it.' His fear of heights made every cell go numb. And yet, frail and brittle, he kept climbing. He didn't dare look down. The higher he went, the colder it became.

He gripped the peeling rungs with damp hands, pulling his scared body after them with a mysterious strength until he reached the top of the tower. Hiking a leg over the edge, he collapsed on the concrete roof, shaking from fright and exertion. For a few minutes he lay there 'like a stricken corpse', gladly letting the chill roughness of the concrete bring him back to life. Then, still breathing hard, he sat up and looked about.

The flat, round roof was ringed by a low parapet topped by a guardrail of metal pipes. In one corner were the remains of the observation post that once had been 'faithfully manned' by a lookout equipped with a mounted searchlight and a bell. White with dust, a few empty sacks and tattered semaphore flags lay abandoned there.

Pinness rose, leaned against the cool metal of the railing to help fight off a wave of vertigo, and unpremeditatedly called out, 'Yoo-hoo! Yoo-hoo!' His cry, however, was too weak to escape the clutches of the branches and the gusting night breeze. Although classified as a Helpful, a barn owl startled him by darting close to his head, as silent as a groundsel's floating seed. 'The harm the barn owl does the poultry is more than balanced by the number of mice it eats,' he had always claimed, greatly angered by farmers who killed it because they feared its noiseless flight and the human look of its white face.

Beneath him lay the village, 'no longer white tents in the wilderness but houses and cowsheds and fields, paved and well-trodden paths, tall trees and rooted men.'

The village was asleep. The wind whistled through the treetops. Yolks formed and clustered in the vitals of the hens. Mixers hummed in the feed shed and sprinklers chattered in the darkness.

Pinness lay in ambush for an hour and a half, during which nothing happened. In the end he climbed down again, terrified, and slowly made his way home.

'I did it,' he thought, hardly able to move. 'Tomorrow night I'll do it again.'

# 32

Towards the end of his life in the old folk's home Grandfather was so feeble that he spent most of his time in bed or in a wheelchair. Shulamit took care of him as best she could, but she too was far from healthy or strong. The smoke of old steamships and railway stations hung in the air between them. They never stopped touching each other, looking at each other, supporting each other, meeting and parting from each other.

The Crimean whore sat watching Grandfather for hours, touching his fingertips and crying as she read the cuneiform writing on his wrinkled neck. Within a few weeks he had grown shorter; his chest was narrower, and his whole body had dwindled. No longer nourished by his sensual attentions, she now scavenged the cells of his body.

His carefully measured love was as dangerously calibrated as the act of a tightrope walker. A single heedless movement could have sent him plummeting into her eyes, choking on the dust of his own bones.

Only now do I understand that there were four people in that room: Grandfather and Shulamit as young lovers and as old ones. Sometimes they were old or young together, and sometimes one was young while the other was old. Time, which I only knew from the setting of fruit and the fermenting of silage, had become in their room a many-faced weather vane that had run out of wind.

Although he could barely swallow the milk I brought him, he still insisted on drinking it all. Sometimes he gagged and spewed up sticky little clots of sour cheese on his chest. On his 'bad days' I carried him to the bathroom and bathed him, his gaze fluttering off into space like a white handkerchief as his tiny soaped body lay cradled in my arms. On his 'good days' he forced himself to smile and asked me about the farm.

I never talked to Shulamit, although there was a great deal I might have liked to ask her. When she first arrived, I hated her – her and all those Russians of hers who had allowed her out. A week after she came, Grandfather began to arrange for his move to the old folk's home. He had told us nothing of his plans, and we were dumbfounded when he sprang them on us. Avraham frowned, while Rivka gasped before huffing, 'Very well, then, I suppose you know what you're doing.' Yosi kept silent. Uri chuckled and said, 'You really are a dark horse, Grandfather!'

I was so frightened that my stomach felt like ice. I knew it was because of the woman from Russia who had knocked on the door of the cabin one day and walked in as though out of Grandfather's trunk.

'Hello, Ya'akov,' she said. 'Won't you offer me a cup of tea?'

Grandfather rose with trembling hands. Not that he hadn't known that Shulamit was about to appear. The pelicans had brought the mail, and Busquilla had festively delivered a telegram from Jerusalem the day before. Busquilla loved telegrams and had trained Zis to bray like a siren when he came with one. 'It makes my day,' he explained.

'This is my grandson Baruch,' said Grandfather. After all those years, those were his first words to her.

She laughed when he absentmindedly rolled an olive in his mouth while handing her the glass of tea, and laid her hand on his arm with a gesture of ownership and confirmation.

The fact of the matter was, I told myself, that she was nothing but an old woman. Tall but stooped, she had thick white hair, a wrinkled face, flabby rolls of flesh on her neck, and a complexion mildewed by age, like the mouldy skin of old olives. Yet beneath her dress she had long thighs, and her tottering ankles were still shapely.

She too drank her tea boiling hot. Not until their glasses were empty did they rise and embrace as though by a prearranged signal. Grandfather put his head against hers and moved with her to a slow rhythm. His moustache against her neck, he tapped out an identifying code on her shoulder with quick, small movements of his hand while sliding the other hand from her breasts to her stomach in an ancient, practised motion that the years had kept stored in some attic of old habits.

Every couple, Uri later explained to me, has their private and limited repertoire of love gestures, established quickly, perfected slowly, and never forgotten.

'Even when their love is gone and they no longer breathe each other's skin, eat each other's flesh, and dive head-first like idiots into each other's eyes, the same movements remain,' he said.

Uri had something against eyes. He always insisted that they had no expression and that all the talk about their mirroring the soul was 'nothing but a stupid optical illusion'. He himself read people by the mouth. That and not their eyes was what he looked at, deciphering the corners of their lips.

Shulamit cried, a shudder running through her body. Gently fingering her skin, Grandfather ran his planter's hands over her. Just as the dam of Time was about to burst and its torrent buckle their old knees, he noticed that I was still in the cabin and broke away from her. They went on sitting and staring at each other, and the air was so thick with all the words and touches that had yet to be taken from their hiding places that I mumbled something about shutting an irrigation tap and wandered off into the orchard.

When I returned two hours later the light was still on in the cabin and the chimney of the boiler was sputtering. They were deep in a Russian conversation.

'What's done is done,' Grandfather said to me. 'From now on Shulamit and I will live together. We don't have many years left.'

'Each time I climbed the tower, I felt weaker and more afraid than the time before.'

One night Pinness had trouble holding on to the ladder. At one point in his descent he nearly lost his grip and toppled thirty feet to the ground. 'For a long while I just hung on with a strength I didn't know I had.' His shaking knees bumped painfully against the cold metal. He was too scared to breathe.

'Why didn't you call me?' I burst out. 'I would have caught you if you had fallen.'

Pinness smiled sadly. 'This isn't a story, Baruch. We're talking about real life. And besides, you may be as strong as your father, but I weigh more than your mother.'

He steadied himself and remounted the ladder, since it was easier to climb up than down, then lay on the wet concrete of the tower while recovering his wits and his breath.

Half an hour had yet to go by when Pinness, who was ready to try another descent, heard quick hands and merry pants on the ladder rungs. He peered down and saw two dark, agile forms climbing limberly toward him. There was no way out. Feeling ridiculous, he crouched behind the old lookout post and tried to make himself small as the two figures drew closer.

Although he was unable to make out their faces in the dark, he could tell from their movements that they were young, sure of themselves and their bodies. 'They had the confidence of youth that its limbs would not betray it.'

The two hurriedly threw themselves down on the bed of sacks. From his hiding place, Pinness heard the soft rustle of fabric over skin as clothes were peeled off, followed by whispered moans of pleasure and the long-forgotten squish of moist membranes coming together. The fumes of love given off by the warm bodies condensed in the cold air and trickled into his nostrils. Trapped in the sinful magic of the moment, the old teacher felt a flicker of excitement in the most deadened parts of his body until he saw the handsome head of the young lover rise above the guardrail, a curly silhouette against the dark sky.

The brazen cry now sounded right beside him.

'I'm screwing Ya'akovi's wife!' it rang out.

Pinness cringed like a frightened mole in its burrow, his head pounding so hard from desire and shame that he thought it would burst. Ya'akovi was the village's successful young Committee head, and Pinness had known his wife since the days when she was his pupil.

'Ben-Ya'akov's granddaughter – the same Ben-Ya'akov who was killed in the Arab riots. A bright, lovely girl: I saw her grow into a fine, hardworking young woman right under my eyes! She was always so shy-looking.'

The cry burst in the wind, its syllables drifting down over the village like the white petals of almond blossoms, waking the sleeping women with dreamy smiles. In the silence that descended again on the water tower Pinness heard only the thumping of his own heart and a soft groan of laughter from the nearby throat of Ya'akovi's wife as she sought to silence her lover by burying his head in her breasts.

They lay there quietly. Slowly the blood in the old man's legs stopped its mad race. He felt the cold creeping over his body, but there was nothing to do but endure it until the two rose, put on their clothes, and started back down the ladder.

Pinness decided to wait a few more minutes to make sure he didn't give himself away. Then, gripping the guardrail tightly, he started down just in time to see several men charge out of the dark bushes and hurl themselves on the couple 'like wild beasts'.

The woman was dragged aside by the hair, while the young man was 'knocked down, beaten, kicked, and pummelled with fists and work boots' in the most horrible of silences, as methodically as if by a machine. The only sounds in the cold air were grunts and groans and the thud of blows on the squirming body.

When the men were gone, Pinness climbed down the ladder and went to have a look at the boy's bloodied face. The minced flesh gleaming like a crushed pomegranate in all shades of scarlet broke the old teacher's palpitating heart.

'He was lying face down. When I turned him over gently, he groaned with pain. It was Uri Mirkin. Your cousin Uri.'

# 33

To this day I feel guilty for not having been there that night to come to my cousin's rescue. Hoping to overhear something about Grandfather's condition in the days before his death, I was outside the village doctor's house, where the health director of the old folk's home was giving one of his periodic reports to the physicians of the area.

'If only I had been there!' I wept to Pinness. 'If only I had been there! I would have saved Uri. I would have killed every one of them.' My hands clenched and opened, the sweat running down my neck.

Pinness told me the whole story after Uri had been made to leave the village. Everyone knew what had happened, but only I heard the old teacher confess that he had been on the water tower that night. When questioned by the Committee members, he had merely said that he was unable to fall asleep, went for a walk, and found my cousin lying senseless by the tower, 'and started cursing at the top of my voice at those gangsters, those Cossacks, those evildoers'.

Pinness asked Uri if he was all right, and failing to get an answer, he hurried to the rose garden by the synagogue, soaked a handkerchief under a tap, and rushed back to wet my cousin's split lips. His slender, savaged body, 'like a fallen, lynched angel's', made a slow, excruciating effort to move its cracked ribs and battered organs.

Pinness took Uri by the arms and barely managed to drag him to his nearby house. 'His collarbone was fractured and one shoulder was dislocated.'

'Why didn't you call me?' I wailed. 'I would have carried him.'

Pinness laid Uri in his bed and sat by his side. Completely undressing the handsome, finely formed, mauled figure, he swabbed the wounds with a soft cloth and disinfected them.

Uri kept tossing and turning in pain. Bright welts covered him like flowers, and the pudendal smell rising from his loins flew up Pinness's inflamed nostrils 'and clogged my sinuses', accumulating behind his forehead like a sweet layer of dew.

Pinness sat watching Uri all night.

'He asked me why I shouted each time and what made the women of the village line up to go to bed with me.'

'His shock and pain were too great for him to answer any of my questions.'

Pinness could not get the sounds – the thumping blows, the splintering bones, the cracking joints, the shriek of flayed skin – out of his mind. He had failed to make out the attackers in the dark, and now he suspected every man in the village between the ages of sixteen and sixty. 'We have become like the beasts of the forest,' he declared, 'each man devouring his brother alive.' His skull bones had thinned to a perforated membrane that could not hold back his sorrow and his wrath. 'All my life I stood in the breach, and now that the dyke had collapsed, I faced the tide of danger by myself.'

In the morning he left tea and biscuits by the bed and went to our cowshed. Avraham and Yosi were busy with the milking, grumbling over Uri's absence. I was unloading a cart of beet fodder in the farmyard.

'Uri's at my place,' announced the teacher.

Before he could say another word, the Committee members appeared on the scene. Avraham left Yosi and me with the milking and went off with them to his house. Before two minutes had gone by Rivka's frightful screams sounded up and down the street. As if being a saddler's rather than a farmer's daughter and the wife of the village's firstborn disappointment were not bad enough, she now had to bear the disgrace of her son's profligacy. For the first time in my life I could hear as much as I wanted without having to crawl, duck, climb trees or creep through the darkness like a thief.

'It's all the fault of that hard-up nursery teacher who let him go around with his head up her arse,' screamed my aunt.

'You don't have to tell the whole world about it,' said Avraham.

'It's all your fault. You were hard up yourself at the age of nine. Your brother fucked cows and your sister went down on every rooftop.'

A huge flock of startled pigeons took off from the roof of the cowshed, the last echo of their wingbeats ringing in Rivka's cheeks. The Committee waited patiently for the rumpus to die down and informed Uri's parents of its decision to 'ask Uri to take a leave of absence from the village'. Ya'akovi's wife, it was announced, had already been driven to her sister in the city that night. Meshulam Tsirkin, who was then a fifty-year-old virgin, admitted afterward that 'if every woman Uri screwed had to leave the village, there would be no one here but Tonya and Riva'.

Uri was taken to the district hospital. I visited him there only once, because he asked that no one come again. 'At least Grandfather's dead and doesn't know,' he said. The nurses who ogled the good looks that showed through his bandages and bruises suspected that women were not to his taste. After his release it was decided to send him to his mother's brother, a wealthy road contractor in the Galilee. Avraham and Rivka accompanied him to the railway station. From the roof of the hayloft I watched them depart via the paths of Pioneer Home.

They paused by Grandfather's grave, passed through the orchard, and diminished like ants in the straw-yellow expanse. That was how I had seen Zeitser disappearing on his Sabbath walks, and Efrayim vanishing, and Grandmother Feyge rushing toward the railway tracks with her comrades, and Levin returning to Tel Aviv after his sister's funeral.

Uri was wearing a light shirt and a pair of pressed blue cotton trousers, and carrying a small wooden suitcase. Rivka walked by his side, and Avraham a few steps ahead of them, his head lowered as if to clear the way. They crossed the fields of stubble, made a detour around the abandoned British ack-ack guns, and reached the station hidden among giant eucalyptus trees. When the train had pulled out, leaving only its whistle behind, I saw Avraham and Rivka coming back. Now it was she who strode ahead, excitedly waving her hands, while every now and then

he bent down to the ground and placed some poisoned seeds in
a mousehole he had spied along the way.

Each time I tried to discuss Uri with Pinness, he told me that I could
not understand what had happened because I had never felt love for
a woman. His old qualms and cautions thrown to the wind, he now
spoke his mind freely. 'You never loved anyone but your grandfather,'
he said. 'Sometimes you remind me of Efrayim's bull. Maybe you
expect to be carried to a coupling on someone's back too.'

I didn't tell him that I had known about my cousin's escapades
all along. I had never caught him red-handed, but more than once
I had unwittingly overheard the shamelessly candid conversations
of women confessing their indiscretions, laughing, sighing, and
nudging each other with fingers and eyes as they spoke about Uri.
Afterwards I would see them in the village exchanging secretive
smiles. Rilov's and Liberson's granddaughters; the wife of Shuka
the cow breeder; the daughter of Gidon the carpenter; Michal
Margulis's mother; Michal herself, who had been a classmate of
ours; the doctor's wife; the vet's wife, who despite her age was as
stormy as wheat in the wind and cried out, 'Efrayim, Efrayim!' –
every last one of them.

'The strangest part of it,' said Uri, surprised by how much
I knew, 'is that they love it when I shout their name. They've
heard about it from each other, and it means more to them than
actually doing it with me.'

The first of them was Rilov's husky-voiced granddaughter
Edna, who had breasts at the age of nine. Once a month
swarms of male emperor moths would dash themselves against
her window blinds.

She was seventeen at the time, two years older than Uri.
Haunted by his looks and mocking manner, she grabbed hold
of him one night and dragged him up to the water tower.

'I had no choice,' said Uri, the old hidden grin on his face. 'She
had a gun.'

He climbed the ladder after her, his eyes glued to her behind,
which glimmered in the dark in its white pants.

'Was she ever hot!' he told me. 'She made sounds like a bare foot in the mud. I wanted to crawl all over her, to get my hands and legs and head and body inside her – only just then I thought of her grandfather with all his bombs and guns and explosives, and of what he would do to me if he found me in his granddaughter's ammunition dump, and I started to laugh.'

'What's so funny?' asked Edna.

'I'm screwing Rilov's granddaughter.' Uri whispered the slow boast into her mouth.

'Then why don't you tell everyone,' she jeered. Before she could stop him, he had raised his head above the guardrail of the tower and yelled at the top of his voice:

'I'm screwing Rilov's granddaughter!'

The words tangled with the night breeze, bounced off the treetops, and burst into meaningless droplets of letters and syllables that none of the farmers ever heard.

Even I, the great eavesdropper, was deaf to them. Not so Pinness, whose ears had never been stopped with earth and whose closeness to insects and children had taught him the art of piecing together jigsaw puzzles of sound. Not so the women of the village, whose monotonous lives had taught them to seek excitement even beneath the hairy leaves of pumpkins and in the foetid drinking boxes of the hens.

The old teacher jumped up in a sweat and rushed outside to lay into the culprit, but the women merely awoke and smiled as one at the darkness. In a flash of blinding possibility, they knew at once whose voice had whinnied like a stallion. A rare and subtle fragrance, a crystal transparency, the touch of youthful flesh or flawless crystal, overcame them where they lay.

'You'll never understand it,' said Uri. 'You don't care for women. But I think of those poor turkey hens in their darkrooms, and of Grandmother, and of Shulamit, and of Hayyim Margulis's sweet fingers, and of poor Daniel Liberson falling in love with your mother when he was three weeks old, and I think of Grandmother's saying that somewhere in the world everyone has a true love. I'm going to find mine.'

'If Fanya Liberson were alive,' said Pinness, 'she would call it your grandmother's revenge. In the veins of the Mirkins the sweet blood of the Workingman's Circle turned into a never-clotting venom. There was your grandfather, who couldn't love Feyge and tortured himself with longing and hate for Shulamit. There was Avraham, who sang his first and last love song at the age of nine. There was Uri, who made us lose all sense of proportion. And there's you, the family ox, Isaiah's wild bull in a net, big, strong, and barren of heart.'

Uri's beating hit the old teacher hard. 'We were wrong,' he wrote in the newsletter. 'Wrong educationally. Wrong politically. Wrong in how we thought about the future. We are like the blind beasts that perish, up to our necks in mire.'

Now, at the age of ninety-five, Pinness looked up to discover that the menacing tides had dried behind the dykes and fresh breezes blew over the earth.

'If only I could tell you,' he said to me, 'what marvellous thoughts I have inside my head! I can feel them flutter there like moths.'

'Only now do I understand,' he wrote in an article that touched off a storm when it appeared, 'that Uri Mirkin was the most original thinker our village ever produced. Like Jeremiah in the Valley of Ben Hinnom, like Elijah on Mount Carmel, like Jotham atop Mount Gerizim – so Uri Mirkin spake in parables from the heights of the water tower.'

# 34

'Everything happened after Grandfather left the village and after he died,' my banished cousin wrote to me. He had finished his army service and was operating a scraper for his uncle in the Galilee, declining to return to the Valley. 'Zeitser and Liberson went blind and died, Pinness lost his mind, Meshulam started reswamping the village, my father and mother left the country, Yosi became a career officer who speaks without using his jaws and thinks without using his head, I was sent into exile, and you of all people have become the richest farmer in the Valley.

'I received a letter from Pinness. He thinks about us. Mirkin's two grandsons, he writes, both dealt him a low blow. One in Death and one in Love. The necrophile and the nymphophile. Quote, unquote. It's a shame that Grandfather isn't around to hear Pinness's language these days.

'What was it about the old man that held everything together?' wrote Uri. 'Who knows who he really was: an angel of green growth or the Satan of poor Grandmother Feyge's Workingman's Circle? Like you, I think a lot about Efrayim. Did Grandfather bring him the mask for Efrayim's sake or for his own? Sometimes I think Efrayim left because of Grandfather alone.'

My big footprints run along the retreating margin of the sandy beach. I look in amazement at this light, poor soil whose grains are so pretty and so worthless. And yet what is it but the soil of the Valley speeded up? Quicker to absorb moisture and quicker to lose it, quicker to blow away and quicker to pile up, quicker to fall apart and quicker to clump together, quicker to imprint and quicker to obliterate.

Damp nubs left by the playful toes of little children, the prints of beach sandals, the balled heels of women leading to the water's edge and disappearing there, and jagged holes torn in the sand by the joggers with their dumb, tormented looks. Were Efrayim to walk here, Jean Valjean's weight would make deep depressions in the sand, deeper even than mine.

I can't imagine anyone leaving because of Grandfather. Deep down I want to grab his shirt and huddle under his wings to this day. 'You're wrong,' I wanted to say to Uri. 'Completely wrong. No one could want to leave Grandfather, not even our uncle Efrayim.'

The search for Efrayim continued until Grandfather's death. A dragnet was spread all over the Levant for a masked man with a big blond bull on his shoulders. Colonel Stoves, who was now serving with the Arab Legion in Transjordan, looked for him everywhere, hobbling on his shattered knee. Old Arab friends of Rilov's brought reports from Syria and Lebanon. The Movement had its own intelligence network in the country. Agricultural advisers, party activists, veterinarians, ritual circumcisers, itinerants of all kinds who ran into varieties of man and beast, were asked to keep their eyes open.

Occasionally Charolais calves were rumoured to have been sired in odd places. Pilgrims returning from Mecca told the headman of the Mazarib tribe that they had seen a huge white bull on the Saudi Arabian coast near al-Magnah. Through their binoculars two Scottish naturalists studying the reproductive habits of coots in the Seyhan marshes of Turkey saw a short-legged blond calf mating with a female water buffalo. A migrant starling that landed in Pinness's garden to beg him to remove an irksome aluminium band from its leg had seen Efrayim swimming across the Black Sea in a northerly direction while Jean Valjean galloped thunderously along the shore.

For a while these reports aroused hopes. But the noiseless and invisible Efrayim, who was a past master at infiltration, camouflage, navigation, and survival, was never found. His route took him over greater distances than anyone had at first imagined. After a few years a French racing motorcyclist found Charolais-like calves in Armenia and Algeria. Jean Valjean's *crème*, so it seemed, could be carried by the wind like pollen.

'He must have taken Jean Valjean to that brothel in Algiers,' Uri said.

'Border crossings never posed a problem for Efrayim,' remarked his old commander Lord Lovat, who arrived for a visit from London. 'Your son was a first-rate soldier and a true friend,' he told Grandfather. 'We kept in touch even after his discharge. He helped us immensely.'

Grandfather bit his lips and said nothing.

Lord Lovat was a slim old gentleman who leaned on a carved walking stick and kept his throat covered with a blue silk scarf. The scarf also concealed a stainless steel pipe that stuck out of his shredded Adam's apple and whistled softly when he laughed. Accompanying him was a tall, attractive middle-aged woman who began to shiver when she entered the village.

Lord Lovat signed the village visitors' book and then, curious to see where Efrayim had learned the art of silent walking, was taken to Rachel Levin's home. He watched in amazement as the bronzed old woman glided over to a rabbit filching greens from her garden and scared it to death by shouting 'Boo!' into its long ear.

Soon after he and Grandfather had closeted themselves for a long talk in the cabin, I was discovered eavesdropping near the timber wall and sent to join the pretty woman in the orchard. She walked among the blossoming trees, pressing their petals to her throat while singing and laughing in low tones.

I was asked to guard her, and I did, walking as quietly behind her as I could at a safe distance so that she could waltz unhindered among the pear trees. Not even Avraham or Grandfather recognised her. I alone caught a whiff of her scent and heard the bulls bellow as they lunged at the fences of their pens.

'Ya'akov,' said Grandfather to Pinness when Lord Lovat and his attractive companion were gone, 'do you remember how Jacob says in the Bible, "My son is yet alive, I will go see him before I die"?'

'And he did see him, Ya'akov,' Pinness said. 'In the end he saw him.'

'This Jacob will never see his son again,' said Grandfather. 'The only thing still keeping me alive is getting even with you all. You drove him from the village, and I'll get you where it hurts the most, in the earth. I'll get Shulamit in the heart, and you in the earth.'

# 35

She had a hard Russian *r* and deep, spongy *l*'s. Once all the founders of the village talked like that, but the local air stretched their palates, widened their larynxes, and diluted the thick saliva in their mouths.

'For sixty-five years your grandfather wrestled with Shulamit in his heart. He wallowed in sands and swamps like an animal to get rid of the smell and touch of her; he tried to purge her from every orifice of his body, rooting her out with the long steel wires of memory. But her skin shimmered at him in the pear petals and from the flank of the blue mountain. No stone skimmed across the ponds of his soul ever sank to the bottom. Each pelican swooping low over Liberson's house showed him her white breast.'

Pinness, now a fat, hungry, curious, sick old man, easily waxed poetic. Camouflaged as an old nature teacher, he clasped me to his breast, jabbing me with reflections and spines of love. When I started to cry in a thick, sticky voice he patted the back of my neck.

'Revenge is patient,' he said, 'as patient as the bulb of the squill awaiting summer's end. Its greatest pleasure lies in ripening and refinement. It takes shape in the deepest recesses of the soul, beneath the thin surfaces of wheat fields and smooth complexions, in hidden clefts and cleavages.'

Towards the end of his life no revenge escaped his notice. He explained to me how Grandfather had wreaked vengeance on the village and on Shulamit, and how the earth had wreaked vengeance on us all. The things he said in those years shocked the village more than anything except Pioneer Home.

'Long accustomed to the stench of saints' bones and the gross feet of pilgrims and legions, this vulgar earth must have split its sides laughing at the sight of us pioneers kissing it and watering it with our tears of thanksgiving, possessing it in a frenzy, thrusting our little hoes into its great body, calling it mother, sister, lover. Even as we ploughed our first furrows and planted our first crops, as we weeded, drained swamps, and cleared thickets, we sowed the seed of our own failure.'

His voice became almost festive as he continued.

'We may have drained the swamps, but the mud we discovered beneath them was far worse. Man's bond with the earth, man's union with Nature – is there anything more regressive and bestial? We raised a new generation of Jews who were no longer alienated and downtrodden, a generation of farmers linked to the land, a society of the grossest, most quarrelsome, most narrow-minded, most thick-skinned and thick-headed peasants! Your uncle Avraham understood that when he was nine, your grandfather understood it when Efrayim disappeared, and I understood it when I saw him let the fruit rot in his orchard while caring only for the flowers. Uri had to have his spleen kicked in before he understood it too.

'There is no such earth,' concluded Pinness, who had clearly been saving up his punchline. 'And there is no such lover, either.'

Old and frail, Grandfather stood facing me and Shulamit.

'I'm going to live with her from now on,' he told me. 'Please understand me, my child. At my age it's the only thing I can do. But I can't do it here. Not in this house.'

I heard familiar steps approaching the cabin. Pinness knocked and entered, followed by Liberson and Tsirkin.

Breathing heavily and embracing, they all burst into horrible sobs. I was so dumbfounded by the emotion gushing from their old Russian hides that I turned around and left. That night I slept among the bales in the hayloft with no Grandfather to cover me. Even when his friends left after midnight, the lights stayed on in the cabin. When I returned in the morning he was slowly making himself breakfast and the Crimean whore was fast asleep in his bed.

'I never showed you this picture,' said Grandfather. He ran his fingers over the paper lining of the trunk, fumbling gently until he found what he was looking for. Taking out his grafting knife, he slit and peeled back the paper, reached inside with two fingers, and drew out an old photograph.

'This is her,' he whispered, nodding toward the bed. 'Back there, when we were young.'

The photograph had been slashed nearly in two from top to bottom, as though with a sickle stroke. It was held together by some old brown masking tape stuck to its back.

In a dark blouse with a round collar and a narrow tie of black velvet, Shulamit was seated on a carved chair. Her eyebrows arched like proud crescents in her vertically severed young face. Her hands, snipped by the hateful scissors, were crossed with an infinite calm, with all the radiant confidence of a beautiful woman.

'When we went swimming in the river at night, in our little nook of reeds and rushes, Shulamit glimmered like a heron.'

She slept with all the officers, I told myself, and with all the old Red Army generals. Everyone knows she did. She was the reason you couldn't sleep at night. She was the reason Grandmother died.

Grandfather rose, stretched himself painfully on tiptoe, and hit me in the face with his fist. He was so old and weak that it didn't even hurt, but I broke into a sweat like a mule ploughing in autumn, and my eyes filled with tears.

Then Shulamit awoke and I ran out. Half an hour later they emerged for a walk around the yard. I followed behind them at a distance. Grandfather showed her Avraham's milking shed, the hayloft, and old Zeitser, who was munching his pensioner's breakfast. The mule regarded her with equanimity. At his advanced age he knew well that the beast hath no advantage over the man and that the life of both is nothing but one long tug at a stuck cart that never breaks free of pitfalls, sand traps, and bogs. They passed the remains of Grandmother Feyge's old earthen stove, whose ruined walls still smelled of bread, pain, and baked pumpkin, and headed for the orchard. From afar I saw Grandfather's long sleeves flap as he showed Shulamit the different trees. I knew that he was waving goodbye – to the peaches, to the pears, to the almonds, to me.

'Just look at them,' said Uri, coming up and standing by my side. 'Straight out of the pages of a Russian novel.'

A month later the two of them moved to the old folk's home. Until his dying day Grandfather retaliated with a deliberate, calculated, and relentless love whose heartless skill and soft old movements of pleasure made Shulamit shed her grey leafage, scratch at the walls, and stamp her feet as hard as her rheumatic old joints would permit.

\*      \*      \*

And then, as Uri later wrote me, Grandfather died and everything began to fall apart. Rivka's screams grew ten times louder, Avraham's silences and crease lines deepened, and I myself all but stopped eating, because a great tuber of yearning was swelling and sprouting in my stomach. The news that Mirkin had left home got around quickly, racing through the pens and sheds and flying over the fields. It took no more than a few days for weeds to overrun the vegetable and flower gardens by the cabin. Black ants, their high abdomens arched almost to their backs, scooted madly across the floor. Three despairing almond trees, their hollow interiors claimed by the bright sawdust of Doubt, collapsed in the orchard. Ruthless cattle flies descended on the yard, and their strong, stout beaks drilled through the skin of man and beast, leaving bloody puncture marks and testy animals who couldn't keep their minds on their work.

When thorny prosopis plants burst through the floor of the cabin, their ugly fruits distended like cancerous glands before my eyes, I rose from bed and called for Yosi. Armed with hoes, we went to the garden and began rooting out the long, tough nodules that had spread beneath the earth as the malediction of branches grew above it. Yosi had had enough after a day. His hands were blistered, and he couldn't straighten his back that night.

'It's hopeless,' he said to me. 'Cut them back above ground once a week, keep dousing them with petrol, and maybe you'll get rid of them.'

But I wanted to go for the jugular, for the hidden body that had waited for Grandfather to depart before reaching out its tentacles and creeping up at me from the earth.

The deep trench I had dug crossed the yard and ran out to the fields. I extended it now towards the orchard, sending clods of earth flying with great whacks of the hoe as I cut through acres of corn and clover and worked my way through the ruins of the British ack-ack positions, to the consternation of moles and centipedes and the dismay of unearthed pot-shards and mole crickets. I rooted out every side shoot I could find, and four days later I straightened up to find myself down by the spring.

Here, by the blackberries where the infant Avraham lay glowing in the dark and Pinness met the old Arab walking behind his plough, there was still a strong sulphurous stench of Bulgakov. His silken hairs floated in the air, and the venomous, spittley breath of the hyena condensed on the elecampane leaves. It was here that I traced the mother plant to its lair.

Suddenly the stubborn root thickened and dived down into the bowels of the earth. I wrapped it around my waist, dug in my heels and began to pull. I was in great shape, nineteen stone of meat and gristle, as tall as my mother and as strong as my father. Slowly the earth lifted as the yellowish root came to light, raising great clumps of soil, rat corpses, buried owl turds, large pewter beer mugs, and crushed tin toys still warm from the hands of the German children who had gone clutching them to their malarial deaths.

I toppled backwards when the rootstalk came out, its white rootlets wriggling like parasitic worms as they looked for something to grip. A great hole remained in the ground, and from it rose a milky, pestilent vapour thick with swarms of mosquitoes. Peering down into it, I saw the dense, murky water of the past swirling slowly, little grubs clinging to its surface and breathing patiently through their short air tubes. Like any old pupil of Pinness's, I could have identified the larvae of the anopheles mosquito with my eyes closed.

A deep gurgle sounded from the hole. Shut up by the founders in the bowels of the earth, imprisoned in the trunks of the eucalyptus trees they planted, the soughing swamp began to surge toward me as it was touched by the sun's rays.

I was seized by fear. All the horror stories I had heard from the old pioneers until they were flesh of my flesh now came to life. As fast as I could I hoed the earth back into the hole, stamping on it insanely with all my weight and strength.

I came home to find the feathery prosopis leaves wilted and moribund, tore what was left of them out of the ground with my hands, and went to sleep. I stayed in bed for days, breathing the smell of the spring, the sappy odour of the cabin's wooden walls, and the fragrance of Grandfather. It was then I first realised that my own life, overpowered in his body's huge shade, had grown like a low fern, mere mould of the forest floor.

Long night after night I lay without a blanket, listening to tiny footsteps on the roof and tremulous chirps of yellow-plumed chicks, until Avraham came to me with a full pitcher and told me that Grandfather had asked for milk.

At about that time I was informed that as an orphan I was exempt from the army. In the village it was rumoured that I had been found psychologically unfit.

'What else could you expect from a child who adopted a mad grandfather as his mother?' asked my aunt Rivka.

Never an easy woman, Aunt Rivka had loathed me openly since Grandfather's departure for the old folk's home. She was so worried he might will the farm to me that she kept begging her sons to visit him. Yosi, though, said he was too busy with the cows, while Uri didn't give a damn.

'I couldn't care less about trees, and I don't intend to be a farmer,' he announced. 'Who wants to live in a place like this? There's nothing to do here but blabber about cows all day long.'

Still, everyone watched his step with me. I was the strongest teenager in the village. At the age of fourteen I was already anchor man on our tug-of-war team. Before each match Grandfather would say to me, 'Just dig your heels in and stay put, Baruch. We'll show 'em!'

I had no one except Pinness, who liked to chat with me, trying out new ideas and answering my questions. Sometimes Zeitser looked in my window and nodded, but he too was very old and hardly spoke any more.

In the mornings I rose feeling weak from the smell of Grandfather, which lingered in the cabin. The olives I cured didn't taste like his. They grew mushy and rotten in no time because I never managed to get the salt right. The fresh egg either sank to the bottom like a rock or jumped out of the barrel as if shot from a catapult.

I was, as Uri put it, 'a lone bird on a roof'. Until he was made to leave the village he came to see me every morning, bringing two pieces of cake stolen from his mother's pantry, one for me and one for Zeitser.

'How can you live like this?' he asked.

Swallows nested in the corners of the ceiling, and grey lichen pocked the walls.

'You can't let the cabin go to pieces like this,' said Meshulam. 'It's one of the last artifacts left from the village's first years.' He had come to borrow Grandfather's old hat for one of his exhibits. It was a grey floppy-brimmed thing that I sometimes liked to wear to the fields.

Alone in the cabin, pacing the floorboards between the rotting walls, I groaned for the grandfather who had abandoned me, for the father and mother who had died, for the uncle who had disappeared, for the stars above to save me from my loneliness and sorrow. My only friends were the spiders jiggling in the corners and the translucent geckos who scaled the walls with their hands and looked at me with black innocent eyes. By day I tended Grandfather's orchard. From the heights of his love nest he had instructed Avraham to put me in charge of it.

'The child needs something to do,' he said. 'And he has a good pair of hands.'

I pruned, notched buds, tied branches, smeared tree tar on wounds, and let the fruit ripen and fall like Grandfather had. Now and then Avraham asked for a hand in the cowshed, which I was always glad to lend. I liked unloading heavy bales from the cart and stacking them in the hayloft, cleaning the sewage ditch, and dragging the giddy, excited young heifers to their first tryst with the inseminator.

Whenever things seemed so hopeless that I felt my bones begin to rot, I would go and wrestle the calves in the feed pen. As I playfully grabbed a half-ton yearling by the horns, Zeitser would raise his wrinkled head from his pile of old newspapers and give me a quizzical look. The calves, gargantuan crossbreeds of Brahma, Angus, and Charolais, let out glad, chesty bellows when they saw me coming, pulling off my shirt as I drew near. They loved me for being the one bright spot in their brief, nasty lives.

Raising beef cattle was a highly profitable business in those days, but the sight of the meat dealers pulling up in their lorries always made my uncle Avraham glower. Wrapping a calf's tail around a fist, they would twist it painfully back and forth while leading the big animals to the lorry ramp. Avraham couldn't bear it. For two or three days after the teary-eyed calves were taken to the slaughterhouse, his muscles were so tense that he staggered stiffly around the yard like a mechanical doll.

Although he never said anything about my horseplay with the calves, a small, slow smile of approval spread over his face when he watched it, smoothing the furrows in his brow. Sometimes, stepping sweaty and bare-chested out of the pen, the veins bulging under my skin, I spied Aunt Rivka hiding behind the thick trunk of a eucalyptus tree.

'Why don't you find yourself a girl instead of laying bulls in their own shit?' she shouted angrily before hurrying off.

In Grandfather's drawers I found old papers and documents, flowers dried by my mother, and letters from all over the country requesting agricultural advice. 'I have such heavy soil that the water stands after a rain,' wrote Aryeh Ben-David of Kfar Yitzchak. 'Do you think I should plant peach trees?'

Grandfather attached a copy of his answer to each letter. He advised 'Dear Aryeh' to plant a hundred and forty-four trees to an acre and to graft them on myrobalan plum stock.

I found bits of gnawed, infected leaves that were sent to him for diagnosis and a note in his own hand that said, 'Shimon, my friend, what I said about pruning back branches does not apply to a new vineyard. At this stage, no shoots from the graft should be touched. Just make sure to remove any suckers coming up from the stock.'

There were other finds too. 'I'm living in a rented room with several other workers,' wrote Shlomo Levin from Jerusalem to his sister in the Galilee. 'Every day I come home with my hands so raw and swollen from cutting stones that I can't touch a thing. Not far from here are a few old olive trees that I go and lean my head against and cry like a small child. Will I ever make a working man? Or am I just a mummy's boy?'

Rain drummed on the roof of the cabin, the slow, full rain of the Valley which turns the earth into a quagmire and a man's flesh into a sponge. I enjoyed walking in it like the old-timers, with an empty sack rolled up over my head and shoulders like a huge monk's hood. Once a week I went to see the film showing at the meeting house, more for the sake of seeing Rilov bounce some trespasser from his regular seat than anything else. Sometimes I walked to the spring, where I lay on my back looking up at the sky through the bushes. It was here that Grandfather had come with his firstborn son, baby Avraham, the night the whole village climbed the water tower to see his magic halo.

'I kept a small campfire going all night,' Grandfather told me. 'It drove off the jackals and made the blackberries and papyrus reeds glow yellow. Avraham slept, and I sat there and thought.'

Three times a week a woman comes to clean my house. At night I sit drinking tea and thinking in my spotless kitchen, picturing the village in the dark.

Our village is shaped like an H. The farmers' houses run along the two vertical arms, their farmyards backing off to either side. The Mirkin farm is in the north-eastern corner, and the school, the meeting house, the breeder, the dairy, the clinic, the store, the feed shack, and the post office are in the village centre. The non-farmers live here too, their homes surrounded by small gardens and auxiliary barnyards.

It's hard to imagine that it was all a wilderness once. The old photographs in Meshulam's boxes – tents in a treeless landscape, poorly dressed men and women, skinny chickens, cows as meagre as those in Pharaoh's dream – look like they were taken elsewhere. Lofty avenues of cypresses and casuarinas now line the entrance to every farmhouse. Slender-trunked Washingtonia palms, planted in those first years, shake their wild heads of hair in the sky.

I planted a dozen such palms myself in a handsome boulevard by the entrance to Pioneer Home. By then the only Mirkins left in the village were Avraham, Rivka, and Yosi. Every Saturday they went to visit Uri. Sometimes they invited me along.

Yosi drove the old Studebaker. Although he didn't have a licence, he was an excellent, careful driver. You could see the road running into his eyes as if his brain were endlessly digesting it. Avraham kept silent, and Rivka, after trying to make small talk about this or that, gave up and sat there like the scolded calf she was so good at imitating.

Her brother, with whom Uri was now living, had left the village after his discharge from the army and become a successful earthmover. He had tractors working for him all over the country and businesses in Africa and Latin America. A small, rich, jovial man, he was immensely fond of me and liked to challenge me to wrestling matches. Slapping me on the back as hard as he could, he asked if I wanted 'a job as a bulldozer' with him.

'I hear you're making money, young fellow,' he said shrewdly, planting his little fist in the great wall of my stomach. 'If you'd like a little power shovel for those graves of yours, just let me know.'

'All I need is a pickaxe and a hoe,' I said.

'Before you know it he'll be buying you and all your power shovels out,' said Rivka.

Although the story of his relocation, which arrived together with him, had made Uri the local girls' dream boy, he led a life of monkish abstinence.

'Do you know what I've been thinking about?' he asked when we were left alone at last for a few minutes. 'I've been thinking about your parents – about your father, who looked up and knew that a woman would fall on him from above, and about your mother, who died hugging him in her sleep, dreaming of meat.'

# 36

After departing with Shulamit, Grandfather returned to visit only once. I remember how my heart skipped a beat when I came home from the fields and saw the ambulance from the old folk's home parked in the yard. Entering the cabin, I found Grandfather lying in bed, with Avraham and the village doctor seated by his side. I was good and frightened, but Grandfather explained that he missed the cabin so much he had to see it again. By the door, the doctor asked to have a word with me.

Doctor Munk was new in the village. Grandfather was already in the old folk's home when he came. He had an amiable blonde wife who made friends with everyone and sometimes substitute-taught in the school, a woman who smelled as clean as a cat and wore summery dresses perfumed with crushed lemon leaves. A month after her arrival, Pinness and all the women heard the cry, 'I'm screwing the doctor's wife.'

The doctor played the cello and even gave a few amateur recitals. One of them was attended by Tsirkin, who announced afterward that if he held his mandolin upside down between his legs, 'it would howl like that too'.

'Grandpa thinks he's dying,' said Doctor Munk with the fake intimacy he cultivated, as his revolting little dog tried to nip my heels. 'I've examined him and there's nothing wrong with him. It's something that happens to people his age, and so we have to try to calm Grandpa down.'

Grandfather's wanting to visit the village had aroused no suspicions in the old folk's home. No sooner did he arrive, however, than he sent Avraham for the doctor.

'I'm dying,' he told Doctor Munk, 'and I'd like to know what it will feel like.'

The odd thing was that Grandfather had never had the slightest use for doctors. He trusted only nurses and medics and couldn't stand our former physician, a strange supervegetarian who had come to us from Scotland long before Efrayim's letters and had been dead for several years. Far in advance of the discovery of penicillin he smeared infected cuts and drippy penises with bread mould, and included in his diet baked bulb of autumn crocus, mesocarp of mandrake, and ground walnut bark. He also made sure to sunbathe every morning, and his guests were offered such refreshments as mallow leaves picked by the roadside and purslane filched from the chickens' feedboxes. His language was a source of general amusement. One of his more famous diagnoses was, 'The cow kicked Rilov in the head, and for half an hour he lay in manure with no sense.'

So healthy and balanced were the foods the Scottish doctor ate that he never aged at all. When as a man of eighty he crumbled to a yellow powder, the last of his cellulose consumed by bostrychids and weevils, there was not a wrinkle in his skin.

Doctor Munk was acquainted with the stories told about Ya'akov Mirkin in the village.

'I've heard a lot about you, Grandpa,' he said, leafing through the clinic's medical file. 'I'm glad to get to know you.'

He phoned the doctor at the old folk's home, took Grandfather's pulse and blood pressure, and performed a cardiogram to be on the safe side.

'Grandpa,' he said, 'you're as healthy as a horse. I wouldn't send you to the Olympics, but you're in fine form.'

'Let's get this right,' said Grandfather, the chill in his voice cheering me. 'In the first place, I'm not your grandfather. And in the second place, I didn't ask for your medical opinion. Don't call me Grandpa, and don't send me to the Olympics. Just tell me what it feels like to die.'

'To tell you the truth, I wouldn't know,' said the offended physician. 'I suppose it depends what you die of.'

'Old age,' said Grandfather. 'I intend to die of something as banal as old age.'

I was up all that night. I was so glad to have him back in the cabin and so scared by the way he talked that I was too tense to fall asleep. He himself, after laboriously rising to cover me and returning to bed, fell asleep like a baby.

As soon as the sun was up I made him breakfast. After we had eaten, Grandfather asked me to take him to the fields. I pushed him along the ruts of the tractor path in his wheelchair. The old milk cows sighed happily to see him as we passed the cowshed, but some of the young calves and heifers didn't know who he was.

'You need to put a salt lick in the feed stalls,' Grandfather said to Avraham, who had just arrived.

'Nowadays there's already salt in the concentrate, Father,' said Avraham.

'Any cow would rather lick her own salt,' insisted Grandfather stubbornly.

We passed the fig tree and the olive. Grandfather gave Zeitser a hug and patted him on his nose, which was as smooth and soft as a colt's despite his great age.

We reached the orchard, which looked wild and healthy.

'Very nice,' said Grandfather, fingering the leaves and branches. 'Go and bring me some fruit.'

He sniffed the Methley and Vixen plums, varieties no one grew any more, and declared that the soil needed nitrogen. Next autumn, he suggested, I should enrich it by sowing sweet peas among the trees.

'Listen to me, Baruch,' he said all of a sudden. 'That doctor knows nothing. I'm dying and I want to be buried here, in my orchard.'

I could feel my face twitch. A frightened smile struggled for a foothold at one corner of my mouth.

'But Avraham wants to keep up the orchard. You yourself asked me to look after it,' I said.

'And so you will,' said Grandfather. 'Don't you worry. I won't take up much room.'

'Listen to me carefully, my child,' he added after a while. 'I didn't come here to visit. I came here to die. I want to do it at home, because it will be easier to bury me here if you don't have to ask anyone's permission or snatch my body from the freezer at the old folk's home.'

'But why, Grandfather?' I stammered.

'They drove my son from the village,' Grandfather declaimed. 'I don't want to be in their cemetery. I don't want any part of them. I'll stand their earth on its head.'

He looked at me sternly. 'You'll bury me here. This land is yours and mine. And after me you'll bury Shulamit, and perhaps there will be others. Don't let anyone move us from here. I'm counting on you, Baruch. You're the only one who can do it.'

Grandfather watched me slowly taking it all in. Suddenly it

dawned on me why he had fed me all those vegetables, raised me on stories and colostrum, saved me from the hyena, weighed me so carefully.

'And now take me back to the cabin,' he ordered.

I wheeled him back, my heart heavy. Never before had I realised what a stupid idiot I was. I felt like an animal that doesn't understand a thing.

After I helped Grandfather into bed, he told me to go back to work. 'I'll rest for a while,' he said.

At noon a hen came out to the field, importantly flapping her wings, and I followed her back to the cabin. Grandfather was getting impatient. He wanted me to go to the co-op and ask Levin for a new pair of pyjamas.

'At my age I can afford to indulge myself,' he smiled.

'Maybe he'd also like some silk sheets for the mule?' Levin jeered.

I returned carrying a pair of soft grey flannel pyjamas with light blue stripes. Grandfather asked me to light the old wood-burning stove and bring his trunk to the bedside.

While the stove's chimney purred, Grandfather picked his way through the old vellum of his papers, arranging them: letters, documents, photographs the colour of earth. Then he walked about the cabin a bit, hobbling from corner to corner. I followed him around instead of going back to work, all but clinging to his tiny body. My big bulk must have bothered him, because suddenly he turned around and scolded me. But even then I didn't leave him. I was afraid that if I looked away for a second he might vanish into thin air.

Towards evening I brought him some milk from the cowshed, but he vomited it all up, lost his temper, and yelled at me to mop the floor. Afterward he apologised and asked me to help him to the shower and sit by his side while he washed. I had kept his old milking stool there, its wooden seat sanded white by the rough cotton weave of his work clothes. He sat on it to keep from slipping on the wet tile floor, running the water so hot that his white skin turned pink and steamy and drops of vapour trickled down the windowpane. He soaped his body and took care to cleanse it well, fussily wielding the scouring pad behind his ears and in between his toes and buttocks while I sat and waited, crouched against the wall beneath a hanger that held my sour work clothes. I could tell when Grandfather wanted to be alone with his thoughts and didn't bother him.

When he was finished I helped him to his feet, wrapped his body in the big old soft sheet he liked to dry himself with, and carried him back to bed like a nurse carrying a baby. He slowly put on the new pyjamas I had bought him, asked me to button up the shirt, and said, 'Bury me in my earth, among the trees.' Then he lay down, placed his glasses on the little night table, pulled the blanket up to his chin, and fell into a deep sleep. It took me six hours to admit to myself that his lost consciousness would never be regained.

Rivka and the doctor wanted to rush him to the hospital, but Avraham said that his father had made up his mind to die and should be allowed to do so. At 1 a.m., when Doctor Munk declared that such a comatose state could last for days, Rivka and Avraham went home to sleep. Grandfather's body went on breathing and quivering and secreting brown, dry, foetid earth.

For three whole days I sat by the wooden wall of the cabin without sleeping a wink. People went in and out, and I was so delirious by then that I no longer knew who came via the door and who via Grandfather's trunk. On the third night, when my body was limp and porous from lack of sleep, there was an end to the eddy of dreams in the room and I knew that Grandfather was dead. I went over to his bed and picked him up. He was small and light.

'The earth, the earth,' he said all at once. 'The earth will lift up its voice.'

I held him in my arms and headed for the fields. We passed the hayloft and the pens of nodding calves. By Efrayim's old hut we stopped to take a pitchfork, a pickaxe, and a spade. Soundlessly we glided past Zeitser, whose twitching body was in the middle of an argument with itself. A jackal yelped far away, startling the turkeys. A heavy layer of dew covered the earth, the blades of grass, and the Fordson tractor parked nearby.

'Here,' said Grandfather.

I broke the earth with several blows of the pickaxe and dug down with the pitchfork, flinging up the heavy clods and then evening out the sides with the spade. I did this over and over, and since I'm strong and was in a frenzy, it took me exactly twenty-five minutes to dig a square pit a yard and a half deep among the pear and apple trees.

I took off Grandfather's pyjamas and laid him in the grave. His smooth white body glistened in the darkness. I covered him with dirt, packed it down with my feet, and marked the site with some heavy stones gathered from the borders of the property. Then I lay down on the damp ground and fell sound asleep.

It was 7 a.m. when I awoke, my eyelids struck by the sunlight filtering through the foliage of the pear trees. Uncle Avraham was calling my name. Doctor Munk stood wanly off to one side while Ya'akovi, the Committee head, gave me a kick in the shoulders and demanded to know what I thought I was doing.

Doctor Munk plucked up his courage and flung himself on me, screaming like a madman as he tried pathetically to shake my body.

'How can I fill out a death certificate? How do I even know he's dead? What's going on here?' He went on asking his idiot questions. Ya'akovi picked up Grandfather's pyjamas with a strange look on his face, as though expecting to find in them a clue to the mystery.

'Put those pyjamas down!' I yelled in a voice I had never used before.

He just stood there. I pushed Doctor Munk out of the way, rose to my feet like a bull, and slapped Ya'akovi in the face so hard that his lips split open like a plum. Hurt and incredulous, he staggered backward like a ludicrous mannequin and sat down on his rear. With two flying steps I was on him, snatching the pyjamas from his hands.

'That's for Grandfather and for Efrayim,' I said.

Supporting himself on his knuckles, he started to rise.

'And no funny stuff,' I warned him.

Though shorter and lighter than me, he was well built and a veteran of several wars, like most of the men in the village. He got to his feet, wiped his bloody chin with his hand, and said dryly: 'We'll be back in an hour to open the grave. We'll bury him in the village cemetery, in founders' row, next to your grandmother. If I were you, Baruch, I wouldn't make any more trouble.'

They left. A short while later Avraham came back by himself, carrying the heavy tow chain from the tractor and a length of two-inch metal pipe. He laid them on the grave without a word and returned to his cows.

He was back again in half an hour. This time there were several men with him, including Ya'akovi, whose face had been cleaned and bandaged, Pinness, and Dani Rilov. By then I had already dug holes for the ornamental bushes I planned to plant around the grave.

I straightened up and braced myself.

'My grandfather asked to be buried here,' I told them.

'We know you were very attached to him,' said Pinness in a friendly tone, 'but this is no way to do things. There's a cemetery, Baruch, and that's where people are buried.' He thought he would outsmart me as the farmers outsmart a calf bound for slaughter, sweet-talking himself close enough to lay his hypnotic hand on my neck. But I knew all the tricks of teachers and cattlemen and jumped back to the pile of rocks on the grave, where I stood without a word.

'Don't waste your time, Pinness, this isn't a civics class,' said Ya'akovi. 'We've had enough trouble from this family.'

He made a hand motion. Out of the corner of my eye I saw the lanky form of Dani Rilov begin moving towards me with his arms out. The heavy tow chain with its wicked hook at one end whistled through the air, whirling over my head in a dark, glittering circle. Dani backed off and the group retreated.

Pinness, who more than once had seen me roll away heavy rocks to look for velvet ants and galeodes, went over to Ya'akovi. So did Avraham, whose angry whisper everyone could hear.

'I don't want any scenes now,' he said, his forehead crawling and contorting. 'Don't forget that we're in mourning. My father is dead, and we want to mourn him in peace.'

Ya'akovi took fresh stock. 'We'll go now,' he said. 'But take it from me, you haven't heard the last of this from the Committee.'

To this day I don't know who was right – Uri, who said that Grandfather had prophetic powers, or I, who argued that he simply had planned the future so long and so exactly that it was forced to flow in the ditch he had dug for it until it reached me and woke me up.

Grandfather knew that no one would move his body. He knew that no one would dare challenge the monster of a grandson he had raised. He knew that I would bury more ticking corpse-bombs and menacing sacks of gold after him.

He knew he would not be dug up because the village never unearthed anything embarrassing. We keep our scandals to ourselves. It takes something pretty grim or horrible for the police to be called in. We have never had a single case of rape or murder, while robbery, assault and battery, and other such irregularities are dealt with by our elected officials, loyally abetted by public pressure and the village newsletter.

I stood guard over the grave for a month. Avraham did nothing to encourage me, but neither did he try to dissuade me. Yosi and his mother seconded the general opinion that I was mad. Uri was amused. Pinness was horrified.

'I can't believe that this hideous dream is taking place right under my nose,' he said.

'Grandfather told me to do it,' I answered.

'It's unspeakable!' Pinness said.

'Grandfather told me to.'

'And such violence – flying chains, iron rods. You're like Cerberus guarding the gates of Hell.'

'Grandfather told me.'

Pinness looked at me sternly. Little by little, however, as though in an abstraction of surrender, he backed down. Grandfather knew that the perplexed old teacher would try to convince me and fail. Out on his long evolutionary limb, Pinness belonged to a generation whose necks were adapted to nooses of words. 'Buried in His Own Earth' or 'Here Lies the Farmer in the Soil He Tilled' were irresistible phrases for someone like him.

'And he died and was buried in the garden of his own house,' he quoted with open envy from the Bible.

Nor did he protest when I buried Shulamit. Fanya had a fit for a few days until she realised it was useless and calmed down. It was only when Rosa Munkin's coffin arrived several months later and her pink tombstone was unveiled next to Grandfather's, marking my professional début as an undertaker, that Pinness was shaken to the core.

The orchard was in its last days then. Despite Uri's prediction that the trees would flourish manured by Grandfather's body, the ones nearest his grave were as quick to die as if poisoned, while those farther away became ill and nervous: they crawled with aphids, rustled their branches in breezeless weather, dropped their fruit before it was ripe, and were mined by the shafts of every conceivable pest. They also flowered fitfully, their blossoms reeking of dead bees and flies killed by their toxic nectar and pollen. Margulis took his hives elsewhere. The wind rolled up the carpet of petals, leaving behind a hard layer of earth. Now and then I picked the fruits that hung from the dead branches, but they tasted and felt like meatballs. At night the owls and the polecats gnawed at them, and Grandfather's orchard soon died and rotted away.

Avraham had Grandfather's name carved on his tombstone with the dates of his birth and death and the verse that had served as the caption of the first tree he had ever planted.

'A green olive tree, fair, and of goodly fruit.'

## 37

During the first spring after Grandfather's death, the earth around his grave began to stir. Red beetles with black-spotted backs crawled out of it, awaiting the tread of more dead. Soon enough they arrived. Pioneer Home was a fact and the village was in an uproar. I refused to appear before the Committee for a hearing, from which Busquilla returned in high spirits to read me what he thought to be the protocol's most entertaining passage.

'"Comrade Liberson: Comrades, for the past year Comrade Baruch Shenhar has been burying dead people on the Mirkin farm. Comrade Shenhar started with his grandfather, whose will he claimed he was executing, without requesting permission from the authorities. A few months later he buried Shulamit Motzkin, a recent immigrant from Russia, whom you all know as the woman Ya'akov Mirkin lived with during his last months. Subsequently he began burying on a commercial basis, even importing the corpses of ex-émigrés.

'"Comrade Rilov: In the past half-year he's put away close to fifty stiffs.

'"Advocate Shapiro: I request that Mr Rilov resort to more dignified language.

'"Comrade Rilov: You're not dealing with just anyone. You're dealing with Committee! The Committee demands that Comrade Shenhar exhume the graves on the Mirkin farm and desist from any more such acts.

'"Advocate Shapiro: If I may be permitted a comment, we are discussing a livelihood, not 'acts'. My client makes his living by providing burial services to interested parties.

'"Busquilla: We've never buried anyone against his will.

'"Comrade Rilov: You shut up, Busquilla.

'"Comrade Liberson: The village has a perfectly fine tree-shaded cemetery on a hill overlooking the Valley, situated more than three miles away in conformity with hygienic requirements. This is not the case with the Mirkin farm, which is in a residential area.

'"Advocate Shapiro: According to the Public Health Act of 1940, subsequently amended in 1946, the Ministry of Health will not refuse a permit for the establishment of a new cemetery if: one, it is satisfied that said cemetery does not threaten to pollute any river, well, or other water source; and two, it is satisfied that on the date of opening said cemetery is at least one hundred yards from the nearest existing residence. Every new cemetery must be enclosed by a permanent fence or wall whose height shall be no less than five feet. Every cemetery must have adequate drainage. My client maintains that Pioneer Home meets these specifications and has been inspected and authorised by the appropriate government commission, in testimony of which I submit to you this licence.

'"Comrade Liberson: Comrade Shenhar is violating the village by-laws. We returned to the earth to farm it and to live by our own labours.

'"Advocate Shapiro: My client is acting in perfect conformity with the ideals of co-operative farming that you speak of. He employs no hired labour and pays all his taxes and dues to the co-operative as required. If I may be allowed to say so, my client is definitely engaged in returning Jews to the earth, and the homage paid by him to the pioneers of your Movement should be a source of pride and honour to it.

'"Comrade Rilov: That's enough of your stupid jokes.

'"Advocate Shapiro: My client quite literally earns his livelihood from the earth. He supports himself by his own labour, considers himself a tiller of the soil, regards the mortuary profession as a branch of agriculture, and uses agricultural tools to excavate, plant, fertilise, and irrigate his prospering business. His graves are drought-resistant, pest-resistant, frost-resistant, and disease-free. I hereby submit a detailed cost accounting demonstrating that an acre of graves is more profitable than any other agricultural crop, both in absolute terms and relative to the investment demanded."

'And that,' trilled Busquilla, 'is what killed them the most. Your profits, Comrade Shenhar. The cash. The fact that we make more money farming than they do.'

# 38

Pinness's scientific reputation dated back to his discovery of the prehistoric cave. 'The village and I were both young then,' he told me. Like all his pupils, I knew the cave well. It was on a rocky slope overlooking the Valley, at the far end of the village cemetery, its entrance hidden by a clump of prickly pears and the stone ruins of the German settlers. At my grandmother Feyge's funeral Pinness had noticed two Little Owls, a male and a female, bowing and curtseying to the mourners while curiously regarding them through slit golden eyes. 'My heart is smitten and withered like grass, so that I forget to eat my bread,' he eulogised his friend's wife. 'I am like a griffon of the wilderness; I am like an owl of the ruins.' Several days later he returned to find that the two small birds of prey were nesting among the stone ruins. Scattered on the ground were the silvery skulls of field mice, dry, hardened bird spew, and the wings of devoured grasshoppers. A stench of carrion arose from two little fledglings in a nest, whose white plumage and angry hisses made him think of a pair of Hasidic dwarfs.

'When I knelt to have a closer look at them, I spotted the entrance to the cave.'

At first he took it to be an ancient monk's cell. Making his way around a large rock, he hacked a path through the prickly pears and entered. The walls exuded a strange, dim odour, a whisper of quenched campfires, dry rot, and the gummiferous smell of frozen time. The flint tools that Pinness found were buried beneath a surface layer of ash and animal dung that was easily scooped away. As he dug farther, he came across the famous cranium that brought a team of scientists all the way from England. In this very cave, so their dig determined, had dwelt *Homo sapiens palestinaeus*.

'*Homo palestinaeus* was never *sapiens*,' I was told years later by Pinness, whose stroke had improved his sense of humour and made him more tolerant of shenanigans like Uri's and backbiting like Levin's.

The archaeologists from London found five human skeletons in the cave, three of adults and two of children. The thought of it gave Pinness the shivers. 'Just imagine them digging up our own graves someday! I can picture the pickaxes poking at Leah, baring the blue little bones of her poor innocent twins trapped between her rib cage and her pelvis.'

Stone weapons, a large buffalo femur split along its length, and the splintered vertebrae of rhinoceros calves told Pinness that the cave dwellers had been hunters and not farmers. An old sense of resentment came over him. The flint knives, the buried arrowheads, the thick, squat, beetle-browed skulls – all reminded him of Rilov.

Stepping back out of the cave, he sat in the entrance looking down on the broad, obeisant, fertile Valley at his feet. The humble cabins of the village, its infant streets and young shade trees, suddenly seemed to float on the fallow, long-historied earth, bobbing on its countless strata. The first geometric fields of the pioneers looked like so much patchwork, mere cobwebbery. He was still a young man, and the thought of vast epochs swinging over the Valley like pendulums induced in him a feeling of vertigo.

The Englishmen included an old professor who, Pinness said, 'took a grand liking to me', and a merry troupe of tall students in pith helmets and wide-bottomed knickerbockers who pitched a large tent on the hill and came down to the village each day to buy eggs, milk, and cheese. They took their midday meals at Riva Margulis's, paying for them in full, and nodding and stamping their stockinged feet beneath the table in surprised approval of the crystal service, the Siberian lace tablecloth, and the gold-rimmed drinking glasses.

'The Committee permitted Riva to use them, although they

were really hers anyway,' explained Pinness, his voice dropping to a whisper. 'They came in the steamer trunk her parents sent from Russia.'

By the time Pinness told me about the cave and its archaeological deposits, Riva's famed luxury trunk had long been buried beneath thick layers of earth and forgetfulness.

'That was one of the first trials we were put to.' Along with my uncle Avraham's poem, the plague of locusts during the Great War, and the death of Leah Pinness, Riva's trunk lay interred at such depths that only a hydraulic plough could have unearthed it.

'After marrying Margulis, Riva wrote her parents a letter about him and his bees telling them how she loved the hard field work and enclosing some photographs of herself – a little maid from the Land of Israel in a dress of coarse grey Arab cloth, scattering chicken feed in the yard and gathering honey from the hives.

'At the time of their wedding,' said Pinness, 'no one, not even Margulis himself, knew that the bride was the daughter of Beilin of Kiev, the richest Jew in the Ukraine.'

Six months later a cart arrived drawn by three span of oxen. Six Cossacks and four Cherkessians, Winchester rifles slipped through their saddles and gleaming daggers thrust in their belts, escorted it on small, nervous horses. It bore a large trunk out of which came ebony furniture, sets of dishes thinner than air, silk pillows, quilts puffed with goose down, blue lace curtains, and Bukharan rugs. Somehow Riva's parents had managed to smuggle out a trousseau under the eyes of the Bolsheviks. That evening Tonya Rilov, beside herself with envy and principles, insisted on convening the Committee, whose members had already noticed a wild gleam in the eyes of the female comrades. The urgently called session made it clear to Riva that the co-operative would not abide such luxuries in the home of a Hebrew farmer. Either she could send the trunk packing, or else she could pack and leave with it.

'I have a better suggestion,' proposed Margulis mildly. 'Riva and I have already talked it over and would like to donate the entire trousseau to the village.'

Choking on the lump in her throat, Riva nodded her agreement, and Rilov and Liberson were sent to take possession of her treasure. For years afterwards she had to watch ragged farmers eating from her family crystal, their grimy fingers clutching her gold forks while they jokingly addressed each other with courtly phrases, bowing, scraping, and dancing minuets in newly reaped fields. I can remember Pinness repeating the word 'narodniks' – Russian nobles – as he told me about it. Liberson, who never missed a chance to make his wife laugh and stay in her good graces, fashioned himself a beard out of corncobs, dressed up as Count Tolstoy, and sallied forth in a long white shirt to his comrades in the fields, greeting them as his serfs and serving them chilled lemonade in fancy glasses poured from a cut-glass jug.

Riva's lacquered Chinese sideboard stood in the Committee tent until it was eaten by oak borers. The silver was traded for six cows and a spoiled, evil-tempered Frisian bull. With one of the Bukharan rugs Rilov bought a disassembled howitzer, while the goose down was divided up among the villagers, each family getting an equal quiltful. Tonya and the village by-laws were satisfied; Riva sulked bitterly, even when Margulis reassured her that his honey tasted better licked from fingers than from golden spoons. He salved her rough hands with beeswax and dripped stalactites of honey on her navel, but she refused to be consoled. Although she seemed to have resigned herself to the village's verdict, 'she sobbed so gustily at night that you could hear Margulis's tent flaps whipping in the wind'.

'What even the Bolsheviks couldn't take from my father our own Reds stole from me,' she said to her husband.

Within two years all the crystal was broken. It was so transparent that it was invisible when empty, and glass after glass was swept off kitchen tables by the rude hands of the farmers.

Margulis spent the days herding his bees among the flowers. When the last cups and dishes were shattered, Riva was left to her own devices with nothing but dust, sweat, utopian visions, and the thick smell of cow manure.

'It was then that she went mad,' said Pinness. 'The normal feminine passion for cleanliness, which is simply a higher form of the nesting instinct, turned into an insane obsession.' Armed with a tightly bound kerchief, an apron, strips of old clothes, and a pair of rubber boots, she went forth to do battle each day.

First she banished the rubbish bin, since the presence of filth, even with a lid on, upset her delicate nerves. Dozens of times a day her children had to walk the hundred and fifty yards to the cowshed, where they dumped cucumber peels, breakfast leftovers, and swept-up table crumbs onto a big compost pile.

'She kept watching the skies,' put in Grandfather.

'Like Grandmother?' I asked.

Grandfather did not answer.

'Everyone in this village watched the skies,' said Liberson. 'For rain clouds. Or homing pigeons. Or locusts.'

'Or migrating birds,' added Fanya scornfully.

But Riva watched the skies because she expected the imminent arrival of dust clouds from the desert and flocks of defecating starlings from the north. 'Filthbirds,' she called them. Around her cabin she set out a dozen large flytraps, wooden crates with nets, a bait of meat or rotten fruit, and an opening below where the flies could swarm in but could not get out again. Such traps are used successfully in the village to this day, but Riva's were perpetually empty, since the flies soon learned that she and her house were poor pickings.

Every day the English scientists regarded her blithely when she made them remove their shoes before entering her house to eat their borscht, chicken, and potatoes; thanked her politely, and returned to their cave accompanied by Pinness.

'I used to join them because I liked their company, until Liberson informed me that no self-respecting socialist would be caught wolfing fried chicken paid for by the English bourgeoisie when his comrades were eating baked pumpkin and wild mallow.'

The English did not understand why Pinness stopped taking his meals with them. He, for his part, could not fathom why they never sang when they wielded their hoes.

After excavating and sifting thirty cubic yards of earth, the archaeologists ran into a huge slab of slate that blocked off the space behind it. There was an ominous rumble when they tried to move it. Pinness recommended consulting an expert mason who could find the fault lines in its veins and even brought such a man from Nazareth, an old Arab who descended into the cave, put an ear to the stone slab, scratched at it lightly with his chisel, tapped it with his fingers, and announced that it was as fragile as glass and would bury them all in a cave-in if they tried to break through. And so the back of the cave remained unexplored.

Eventually the Englishmen packed their finds and belongings and went home. The district governor had an iron door made for the cave entrance, locked it, and gave Pinness the key. None too gently, Rilov demanded that the cave be used for hiding dynamite and corpses and conducting secret initiation rites, but Pinness adamantly refused. With a surprisingly mulish show of courage he told Rilov that any sign of the door's having been tampered with would be reported to the governor at once.

The cave became his retreat. 'Everyone needs to bury himself somewhere,' he chuckled. Best of all he liked to sit in the entrance looking down on the Valley from an unconventional perspective of time and space. Though he never slept in it, fearing not only cave fever but all kinds of prehistoric diseases that the ticks which lived there might infect him with, odd strains of Neanderthalian typhus and even more primitive and incurably pre-anthropoid illnesses, he visited it often for research and meditation.

There in the bowels of the earth Pinness discovered blind snakes that lived off thallophytes, pallid salamanders that metamorphosed more slowly than their surface-dwelling cousins, and African wood lice that were unknown in Palestine. 'Living fossils,' he called them, struck by a mind-boggling thought. Not far from the cave grew a small stand of *Acacia albida*, 'the only surviving remnant of the African flora that invaded this country millions of years ago', and Pinness conjectured that the wood lice were relics of the same period. As he crouched watching these crablike immortals scuttle over the ground, the cave startled him by becoming the aperture of a time tunnel. The perseverance of such 'exceedingly wise lilliputians', who had managed to create an enduring society despite their lack of Movements, utopian visions, and historical traditions, filled him with a warm glow. With its exotic acacias, the cave seemed to him part of a primeval bubble unburst by time. Often he had to take a deep breath before entering its subterranean labyrinth, where he felt that he was sinking into the strange, viscous depths of a pocket of still hardening amber.

For years he brought his pupils to the cave. We would tramp for close to two hours through fields and up the steep hillside to plunge all at once into the cleft of a rock. Taking the key from his pocket, Pinness would open the grating iron door, releasing a chill, thick eddy of air that crawled inquisitively over our faces and bare legs. First he made us sit in the front of the cave by a small pool of water so old it had no taste at all, its sediments having long since settled to the bottom. Eyeless little creatures jetted back and forth on it. Though the aeons of darkness stored in their bodies blinded anyone who looked at them, their soft forms could be felt as they brushed the backs of our hands.

Pinness showed us how to make blades out of flint, made us try lighting a fire by rubbing stones, and shepherded us back to the ledge outside the cave for a view of the Valley and the village.

'The cavemen,' he told us, 'sat looking down on our Valley from here too.' There were large sumac and oak trees then, ash and juniper, and wild animals – 'the spotted leopard, the roaring lion, and the charging bear'.

He rose to his feet. 'And the land was watered like a garden of the Lord,' he declaimed. 'A stream of pure water ran through the Valley, whose white mists hid the earth. Large herbivores pastured in the reeds – wild boar, hartebeests, hippopotami, and bison. The cavemen descended to the Valley to hunt them and split their bones on this ledge with stone hammers and knives.'

Pinness could all but hear the bellows of the slaughtered wild oxen and the rip of hunters' bellies slashed by the tusks of the boar. His eyes unpeeled the earth, plunging into the quicksand of the past as he told us about the primeval rain forests that had once covered the globe and about the cichlids and wild ostriches that had migrated to the Valley from Africa long before the first human beings. That tiny killer, the shrew, must have migrated from the glacial north; the rabbit and the agamid lizard from somewhere across the Mediterranean; and the sparrow and the genet from the distant steppes of Asia.

Avian wings, anthropoid legs, bovine hooves, and carnivorous claws lay all around him in the earth. Canaanites, Turkomans, white wagtails, Jews, Romans, wild goats, Arabs, swamp cats, German children, Damascene cows, and English soldiers had vied to leave their prints in the crumbling and amnesiac soil.

He was not a historian, just a modest and inquisitive peda-gogue, 'a folk teacher', as he liked to call himself, whose subjects were Nature, the Bible, the cycles of the year, the extinction of species, and the resurrected bodies of ancient gods and visions.

'I'm a woolly mammoth, frozen in ice,' he told me, spewing bits of food as he laughed. 'Whoever digs me out will find I'm still edible.' In the course of his own lifetime, 'which is but a blink in the evolutionary process', he had seen the griffon vulture disappear from the skies of the Valley, had witnessed the introduction of animals that understood human speech, and had heard the warble of the blackbird, which had left its old habitat in the hills of the Lower Galilee to settle in our village.

His mind was still whole in those days, well rounded and defended, before his illness had made heretical inroads. And yet even when younger, he had felt the futility of all things. The famous Via Maris, 'the Way of the Seal', along which countless conquerors and traders had crossed the Valley, was nothing but a wretched scratch on the surface of the earth. The ancient walled city of Megiddo to the west, with its mighty fortresses and bottomless storehouses, was a crumbling pile of ruins at the foot of the blue mountain range. The once living stream, 'that ancient river, the river Kishon', in which the nine hundred chariots of Sisera had sunk, was now a mendacious sewer. Field marshals and altars had been swallowed up by the depths, palaces had crumbled like bones, like old aqueducts, like ancient terracing, like the vineyard of the nearby kibbutz. Barely two generations had passed since Liberson's elopement through the grapevines with Fanya, and already it was uprooted, covered with concrete and a plastics factory, the entire story forgotten.

Pinness envied the caveman, who had wandered to this guileless land without biblical get-thee-outs to find it unpossessed and unscarred by the petty footprints of human loyalty and love, 'driven only by his own hunger and thirst and an innocent appetite, retained by every living cell to this day, for that warm, moist thing we call life'.

He also envied Meshulam, who, caring nothing for the long pinions of Time, chose to follow its winged flight only from the day the founding fathers first alighted in the Valley. Oblivious to the forces of disintegration and rot, Meshulam shut his eyes to the chalk-white bones, the fossilised ostrich eggs, and the broken slivers of giant shells that Pinness lovingly collected. Everything that had happened before the founding of the village seemed to him one long, superfluous column of negative numbers.

'Meshulam is convinced that it was the founders of the village who drove away the cavemen and the swamp flora and poisoned the mastodons and the cave bears before weeding the crabgrass and planting vegetables. He thinks the earth just sat here waiting for them, trembling like a bashful bride.

'And for whom? For whom? Waiting for whom?' chanted the old teacher in a thin, mocking voice. Towards the end of his life he had mastered all the subtleties of sarcasm. He understood now how easily the earth shook off whatever trivial images men cloaked it in. 'Why, it's nothing but a tissue of poor fictions anyway, the earth!' he exclaimed. 'A thin crust beneath which is nothing but pure selfishness, a speck of dust at the far end of a minor galaxy.

'The earth cheated on us,' Pinness informed me with a salacious smile. 'She wasn't the virgin we thought she was.'

# 39

Now, old, heavy, and myopic, Pinness could penetrate at a glance so far into space and so deep into earth that he suffered from attacks of vertigo and fainted on the floor of his room amid bits of leftover meatloaf, preserved caterpillars, and dry crusts of bread. This was the state Meshulam found him in when he arrived one day, devastated by a new piece of research that dealt with our very own village.

He shook Pinness awake and helped him into bed before furiously waving under the old teacher's nose one of the many journals he subscribed to. It was a publication called *The Land of Israel Historian*, and on its cover was a large, oddly reddish fish curled around the Cave of the Patriarchs with its nose in the scales of its tail.

'The latest is that they say there were no swamps here,' shouted Meshulam irately. 'What doesn't pass for research these days!'

With his grey hair and clawing fingers Meshulam resembled an irritable Egyptian vulture. Turning the pages until he came to an article entitled 'The Swamps of the Valley of Jezreel: Myth and Reality', he began reading out loud, his shaky forefinger jumping from line to line.

'Listen to this! "For propagandistic and political purposes, the Zionist movement created around the Valley of Jezreel a symbolic mythology of swamps, malaria, and death. In fact, ninety-nine per cent of the Valley was not swampland at all."'

Pinness, who was by then being touted by febrile journalists as 'one of the last pioneers of the Valley of Jezreel', clutched at Meshulam's words as if they were straw that might rescue him from his swoons of heresy, or an anchor whose stability amid the labyrinthine caves of time and the treacherous chutes of space could restore him to the safety of his old beliefs.

'Go on,' he said.

'"The evidence indicates that at the beginning of the period of modern Jewish settlement, swampland in the Valley of Jezreel was not widespread,"' Meshulam recited. '"This, of course, is at variance with the picture given by Zionist sources, which created the Myth of the Swamp. Although the actual extent of the swamps was small, their imaginative appeal was enormous."'

Meshulam repeated the words 'imaginative appeal' several times with barely suppressed fury, sipped some tea, and declared that 'they', those '*muzhiks* who call themselves historians', had even cited his father's and Liberson's memoirs 'to advance their tissue of lies', making a mockery of the truth by 'quoting selectively at their convenience'.

'But they don't know who they're up against!' he roared at the ceiling. 'I've got all the documents and proofs. Now you see why I saved all those papers even when everyone laughed at me.

'Look at this,' he said, pointing at the journal. 'The frauds actually mention my father!'

He began to read again. '"Before the village was established, its founders surveyed the site. One of them, a certain Tsirkin who was nicknamed 'Guitar', wrote in his memoirs: 'We went to have a look at our first swamp and saw a clump of bright green willow trees. Swamps like this, we were told by those who knew, were nothing to be afraid of, because ordinary drainage ditches could lower the water level until they disappeared.'"'

'Guitar,' gagged Meshulam, glancing at Pinness to see if he was similarly aghast.

'Read on, Meshulam,' said Pinness.

'Now I'll read you what my father actually wrote, the part these so-called scholars never quoted,' Meshulam said, opening the familiar green volume of his father's memoirs, *On Native Paths*, which he himself had edited, published, and given a copy of to every family in the village a few years previously.

'"A green carpet of brackish water that collected in sinkholes and hollows lay everywhere, infested with all kinds of pests."' He leafed through the pages until he found the famous passage that had once appeared in *The Young Worker* and could still be found in school readers. '"We looked all around us at the green pools with their stagnant water and were far from overjoyed. The rank green rushes were taller than a man. The swamp was green too. But it was deep with promise, though its big and little marshes were crawling with mosquitoes."'

That evening, when I had returned from my graves and was helping Avraham with the milking, Meshulam appeared at our place too. Over the whirr of the electric motors and the blasts of compressed air he vociferously told me, Avraham, and the sceptical cows how the founding fathers had 'drained the evil waters' until 'they shook all over from malaria', wallowing 'waist-deep in muck' while laying clay pipes in accordance with the Breuer system and singing the pioneer ditty 'Friend of the Frog'.

'"Despite the warnings of Doctor Yoffe and the fever we all came down with, we cut papyrus with our sickles until our arms ached and our shoulders felt like stone,"' he held forth from his father's memoirs. '"Under absolutely no circumstance must you try settling in such a place,"' he quoted Doctor Yoffe, the country's leading expert on malaria. Meshulam knew a large portion of the documents in his possession by heart.

We were busy opening and shutting air valves. By the time Avraham switched off the Alfa-Laval vacuum pump, Meshulam had moved on to the high ground of principle, castigating 'the epidemic of cynicism that has infected the public' and 'the pathetic hunger for publicity and sensationalism that you find among academics, which will soon spread throughout our society, this village not excepted.'

In those days Avraham no longer brought his milk churns to the dairy. His cows yielded such prodigious quantities of milk that he had installed his own refrigerator in the yard, and the village tanker emptied it every day. Now, checking its temperature, he remarked that perhaps Meshulam should write an article for the papers. But Meshulam merely spat angrily and said that the press was 'part of the conspiracy' and that 'something drastic must be done to set this country on its ear'.

'It's scandalous,' admitted Pinness, grateful to be released for a while from the clutches of the cavemen and the slow crumbling of the Via Maris into a world that had reassuringly contracted to the dimensions of a local outrage. 'Today it's Guitar Tsirkin and tomorrow they'll say there were never any pioneers to begin with. Why, Doctor Yoffe was here in person and declared that this place was every bit as bad as the swamps of Hadera.'

He wrote a long article and sent it to the Movement newspaper, which not only failed to print it but did not even bother to return it. Pinness was cut to the quick. Resentfully he recalled all the pieces that he and his fellow pedagogues had regularly published in Movement dailies and periodicals in the past. 'A little poem' of his had even been printed in *The Young Worker* in a special box bordered by flowers, and had been set to music by Mandolin Tsirkin. Every child in the Valley could sing its refrain in a piping, confident voice:

> Say ye not the flesh is weary,
> Say ye not the dream is fled.
> Be in this land a pioneer, ye!
> Never shall ye bow your head.

In the end Pinness turned to the village treasurer and asked for a grant to publish the article at his own expense. He was given the money and the piece appeared, but the words 'Paid Advertisement' at the bottom seared his soul like a humiliating tattoo.

Under the title 'A Land That Devoureth Its Inhabitants', Pinness referred to the Swamp Revisionists as 'promiscuous-mouthed hypocrites' and related his own memories.

'On our visit to the site we saw the graves of the Germans who had tried to settle there before us and died of malaria. Later we met an old Arab who was ploughing with a team of oxen.

'"Don't you suffer from swamp fever?" I asked him.

'"No," he said. "If you come to live here, you will have four years of war, because that's how long you will fight your own blood, but if you are alive at the end of them, you will go on living."

'"What about your children?" I asked. "Do many of them die?"

' "Yes," he said. "The old people live, but the children, Allah takes them."

'A year later my wife Leah died of malaria with two infants in her womb, sinless twins who never saw the light of day. As the chief butler says to Pharaoh, "I do remember my faults today." I sought to take my own life, but my comrades snatched my gun from me. My wife and twins were the victims of the imaginary swamps of the Valley of Jezreel.'

In the village, the old argument over Pinness's rifle was revived.

'What is he yacking about that gun again for? He forgot to take it with him,' said Meshulam, who considered Pinness's article a red herring.

'Rilov removed the firing pin,' said Levin.

'You weren't even here then,' Levin was told.

'Rilov was carrying on with Leah Pinness,' declared Riva Margulis.

'That whore never died of malaria. She died of cave fever,' said Tonya Rilov.

'Whoever should know knows, and whoever shouldn't doesn't,' said Rilov, sticking his head out of his septic tank for a breath of fresh air before resubmerging and vanishing from sight.

# 40

I was thrilled by the publication of Pinness's advertisement. For the first time, I saw the words of the stories I knew spread out on the printed page for all to see. I looked back at the mountain, searching once more for the figure of Shifris, the green of Efrayim's eye, the glimmer of Jean Valjean's horns. Uri scoffed at any mention of this trio and asked me in his sardonic letters whether Efrayim would also carry Shifris on his back or Shifris would carry Efrayim and Jean Valjean on his.

Nevertheless, although Pinness's article aroused a degree of interest in the village and the area, the great public debate he had hoped for failed to materialise.

Meshulam, as bitter as the leaves of a cornflower, exclaimed, 'I told you so. This country needs a shaking up!'

Returning to Founder's Cabin, he settled down among his old rolling pins, washboards, sooty lanterns, clay pots, sieves, winnowers, butter churns, millstones, and oil incubators to launch a new project, namely, a diorama of the swamp and its draining. Visitors, so he hoped, would come from all over the country to see it.

With no little effort he dug a large, shallow pit in his yard and filled it with water. 'I'm founding a swamp,' he answered all inquiries, and since the heavy black Valley soil is not very porous, the water remained there for several days. I went to have a look at it. It was already a little swamp of sorts: mosquitoes and dragonflies had come to lay their eggs in it, protozoal algae had tinged it a mythical green, and a loudly singing Meshulam had hastened to dig drainage ditches and plant a few eucalyptus branches in the mud. At that point, however, his neighbours, unable to stand the mosquitoes and the oestrous croaking of the frogs, broke into his yard at night, gave him a good beating, and drained the little bog with a sewage pump hooked up to a tractor engine. The issue came up at a general meeting of the village, at which Meshulam announced that he had just begun to fight. And indeed, in the days that followed, his annoying puddles turned up in the most unexpected places, such as the entrance to the village, the lawn in front of the meeting house, the public war memorial, and the nursery.

Following Meshulam one night, I saw him drag a fireman's hose from the school hydrant to the nursery playground, where toddlers arriving at seven-thirty in the morning discovered that the sandpit built years ago by the Gang was completely flooded, its contents blasted all over the yard by the pressurised water. In it stood a shirtless Meshulam, his trousers rolled up to his knees, waiting to be carried off by malaria. The hair on his chest was a furious grey, his head was streaked red by his father's gypsy bandanna, and plastic toys in all colours floated around his legs.

The sight of the blond, innocently chirping youngsters coming upon such a scene alarmed me. I knew it was silly, but it did.

Not that anything happened. The children were of course frightened, and two became totally hysterical; one, Ya'akovi's son, stuttered for months afterward; but that was all. Meshulam, standing in the middle of his swamp, was not bitten by a single anopheles mosquito, although a sudden, mocking breeze blew the hair of some processionary moth caterpillars out of the nearby pine trees, which did make his shoulders itch for a long time to come.

That same week we went to visit Uri. He asked about Zeitser, whom he called 'Productivus Bound', and inquired after Pinness, whose 'adverticle' he had seen in the newspaper. I told him about Meshulam's latest madness. 'King Jonquil of the Swamps,' pronounced Uri, and we both burst out laughing. When Rivka said that she saw no difference between Meshulam's swamps and my cemetery, however, Uri grew suddenly serious and told his mother that the village had more surprises in store for it, and that now, from a distance, he could more clearly see the processes of disintegration that he himself had played a part in.

We drove home in time for a nap. An onerous heat lay over the yard. The cows were asleep in their pen. The refrigerator motors hummed quietly in the milk shed. Farther off we saw Zeitser lying under his fig tree with his head covered. No one gave it a second thought, because Zeitser liked to shade himself in hot weather with an old green cloth, but when we rose from our nap the waning sun's rays glinted off an army of green flies. Avraham let out a great bitter cry and ran to the old mule, whose head was wrapped in the necrophagous blanket of the outdoors.

Zeitser was still breathing. His ribs rose and sank slowly. An odd, sticky, round object lay on the ground by his neck. It took a few seconds to absorb the full horror of what we were looking at and to realise that it was the mule's left eyeball, which a flying stone had dislodged from its socket.

A puddle of blood, scattered stones, the tracks of familiar work boots, and the imprint of frantic hooves made what had

happened all too clear. Taking advantage of our absence, Shlomo
Levin had stolen into the yard during the hot noon hours when
everyone was closeted indoors and stoned Zeitser from a safe
range until he succeeded in knocking the mule's eye out.

Avraham called for the vet, a kindhearted man who had
never given much thought to the true relations between farmers
and their animals. They crouched together by Zeitser's side to
examine the terrible wound.

'It's a bad one,' said the vet. 'He's very old. We'll have to give
him a shot.'

'A shot?' said Avraham.

'Between the eyes,' replied the vet, getting to his feet.

Avraham threw him out of the yard. He brought a cattle
hypodermic and some sulpha from the medicine cabinet in
the cowshed, cleaned, disinfected, and bandaged the mule's
eye socket, and pumped a quart and a half of Biocomb into his
veins. Tears kept running down his cheeks, but his hands were
sure and steady. He sat by Zeitser's side for three whole nights,
and then, despairing of conventional remedies, filled some baby
bottles with sweetened skimmed milk, barley gruel, and brown
rice in poppy aspic and fed him as though he were a newborn calf
critically ill with dysentery.

The old mule just wheezed and kept dying, too weak even to
open his good eye. In the end the only thing that saved his life
was Grandfather's black tree tar, a can of which I kept in the
cabin. Taking a chance, Avraham applied a whole handful of it
to the deep, abscessing hole in Zeitser's head, and within a few
hours the stubborn old creature revived and my uncle went home
to sleep.

I watched him from behind the trunk of the olive tree, walking
slowly with his head down, the air eddying around him while the
night light of the cowshed dripped shadows from his feet.

I always liked Avraham. Though he never talked much or
displayed physical affection, I felt I knew what he suffered inside
himself. He had added a wistfulness of his own to the yearning
inherited from Grandfather and Grandmother. I haven't seen him
for years, but when I think of him today it's still crouching by

Zeitser's big body, or bent over the milk jetting out of his cows, or crossing the yard in his yellow rubber boots and blue work clothes, his frightful forehead carving furrows in the air.

Levin never showed his face at our place again. 'Efrayim would have put a bullet in him,' said Yosi when he came home on his first leave from basic training. He was all for such military retaliations against Levin as kneecapping or antipersonnel-mining him, but Avraham convinced us to let the matter drop and keep his uncle's heinous deed a secret. Eventually, though, word got around. It was the old itinerant barber who spread the tidings over the Valley, from every corner of which Zeitser's friends came to visit him.

They were old, these last founding fathers. With their worker's caps, grey shirts, and rheumatic, work-gnarled fingers, they all looked like Grandfather. Each having withdrawn into a shell of his own, they hadn't had such a reunion in years. Some hadn't seen each other since my parents' wedding. Now they strolled about our yard and descended as one man to the fig tree, ploughed earth beneath their feet and tall skies of words above their heads. They were as tough as nails, it was said of them in the village, a generation of titans and tribal chieftains. Once, when Grandfather was alive and still his old cynical self, I remembered him saying to Pinness that his comrades' suspicions and disputatiousness would eventually lead them to the ultimate in factional splits: schizophrenia.

After visiting Zeitser, they trooped on down to my cemetery, a single grey monolith, stopping at the graves of their friends, sniffing the flowering ornamentals, and conversing in quiet tones without rancour. I stood off to one side, not daring to approach them.

Like Grandfather, many of them had grown small and short, the first sign of their impending death. Years of loving too much, hating too long, being disappointed too often, and searching their souls too hard had burned out their cells and sapped their vitality. 'We were the sour orange stock onto which the Jewish state was grafted,' said Eliezer Liberson to me a few days before he died, though not wishing to sound boastful, he added at once that the sour orange was 'a most horrible-tasting fruit'.

Half hiding behind my back, Busquilla whispered timidly, 'You'll see, Baruch, everything will be all right now.' He already knew some of the old-timers well, those who had ventured to buy a plot for themselves while still alive.

The pioneers surveyed their future resting place as they had surveyed the earth of the Valley upon arriving there years before. Each step they took was met by answering vibrations from Grandfather. His old comrades did not even have to put their ears to the ground, because the broad soles of their feet conveyed his sound to the panniers of their bodies. Though I did not have the nerve to follow them, I knew from my vantage point by the hedge that Busquilla was right and that my quarrel with the elders of the Valley was nearing its end.

Once they had gone home, it became clear that Grandfather's rotting body, Rosa Munkin's moneybags, and the other capitalist traitors I had buried had not merely poisoned the orchard and sowed confusion. Within a few weeks, as though by mutual consent, the voice of the old pioneers was raised in lament across the Valley. Pinness, who was accustomed to painstaking observation and precise notation, was the first to understand what was happening. Once recovered from the initial fright of his own uncontrollable crying, he began to make out the sobs and snuffles of the others and to realise that he was hearing something more than the smothered threnody of cornered moles or the wailing of fruit sprayed with pesticide.

'A voice is heard on high, lamentation and bitter weeping,' he pronounced.

The barely audible yet all-penetrating sound of deeply cleared throats, loudly blown noses, and painfully swallowed lumps made the night air shudder. No jaw was clenched tightly enough to stop the sobs that escaped it. Softly these flowed from the wrin-kled vulture throats of the founding fathers, easily overcoming the resistance of bald gums and rumpled lips. 'They're softening up the earth,' declared Pinness, who told me about the amazing digging capacities of certain insects.

Soon word began to reach us from other villages, travelling as fast as a dust devil. The old itinerant barber, who came once a month on his ancient motorcycle, told us that Yehoshua Krieger, the chicken breeder from the kibbutz of Nir Ya'akov who had invented the fuelless incubator and drafted the first workers' manifesto in Gedera, claimed to be growing roots. Krieger's announcement was made at his ninetieth birthday party, which was celebrated by a large crowd, and would not have bothered anyone had he not planted himself by the water pipe leading to the grain fields, thus interfering with the laying of irrigation lines and the tractors finishing the autumn ploughing. Each time they tried to remove him he began to scream horribly, insisting that he was in devilish pain because his little rootlets were being torn.

In the end, said the barber, Krieger had to be dug up with a great clump of earth clinging to his feet and replanted among the cypresses by the approach to the kibbutz, where he stood waving at whoever came and went, harassing embarrassed young female volunteers from abroad, and pestering everyone with incorrect weather forecasts.

Yitzchak Tsfoni, who had ploughed the first furrow at the Valley's eastern end, pressing down on the ploughshare with one hand while firing his gun wildly with the other, took to wandering around the centre of his village with baskets of reddish soft-shelled eggs that he said he had laid himself. Believing they would bring him eternal youth, he ate them avidly and tried to get his children and grandchildren to do so too.

'It's not illogical,' said Pinness, straining to catch a glimpse of the back of his new haircut in the mirror. 'Eating your own eggs could turn the linear flow of time into a circle.'

Ze'ev Ackerman, who had lived on the kibbutz next door, completed construction of a revolutionary new food machine with which he appeared one day in Pioneer Home, accompanied by his sheepish-looking son.

I remembered them well from my visits to Grandfather in the old folk's home. Ackerman had been the kibbutz plumber for years and had always complained bitterly about the snobbery of the field hands. When these 'princes of the wheat fields', as he called them, came to the communal dining hall smelling of earth and hay, he, reeking of linseed oil, soap fumes, and sewage, would sit there watching them jealously.

Now, in the old folk's home, he toyed with the kibbutz members who came once a month to beg him to reveal the location of the underground water and sewage pipes he had installed years before. He alone had a map of the system, and the kibbutz gardeners were forced to look on distraughtly while three whole lawns were dug up to find leaks, blockages, and the whereabouts of pipes that the angry old man kept a zealously guarded secret.

He himself devoted his spare time and vast technical knowledge to a single all-consuming project, his 'constructivist revenge', as he called it, a machine made of pipes, tanks, and shiny little solar receptors whose valves he had turned on the lathe belonging to the old folk's home's handyman.

Old Ackerman was overcome with emotion when Grandfather came to the home. 'There was so much we could have done together if it hadn't been for that oversexed friend of yours, Eliezer Liberson,' he said, reminding Grandfather of the incident of the cow.

He asked about Mandolin Tsirkin and the Feyge Levin Workingman's Circle, wiped a tear as he thought of Grandmother, whom he called 'a pioneer's pioneer', inquired after Zeitser, who had worked with him in Yavne'el, and then, grabbing Grandfather by the sleeve and sitting him down on his bed, began haranguing him about his machine, which would revolutionise agricultural life.

'No more hard work and farm animals, day and night, rain or shine. My machine will manufacture food from earth, sunlight, and water. It will drink and breathe, photosynthesise and flower, store nutrients and produce fruit just like any plant.'

He filled a large pan at the bottom of the machine with earth. 'Now I'll add some water with the necessary chemicals at this end, while at that end the good sunshine of our Valley is concentrated by the receptors. Those are the controls over there.

'Look, Baruch,' he said to me when a muffled clank came from the machine's depths. 'We have reaped a bounteous harvest, the aubergine and radish together.'

He cranked a few handles, and indeed, with a great deal of clicking and grinding, a slow, grimy trickle of something resembling mashed potatoes flowed from the machine. The old man scooped up a spoonful of it and thrust it radiantly in my face.

'Go on, try it,' he urged. 'It tastes exactly like radish. You'll never know the difference.'

'That's enough, Father. Stop,' whispered his embarrassed son.

Whenever I brought Ackerman the cakes and fruits his son sent him, he would give me a mocking smile and say that cake was bad for the system, and as for fruit, he had all he could eat from his machine, stoneless and easy to chew. Aggrieved, he told me how none of the places he had written to had taken his invention seriously.

'Even the milk,' he added, 'even the milk you bring your grandfather, though it's certainly good of you to do so, can be taken from my machine. Milk and honey too – both, if you don't mind my putting it crudely, nothing but animal secretions. And when my machine is old, no one will put it on the chopping block or throw it into an old folk's home. No, indeed. They will not!'

I was so upset by Ackerman that I told Pinness about him.

'We never thought we would grow old,' said Pinness, who had grown weak from despair and very old himself ever since Uri's beating at the foot of the water tower. 'Having come to this country together, and worked together, and settled the Valley together, we were certain we would die together too.'

'It's a fact,' confirmed Meshulam. 'You won't find a single document of theirs referring to old age. They discussed everything under the sun – the proper diet for a pregnant comrade, the fairest way to divide up work clothes, whether to invest in a pair of city shoes for the village treasurer. The only subject that never came up was what to do about themselves when they grew old.'

'The battle with old age is a very private one,' sighed Pinness. 'It was never a matter for the Movement. When it's time for me to depart this world, all I ask is a clear mind to face my death with.'

Today Ackerman is buried in row six, plot seventeen of my cemetery. His food machine lies behind the kibbutz cowshed, shiny, abandoned, and silent. Some experts from the Institute of Technology who had heard of it tried to operate it and gave up. No one besides Ackerman could get it to work, just as the sour orange tree by our cabin, which had borne, so it was said, lemons, pears, apricots, and quinces, stopped yielding when Grandfather died. Green, unfriendly, and infertile, it stands in the yard with the rude nests of sparrows, impudent patchworks of straw and stolen feathers, hanging from its branches.

Only Zeitser, in whose honour the old people had come to our village, bore his suffering in silence, as if determined to live out his life with as much circumspection as possible. Now and then I untied him and took him to the cemetery, where he stood in the cool shade of the trees, unrebuked by me if he cropped the grass or trampled a flower on his blind side.

Meshulam's swamp fever seemed to have passed too. 'Tsirkin is down with his final illness,' said Pinness of Meshulam's father. Meshulam so wished to give the old man some pleasure in his last days that he even began working on the farm. And yet, said Pinness, like all revenges, Tsirkin's too was ripening poignantly, deep beneath the fragile membranes of broad wheat fields and smooth skin.

A few weeks before his death Mandolin Tsirkin asked to see me. He still lived at home and was dead set against going to the old folk's home. 'I don't need to have my fingers broken by some physiotherapist while a young intern sticks tubes up my backside.'

Irritable and grumpy, Tsirkin could barely walk. Meshulam pushed him around the village in a wheelbarrow padded with sacks.

'Who but a good-for-nothing like him would have time to take care of his old father,' grumbled Tsirkin. 'At least he's finally found something to do with himself.'

'You're not going to catch me riding around in one of those Odessa *droshkies*,' announced Mandolin when Meshulam suggested buying an electric car like those used by old people on the kibbutzim.

He felt bone-weary. He couldn't work any more. His rich fields with their fine fruit trees and the best hay, wheat, and cotton in the village fell fallow. Bindweed, creeping grass, and prosopis spread their wild, ominous drapery over the Tsirkin farm. Whole families of mice escaping from poison in the neighbouring fields found shelter in the abandoned soil and used it as a staging post for raids on their former territories. Although the Committee kept demanding that Meshulam stamp them out and farm his fields, this was simply beyond his capacities. The farmers consulted Liberson, who racked his brains and remembered that the village had been visited in its first years by an eccentric Egyptian agronomist who claimed that mice had a horror of broad beans. And indeed, when the fields surrounding Meshulam's were planted with these beans on Liberson's orders, the inexplicable magic worked its spell. The mice kept to Meshulam's property, where they multiplied steadily until hunger, overcrowding, and internal dissension caused them to grow long fangs and turn into predators. Every night we could hear their hoarse death groans and roars of vengeance as they devoured one another. The broadbean barrier, explained Pinness, had turned Tsirkin's fields into an evolutionary cul-de-sac whose inhabitants could never mutate back again.

Meanwhile, their udders bursting, Mandolin Tsirkin's cows screamed and cursed in pain while the old man sat in his wheelbarrow trying to teach his son how to milk. Never before in his life had Meshulam held a female nipple.

'For years we milked by hand,' thundered the old man. 'By hand! And you mean to tell me you can't even open the stopcock of a milking machine?'

'She's got an infected udder, you imbecile, can't you see? Why are you torturing the poor thing?'

His arthritis drove Tsirkin mad. Warped like a kite's talons, his fingers froze. The calloused skin of his palms dried and split into a network of deep fissures that caused him terrible pain. He could no longer milk, prune trees, or play the mandolin. One day he was told by Tanchum Peker the saddler that the old peasants of the Crimea cured rheumatism with bee toxin. The next morning I took him to Margulis's grave, where he pulled off his shirt, rose with difficulty from his wheelbarrow, let down his trousers, and stood leaning against the gravestone, his body gleaming in the sun while he waited to be stung by Margulis's inconsolable bees. Tonya gave him an angry look but said nothing. Removing what was left of her fingers from her mouth, she vanished into the trees – among which, clustered like fruit in the dense foliage, two generations of village children were hiding in the hope of getting a glimpse of a founding father's behind.

In pain and impatient, Tsirkin shouted and waved his hands at the bees to no avail. Long years of work and music had made him smell so good that they took him for a giant flower rather than a honey thief and landed in swarms on his shoulders, crawling docilely over his back and bare bottom.

After an hour of this, he asked to be taken home. The bees had left orange pollen in the wrinkles of his neck and the cleft between his buttocks. Busquilla cleaned him off carefully with a large, soft brush, helped him to put on his shirt and knot the rope belt on his trousers, and followed us back to the village.

The three of us sat on Tsirkin's bed beneath the mulberry tree. He had taken to sleeping outside again on summer nights, because the heat brought Pesya's damnable perfume steaming out of the walls of the house, torturing the old man's nose and principles.

'Listen here, Baruch,' he said to me. 'I'm not long for this world. I want you to set aside a good place for me next to your grandfather.'

'It's yours for the asking,' said Busquilla.

'If you don't mind, I was talking to Mirkin's child,' said Tsirkin in an icy tone. He paused for a moment. Tsirkin never uttered a sentence without making sure that the sentence before it had been understood.

'I want you to bury my mandolin with me, like you did with

Margulis and his honey. Like all those little Pharaohs in Egypt with their ivory toys and dung beetles.'

'Fine,' I said.

'It's not so simple, because Meshulam took it to his museum when I stopped playing.'

Getting Meshulam to surrender a historical artifact was an impossible mission, but Tsirkin had thought of everything. 'On top of the beam in my hayloft, in the far corner, you'll find a little box. Bring it to me. Don't worry, Meshulam won't catch you. He never goes to the hayloft unless he's forced to.'

I cleaned the pigeon droppings and spider webs off the box and brought it to him.

'It's got all kinds of old papers and crap in it,' grinned Tsirkin. 'A shopping list of the Workingman's Circle from June 1919, a letter to me from Hankin, and a letter from Shifris that the pelicans brought from Anatolia ten years ago. No one knows it except me and Liberson, but that mad old man is getting closer all the time.'

'Should I give it to Meshulam?'

Tsirkin looked at me as though I were a moron.

'Of course not!' he screeched. 'Just tell him that you'll trade it for the mandolin. If he's the idiot I think he is, he'll agree. There's nothing he loves more than papers. I want you to bury the mandolin in the coffin with me so that the worms can play me music on it.'

# 41

Two weeks later, in the middle of the night, Zeitser broke free without warning from the rope that tethered him to the fig tree, went to Shlomo Levin's house, raised one hoof, knocked politely on the door, and stepped aside to wait. Levin came out to see who it was, but by the time he recognised the mule's huge silhouette lunging at him in the darkness, he knew it was too late. Cocking his head to see his foe with his good eye, Zeitser bared his yellow teeth, sank them in Levin's upper arm, and bore down as hard as he could with all the powerful hatred left in his old jaws. He tore the flabby biceps to tatters, splintering the crunchy humerus as a froth of thin blood bubbled up amid the shreds and slivers. There was no time for Levin to scream. He passed out on the spot while Zeitser padded quietly back to his barrel of feed and his fig tree.

In the small hours of the morning Rachel Levin noticed that her husband was not in bed and hurried outside to find him green and moaning among the garden plants. Her screams woke the whole village, and Yosi drove Levin to the hospital. At first there was talk of a new hyena, but that afternoon Avraham came to the Committee office to confess that the culprit was Zeitser. The district veterinarian was called for, and following an investigation he ordered that Zeitser be shot as required by law.

There was an uproar. Avraham ran berserkly home, sobbing and slinging earth. When the vet appeared with a policeman, Zeitser was gone from the yard, because my uncle had already hidden him in the thicket by the spring. I had been busy pouring concrete that morning for the erection of two new gravestones and only heard the news when I returned home in the afternoon. Avraham refused to tell me the mule's whereabouts, but when I went down to the spring to be alone the next day I discovered him there, his empty eye socket shedding slow tears of pus.

'I'll bring you some barley,' I said. But Zeitser was beyond all that: ambling in his dreams along familiar paths, he was smelling blossoms whose names had been forgotten, the likes of which could only be found in my mother's old album of dried flowers. In the evening Avraham came to stand guard against wild beasts and bureaucrats. Close to midnight, however, he dozed off, and Zeitser, taking advantage of the opportunity, slipped away to the fields.

It was dawn when we towed his big truncated body back from the highway. Zeitser knew that at 3 a.m. every day the milk lorry started out for the city, and he had waited for it by the roadside.

'He jumped out and lay in front of the Mack's wheels,' related

Motik the driver, still in a state of shock. 'With twenty-eight tons of milk in the tank, there was nothing I could do.'

Chipped and falling apart from years of hard labour, Zeitser smashed against the tanker's big bumper like a clay doll. Tyre marks, tufts of hair, dusty bloodballs, rashers of mule meat, and cracklings of old skin were strewn along three hundred yards of road, up and down which Avraham ran shouting to drive off the gathering jackals.

When Shlomo Levin returned from the hospital a month later with his stump of an arm swinging in an empty sleeve, no one even said hello to him. The late Zeitser, as Eliezer Liberson phrased it in a speech given at a memorial in the meeting house, to which he had come especially from the old folk's home, had been 'one of the monumental figures of the Movement'.

The wretched Levin was never his old self again. Day after day he sat wasting away in Rachel's garden, nibbling whole sheets of *kamardin*. He was particularly angry at Zeitser because, having stolen the limelight in his lifetime, he had now conspired in his death to pre-empt the glorious suicide that Levin had long dreamed of. His only visitors were Avraham, who still remembered from childhood his uncle's gifts and kind hands, and Uri when he returned to the village.

When Levin felt that his time was up, he sent for me and offered me a large sum of money, which I refused to accept, to bury him with the pioneers. 'With the productive sector of the village,' he said bitterly.

I granted him his request. He was, after all, genuine Second Aliyah. On his gravestone I got the masons to carve the inscription he composed for himself: 'Here lies the Pioneer Shlomo Levin Who Took His Own Life by Mule Bite.'

Busquilla and our lawyer, Shapiro, argued with me every week about the need to invest my earnings wisely. I never listened to a word they said.

Busquilla now had an agent working for him in Florida.

'They're all down there,' he said. 'All the old Jews. They even have swamps, and a sun as killing as ours.'

He bought a black van with 'Pioneer Home' painted on the doors in gold letters and managed me and the business expertly.

'It isn't right for me to sit in an office while you dig graves and lug a garden hose,' he said to me. 'You're the owner, Baruch. Why don't you let me employ someone to do the dirty work?'

I did my best to explain the importance of agricultural work and the village's opposition to hired help, but Busquilla forbearingly dismissed the ideals of co-operative farming.

'That doesn't convince me,' he said. 'I'm an observant Jew myself. Everyone has his own rituals and commandments, and yours are sometimes worse than ours.'

Another time he asked me, 'Why don't you ever take a trip abroad? Go on a holiday, have a good time, meet some girls.' When I failed to answer, he persisted.

'What's the matter, can't afford it?'

Busquilla had a plump, pretty, likable daughter who was younger than me. Often he spoke of introducing us.

'What for?' I said, blushing each time. 'I'm happy as I am.'

'I'll send her to Pinness with some food,' he ventured at last, ceasing to beat around the bush. 'All you have to do is be there. She'll make you a good wife, not like the women you have around here.'

'Stop it,' I said, feeling my forehead crawl with centipedes.

'It's no good, your living like this. You're a healthy young man. You ought to be married.'

'Not me!' I said firmly.

'When a Moroccan wants you to marry his daughter, don't think he'll take no for an answer,' Busquilla warned me.

'I don't like girls,' I told him.

'Well, you can't have my son,' he joked. But there was a frown on his face.

Sometimes he watched me while I worked, marvelling at my size and strength. 'You're not at all like the rest of your family,' he said. 'You're a big, dark, hairy hulk of meat who's never been bitten by the love bug. Now, that cousin of yours, he's something else! He's slept with every girl in the village, but you just go your quiet way.'

'Stop it, Busquilla,' I said. 'What goes on in the family and the village is none of your business.'

'You've all got a screw loose somewhere,' he needled me, testing the limits of my patience.

Sometimes he told me about his first days in the village. 'Everyone looked down their nose at me. It was like being on permanent probation. I was put to work digging onions to see if I would make a decent postman. Even Zis thought he was better than me because his father once hauled water from the spring, until I gave him a right to the jaw and he began to act like a human being.'

He observed people with unconcealed curiosity, quickly grasped the fine points of village life, and annoyed me with his maxims.

'A man who spends all his time in a septic tank must be afraid of something.'

'No woman ever forgets the first finger that touched her.'

'A good grandfather is better than a father. A bad one is worse than anything.'

'What's all this earth, earth, earth stuff all the time? It's enough that we come from it and return to it. In between a man needs to rest.'

'You people, if you hear someone say something stupid when he's nine, you think he's stupid till his dying day. You're sure you've got him worked out.'

As a letter carrier he had knocked on every door in the village and remembered exactly which had opened to offer him fruit or cold water and which had stayed shut while suspicious eyes studied him through the window. Busquilla was the first to know that Margulis and Tonya were back together, that Grandfather received foreign mail via channels other than the post office, and that if Grandfather never gave him the time of day, it was because of a deep anguish and hate that had nothing to do with him personally. Busquilla also knew that apart from the historical journals he received, Meshulam subscribed to other magazines whose chrome-and-flesh-coloured contents winked and tittered through their supposedly opaque brown wrappers. He chuckled too whenever he brought the Libersons their post, because he knew that a good part of it, including letters that appeared to come from abroad, was from Liberson to Fanya.

'He sends them without a return address to surprise her when she opens them.'

# 42

When his compulsory army service was over Yosi signed up as a career officer, while Uri became a heavy equipment operator for his uncle in the Galilee. Thus, there was never any problem about who would inherit the Mirkin farm.

It was Meshulam who explained to me that when the founding fathers came to Palestine and saw how the fields of the Arab peasants had been whittled to thin shavings by the jack-knife of inheritance, they decided to bequeath their farms to one son alone. From the day a boy was born, he was under constant scrutiny to see if he fitted the bill. The experienced eyes of his parents, teachers, and neighbours measured his first steps, the development of his back muscles, his success at predicting rain, and the presence or absence of the green fingers that every good farmer had to have. By the time he was ten the boy knew if he was destined to remain in the village or to seek his fortune outside it.

The failures first cloaked themselves in injured silence, then burst into stormy protest in the hope of reversing the decree, which was, however, irrevocable. Their fate sealed, they were sent out into the world with the ways of the village stamped in their flesh like a cattle brand. Some became farmers elsewhere; others went into business or to the university; all did splendidly in their new lives. Years of growing up in the village, of hard work, responsibility, and an intimate knowledge of nature and animals, made successes of them all.

Gradually, each father transferred part of his farm to the chosen son, consulting him about the harvest of various fertilisers and carefully weighing his answers and opinions. As a hive raises new queen bees, so the village raised its next generation of farmers.

Sometimes mistakes were made. Daniel Liberson, whose infant passion for my mother was taken as a sign of a nonagricultural personality, turned out to be a first-rate farmer. Having no one left to love or hate once my parents died, he devoted all his talents and energies to tilling the soil. Eventually, after working as a dedicated and much-praised adviser in an immigrants' settlement, from which he brought back his Romanian wife, he became a thriving grower of chickens, cotton, and mushrooms. The latter were cultivated in a secret formula of straw, soil, and horse manure that Daniel found in an old Russian farmer's almanac he got from Meshulam in a swap for Hagit's original milking stool. According to the almanac, the best time for picking the mushrooms was when they gave off 'a strong foresty smell', and every few weeks when a new spore cycle ripened, since Daniel had no idea what a Russian forest smelled like, he tore his old parents away from their amours to have them sniff the dark fungal beds. Never once did they disappoint him.

Meshulam, on the other hand, made it clear from an early age that as Uri put it, 'the only thing that ever drew him to the earth was the force of gravity'.

Uri himself never thought of remaining in the village, and his determination to leave came as no surprise. His love of books, ardour for his nursery teacher's behind, tendency to tire easily from hard work, and quips about the frustrated lives of the hens or the over-intimacy of the inseminator with the heifers, along with other signs that could not be dismissed lightly, cast doubt on his character long before his escapades on the water tower, which were the last straw.

Though everyone liked Uri, it was obvious that Yosi would be the one to step into his father's milking boots. He was a thorough, conscientious boy with a fund of technical knowledge and a born knack for planning and organisation. The one thing that worried Avraham was the violence pent up in him beneath the surface. Yet while my uncle was afraid that Yosi might harm an unruly or stubborn animal, he entrusted him with the morning milking at the age of fourteen, and even Grandfather, who saw in Uri a distant reflection of his lost son Efrayim, turned to Yosi when he needed someone to harrow the orchard without damaging the tree trunks.

And so, when Yosi announced that he too was not coming back to the village, Avraham looked up from the earth, which was something he had rarely done before, and shuddered at the sight of his life stretching desolately out before him as far as the horizon of his death. He was seized by despair. Though I tried to help him with the farm work as much as I could, I was far more interested in cultivating my field of dead bodies in Grandfather's ruined orchard.

'Not one of Mirkin's grandsons will be a farmer,' said Rilov. 'The Committee should make them sell the farm.'

'Don't let him worry you,' said Busquilla. 'Who would be crazy enough to buy it? Who's going to dig up all those bones or grow crops between gravestones?'

Grandfather's revenge was taking shape. The graves burned like a chastisement in the earth of the village, like a terrible mockery of its way of life, a rank challenge to its very existence. People stared and whispered as I walked down its streets, appraised my stiff neck that would not be yoked to the founders' vision, and imagined the money in my sacks. I paid no attention to them. The eyes fixed on me were a protective bluff that did not scare me. Busquilla, who kept a record of our running battle with the village authorities in his well-organised filing cabinet, thought it was all very funny. Again and again he told me not to take the threats against me seriously.

'You may know more about farming than I do,' he said, 'but I happen to know something about graves. There are six hundred and sixty saints buried in Morocco, and still more of our rabbis crossed the sea to the Holy Land in order to be buried here.'

'It's not the same thing,' I said.

'Of course not,' chuckled Busquilla. 'We Moroccans charge money to visit a saint's grave, while you Jews from Europe bill the saints themselves.'

Avraham alone did not mind my field of graves. Morose and past hope, he immersed himself in his dairy operation, at which he worked harder than ever. He invented new feeding techniques, disinfected the pens with special sprays that killed all internal and external parasites, enlisted the help of two engineers to develop a flow-sensor system that monitored air pressure in each teat, and experimented with different kinds of music during milking. Ever since my father had hooked his phonograph up to Rilov's cowshed, the farmers had known that music meant more and better milk, but only Avraham matched his records to each cow's personal taste. Large earphones on their broad heads, the solemn-looking animals stood dreamily swaying to the strains of flutes and string sections that coaxed the milk from their udders.

He also did away almost entirely with the weekly supplement of roughage in the cows' feed, preferring 'more for psychological than nutritional reasons' to take them out to pasture once a week. The milking machines that whirred nonstop made him smile at the old argument over whether a cow should be milked two times a day or three. 'It's not a scientific issue,' he explained. 'It's simply a matter of weighing the farmer's convenience against the cow's.' His own cows were milked four times a day and kept the vacuum pumps working around the clock. And though the puniest of his animals gave three times as much milk as the renowned Hagit, Meshulam, whose depressive wanderings through the village brought him to us too, declared that none of them would be exhibited in a museum or listed in a record book. 'History is not what is done,' he said, 'it's what gets into writing. That's what makes that damn swamp study so dangerous. And it's Hagit who will go down in history, not any of your uncle's milk wells.'

Having ceased to bring his milk to the village dairy like the other farmers, Avraham was excluded from their daily social chat and withdrew into himself like a mole cricket into its underground chambers. Every morning as Motik skilfully backed all twenty-two wheels of his huge tanker into our yard, I heard the sound of the big diesel engine and the gasps of the power steering, followed by the inevitable conversation.

'Good morning.'

'Good morning.'

'Can I start pumping?'

'Yes.'

'He jumped right in front of me. There was nothing I could do about it.'

'I know. It wasn't your fault.'

Off in a side room two big separators whirled ceaselessly. From one end flowed cream that tickled the taste buds of visitors to Pioneer Home and drew them to the cowshed, where Rivka sold them clandestine jars of it in violation of the co-operative's by-laws. From the other end came skimmed milk, which was piped back into the cows' drink, enriched by minerals. Avraham was the first dairy farmer in the village to understand that far more than solid food, liquid intake was the most important factor in a cow's metabolism. That was why he had never had a cow go dry on him while still in its productive years. 'A cow should drink five quarts of liquid for every quart of milk it gives,' I once heard him tell Yosi as they were cleaning the white terrazzo floor of the milkshed with clear plastic high-pressure hoses. All his piping – for water, for disinfectants, for air, and for milk – was transparent, as were the constantly filling and emptying glass tanks. 'It's so the cows can see what they're doing,' said Uri, who had a revolutionary proposal of his own for increasing production. 'Why not,' he asked, 'add the water directly to the milk instead of to the cows?'

Only now did the village understand Liberson's prophecy. The hard olive stone had split and germinated. The promise of the firstborn son had been fulfilled. In his white smock and yellow rubber boots, Avraham had professionally outclassed every other first son in the country. And yet there was something frightening in the mechanical way he moved his hands when he worked. His fingers no longer massaged the cows' udders but rubbed them as though they were strangers, and he never smiled with pleasure any more when their teats grew erect, or slapped the rump of a heifer in heat, or handfed clover to a favourite milker. Like giant stuffed animals, his cows strode to their places while he fitted them to the rubber cups of the machine as though he were a new piece of automated equipment himself. Still, so much milk gushed from them that more than once he had to dump surpluses, forming bogs covered by a sour scum.

One evening when he was throwing out several hundred quarts of milk, Rivka came to the cowshed to inquire coquettishly why he did not offer to give her a milk bath like those the Roman empresses took. Avraham flashed her a smile whose tail end smouldered with an anger she had never seen in her life. The furrows deepened in his forehead, branching up into his thick hair, and for a moment his face was so contorted that he reminded her of his missing brother. Suddenly she grasped the full danger he was in. Remembering how quick the Mirkins were to hide behind tree bark and beekeepers' nets, she realised what I had known all along, that her husband was drowning his anguish and wrath in his cows' white lakes.

Meanwhile I ploughed and cultivated my earth, sowing it with lupin, while Busquilla brought in several lorryloads of red gravel and got masons to lay borders and polish square blocks of white marble into gravestones. I extended the paths to the ends of the property, ploughed the lupin under when it flowered to green-manure the soil, planted handsome ornamentals, and installed stone and wooden benches. Magnificent birds never seen even by Pinness descended to rest from their migrations, hopping on the tree boughs, and quiet little animals appeared among the flowers as though created there. At dusk I would stroll through the garden, polishing the copper letters, breathing the cool air that had formed in the shade of the trees, and naming the birds and animals.

It was utterly peaceful. The old pioneer songs had died down into a quiet murmur, the great manifestos were silent in the sweet clods of earth, and the flaming swords of debate no longer turned every way. Couples came from all over the Valley on summer nights to make love on the cool headstones. I could hear the wind carry off the soft moans and gasps of the women, and sometimes there was a dull explosion in the earth as a newly buried stomach swelled to the point that the flaccid abdomen popped loudly from the pressure. I knew that as the guts came spilling out, the hordes of white maggots knocking madly on the coffin burst inside. Except for Grandfather, who was laid to rest in nothing but shrouds as is the Orthodox custom, everyone in Pioneer Home was buried in a coffin. This has been the practice in Movement villages and kibbutzim ever since Liberson denounced the Orthodox for returning to the earth the easy way.

Eliezer and Fanya Liberson came to all my funerals. The old man always stood in the front row with one arm draped around his wife, his fingers grazing her breast, but he was still firmly opposed to my booming business. Like all his friends, he was carefully calculating the days he had left and his prospects of living them out.

Apart from sniffing the mushrooms, his entire farm was now in Daniel's hands. Utopian formulations, polemical swordplay, and the trench warfare of ideology no longer interested him. Such phrases as 'our inner world has ceased to be inviolable', 'in times of drift and doubt', and 'the question of economic self-sufficiency must be examined in historical perspective as well as in light of this generation's inward experience' now rolled off his pencil and out of his mouth with a painful, frustrating ease. Fanya alone, with her merry laugh, white hair, and keen eyes, was not to be taken for granted. She was still his holy grail of love, an airy butterfly of the vineyards whose polka dot dresses and bright head were the last lights his ailing eyes could make out.

Every year Eliezer celebrated their first bucolic meeting with a picnic in the lap of nature. In the old days Tsirkin had joined them with his mandolin, but now that he was confined to a wheelbarrow, this custom had ceased.

For the fiftieth anniversary of their falling in love, Liberson prepared a basket of bread, a wheel of farmer cheese that still showed the marks of the cheesecloth, some pickled herring in sour cream and green apples, and a few late-ripening cucumbers, in one of which was a note. He had implanted the little tin tube in the pistil of the flower several weeks ahead of time, as it was beginning to swell among the wilted petals, and the cucumber's green flesh had formed around it. Fanya packed dishes and silverware, Liberson filled a thermos with clear pomegranate juice, and the two started out for the fields.

They walked slowly along the border of the planted crops, tottering happily. The first autumn rains had fallen the day before. Tender sprouts grunted their way up through the earth, which emitted the usual vapours of pure promise that made the farmers drunker every year. It was the season when I used to go with Pinness to watch the burrowing insects, who waited for the first showers to soften the ground before digging themselves and their offspring a new domicile.

Fanya and Eliezer headed for Margulis's old vineyard. Liberson, with his thick-lensed glasses, carried the picnic basket, and Fanya, weak and light, rested her head on his shoulder, joking with her husband about the impudent spermlike aroma of the stamens of the carob trees. 'Fanya, at your age!' said Liberson, turning pink with love.

Both leading and clinging to each other, they walked along the cart tracks, thoroughly enjoying the smell of the rain and the clouds from the cave in the blue mountain. They spread a cloth beneath the ancient grapevines, held out their hands to help one another settle slowly down into the high grass, and ate without taking their eyes off each other.

There was not a soul in sight. Margulis had planted the little vineyard years ago for the exclusive use of his bees. He had never picked the fruit, believing that would make his honey winier, and the vines, untended since his death, grew over their rotting trellises in a jungle of sturdy, wildly intertwining shoots. Large silvery argiopidae wove sparkling curtains between them. Skinks warmed themselves in summer's last rays on fresh molehills, looking fondly at the loving couple.

Liberson sliced the pickled fish with slow precision and spread sour cream on the rolls. 'How about a cucumber, Fanya?' he suggested slyly.

'Later,' Fanya answered. Not wanting to make her suspicious and spoil his surprise, Liberson did not press her. He settled back against a rock while Fanya lay on her back in the grass with the bright halo of her head on his thigh. It was mid-afternoon, and the soft autumnal sun, as pale as the yolk of a refrigerated egg, bathed their bodies, working its way into their old joints and filling them with amatory pleasure.

'Look,' said Liberson. His dim eyes had discerned some blurry dots flying towards him in the still air, bright with a black, translucent glow.

Fanya opened her eyes. 'Queen ants,' she said. 'The queen ants have come out for their wedding flight.'

The winged queens of the harvest ants had emerged by the hundreds into the autumn light, flying or crawling over the ground. Many were hunted by the open beaks of swallows or trapped in spider webs. Others glided on air, each with a tiny male attached to it.

'How beautiful they are,' said Fanya. 'How beautiful on the one day of light and love they'll ever have.'

Liberson stared straight ahead, struggling to make out the glossy queens. Fanya shut her eyes again and stretched delicately out on the ground, her head turned to one side with her cheek on her husband's leg. Feeling her light, winged touch, Liberson raised his hand to clasp her fingers and found himself gently clutching a queen ant.

'Look,' he said to Fanya. 'Here she is, the queen. And I, my precious, I thought it was you.'

'It is me,' said Fanya. 'Come fly with me.'

The swallows clove the air with their sharp cries and black sicklelike wings. Her eyes shut, Fanya let the sunlight pinken the darkness beneath her lids. She smiled as she heard the shrill calls, and Liberson felt love's sweet pleasure steal from her body into his. He held the queen up to his frail eyes to examine her shapely figure.

'When Pinness was in his prime,' he said, 'he would have given a speech about the power of love that makes the queen ant grow her wings.'

'You could still give one,' said Fanya. As though she were already asleep, a swift dreamlike breath escaped her slightly parted lips. Her hand dropped to the ground, and her white hair moved in the wind. Liberson looked at her, feeling her body relax. Careful not to wake her, he stretched out on his back, laid his head on the rock, and gazed up at the vast sky while his hand played slowly with a tuft of hair on her neck. Their long years together had taught him to cultivate the passion for life, which burned in him ever more strongly as he grew old. 'The eternal flame' was his private phrase for it. He was grateful to God for liking him despite his unbelief and giving him the strength to nourish this flame daily, and to the kibbutz and Mandolin Tsirkin for providing him with such a gift, the bright butterfly who was his very own.

A few queen ants landed on Fanya's dress, and Liberson, before dozing off too, blew on them gently to keep them from disturbing her sleep. An hour later he awoke shivering from the chill that had crept into the air. By the time he realised that it was not the frost of autumn but of his wife's dead body, the cataracts on his eyes had curtained off his last sight, leaving him totally blind. In the darkness that descended on him, his fingers probed Fanya's icy skin while he listened to the buzz of the green flies that could scent death moments before it arrived. From the tall grass among the grapevines where I lay in hiding, I saw him shaking her corpse.

Liberson rose painfully to his feet, wrenched an old trellis out of the ground, and began groping his way between the rows of grapes with groans and shouts. I knew where he would go and followed him, making sure that no harm befell him. For six hours he stumbled over the black earth of his blindness, colliding with trees and rocks and tripping on bumps and irrigation pipes until he reached his destination. It was night-time now, and I hid again behind a slight rise in the ground.

'She was my light,' he kept saying as he tried to explain the situation to the night guards of the kibbutz. Hearing the alarm go off in the plastics factory, they had hurried over to find an old man whose filmy eyes shed chalky tears as he strove to pierce the concrete floor with a rotten piece of wood. Liberson was unable to convey to them how he had managed to pass through the security fence, the iron gate, and the beams of the searchlight in order to kneel by the plastic rolling mills on the spot where the muscat grapes had once grown and a young man and woman had eaten fruit and cheese while flirting to a mandolin's fading notes.

'This is where I met Fanya,' he told them, six miles from her corpse.

The two handsome youngsters had no idea who Fanya or Liberson were, and did not know that the long, stubborn feud between their kibbutz and our village had started right there under a layer of concrete.

I watched them trying to decide what to do while holding Liberson up and patting him on the head. Assured they would not harm him, I slipped away and returned to the village in the dark. From afar I saw the sobbing red light of an ambulance pulling out of the kibbutz. I knew that Liberson was inside it, limp but irate, muttering incomprehensible phrases about cucumbers left uneaten in the fields. Fanya's body had already been retrieved, and now two green flares shot up from the Rilov farm to recall the search parties.

Daniel Liberson and Ya'akovi were waiting for me by the cabin. 'Where were you?' they asked angrily. 'We've been looking all over the place for you.'

A determined Liberson wanted to see me. He came straight to the point. In no mood to be brooked or reminded of his former opposition to Pioneer Home, he informed us that he wanted Fanya to be buried 'in Baruch's new cemetery'. As great as his grief and sense of loss were, he was not angry because of them but because of the fact that the death of his beloved had taught him nothing new. 'The anticipated sorrow of parting never lets us down,' Grandfather had written years before in one of his notes, and nowhere in the Valley was there a greater expert at reckoning separations and longing.

'Unlike most lovers,' Liberson wept, 'I was struck blind when my love was taken from me, not when I first met her or lived with her.'

He refused to let the doctors treat his cataracts.

'She was my sun, my moon, my stars, the light that ruled my day and night,' he groaned as I dug her grave the next day. 'A horror of great darkness has fallen on me.' Although I remembered his angry diatribe at the Committee meeting devoted to my cemetery, when he had called me 'a rotten apple', 'a death merchant', and other such names, I was not surprised. By now I was used to Grandfather's guiding hand hoeing the earth ahead of me to direct the flow of the future. Every night I lay down to sleep in a ditch he dug and woke shivering, smelly, and wet when the stream of his prophecies reached me.

Liberson instructed Daniel and me to save a place for him next to Fanya, and that was the end of the great cemetery debate. No one bothered me after that. The old man cloaked himself in his blindness and was sent to the old folk's home, where he shared Grandfather and Shulamit's former room with a hundred-and-four-year-old Bulgarian Jew.

The Bulgarian's age impressed him greatly.

'Yoghurt?' asked Liberson appreciatively.

'Brandy and chocolate,' replied the Bulgarian, introducing himself as Albert.

And so Liberson surrendered one more article of faith while deepening his knowledge of human nature. Having lost his wife and left his land in a single week, he befriended the old Bulgarian quickly and unreservedly. They both knew that the home was their last stop and were determined to make the best of it. Liberson never argued with Albert or sought to convert him to his idea of the correct life, and Albert repaid him with a smile that could be felt if not seen. Their brief, friendly conversations led to a mutual understanding that few friends ever achieve. Liberson did not try to be funny or impressive. He told Albert neither about the Workingman's Circle nor about the swamps and the pelicans, but only about the death of his wife and his childhood in the Ukraine. Between these two things a dark curtain hung before his eyes.

The Bulgarian lay in bed all day long with the covers pulled over his chest, his eyes burning brightly and his wet sheets smelling faintly of bedsores and septic tanks as he told Liberson about the wonders of the famous wrestler Podumov, the magnanimity of King Boris, and the taste of the black bread in the Plovdiv of his youth. Liberson was unaware that Albert was naked from the waist down beneath the armour of his ironed white silk shirt and shiny bow tie resembling a thirsty black moth that had landed on his throat, but he would not have minded had he known.

# 43

Time passed. Milk flowed. Corn ripened on the stalk, its lancelike leaves cutting the skin. Granaries filled. Fig trees set their fruit. More wars were fought. And one day a powerfully built old worker named Yehoshua Ber turned up in the feed shack.

'I know you from somewhere,' said Rilov. 'And I'll find out from where.'

Whenever a newcomer arrived in the village, the old Watchman scrambled out of his arms cache 'to look him over'. I liked to watch him emerge from his rancid lair, stand for a moment in the sunlight until he could move his limbs freely again, mount his horse, back it out of the yard with a wonderfully adept swivel of hand and hip, and fly off about his business. That was how all the old folk moved when holding some tool in their hands, an ancient fork for digging in the garden or a sickle for reaping the first symbolic ear of wheat. That was how Grandfather caressed Shulamit.

Yehoshua Ber smiled uneasily. He was a balding, wrinkled giant of a man, more good-natured than clever.

'I've been around, for example,' he said.

'We don't like people who've been around too much,' said Rilov. 'Moving targets are harder to hit, even when they're as big as you.'

'Leave him alone,' said the manager of the feed shack. 'He's a good worker. What do you want from him?'

'Nothing,' Rilov said. 'But if the two of you want to die in your own bed, make sure he stays clear of my yard.'

'We don't share no bed together. What kind of way is that to talk, for example!' said Yehoshua Ber angrily.

Rilov, however, was already spurring his horse's flanks. 'And stop saying "for example" all the time,' he called back as he rode off, his granitelike back repelling the stares that sought to follow him.

Yehoshua Ber liked to play with the village children. During his lunch break he would go to the co-op and buy a loaf of bread, a quarter of a pound of butter wrapped in waxed paper, and three cloves of garlic. That was his afternoon meal.

'The bread is for health, the butter greases your guts to help you shit, and the garlic makes you strong, for example, and kills the worms that come to eat the butter,' he explained to the toddlers who huddled like baby chicks around the big brooder of his rugged, heat-giving body.

In Poland he had been a famous wrestler. 'I'd get dressed up in a leopard skin, for example, put on a Roman belt, and beat the hell out of the Christians.' He even excitedly showed us an old photograph of himself wearing a gold cardboard helmet with a horsehair plume, his huge calf muscles laced in the leather straps of a gladiator.

Yehoshua Ber rented a room from Rachel Levin and pleased the feed manager with his untiring hard work. Every morning he jogged and exercised out in the fields, his great buffalo gasps audible all over the village. Twice a week he coached the teenagers in those two forgotten arts of British Mandate days, jujitsu and hand-to-hand combat. 'You don't even have to pay me, for example,' he told them bashfully. And then one day, when he was demonstrating how he could lift a feed sack with one hand, his face flushed with pleasurable exertion, Rilov came charging out from behind a heap of sorghum seeds, drew his Russian revolver from his belt, and declared:

'I've got it! I know who you are. You're Zeitouni's strong man.'

Now everyone remembered. Although the years had stripped him of his great mane of hair, he was the same performer who had smashed bricks and twisted nails for Zeitouni.

Dani Rilov and Ya'akovi took Yehoshua Ber to the Committee office and sent for Avraham.

Avraham was excited and edgy. 'Where's my brother?' he demanded at once.

The strong man, however, was unable to be of any help.

'Your brother was only with us for one day, for example,' he said. 'Zeitouni billed him as Alfonso Corrida, the Strong Man of Toledo.'

The repulsive stage name made everyone groan and shudder with disgust.

'He followed us all day with that cow on his back,' said the strong man.

'Bull. It was a Charolais bull,' said Dani Rilov.

'He just walked along with it. I couldn't believe my eyes. I sat in the cart, for example, and all the time I kept looking back at him. He had this mask on his face and kept walking with the cow. He wasn't even breathing hard, for example. That evening we camped in an Arab village. From the moment your brother joined us, Zeitouni never stopped insulting me. He even made me cook supper for everyone.'

Before the dumbfounded eyes of the Arabs, who were sure he had a djinn in him, Efrayim lifted Jean Valjean to his shoulders ten times. The beekeeper's mask with its gleaming green eye frightened them too.

'That cow was the only thing he had strength for,' said Yehoshua. 'I could have pinned him to the ground with one hand. He couldn't pick up two hundred pounds. Not even one hundred, for example. Just that cow, for example.'

'If there's one more "for example" out of you,' said Rilov, 'I'll make you eat this whip.'

Pinness opened the door, came in, and sat down.

There had been a good gate that evening, and Zeitouni was in a fine mood.

'After supper he let your brother have the rubber girl.'

Avraham had tears in his eyes. 'What did we do to deserve all this? What?'

'How wretched a man must be to stoop to such things!' mused Pinness.

'No one had ever messed around with her before,' said the strong man. 'Only Zeitouni. She didn't even need men. Whenever she had the hots, she went down on herself, for example. The way she tied herself into knots could drive a man out of his mind.'

Pinness fidgeted and said, 'You can skip the lurid details. Stick to Efrayim, please.'

'Zeitouni put her in a tent with your brother,' continued the strong man, 'and they had a go at it until pretty soon we heard her howling like an animal. Just then along comes that cow of his, opens the tent flap with its horns, and stands there watching them. They were glued together, for example, she had herself plastered all over him. Your brother was naked except for that net on his face. He gave the cow a kick in the *schnoz*, his nose, but the cow, it didn't want to leave.'

'He was watching Efrayim just like Efrayim watched him,' said Avraham in a shattered voice that could have been Grandfather's speaking from the earth.

'Well, he stood up with the girl still wrapped around him and began to walk off. The cow, it picked up his clothes in its mouth and started to follow them. After a couple of yards there was this big pop, for example, and the girl, she came loose like a wet rag.' The strong man stuck a straight, thick finger in his mouth, pressed it against the inside of his cheek, and plucked it out like a disgusting cork.

'That's what it sounded like,' he said.

Zeitouni ran after them, pleading and shouting. 'But that cow just turned around with its head down, for example, gave him a look and a snort, and put its foot in the ground, here, just like this. He didn't dare come closer.'

'Where did Efrayim go?' asked Rilov.

'At what o'clock?' asked Dani. His son Uzi was doing his army service, and he had picked up some military expressions from him.

Yehoshua stopped bellowing ominously and pawing the ground with his foot. 'It was like a dream, for example,' he said, his coarse face growing bright and soft. 'It was like having a dream in a dream. He just put that cow on his back, and off they went into the trees and clouds.'

'But where?' shouted Avraham. 'Where?'

'I don't know,' said the strong man. 'Zeitouni looked for them a bit. He thought your brother might change his mind. But he just walked away. I've never seen anyone like him in my life. That morning I was jealous of him, that afternoon I was afraid of him, and that evening I loved him.'

The next day Zeitouni bought a small calf from the villagers and made the strong man begin practising bull lifting.

'I said to him, "How much can I lift? A thirty-stone cow? A forty-stone cow? That still doesn't put me in his class. I know something about strength. That's my line. But what he's got, for example, that isn't strength, that's something you've got to be pretty desperate to have. Or maybe two men who were friends could do it together, for example."'

I heard a deep sigh on the other side of the wall and the scrape of a chair leg. Avraham rose wearily and walked out. Yehoshua Ber sat there for a moment and then ran to the window and shouted after him, the words sailing over my head, 'I think that cow didn't want your brother to do it with the rubber girl.'

Ya'akovi and Dani shoved him back into his chair.

'What made you come back here, Yehoshua?' asked Ya'akovi.

'I left Zeitouni. I didn't want to work for him any more. That was a long time ago. After that I had all kinds of jobs. I was in the building trade, carrying cement sacks, and I worked tying ships in the port, for example. I was already living in this village before I even remembered that that bloke with the cow came from here.'

I heard old Rilov rise from his chair and knew he was about to grill the suspect until the hackles stood up on his neck. 'That was a lovely bull story,' he said. 'We've already heard it all before. Now listen carefully and watch your step. Did you run into any English on your way?'

'No.'

'I'm going to ask you again. Did you see any English talking with Efrayim, taking anything from him, giving him anything?'

'What kind of English, for example?' Yehoshua was getting annoyed. 'The English are gone. This is our country now.'

'I've dealt with men twice your size,' said Rilov with genuine nostalgia. 'Think it over. Maybe an English officer with a limp and a cane? Or two Scotsmen?'

'What's a Scotsmen?'

'Don't leave the village,' said Rilov. 'I'll check your story with some friends in the Galilee, and I'll get back to you. Don't think you're dealing with just anyone. I'm Committee!' His voice had acquired a hollow resonance with age, and his words kept on ringing in the air after he had left the room.

Avraham came back from Yehoshua Ber's interrogation a devastated man. He went straight to the cowshed, where he started to bellow and spin around with his arms out, staggering this way and that like Shoshanna when Grandfather slaughtered her, the deep creases in his forehead white from pressure. Yosi was in the army, and Uri was with his uncle in the Galilee, so Rivka grabbed me and dragged me to her husband to keep him from smashing his head against a wall. I waited until he collapsed on the floor and carried him to his house.

It was easy for me. Effortless. I'm a strong man. As big as an ox. An obedient brawler of a grandson, broad of back and stiff of neck. Why else did Grandfather cram me with so much strength? To carry him when he died, to carry Pinness when he was sick, to carry that half-drowned surfer by the sea. And the exhausted Shifris. And my sacks of money. And my barrels of stories. And my beautiful, tall, burned mother.

Mandolin Tsirkin died in his bed in the yard. Pesya, who passed away a year later, did not even know about it. Alone in a little room in a Movement geriatric institution near Tel Aviv, paralysed on her right side, she lay holding subtle but demented conversations in a loud voice with the minister of the treasury, Fanya Liberson, and someone named Ettinger. She had no idea whom Meshulam meant when he came to tell her about his father's death. Repeating the words 'gizzard flowers' over and over, she begged him to rescue her slip from the flames.

Tsirkin died noisily, unco-operatively, shouting his objections at the top of his lungs. The whole village heard him wrestling with Death.

'Why didn't anyone tell me that it hurt?' he cried out in bitter astonishment.

Meshulam and Doctor Munk stook by his bed. Assisted by Eliezer Liberson, who had been brought from the old folk's home, they tried to get him to the hospital. He argued with them, squirmed, refused.

'It'll be over in a few minutes anyway,' he said.

'The interns will stick tubes up me,' he moaned.

'Call for Doctor Yoffe,' he commanded in a fog. And briefly pausing, he went on: 'Come, join us, Feyge. I've made some baked pumpkin with flour and eggs. Come, they're both gone now. Jump into the water with me, it's not cold at all.' Suddenly he shouted, 'Comrades Tsirkin, Mirkin, and Liberson will make no dishonorable advances.' I alone knew what he meant.

He calmed down a bit, his chest rising and falling heavily.

'I have to keep breathing,' he told himself. 'I mustn't stop even for a minute.'

A fresh attack of pain racked his body, making him shout out loudly and curse the 'hole counters' – a familiar term so old that no one knew what it meant any more. 'It all started with those damn idiots the hole counters,' he swore.

'Who were the hole counters?' I asked Meshulam several weeks later.

'It's just something my father made up,' he replied.

I never gave him the letter that Mandolin wrote to Grandmother Feyge. The other documents in Tsirkin's box he read aloud at his father's funeral. He was thrilled to come across an original letter from Hankin having to do with the removal of Arab sharecroppers from land purchased in Ein Tab'un, and to discover a shopping list of the Feyge Levin Workingman's Circle from June 1919. 'Two *rotls* of flour, a bottle of sesame oil, four shirts of Arab cloth, a straw hat for Mirkin,' it said.

Meshulam claimed that Shifris's letter was a forgery. 'It's a bad practical joke,' he said, though he kept it in his archives. 'If you ever want to swap it for the constitution of the Workingman's Circle, I'm ready to talk,' he told me.

We lowered the coffin into the ground, and Meshulam hoed some earth onto it. After a while his place was taken by blind old Eliezer Liberson, the last survivor of the Workingman's Circle, who finished the job with a few practised scoops of the spade.

'What did you do with my father's mandolin?' asked Meshulam as the crowd dispersed.

I pointed at the grave.

'What?' he yelled. 'You put it in the coffin?'

'As per the request of the deceased,' said Busquilla.

'It was your father's idea,' I explained.

Meshulam gave us a look that could kill, reached for the spade, and began to exhume the fresh grave. At first I made no attempts to interfere. As he dug deeper, however, the sounds grew louder, and I stopped him.

'Listen, Meshulam. Listen.'

He kept on digging. I grabbed the spade from him and threw it away.

'Listen carefully, Meshulam.'

The people of our village are always hearing things in the earth: snails waking from their summer sleep, the malarial chirps of the German children, the suffocating gasps of Sisera's army. Meshulam heard every tendon, sinew, and eyelash of his father's body shouting at him to desist.

A flabby old orphan who had never planted a tree or known a woman in his life, Meshulam began to sob. 'Forgive me, Father, forgive me,' he cried, flinging himself face down on the ground.

# 44

In summer the cicadas thundered in the cemetery, clinging to the jasmine bushes and the branches of the olive trees. They drove their short beaks into the bark, sipped the fresh sap from the veins of the plant, and sounded a long and monotonous cheer of pleasure. It was the same deafening roar that had accompanied the earth and its denizens immemorially, from Pinness's primitive cavemen to the Feyge Levin Workingman's Circle, greeting conquering armies, caravans of pilgrims and immigrants, and travelling merchants and circuses.

The ear-blinding sound of the cicadas can drive anyone not used to it out of his mind in a few minutes. For us people of the Valley, however, they were the beloved poets of summer and field.

'What makes them sing?' Pinness asked himself and me. 'It's not a mating song, because the females don't seek out the singing males. It's not territorial, because male cicadas don't defend territory. Besides which, they're practically deaf. What makes them sing, then?'

He looked at me, waiting for an answer. But I was a ten-year-old boy, a big, bearlike sack of stories that had no answers in it.

'They are the true song of this country,' Pinness explained, 'an obstinate trill that has no melody or notes, no beginning or end, nothing but the jubilant and admonishing proclamation of Existence that says, "Here I am!"

'I want you to know, Baruch,' said Pinness, 'that this humble insect is the true hero of the famous fable of the cicada and the ant. Incompetent translators called it a grasshopper, and the whole ridiculous parable is one big testimony to ignorance.'

He took me to the orchard. The sun beat down on the broad fields, and there was not a bird in the sky. The calves stood with their tongues out in the shaded squares of the cattle pens, and the spiders had retreated to the bushes from webs rigid with heat. Blue butterflies fell to the ground like burning feathers, their wings in my hand as hot and stiff as copperplate. Only the sturdy, boxlike cicada kept up its lusty dry heat-chant, its orange voice sawing through the branches, challenging the fury of the sun, mocking the furnace of the earth.

Pinness was an artist at catching cicadas. Every child in the village knew that cicadas fell silent and flew off when approached, but it was Pinness who revealed to me that their sharp vision was offset by their near total deafness.

'Fabre set off explosive charges by the chestnut tree in his garden, and the cicadas didn't even budge,' he told me. Jean-Henri Fabre, the French entomologist, was a favourite of Pinness's. 'He may not have kept the most exact records, and he opposed the theory of evolution,' he admitted, 'but I must say that he had all the innocence and curiosity of a child.'

We approached the bushes together. Pinness whipped out a hand, there was a screech of terror in the branches, and the cicada was gripped between his fingers. He pointed out to me its big checkered eyes, its transparent, veined wings, and the sound plate on the side of its abdomen. Drawing a thin straw across it, he managed to produce a brief chirrup.

He then described for me the extent of human ignorance. Aristotle, he said, believed that flies were generated from rotten meat. The Bible held that the rabbit and the hyrax chewed their cud. 'The poor fools,' he whispered, lowering his voice as he always did when holding an insect. 'The ignoramuses! And for sheer misinformed stupidity, nothing beats that fable of the cicada and the ant. Why, the cicada winters underground in larval form and doesn't need any favours from the ant! And in summer it's the ant, more rapacious than industrious, that robs the cicada of its labours.'

I was ten years old. I still remember the feel of the cicada's hard body between my fingers as it struggled to kick free with sturdy legs. Pinness showed me how it sucked juice from the bark of an apple tree while a long row of dark little ants, attracted by the sweet smell, ascended the tree in a black stream. The lead column attached itself to the cicada's beak and clambered over its back, sipping the drops of juice that trickled from the apple bark and giving off a bad, aggressive smell of formic acid.

'Take a good look,' said Pinness. '"Go to the ant, thou sluggard" – to that beggarly swindler of a parasite that practises its piracy in broad daylight under the aegis of King Solomon and his proverbs and of that bourgeois Aesop, La Fontaine.'

Grandfather was not interested in creatures like the cicada.

Insects that neither helped nor harmed his fruit trees did not concern him. Sometimes, to be sure, the cicadas left a red ring on the peel of the fruit, but Grandfather did not consider this a defect. Once, hoeing next to him in the orchard, I found a cicada larva in its deep tunnel, living in utter night and clinging to a root from which it sucked its sustenance. Pale, clumsy, and bleary-eyed from the darkness, it wriggled slimily in my hand.

With Pinness's help I also saw the final stage of the cicada's metamorphosis. 'It's a matter of luck,' he had warned me – and just then a pupa emerged from the ground and looked for a bush to ascend. It was slow and awkward, but its eyes glittered blackly.

'The matrix is now ready to receive light and form,' Pinness whispered. 'For the light is sweet and a pleasant thing for the eyes to behold,' he said. We sat down on the ground, and my teacher put his hand on mine. The pupa gripped the bush, began to climb, and stopped. As though slit by an invisible knife blade, the chrysalis split lengthwise down the back.

Little by little the adult cicada emerged from its baby suit. Still moist and weak, it wriggled its legs slowly while the damp robe of its wings began to harden. We sat watching for three hours as the sunlight and air filled its veins and its yellowish hue turned green and then grey-brown. Suddenly it let go of the shrub and flew off, and all at once – drunk with the pride of accomplishment, the passion for life, and its own existence – it joined its loud, exhorting voice to the chirps of its comrades.

Pinness grew pensive. 'You've seen something today that few people ever see,' he said to me as we walked home. He took my hand.

'All his days he eateth in darkness,' he quoted. 'For four years he burrowed in the ground, and now he has four weeks to sing in the sweet light of the sun. Is it any wonder that he's so lusty and loud?'

Those words impressed me greatly. When I related them to Grandfather, however, he dismissed them with a wave of his hand. 'Pinness knows a great deal,' he said, 'but he spins a

lot of tall tales around his insects. How does anyone know
that the larva in the ground is sad? Or that the cicada in the
tree is happy? Pinness takes human feelings and gives them to
insects.'

But back then, in the fields of my childhood, my teacher looked
at me and smiled, happy to give, to educate, to influence. Young
though I was, I understood that he was doing his best to make
something of me. I knew that he and Grandfather sometimes
argued about me, and I stretched out my neck like a big calf to
be lavishly petted by both of them.

'Isn't being an orphan enough without your burdening him
with all your tragedies?' Pinness asked over a nocturnal bowl
of olives.

I lay in bed with Fabre's insect book on my chest, a loan from
Pinness, feeling blissful when I heard Grandfather reply:

'He's my child.'

It was only years later that Pinness admitted his entomological
rhapsodies were baseless and had been uttered simply for their
effect on me, to win me over to the study of nature. 'The magic
spell animals cast on human beings is nothing more than a form
of egotism that confirms our own prejudices. We domesticate
cattle, train birds, and dress monkeys in top hats to reassure
ourselves that we are the crowning act of Creation.

'Curiously,' continued Pinness, 'the biblical creation myth and
Darwin's theory of evolution have a similar attraction. Both
portray Man as the ultimate achievement. And yet, my child,
what right have we to assume that Nature is purposeful and
has goals? Is it not just as likely to be an accidental chain of
developments that automatically eliminates its own mistakes?'

He opened his big Bible and showed me 'an important verse'
from the Book of Ecclesiastes. '"For that which befalleth the sons
of men befalleth beasts; even one thing befalleth them; as the one
dieth, so dieth the other; yea, they have all one breath; so that a
man hath no pre-eminence above a beast."'

'None of the commentators ever understood this verse,' he
said, slamming his Bible shut. 'The key word in it is not "dieth"

but "befalleth". It's not death that best expresses the equality between man and beast, it's the randomness of life.'

He watched me carefully, as pleased as punch to see that I was looking back at him attentively.

'"For that which befalleth the sons of men befalleth beasts",' he declaimed. 'Both are the products of accident, and both are subject to the quirks of Chance.' He burst out laughing. 'To say nothing of the work animals in our village, who are our social equals as well.'

'Does the cicada remember its four years underground?' wondered Pinness out loud beneath the apple tree. 'Or the pretty swallowtail – does it recall having been a clumsy caterpillar on leaves of rue?

'The pupal period,' he explained to me, 'is not just a stage of maturation and quiet readying for a new life. It is also one of forgetting and oblivion, an impenetrable screen between the larva and the imago, those two so contradictory life phases of a single creature.

'Whereas we,' he lamented, 'have been given this most terrible of gifts. Not only must we bear on our backs the camel's hump of memory, we are not even recompensed with a brief life of flight, song, and love unburdened by the constant urge to eat, accumulate, and grow fat.'

I watched entranced as the stream of marauding ants attacked the cicada, drove it off, and plundered the juicy well it had dug. Pinness studied me to see if I was ripe for his final peroration. 'Why, then, did Solomon praise the ant?' he asked. 'Because he was a king, and kings have always preferred ants to cicadas and bees to dung beetles. Just like that stinker Michurin. They have always thought of us as a huge, blind mob of slaves whose acquired submission to servitude is genetically transmitted.'

Bringing me back to the cabin, he took the volume of Burbank from Grandfather's bed and read aloud to me from it.

'"Nature takes just as much cognisance of the deadly snake as of the greatest statesman."'

'Why? Why?' Grandfather roused himself from the kitchen table. 'Why must you put such things into the boy's head?'

And so I never heard the end of Pinness's lesson until I was grown up and the ailing old teacher had lost all inhibition. 'It's better to roll your own ball of shit than to eat the higher-ups' honey,' he informed me, chuckling as he champed on Mrs Busquilla's Moroccan treats.

# 45

Now only Rilov, Pinness, Tonya, Levin, and Riva were left in the village. I asked Busquilla to drive them to the old folk's home now and then to visit blind Eliezer Liberson, and he was 'honoured to do it'. Liberson, however, did not show much interest in them. It took Levin's attack on Zeitser to get him to react in his famous article, while when Rilov's septic tank blew up, he heard the explosion, knew at once what it was, and came for the funeral.

Rilov was very old. Sometimes he emerged from his arms cache to get a breath of air, go for a ride in the fields, take in the sun, and see what was new in the village. Visitors came from all over the country to see the Watchman, who was as tough as an old boot and could still sit in the saddle for hours. 'They don't understand that the poor old codger climbs up there and rides around for two days at a clip because he's embarrassed to ask for help to climb back down again,' wrote Uri in reply to a letter from me about Yehoshua Ber and Rilov's suspicions.

Most likely, I imagine, the uric acid fumes that penetrated the cache's sealed ammunition crates also ate their way into the chemical time fuses. The blast shook the whole village. Thousands of old Mauser cartridges and percussion grenades and tons of TNT and dynamite sticks blew sky-high in a great tidal wave of sewage, milk, mangled earth, and twisted Sten guns.

When the yellow vapours had settled, it emerged that half of old Rilov's farmyard was now a canyon. His son Dani's calf pen had become a ruin of blackened posts and veal cutlets. Nothing was left of the hayloft but a few foul-smelling brands of charcoal hissing and sputtering beneath the endless drops of rain that started to fall. 'Fourteen milk cows went to their deaths without disclosing the whereabouts of the hidden arms,' was Uri's journalistic summation. Rilov himself was scattered over a radius of hundreds of yards. Trained in the conspiratorial tradition of their family, his son Dani and his grandson Uzi managed to convince the police investigators that they were confronted with a work accident caused by mixing large amounts of red phosophorus with potash and sulphur salts used for fertiliser.

The search for Rilov's remains went on all over the village for several days, but the old man was never found. It was months before the horrid smell of ammonia, roast meat, and smoke dissipated and the old Watchman's spiked army boots turned up, each with a rotting lump of flesh inside it. The right boot was discovered in the bushes by the spring, while the left was found in the bougainvillaea vine twining up the columns of the water tower. Both were put in a plastic bag and buried in my cemetery in the presence of a large crowd.

The funeral of Rilov's boots was attended by the last surviving Watchmen, veterans of the Haganah, and hundreds of pallid, unknown old men who emerged from airtight compartments and underground cellars and chambers. Once the grave was filled in, they gathered beneath the shade trees to update passwords, synchronise watches, and trade secrets.

We had always known that Rilov continued to stow arms away for the defence of the village and the Movement even after the establishment of a Jewish state, but no one had had any notion of the quantities he had managed to secrete. 'Rilov could have armed two whole divisions,' proclaimed one of his eulogists, fixing his yellow eyes on the assembly. 'We weep for you, Comrade. We weep for your arms cache. We weep for Tonya, your partner in subterfuge. We weep, ah, bitterly, for so many good weapons gone forever.'

Having learned from her life with her husband that death is no excuse, Tonya walked away from his fresh grave, went straight to Margulis's tombstone, and sat down in her usual place in sight of the mourners. The shape of her body was waiting for her there in the swarm of hovering bees, and she quickly slipped into it, licking and sucking her decomposing fingers.

Liberson too remained in the cemetery after the funeral, groping up and down among the graves with his cane of sour orange wood. He ran a hand over my face and shoulders when I approached and recognised me at once. 'How big you are,' he said. 'You have your father's strength and your mother's height.' Asking me to lead him to Fanya's grave, he sat down on the white stone and took a deep breath of air. 'So Rilov's gone too,' he said. 'That madman. It's a great loss. Pinness and Mirkin couldn't stand him, but if not for him and his friends, we wouldn't be here today. His type is needed also, indeed it is.'

He was glad to smell the flowers and ornamentals. 'You should plant vegetables too,' he said to me. 'Vegetables would do well here.' In Russia, he told me, there was a Crimean farmer who planted squash, onions, watermelons, and potatoes between the rows in the village graveyard with fabulous results. His potatoes were as big as melons, his watermelons were unusually red and sweet, and 'he once grew a pumpkin weighing six poods – nearly as much as you, Baruch – that was taken by *troika* to the summer home of Czar Nikolai.

'The blood of the dead ran in its veins,' he explained. 'I want you to plant roses and aubergines on my grave, and I'll nourish them with my old body. Verily, I shall blossom in the Land of Israel.'

Liberson took his wooden-handled grafting knife from his pocket. It was just like the one Grandfather had and sometimes used for whittling. Cautiously I sat down beside him, afraid of his wrath if he sensed me on his wife's grave. He began to peel an apple that he also produced from his pocket. The skin came off in a red ribbonlike strip that kept getting longer until it was all peeled and he commenced to chew with his corniculate gums.

'Over there in the kibbutz,' he said, 'where the factory is now, there used to be a lovely vineyard. That's where I met Fanya.'

Toward evening Busquilla drove us to the old folk's home. Frail and faded, Liberson sat between us in the black farm truck. 'Next time,' he said, 'I'll be in a box in the back.'

When we arrived I took him gently by the elbow and led him to his room. The old Bulgarian lay in bed in his silk shirt and black bow tie and smiled up at his friend.

'Good evening, Albert,' said Liberson.

'Back so soon?' Albert asked.

'It's all over.'

'After a Bulgarian funeral, everyone goes to the dead man's house for a huge meal,' said Albert longingly. '*Pastelikos, apyu,* cold beans. And of course a drink or two.'

'After a funeral in the village, we just go on eating hay,' said Liberson.

The two old men laughed. 'I once had a girlfriend in Varna,' Albert declared. 'You should have seen her breasts. They weighed seven pounds each. They're pushing up the daisies now.'

Liberson signalled me to go home, and I did.

# 46

As if they had planned it together, the old folk were dying off one by one. A great deal was said at their graves about 'the vacuum left behind', but although Pinness had taught us in school that Nature abhors a vacuum, nothing rushed in to fill this one.

One night I went to spy on Meshulam. Through his window I saw him bent over his documents, his face lined with contrition and framed with the new white fuzz of a mourner's beard. His visitors heard him regret having shortened his father's life with his shirking, denounce his own petty-mindedness, and list the principal differences between the anopheles and the house mosquito as smoothly as if humming a melody. Whereas the larva of the latter has a long breathing tube and lies in the water diagonally, the larva of the former has a short breathing tube and lies in the water horizontally. The house mosquito has short antennae and a drooping stomach, the anopheles has long antennae and an arched stomach. Asked why he should bother to recite basic facts that every schoolboy in the village knew by heart, Meshulam answered modestly that the memory of the Jews of Israel was going soft and some things needed to be saved from oblivion.

When the month of mourning was over, Meshulam looked in the mirror and decided to keep his beard. 'It's the first crop he ever managed to grow, so of course he can't stand ploughing it under,' wrote Uri, who kept asking me to send him news of the village.

As sometimes happens with beards, Meshulam's flourished splendidly and gave him a sense of his own rectitude. Every day he came with new queries to his father's grave, where his appearance caused a stir among the visitors. With Mandolin Tsirkin's old work clothes and rope belt and his own great shock of salt-and-pepper hair, Meshulam was the spitting image of Hankin, Gordon, or the prophet Isaiah. American tourists and visiting schoolchildren looked at him admiringly and asked to have their pictures taken with him. Busquilla suggested paying him 'a modest salary' to hang around Pioneer Home all day 'with a worker's cap and a hoe', and even wanted to sell picture postcards of him. As far as I was concerned, though, Meshulam was nothing but a pest. Since Avraham and Rivka had gone abroad, he had become more obnoxious than ever. He even insisted that 'we must' – *we*, no less! – put Hagit's stuffed body by his father's grave. Now that Grandfather and Avraham were gone and the farm was mine, I had no more patience for him.

'I don't need that mangy cow of yours in my cemetery,' I told him. 'If your father had wanted her next to him, he would have told Liberson.'

Busquilla was poised to recite our usual disclaimer about the candidate not meeting admission requirements, but Meshulam, his face limned by the golden aura of swamp drainers and desert blossomers that he had managed to acquire from a prolonged study of old photographs, chose not to argue.

For several weeks he tried to make a farmer of himself, getting some Rhode Island broilers for his yard and even attempting to plant vegetables. Bashfully approaching Rachel Levin, whose greens were famous throughout the village, he tendered her one of his prize exhibits, a book by a farmer named Lifshitz entitled *Vegetable Growing in the Land of Israel*. Rachel, however, looked doubtfully at the old paperbound volume, on the cover of which two fat children and a huge lettuce graphically symbolised the bounty of the land, and pointed out to Meshulam that the book was older than the village and badly out of date in its advice.

Nevertheless, Meshulam was smitten by Lifshitz's prose style. '"Your aubergine delights in light and well-mannered soil",' he read aloud to me, his lips curling as though tasting the aubergine's delightful nourishment. The two sentences he found most spellbinding were: '"The most suitable of radishes for the Land of Israel gardener is the Giant White of Stuttgart",' and '"The smaller the animal, the finer its manure: sheep droppings are finer than cattle droppings; songbird droppings are finer than pigeon droppings; but finest of all are the droppings of the silkworm".'

'He must dream of giant Nazi radishes getting fat on protozoa shit,' wrote Uri, adding that Meshulam would go down in history as 'the first farmer in the Valley to manure his crops with a tweezers and a magnifying glass'.

Meshulam got hold of some silkworms, and Rachel, patient and good-natured as ever, showed him how to feed the little creatures fresh leaves from the mulberry tree in his yard. But not even their magic guano could do any good. The timidity of Meshulam's touch made the earth go into spasms and vomit up his seed, while his starving chickens called him names behind his back.

Meshulam did not give up. Filled with the great deed for which he was preparing himself, he went around with a pregnant expression. The villagers knew that look well from their cows and their wives but failed to recognise it on a face with a beard, misinterpreting it as grief.

The product of his father's obstinacy and his mother's shame-lessness, Meshulam was now abetted by these two qualities. He hired Uzi Rilov to give his land a good ploughing, borrowed the village's chain mower and heavy harrow, and uprooted the rank carpet of wild carrot, mignonette, and yellowweed from his property.

The last carnivorous mice, snakes, centipedes, and ichneumons fled in panic from the land that had been their home ever since Mandolin Tsirkin's last illness. The green John Deere tractor crushed the burrows of the voles, splattered the eggs of the lizards, and bared the angry mole crickets to the depredations of the sun. Uzi piled all the weeds in a big heap at the field's far end, and Meshulam set them on fire and stared at them, mesmerised by the tidings of the great, all-purifying flames.

'So Meshulam's decided to be a farmer at last,' said the farmers to each other at their evening meetings by the dairy. They would have been happy to give him advice, because he knew absolutely nothing about agricultural equipment except for the ancient Kirchner and Zirle mouldboards pictured in 1920s farming journals, but Meshulam was not looking for help. On his own initiative he had the district digger build a five-foot wall of earth around his land, the purpose of which, he explained to his startled neighbours, was to plant an experimental rice paddy.

'Rice,' he announced, 'is an important and nourishing food whose cultivation had been neglected in this country.'

By now, however, no one believed a word he said. It was obvious to everyone that behind his white beard and show of ploughmanship and filial bereavement, Meshulam had swamps on the brain. It was decided to discuss the matter at the next general meeting, where it would share the agenda with new contracts for the fodder dealers, the acquisition of some old railway track for the construction of additional cowsheds, and also, I was extremely happy to hear, the request of my cousin Uri to visit the village.

He had now been in exile for several years, and tempers had cooled. Bearing a quiet halo of proud reconciliation and new ideas from the city, Ya'akovi's wife had returned long ago, and when Uri wrote to ask the Committee's permission to come home for the autumn holidays, I was sure his petition would be granted.

The general meeting was never held, however, because Meshulam struck sooner than expected. The night before it was to take place he set out for the fields, wearing his father's work boots and carrying a new ten-pound pick he had bought in the village store. Never in his life, not even when he discovered letters to Liberson from Slutzkin and Berl Katznelson in a cardboard box in the Committee office, had his heart pounded so loudly as it was pounding now, as he walked along the main irrigation pipe smashing the large water taps one after another without stopping once to look back.

Fountains shot up and kept jetting. At first the water sank into the soil, but then, gluing the thin particles together, it turned the field into a huge basin of mud in which it slowly began to rise.

Meshulam did not go home. All night he sloshed around the field, climbing up to perch on the earthen wall when the water reached his boot tops. By the time worried cries rose from the cowsheds and poultry runs, waking those responsible for noticing a drop in water pressure, the Tsirkin farm was flooded and the village had lost three weeks of its national irrigation quota.

In the morning we all turned out to have a look, unable to believe our eyes. The silt had sunk to the bottom, and the new lagoon lay sparkling in the sunlight, the shimmering reflection of the blue mountain visible in its calm water from the angle at which I stood. Apart from an inexpressible fear, we all felt the hidden passion of the farmer for whatever is cool and clear, flows and bubbles, and mirrors the images of clouds. Pinness was the first to realise what had happened. After years of sowing and reaping, of tears, joy, and mockery, the floodgates of the earth had been sprung.

'I stood there thinking of the day Avraham Mirkin recited his poem,' he testified much later before the Movement commission

of inquiry that investigated the events. 'Then too not everyone sensed the approaching disaster.' The commission members
looked at him, looked at each other, thanked him politely, and
told him he could go.

Even after the crowd had dispersed, I couldn't bring myself to
leave the Tsirkin farm. The longer I stood watching, the more
stagnant the clear water grew, forming a green nightmare of slime
before my eyes. Lured from their lairs by the odour of legend and
doubt, sedge and loosestrife sprouted alongside great snails that
had waited all their lives for such wet tidings.

From his place atop the earthworks, armed with his father's
gypsy bandanna and a curved papyrus sickle that he had removed
from the walls of Founder's Cabin, Meshulam proclaimed: 'A
swamp is born!'

'There'll be mosquitoes!' shouted Ya'akovi the Committee
head, who was close to collapse from the late summer busy
season and the cost of the lost water.

Meshulam raised a hand. 'So there will,' he called out. 'The
Jews of this country have forgotten what a swamp is. The time
has come to remind them.'

Ya'akovi did not wait to hear the rest. Shouting, 'You're out
of your mind!' he ran for the digger and started up the engine.
With a thud the steel scoop rammed the earthen breastwork
and battered a two-yard breach through which Meshulam's lake
began to flow, flooding the neighbouring fields.

'Mend your ways!' cried Meshulam, consciously adopting the
hortatory tone in which Pinness declaimed the jeremiads of the
prophets during Bible lessons. 'Drainage ditches must be dug!
Clay pipes must be laid! Our comrades from the press must be
invited to see us plant eucalyptus, sing, catch malaria, and die!'

There were loud guffaws. And yet Pinness, Tonya, and Riva, I
saw, were standing off to one side, apprehensively holding hands.
I knew that in the old folk's home Eliezer Liberson must have
stopped chewing his breakfast as he caught his poignant first
whiff of the forgotten old smell. 'I don't feel well,' he said
to Albert, and vomited up a glob of oozy green muck onto the
tablecloth.

'The thin crust has burst, the abyss has opened its jaws,' said Pinness, thinking 'circularly' about the inundation of his own brain by the stroke that had swamped it in a cloud of forgetfulness. Only the top of the blue mountain remained, protruding like a lonely isle of memory. Ravenously hungry, the old teacher summoned up the last of his strength to go home and drown his worries in a pot of squash with rice and tomato sauce.

Tonya Rilov stuck two fingers in her mouth and resumed her vigil at Margulis's grave. By now the skin around her fingernails was as white and porous as a wrinkled crust of boiled milk. Riva, whom the swamp had caught scrubbing windows, went back to work. Meshulam was in high spirits. His knowledge of Visionary Pioneering's practical fine points was a sure guide to the future, and Ya'akovi's assault on his earthworks had only strengthened his resolve.

From then on everything happened according to the ineluctable laws of cause and effect. Meshulam's water flooded an adjacent patch of clover, decimating the shoots, and malignantly washed away a corn field, reducing it to spongy splotches of foam. Huge, gurgling, atavistic bubbles formed and burst, releasing a horrible stench. With a great squish, a cloud of high-bellied mosquitoes flew up from the bog and circled over it.

Only now did I understand that none of this was accidental, and that the secret, invisible skeins tying us to the earth ran far deeper than I had imagined, intertwined fathoms down with rootlets, corpses, and hoofprints. I thought of poor Levin wringing his blue fingers while insisting that 'this land never gives the slightest strength to anyone who walks on it but simply suffuses the soles of your feet with its madness.'

Grandfather's flight from Shulamit, Efrayim's vanishing, Uri's banishment, Avraham's going abroad, Daniel Liberson's undeciphered love furrows – all these were merely the fissures through which the never-clotting venom could circulate.

Pinness, I told myself, was wrong. He had plugged the wrong holes with his fingers. We were not the products of accident – not unless you considered Pesya Tsirkin's breasts two random

cornucopias whose effect on Mandolin Tsirkin brought their
addlebrained son Meshulam into this world.

That afternoon a few unemployed men Meshulam had hired
in the nearest town arrived on the scene. Smiling sheepishly in
the old peasant's blouses and Russian worker's caps he had
dressed them in, they looked pathetic and ridiculous. Meshulam
gave them sickles and hoes and took them to his swamp, where
to our astonishment they burst at once into the old swamp
drainers' song:

> A friend of the frog,
> Of the frog
> Am I,
> And just like the frog,
> Like the frog
> I cry:
> Give me water,
> Or I die.

Though at first they were embarrassed, little by little their voices
gathered strength and their arms began to move in sweeping
motions. Within an hour, however, several big tankers appeared
on Ya'akovi's orders, sucked up Meshulam's swamp water, and
drove off to dump it in the nearby wadi. On their heels came
dumper trucks loaded with earth that they spread over the wet
fields. Before the day was out the fresh soil was firmed down
by angrily vibrating rollers and the entire bill for the water,
labour, materials, and heavy equipment was presented to the
Tsirkin farm with a strongly worded threat of seizure in case
of non-payment. By the time I drove to the railway station that
evening to pick Uri up, the morning's events seemed simply one
more story I had heard, a nightmarish figment of my imagination.

I drove the farm truck through the fields. I don't have a licence
and only drive on the tractor paths around the village.

Uri jumped down from the train, and we gave each other a big
hug. As I embraced him I could feel how much stronger and older
he had grown.

'You're crushing me, you big ox,' he groaned, half laughing. 'You don't know your own strength.'

He looked good, as slim, sardonic, and handsome as always. As we drove back, he stared at the farmed fields. White beards of cotton were flowering all around, and the first pomegranates were turning red on the trees, taking over from the last Somerset peaches. Far in the distance a big red International was beginning the autumn ploughing. We turned into a path that ran along the wall of Pioneer Home. Uri kept silent as he looked in amazement at the gravestones, the greenery, the flowers, and the ornamentals.

'What do you do with all the money you make?' he asked as we entered the cabin. 'Nothing has changed here.'

I still slept in my old bed and dried myself with Grandfather's soft old sheet after showering. Grandmother Feyge's glass plates and big tin spoons were still in use in the kitchen.

We drank tea and ate some good cake Uri brought me. I suggested that he sleep in Grandfather's bed, since at the request of the Committee I had put his parents' house at the disposal of the cantor who had come to the village to lead the High Holy Day services.

We stayed up talking all night.

'Tomorrow,' Uri said, 'we'll go and see Pinness. And maybe we can visit Eliezer Liberson in the old folk's home.'

That surprised me, because when Grandfather was in the home Uri had rarely bothered to visit him.

'Working on the bulldozers has given me a lot of time to think,' he said. 'Of all the old folk in this village, Liberson is my man. More than Pinness. More even than Grandfather.'

'Everyone's looking for a model,' I answered him. 'Busquilla still thinks that Pinness is a holy man, and Pinness wrote in the village newsletter how special you are.'

'All I am for Pinness is an exotic species of mammal.'

His laughter in the darkness made my skin tingle pleasantly.

'I'm sorry about it,' he said after a few minutes. 'I'm sorry about that whole water tower business. I was a kid and they seduced me. I was just a toy for them to have fun with or to help them get even with the village. I should have gone straight to Eliezer Liberson as soon as the whole thing started.'

'He would have chucked you out,' I said. 'Especially after you screwed Daniel's daughter.'

'He would have done no such thing,' replied Uri. 'He would have talked to me. But it doesn't matter any more. In the end I learned the hard way. You're talking to the most monogamous man not only in the Valley but in the whole world.'

'Not everyone can find a woman like Fanya who's worth devoting a lifetime to,' I said.

'You don't know a damn thing about it,' said Uri. 'Every woman is worth devoting a lifetime to. It has nothing to do with her. It's just a matter of deciding. The only thing special about Fanya was Liberson's love for her. She was just a mirror he kept polishing to do his jetés and pirouettes in front of. He danced and he sang and he thought a great deal of himself. That's all most women ever are.'

'And Grandfather and Shulamit?'

Uri lifted his head. 'Grandfather also decided that Shulamit was worth a lifetime's devotion,' he said deliberately, as if he had thought it through long ago, in the same tone Grandfather used to give his they-drove-my-son-from-the-village speech. 'Not that she was worth two minutes of it. But he went ahead, even if it meant killing Grandmother and living his whole life hardly seeing Shulamit at all.'

'You sound just like your mother,' I scowled.

Uri laughed. 'You and my mother didn't get on very well, but I want you to know that she's not a stupid woman. Far from it. She got my father out of here in the nick of time, just before he blew his fuse.'

He switched on Grandfather's reading lamp and sat up in bed, baring his thin, splendid torso. A single broad scar was all that was left of the boot mark above his left nipple. 'I got a letter from them,' he smiled, producing some photographs of a large white house surrounded by palm trees. Rivka, in a yellow dress, was sitting on a wooden veranda sipping a reddish iced drink from a huge glass, her round eyes shining happily over the rim.

Avraham, in shorts and a grey undershirt, the creases in his forehead soft and damp in the tropical sunlight, was instructing a group of blacks in a barn that looked like a cross between a laboratory and a palace.

'Yes,' I said. 'So she did. I don't blame her. You're lucky you didn't have to see your father coming back from Yehoshua Ber's interrogation.'

I can picture her perfectly, looking as grimly determined as any dim, obstinate hen on its eggs. She had her whole birdlike brain set on it. Convinced by her husband's collapse in the cowshed that he had to leave the village at once, she hurried off to see her brother, who was on good terms with earth-moving contractors, arms dealers, invisible middlemen who were perfectly transparent, and secret entrepreneurs whose tentacles spread all over the world. 'My brother will think of something,' she kept telling me, unexpectedly arousing my sympathy. 'I'm going to talk to him. Is there anything you'd like me to tell Uri?'

She went, came back, and kept mum. A few days later three strangers came to visit the farm. Cool and reserved, they walked around the yard at a fixed distance from each other, like the little flies in the hayloft. They made measurements, took an inventory, and talked at length with Avraham, observing him for hours as he worked in the cowshed, their Dacron suits as shiny as the breasts of preening pigeons. Not a speck of dust or a wisp of straw stuck to their well-groomed hair or the mirror-bright tips of their shoes. If you could have bred Rosa Munkin's lawyer with a Scottish commando, that's what their children would have been like.

One of them photographed the milkshed while jotting down numbers and charts, and a month later the lorries and dealers arrived. Avraham sold all his cows and his electrical and pneumatic equipment, left me his blue Fordson-Dexta, and took off for the Caribbean with his wife, four pregnant heifers who kept mooing apprehensively and stretching their necks to look back, and a few dozen test tubes of frozen sperm. Awaiting him there were a government contract, 'milk-starved natives', unlimited budgets, and simple, high-spirited soil that had never been cursed by the bones of saints or the poisonous salts of long-awaited redemption.

I stayed in the cabin even though they left me the key to their house. Now and then I went to have a look at it, opening taps to keep the pipes from clogging and windows to air the place. Thick cobwebs covered the milking stalls in the cowshed, jumping spiders and geckos hunted midges in the wall cracks, and at night I could hear the faint tinkle of floor tiles shattering all by themselves.

It was a few weeks before the last music of milking and the last chomping of hay stopped echoing in the feed stalls and the whistle of compressed air and the soft plop of dung faded away. The cascades of milk dried into a thick layer of yellowish powder that covered the floor and felt good beneath my bare feet.

The village smithy, I thought, must have looked the same way when the Goldman brothers walked out of Grandfather's stories and off to war.

'He only waited for Shulamit to get back at her,' I told Uri.

'My child,' Uri said, 'you don't understand a thing. Do you remember when Pinness wanted to teach us about oxygen and the lungs and stood you in front of the class with a bag over your face?'

'You bet I do,' I said. 'I passed out.'

'That's because you were such a good boy and Pinness forgot to tell you when to stop,' Uri grinned.

'So?' I felt hurt.

'Grandfather lived all his life with a stupid bag named Shulamit over his face, breathing the poisoned air of hopeless love. That's what made him ill, that's what drove him mad, and that's what killed him when she came. Why do you think he died so soon after and even knew that it was going to happen?'

'He was old,' I said. 'That's what he told Doctor Munk.'

'I never believed Grandfather like you did, and I screwed Doctor Munk's wife the month he came to the village,' said Uri disdainfully. 'Take my word for it, he doesn't know anything either. Not about love and not about how ill you can become from it.'

\*   \*   \*

That night the square in front of the dairy was flooded. Pinness was not in when we went to visit him in the morning, because he had gone to watch the workmen who had been rushed to the village centre. Rotting, ice-cold liquids seeped up from the cracks that yawned in the concrete. Arriving in the morning with their milk, the disgruntled farmers found Meshulam dancing with his red bandanna and crooked sickle while singing ecstatically. This time Ya'akovi had no qualms. He had had enough, and hit Meshulam in the face.

'Just let me catch you near a water tap once more,' he said, looming over him ominously, 'and you'll end up in that stupid museum of yours with your belly full of absorbent cotton.'

Despite the blood that ran from his nose and stained his white mourner's beard scarlet, Meshulam merely smiled. The workmen cleaned up the mess, made forms for pouring new concrete, sealed the cracks, and sprayed everything with insecticide.

When Pinness hobbled to the office to explain to the weary and furious Committee members that this was one swamp that public works could never drain, Ya'akovi screamed at him so loudly that a crowd formed outside the windows. 'What the hell swamp are you talking about? We have a madman who goes around opening water taps, and it's about time you stopped talking at us. We're not your students anymore.'

Pinness was too shocked and hurt to notice Uri standing there. The Committee head saw both of us, though, and his anger exploded as forcefully as a high-pressure sprinkler. The scar on his lower lip, split by me on the day of Grandfather's death, turned white.

'They're all here,' he spluttered. 'The whole damn family. I'm supposed to put in a seed bid and find tractors for the grain fields, and instead I have my hands full with Mirkin's two idiotic grandsons, the mad fucker and the mad undertaker, a swamp revivalist, and an insane old beetlemaniac.'

Pinness put a restraining hand on my neck, Uri took his arm, and we went off to the old teacher's house to have tea.

'Maybe now that he has a swamp to drain, Shifris will finally turn up,' Uri said.

'Or Efrayim,' I added.

'We've seen the last of them both,' declared Pinness.

# 47

No one knew the name of the Valley's old barber. Everyone called him 'the Rabbi', and though he always insisted, 'I'm just an ordinary Jew,' he seemed to like the title. A resident of a co-operative farming village of religious Jews in the north-west corner of the Valley, he also doubled as a cantor and circumciser.

Once, in my childhood, when Grandfather was asked to treat a sick orchard there, he took me along. As we set out on the track that ran through the fields, he let me hold the reins. Zeitser covered the whole distance in an easy, steady trot. He enjoyed these breaks in his daily routine because they took him all over the valley, and he returned from them raring to go to work more than ever.

Grandfather spoke to the bearded planters in a language I didn't understand. It was not the language he wrote to Shulamit in but the one Levin used when talking to the wholesalers in his store. On our way back he humorously described for me how the religious farmers got around the biblical injunction against sowing mingled seed in one field. 'One goes and sows hay, and the next day another comes back and sows legumes, pretending he didn't know the first was there.'

These religious farmers were odd types. They never swore when they looked up at a cloudless sky in autumn. Though they weren't supposed to work on the Sabbath, they milked their cows to keep them from suffering, putting a floor tile in each bucket to make God think that the milk had been spilled on the ground. On Passover they saw to it that their livestock ate no leavened food, which so tickled the fancy of Eliezer Liberson, it was said, that he rode off to their village to sing their cows a comic Passover song called 'Moo Nishtanah'.

Being good-natured folk who had a sense of humour, they did not take it amiss, and as soon as the holiday was over they sent a delegation to Liberson's farm. With it came a crate of bread, jars of red horseradish guaranteed to bring tears to the eyes, bottles of home-made schnapps that packed a wallop, and cans of pickled herring that drew founding fathers from all over the Valley by magic fetters of longing. When the peppery, cockles-of-the-heart-warming banquet was over, the visitors winked at each other, trooped off to Liberson's turkey run, and shouted, 'Hurrah for Socialism!' in a mighty chorus.

The moronic birds cackled an enthusiastic chorus of agreement, and even Fanya Liberson burst into loud laughter and told her mortified husband that he had been bested.

The cantor-barber-circumciser was now very old. He had first arrived in the Valley long ago, brought in a cart from the city beyond the mountain to circumcise my uncle Avraham. The wagon skimmed over the resilient paths of spring, a good smell of horses and flowers filled the air, and the young man, whose long beard hid a soft, pale complexion, was enthralled by the purring magic of the land. He went on dreaming of it after returning home, and when he looked at our blue mountain from the other side, the Valley appeared above it in fair weather like a mirage, its upside-down image so tempting in the sky that it gave his heart no rest. When he heard that a group of Hasidim had decided to form a farming village there, he hurried to join them. A year later, however, a full cart ran over him, the wooden wheels smashed both his knees, and he was forced to return to his old profession.

His work took him all over the Valley. One day in a field he saw a hefty woman, her chin adorned by several bristly hairs, harnessed to a light Arab plough on whose handle leaned a ten-year-old boy. Captivated by the girth of this Astarte's columned legs, by her grunts of exertion, and by the sweat stains tracing her armpits, the Hasid stopped to ask about her. Her name was Tehiya Fein. Her husband, he was told by the local farmers, had divorced her and gone back to Bolshevik Russia 'to light the world with the torch of Revolution', leaving her hardened and embittered. The ten-year-old, they hastened to add, was not her child but the son of neighbours who felt sorry for her.

The Rabbi asked the villagers to arrange a match for him. For their part, they were only too happy to be rid of the woman, who had sorely tried the principle of mutual aid they all subscribed to. Before two weeks were up she had covered her hair with a kerchief like a good Hasid's wife and followed her new husband, pulling after her by a rope a small calf and a donkey loaded with all her possessions.

Though the Atlas of a bride was infertile, she was industrious and good-humoured. She learned to observe every jot and tittle of Jewish law and worked the Rabbi's farm for him, producing bountiful harvests in place of children while he continued to wander the Valley. At first he made the rounds of the kibbutzim and villages on foot, kosherly slitting the throats of chickens, pedicuring cows, clipping locks and foreskins, and marvelling at the bare thighs of female pioneers and the fragrance of freshly tilled earth. With his earnings he bought a small two-wheeled cart hitched by a tall light-footed Cypriot donkey, and after the war he acquired an old BSA motorcycle with a sidecar from British army surplus.

When I was a boy he visited our village once a month. First you saw from afar a speeding grey cyclone crossing the fields like an autumn dust devil, next you heard the muffled chatter of his old piston, and then came the moment you were waiting for. Squeezing the throttle of his cycle, the old Hasid raced it down the bank of the wadi and flew heavily across to the other side with a loud cry of 'Yippee!' His face beamed. His grey coat and the ritual fringes of his undershirt flapped in the wind. On his head was a leather pilot's helmet with his thick sidelocks stuffed inside, shielding his eyes was a pair of tractor goggles, and in his sidecar rattled an astonishing wooden chest that opened up into a barber's cabinet. Collapsible legs unfolded from its bottom, while out of its drawers came razor blades, scissors, a stained sheet, and a manual clipper. Spreading the sheet over his customer and a newspaper over the table, the old barber wagged his shears and tongue and gossiped about the surrounding villages.

He was an unfailing source of news and information from all over the Valley. It was he who took Shlomo Levin's letters to the matchmakers and drove him secretly to Tiberias for his first meeting with Rachel. He transmitted clandestine notes to and from Rilov, tipped us off that the boys from the next-door kibbutz were planning to waylay us with stones, brought word that the new stud horse at the experimental farm was possessed of prodigious powers ('His sheaf arises and also stays upright like Joseph's in his dream,' he told us with a grin), and devoutly spread the word about Uri's escapades after my cousin was caught. Taken with a grain of salt, his reports were of considerable value. He also volunteered to sniff around for news of Efrayim, in whom he took a special interest not only because he had cut his hair in the privacy of his room, but also because it was my uncle who had obtained his pilot's helmet for him from the British air base.

He was our village barber for half a century. He had cut Grandfather's hair, Efrayim's, Avraham's, my mother's and father's, Uri's, Yosi's, my own, everyone's. 'The same teacher, the same barber, the same earth,' Uri said. 'What a cosy sense of continuity!' Early each summer all the children were sent to him to have their heads shaved, which saved the village money as well as strengthening the roots of their hair. The indignant youngsters squirmed and had tantrums in the barber's chair, but I, acting on Grandfather's orders, sat there 'as quiet as a mouse', the only child who did not have to be subdued by sheer force while the Rabbi's pinchy clippers made a single broad part from the victim's forehead to his neck. 'Make haste, my beloved,' he would sing as he released the partially shorn child, who would jump up and run for dear life, only to return before long with the plea that his tormentor finish the job.

Every year the Committee hired the Rabbi to lead High Holy Day services for the handful of villagers who attended our little synagogue. When the holidays were over he returned home with a wad of notes, several trussed hens, a crate of pomegranates, figs, raisiny late grapes, and – if the year had been a good one – a large jar of cream.

Now that he was old, so that 'his hands shook from long years of prayer and motorcycling', he was no longer entrusted with such delicate tasks as haircutting and circumcision. Eventually, having grown too weak to sing or blow the ram's horn, he found us a new cantor, an extremely Orthodox cousin of his from the city beyond the blue mountain.

The Committee sent Uzi Rilov in an open jeep to pick them up at the railway station. The Weissbergs – the new cantor and his wife, their adolescent daughter, and their little twin boys – were equally shocked by the jouncing, dusty ride through the fields and Uzi's immodestly bared shoulders. Mrs Weissberg and her daughter chastely declined the offer of his hand to help them down from the jeep. Soon after their arrival a good smell of sweet and unfamiliar cookery came wafting from Avraham and Rivka's house.

The new cantor was unlike his predecessor. He did not know anyone in the village, and the earth of the Valley held no appeal for him. On the morning after they came his wife hung clothes on Rivka's washing-line the likes of which we had never seen before, and a little later Weissberg stepped out onto the porch and began to practise his ram's horn, slicing the air into shivering strips that sent hundreds of roof-roosting pigeons high into the sky.

The cantor's twin boys startled the village youth with their long sidelocks and socks and the huge velvet skullcaps that covered their shaven heads. Overwhelmed by sun, fresh fruit, and the smells of cowshed and field, they tiptoed through the farmyards gaping at the poultry and livestock while lisping to each other in a rapid speech whose strange diction could not be understood. They were especially frightened by the cows in heat, mounting each other brazenly, and by the mules, those half-asses and half-horses that seemed to have stepped out of the pages of a devilish bestiary. The village children pointed and jeered at them from a safe distance, afraid to approach such exotic creatures too closely. Even Pinness, who stared at them as if straining to remember, was unable to connect them with the childhood that had been erased from the lobes of his brain.

'I know them from somewhere,' the old man kept saying, 'but I can't seem to place them.'

Dark and sombre-looking like her father, the Weissbergs' daughter spent most of her time in the house, although I sometimes saw her towards evening, garbed in long dresses, strolling arm in arm with her mother along the village's palm-shaded main street. They were not at all like our own freckled women and girls, whose fruity, gullible charms were blown afar by the breezes. As they walked with lowered eyes and small steps, talking in low tones, mother and daughter appeared to be fleeing the burly farmers and their bare-chested sons, defending their virtue with the little handkerchiefs they clasped in their hands, their ceaseless murmuring, and the armour of their clothing, which precluded all conjecture concerning what lay beneath it.

Late one afternoon Busquilla invited the Weissbergs to visit the cemetery. Uri and I were weeding the flower beds while Pinness sat nearby. When Busquilla finished explaining the nature of our enterprise to his guests, the cantor nodded and said, 'It is a great commandment to bury the dead properly, a great commandment.' He did not know, of course, that we broke all the rules by burying them in coffins, without prayers or pious beggars to give alms to.

I straightened up as they approached and greeted us, struck dumb by the beauty of the cantor's daughter. Her complexion was a heart-rending mixture of peach and olive, and her dark eyes were lowered beneath prominent brows curved as finely and sharply as a sickle. Until then the only women I had ever known were the women of the Valley. Half were too old, and I had seen so much of the other half since infancy that they held no interest for me.

'Allow me, Cantor, to introduce our teacher, Ya'akov Pinness,' said Busquilla. 'This is Baruch, my boss, and this is Uri, in whose parents' home we have been privileged to house you.'

'Welcome to our village,' said Pinness dryly.

The cantor smiled.

'Weissberg is the name,' he said. 'I'm pleased to meet you. You've been very hospitable.'

'Be careful in the kitchen, Cantor,' said Uri. 'There may be some old bread lying around.'

'That will do, Uri!' said Pinness, instantly on guard.

'Bread?' The cantor did not know my cousin yet.

'Isn't Yom Kippur the day on which you eat only *matzo*?'

'That's enough, Uri. You should be ashamed of yourself,' scolded Busquilla. 'Please forgive him, Cantor.'

'We brought our own food from home,' laughed the little twins. A frown on his face, their father hushed them sternly.

An end-of-summer melancholy hung in the air, causing us all to fall silent. From the orange groves came the pungent smell of autumn manuring, and you could hear the mournful death of summer in the clucks of Ya'akovi's geese as they flung themselves against the wire of their pens, quacking painfully at the sight of the Africa-bound birds overhead.

'Summer and winter, swallow and heron,' said Pinness in the solemn tone he generally saved for his classes in biblical poetry. I could tell from the enigmatic smile on his lips that the old man was once again listening to the seasons changing inside him.

'As the last fruits of summer, as the gleanings of the vintage,' answered the cantor, matching scripture for scripture. Relaxing, he permitted himself to smile.

I could feel summer ending in the burning leaves that whirled in the orchard, in the subtle way the wind grazed my bare shoulder, in the sudden silence of the rock doves, in the ragged nests of the paper wasps. No longer the same old busybodies, Margulis's orphaned bees hovered lethargically, hoping to find a last grape or fig that had eluded the harvesters. Returning from my late-night walks, I saw the stiff forms of baby crows lying on thin layers of frost beneath the cypress trees. There was more dew at night, cold little pools of it collecting on the tractor seats in the dents made by the farmers' behinds. Fleecy clouds gathered in the afternoon skies of the Valley. Pinness, Rachel, Riva, and Tonya planted their radishes and cauliflower, dug up their potatoes, and pruned the dead branches on their tomato vines. Only the pampered and well-fed flowers of Pioneer Home refused to acknowledge the turning of the year, tinting the air with their brilliance like the cantor's beautiful daughter.

A year later I left the village. I may not have read all the signs at the time, but I did feel the autumn more sharply than ever that year. The air was thick with finality and parting.

'Summer's end is more terrible than summer,' the cantor quoted the rabbis to me, watching the expression on my face.

People who don't know me try all kinds of ways to get on my good side and work me out. They'll send up a trial sentence to test the thickness of my cranium or extend their hand to my nose for me to sniff. I don't hold it against them. I know that Grandfather saw to it that I am part animal, part tree. Now, though, I was overcome with revulsion. The hissing way the cantor said 'summer', the wet, disgusting pop of the 't' in 'terrible', as if produced by a straight, thick finger in his mouth: I felt a sudden dislike for this man, whose long black coat made him look like a rootless scarecrow in somebody's vegetable patch.

# 48

On Rosh Hashana eve I went with Uri to visit Eliezer Liberson in the old folk's home. Busquilla sometimes drove there on business, and I had planned to hitch a ride with him in the farm truck until Uri said, 'Let's walk.' Once again I set out on the familiar path that seemed to flow from the soles of my feet and crawl in front of me like a warm, submissive snake of earth.

Most of the old folk were in the home's synagogue, singing in childishly insistent voices as if to pave their way to the next world, but Liberson had never had the slightest use for anyone else's prayers, and Albert was in bed as usual, quiet and majestic. His white silk shirt rippled in and out with each breath while his black bow tie fluttered its wings at his throat.

'We Bulgarian Jews don't go in much for religion,' he said with a bright smile. '*Por lo ke stamos, bendigamos.*'

'"It's enough for us to count our blessings",' translated Liberson from the Ladino. He already knew most of Albert's sayings. Usually they spoke in Hebrew, but sometimes they whispered together in Russian.

'Bulgarian is very close to it,' Liberson said. 'And in my old age I've picked up a bit of Ladino.'

He sat facing his friend with his sour orange cane between his knees. He knew who I was as soon as he touched my face and turned his blind, dirty-white eyes on me. 'How big you are,' he said. 'You have your father's strength and your mother's height.'

Only now did he sense Uri's presence. Gripping his elbow, he pulled him nearer and ran his antenna-like fingers over him. He caught his breath as they descended from the forehead, gently plucking and pinching the cheeks and skimming longingly over the bridge of the nose that was broken on the night of Uri's beating.

'You've come back,' he said. 'I always knew you would.'

'I've come back,' said Uri.

'And you're all healed,' added Liberson. 'Everything is all right now.'

'Yes,' said Uri. 'I'm all right now.'

'And your French calf?'

The touch of horror made my heart a tight fist. The blind man had peeled Uri like a fruit and put his finger on the poisonous, sore kernel.

'I'm Uri Mirkin,' my disconcerted cousin whispered.

The old man's hand jumped back as if burned by a live coal.

'Uri Mirkin,' he said. 'Of the water tower?'

I glanced back and forth from the ugly old man who had held one woman in thrall to my handsome cousin who had slept with every woman in the village.

'I came to say I'm sorry,' said Uri hoarsely.

'Who isn't?' Liberson asked.

'Did he do you wrong?' asked Albert.

'Oh, no,' said Liberson. 'He's just a wild shoot that sprang up in the village fields.'

'He is a fine-looking boy,' Albert said.

'If I had his looks,' said Liberson, 'my life would have been unbearable. The girls would have thrown themselves at me like ripe fruit falling off a tree.'

'*Non tiene busha*,' said Albert. 'He has no shame.'

'That's not how it was,' Uri said.

Liberson rose and asked us out to the terrace. He walked up and down the balcony, the light breeze picking up from his skin its mossy old farmer's smell of steamer trunks, dried dung, clover, and milk. His sturdy cane and grey work trousers lent him a presence that had not been passed on in his genes, Michurin notwithstanding.

Lifting the cane, he pointed towards the horizon.

'Do you see that wadi way out there? That's where we came from, Tsirkin and I, with your grandmother and grandfather, to have a look at the Valley. That good-for-nothing brother of hers was a bank clerk in Jaffa at the time.'

Though he paused to make sure we hadn't missed the dig at Levin, we said nothing. Eliezer Liberson viewed the Valley as a relief map of his memories, its co-ordinates given by the smells and shadows that reached him. And yet, despite their confident precision, the movements of his cane in the darkness that shrouded him filled me with sorrow.

'The roads were full of bandits,' he continued. 'The Valley was one big vale of tears. Here and there pus-eyed sharecroppers worked tiny patches of land. Jackals and hyenas walked around in broad daylight.'

He ran his cane over the landscape like a master of generations. 'And over there by those two oak trees, do you see? That's where Jael had her tent, the wife of Heber the Kenite. But we only got as far as the Germans' abandoned site and then left by train.'

'King Boris stood outside the railway station and said, "You're not taking my Jews." That's what he told the Germans. They didn't scare him.' Albert's voice sounded huskily from inside the room, strained with gratitude.

'That's the same Boris who cooled his heels while Katchke was talking to the King of England,' said Uri.

The blind man gave us a loving and compassionate smile. 'Albert tends to daydream,' he said. 'The Balkan Jews aren't like us.' He resumed the thread of his discourse. 'We worked by the Sea of Galilee and on the road to Tiberias, and at night we swam in the sea. We were already bare-bottomed in the water, splashing your grandmother, when she took off her dress and stood on the shore tall and naked, like a beautiful heron on the rocks. We swam back to her and climbed out.'

'Seven pounds each,' said the soft voice within the room.

'What is he talking about?' whispered Uri.

Liberson went to the door. 'Shhh, Albertiko. Shhh,' he said.

We continued to sit on the terrace. The earth underneath the garden of the old folk's home was alive. Seeds waited. Cicada larvae nursed. Earthworms and carrion beetles laboured over putrefaction.

'We were no better than you are,' said Liberson. 'The time and place made us what we were. Many of us couldn't take it and left. That's something you know about, Baruch, because now they're coming back to you.'

'Tell us a story, Eliezer,' I said all of a sudden. 'Tell us a story.'

'A story,' said the old man. 'All right, I will.'

'A few days after we arrived in this country,' he began in the old familiar tone, 'before we met your grandfather, Tsirkin and I found work digging holes for new saplings in an almond grove near Gedera. It's awful work. You feel your spine is splitting, your hands are full of blisters, and the Arab coolies beyond the acacia hedge are waiting for you to break so they can get their old jobs back again. Just then one man threw down his hoe and said he was going for water, and another went along to help him. They came back with a jug and poured everyone a drink, and when they had finished that they said they would count the holes.'

He sniggered. 'Did you hear that, Albert? We dug and they counted.' Since Albert said nothing, he continued. 'Every group of workers had its hole counters. First they went for water, then they poured it, then they counted the holes. Soon they were counting people, and before long, party members. Within a year they were travelling to Zionist congresses in Europe, and from there to raise money in America, which gave them even more to count.'

Liberson laughed. 'Tsirkin hated them. The hole counters became big-time politicians and never gave us enough money. We were always on the verge of making it, on the verge of getting in the harvest, on the verge of starving to death.'

'*Non tiene busha*,' repeated Albert from his bed.

'Once,' continued Liberson, 'Pesya brought home some member of the Central Committee. Meshulam was a little boy. He sat there hypnotised all evening, asking all sorts of questions. The man, whose name I won't mention, was thrilled by how much the boy knew. After he had gladly answered all his questions, Pesya took him to the cowshed to see Tsirkin milk the cows. Tsirkin took one look at him and recognised him at once.

'"Well, look who's here," said Mandolin. "It's just like the good old days. I'll milk and you can count the cows."'

Liberson turned back towards the Valley. He moved his hands and cane slowly, feeling his way across the map of his longings. 'We came to build a village. A place of our own. There, that big green blotch way out there – that's the eucalyptus woods we planted. The trees sucked up the swamp. Cut them down and it will be back, as far as the eye can see.'

He did not know they were gone already. The big, sappy trunks had been felled the year before, and nothing had happened. The stumps were rooted out, and cotton was planted in their place.

'Beyond the woods is the wadi where Pinness ran to kill himself when he found Leah with Rilov. Who would have believed it? A pregnant woman! We ran after him and brought him back, and only found his gun a year later during ploughing. It was rusted and useless, and Leah was dead by then too. She came down with some rare cave fever that even Doctor Yoffe had never seen.'

He drew a quick stroke in the air with his cane, from west to south. 'There, on that far mountain, Elijah saw the little rain cloud and ran before the chariots of Ahab. He raced the king's horses all the way to Jezreel, over there, and reached it before them.'

We went back inside. The room smelled of the sweet crimson perfume of overripe Astrakhan apples, Liberson's approaching death, and Albert's sheets.

'You've caused quite a rumpus, you two boys, eh? You with your graves, and you with your girls.'

'I drive a tractor now,' said Uri. 'I'm a working man.'

Stripped of his sense of humour, Uri was alone and defenceless against Liberson. The old man sat wearily on his bed. I felt bad about taking up so much of the small room and making him huddle against the wall.

'The Movement likes to think of us as one big happy family,' he said. 'The tribe of pioneers. Together we came, together we redeemed the land, together we farmed it, together we'll die, and together we'll be buried in a nice photogenic row. In every old photograph there's a row sitting and a row standing, and two more of them on a crate in the back, looking over the others' shoulders, and two more lying down in front, propped on their elbows with their heads touching. Three rows out of four eventually left the country. In every photograph you have the three rows, the heroes, and the zeroes.'

'Grandfather once said something like that too,' said Uri. But enveloped in darkness, Liberson was not listening. Only the memory of love could still catch his light-deprived eyes. He faced the window. I knew what he would say. 'Over there, where the kibbutz has its factory, there was once a lovely vineyard. That's where I met Fanya.' He turned toward, me with tears in his white eyeballs. 'You did right, Baruch, to let me go there by myself. Anyone else would have tried to help me.'

I told him about Meshulam's swamp. 'How silly can you get,' he sighed. 'Who cares about all that any more? It's just a big waste of water.' The details didn't interest him.

'I hate this place,' he said to us. 'They make me weave lampshades out of raffia and eat supper at four o'clock.'

Uri wanted to hear more about Liberson's adventures with Fanya, but Liberson's mood had taken a turn for the worse. He was already somewhere else. He had left us and dived back into a world in which we did not exist.

'The old geezer,' raged Uri on our way home. 'He doesn't give a damn. I planned this meeting for so long, and the two of you had to go and ruin it – you with your nonsense stories and him with his textbook memories. Lecturing us with that cane. Even when they're blind, those founding fathers of yours, they have to see more and know better than anyone.'

'What do you want from him?' I asked. 'His wife is dead, his friends are dead, and Meshulam's swamp, if you ask me, scared him more than he let on.'

'I'd rather he did chuck me out than treat me so condescendingly. They were always blind. They stood up to their knees in mud with earth in their ears and never saw more than one thing.'

'But why should he give a damn about your problems? What did you ever do for him?'

'I suppose it's just as well,' Uri said. 'Maybe all my feelings of guilt just came from missing this place.'

'He only thinks about Fanya,' I said. 'That whole performance on the terrace was just to show us that he remembers where the vineyard was.'

'He's a sick man,' Uri said. 'He's demented. He could easily have an operation to remove those stupid cataracts. He wants to be blind. I swear he does.'

'What's left for him to see?'

'My mother was right,' Uri said. 'All those crazy people really drove you mad.'

I didn't answer him.

'You can't imagine how much I missed this place,' Uri said. 'In spite of the scandal. In spite of being beaten and made to leave. Twice I even came secretly at night, but both times I left right away.'

He looked at me for a moment and laughed. 'What a waste for you to walk around like this. You should be hitched to a cart or a plough.'

'Suppose I carried you in my arms,' I suggested.

'Fat chance,' he said.

'It's no problem for me.' I smiled with forlorn hope. 'I could easily carry you home from here.'

'What's wrong with you?' he asked. 'Why don't you find a nice bull to lay instead of picking up boys?'

Uri can be as vicious as a weasel.

'I can carry you in my arms, on my back, on my shoulders, any way you want,' I persisted.

But he wasn't having it. 'Stop it, will you!' he said, and now his voice sounded jagged and scared.

We walked on in silence. As we approached the village, we saw a crowd of men by Ben-Ya'akov's pear orchard. We could hear shouting in the distance, and when we came closer we saw that it was Meshulam again with his sawtoothed sickle and sickening bandanna.

'What am I supposed to do?' Ya'akovi was yelling. 'Station a guard by every water tap?'

The earth moved like jelly around him. Squishily it threw up from the depths dark refuse, sludge, bones, and thick, pale worms that coiled around the pear trees and dragged them down into the pestilent muck. In their place sprang up reeds and rushes as tall as a man, which Meshulam charged brandishing his sickle. An old Arab he had hired ploughed lazily by the swampside, mumbling familiar words. A small herd of wild boars came grunting out of Grandfather's stories. There were several large males, some brutish-looking females, and a dozen or so bristle-haired piglets with stiff, erect tails. Trotting up to the swamp, they sloshed in to wallow in the deepening mire. I glanced at the sky. Black dots soared overhead and swooped closer. Shrieking madly, they circled above me.

I looked at the hysterical Ya'akovi, at Uri, at the crowd of angry farmers. Through the thin veil of their work clothes, sun-parched skin, and strong bodies, I could see the great mud fossils that had been waiting these many years in the earth.

Now the ponderous water buffalo approached, their deep, moist nostrils flaring excitedly at the first signs of human apostasy. They didn't scare me. I was used to animals. A huge blond bull strode among them. The girth of its shoulders, the thickness of its hooves, and the hot vapours blowing from its wet muzzle made my heart beat faster. I began running towards them, and as I drew near I saw the young man in khaki trousers and a beekeeper's mask supporting a stumbling old man who carried a decrepit pack. Yet soon the whole drove crossed the field and vanished beyond the distant cypresses, and when I returned to the flooded orchard and the questioning looks, I realised that no one else had seen a thing.

# 49

After Rosh Hashana Yosi came home on leave. I heard the tyres of his jeep screech to a stop, the loud crackle of a two-way radio, footsteps running and climbing stairs, and last of all, a loud girlish scream from Avraham and Rivka's house.

The cabin door swung open. Standing there in his uniform with his officer's bars and paratrooper wings, Yosi demanded to know the identity of 'the pious bombshell in my parents' house'.

Uri burst out laughing. The twins laughed. I could feel my gorge rise at the affection they displayed despite the differences between them. Yosi had also received mail from his parents, and now the two of them sat down to compare letters and photographs.

'It's about time Father got some fun out of life,' smiled Uri, though Yosi thought that 'instead of teaching all those darkies', Avraham should have found work as an adviser in some new settlement on the Golan Heights.

I stood by the sink, slicing vegetables for a salad. First the onion and tomatoes, then the cucumbers and green pepper. Perhaps their fresh tang would be wafted far away, as far as the ends of the earth.

I liked being with Uri, and Yosi's appearance annoyed me. I

knew I would have to put him up in the cabin and regretted having agreed to give Avraham and Rivka's place to the cantor.

'Why don't you two take a walk,' I said. 'Supper will be ready in half an hour.'

'What's the matter, Baruch?' asked Yosi. 'Don't you like being with your cousins? Or are you afraid we might sting you for a loan?'

'I'm not afraid, and I'll be glad to get out of here as soon as either of you wants the farm back,' I said.

'Who said anything about wanting the farm back or you leaving it?' asked Uri. 'Why do you always take everything so seriously?'

'It would take a heavy infantry company to get you out of here,' said Yosi in the clipped military tone he had learned from Uzi Rilov. He began chuckling too loudly with that wrong-way laugh of his, breathing in instead of out in spasmodic, infuriating jerks. The muscles in the back of my neck tensed.

'If Uri wasn't here now,' I told him, 'you'd go flying out the window, right back into that damn jeep of yours.'

'Comrades,' said Uri, 'suppose we all calm down, okay? My dear Baruch and Yosi, in these difficult times when the entire Movement is looking for new horizons, let us not waste our energy on sterile disputes. The three of us haven't been alone like this for years. The three grandsons of the one and only Ya'akov Mirkin, pioneer, swamp drainer, and desert blossomer. Let's give him a hand, people!'

'Two grandsons and one Jean Valjean,' corrected Yosi.

'I'd rather be Grandfather's calf than your mother's son,' I shot back.

Yosi rose, said he was going to remove the radio from the jeep, and left the cabin.

'Just what was that brilliant Chinese proverb of yours supposed to mean?' asked Uri.

'At least you have a mother,' I answered.

'Stop the dramatics,' he said crossly. 'This isn't the first time I've heard you talk crap, but I know you well enough to know when you mean it.'

'Why don't you call your brother,' I said. 'The salad is ready, and I'll make the eggs when you're at the table.'

Uri went out and came back with Yosi half an hour later.

'We were at the cemetery,' Yosi said. 'God Almighty, what have you done to our father's farm?'

'It was your father's decision to go abroad,' I answered him. 'And since you both announced that you weren't coming back, you have no right to complain now.'

'Enough,' said Uri. 'Either we eat or I leave you here by yourselves and find someone to climb the water tower with.'

When supper was over and we had calmed down, we went to wrestle in Meshulam's abandoned hayloft, since the Mirkin farm was out of hay.

'It's the Twins versus the Monster!' panted Uri, riding my back and trying to strangle me while Yosi bobbed, weaved, butted, and punched me. The three of us couldn't stop laughing. The straw stuck to us, getting in our hair and all over us, until at last I threw Uri down on it and pinned him with my foot while lifting Yosi in the air by his belt. This time he did not cry. His mouth opened wide and he shouted battle cries, choking on his laughter.

A oil lantern approached us from the direction of Founder's Cabin, bobbing up and down in the dark. Frightened and angry, Meshulam stepped into the hayloft.

'Attention!' cried Yosi.

Uri jumped at Meshulam and snatched the lantern away. 'Are we back from a rendezvous with a water tap?' he asked. 'Or have we come to set fire to the hayloft?'

'What do you think you're doing here?' demanded Meshulam furiously.

Touchingly wrapped in Pesya's wet black slip, he looked like a little baby crow.

'Moron!' said Yosi.

'We were just having a little fun, Meshulam,' I said. 'Let's get out of here, boys.'

Uri walked out backward, his sardonic face toward Meshulam. 'You know the rules,' he said. 'You have to count to a hundred before you can look for us.'

My high spirits had faded. We started back for the cabin, but halfway there Yosi asked to go to the cemetery. 'It must be awfully nice there at night, with all those white flowers and gravestones.'

I opened the gate. The gravel crunched beneath our feet. Crickets sang all around. The twins leaned on Grandfather's grave while I sat on Rosa Munkin's pink tombstone.

'How much do you charge for a grave?' Yosi asked.

'That depends. For a rich old American it's about a hundred thousand dollars. Busquilla could tell you exactly.'

'That makes you a millionaire,' said Yosi in a voice that was higher than usual. 'You're a millionaire, do you know that?'

'I'm not anything,' I said. 'I'm just keeping up the farm. I'm doing what Grandfather wanted.'

'It is nice here,' said Uri. 'It's awfully nice.'

He rose and went over to the wall. We heard him peeing there.

'Didn't the army teach you how to take a leak quietly at night?' called Yosi. 'Wag it.'

'I'm trying, but all my life it's wagged me,' came Uri's voice from the darkness. 'I'm going to bed. I'll see you in the morning.'

'What a character,' said Yosi. 'He's a character, that Uri.'

Now that we had fooled around and it was too dark to see his mother's face looking at me from his own, I felt more comfortable with him.

'So what's going to happen with you?' he asked.

'What's worrying you? Didn't you say I was a millionaire?'

'Why are you always so edgy with me?'

'Because you get on my nerves.'

'And you don't get on mine? You're a pain in the neck. You made the whole school laugh at us. To this day everyone in the village thinks there's something wrong with you.'

'Let them,' I said. 'They're just jealous. They drove Efrayim away from here. It's time they realised.'

'Stop quoting Grandfather all the time,' said Yosi. 'And if you ask me, it's a bit odd that no one but you ever heard Grandfather make such a strange request.'

'What are you getting at?'

'That if that was his will, you didn't do badly by it.'

'Pinness heard it too,' I said.

'Pinness,' snorted Yosi. 'Well, well.'

For some reason I was enjoying the conversation.

'This is the first real talk you and I have ever had,' said Yosi.

He rose, about-faced, bent to smell the flowers, studied Shulamit's grave, walked back and forth, and sat down beside me.

'Why did you bury her here? Who the hell was she?'

'It was Grandfather's wish,' I said.

'Grandfather's wish, Grandfather's wish! Don't you ever get tired of it?'

'It's what he wanted.'

'So you just went and took her?'

I went and took her. Her coffin was the only one I never opened before the funeral.

'She was all alone in this country. She had no one else.'

'You're making me cry,' he said. 'Tell me, you saw the two of them together in that old folk's home. What was there between them?'

'I don't know anything about those things,' I answered, thinking of Grandfather's wrinkled neck and bald head in the flesh of Shulamit's dead thighs.

'What did you say?'

'Nothing.'

He looked at me suspiciously. 'But you must have spied on them like you did on everyone.'

He waited for an answer, then went on. 'You think we didn't know that you snooped and peeked through windows?'

'Suppose you did. So what?'

'When we were little, my mother once said that if she ever caught you at it again, she'd give you a licking. My father told her that if she so much as laid a finger on you, he'd break her arms and legs.'

I said nothing. I thought of the looks Rivka gave me when I wrestled with the big calves and of her hatred for my mother, whose wedding dress and flawless bell-clapper legs went on ravaging my aunt's life even after they had gone up in flames.

'I always envied your living with Grandfather,' Yosi said suddenly. 'You were his child.'

'I thought so too,' I said, swallowing a dry dungball of mucus in my mouth. 'I'm not so sure any more.'

'I envied your being an orphan,' he said. 'Once, when we were six or seven, I told Uri that I wished our parents would die so that Pinness would take us for hikes too and Grandfather would bring us up.'

'But neither of you would have buried him like I did,' I said. 'Ya'akovi would have made you back down, and Uri couldn't care less.'

'You were always so strange, always hanging out with the old folk, with Pinness and Grandfather and Tsirkin and Liberson. You frightened everyone from the time you were six. Do you know that no one ever dared pick on me or Uri because of you? They were scared of you.'

He slipped off the grave and sat on the ground, running his hand over the soil and rolling some between his fingers, which were short and stubby like his father's. It was a habit the pioneers had picked up in the Valley and passed on to their children. Their grandchildren were born with it.

'I would have stayed on here,' he said after a pause. 'I swear I would have, and you know I could have made a decent farmer. It was only these graves that made me decide to leave home, and Uri will never come back. In the end you'll be the only one left. You'll show the village and the world, and you'll make more money than the old folk ever dreamed of in their wildest visions.'

'Why does everyone keep talking about the money?' I asked. 'You can see for yourself that I don't spend it. Have I bought anything for the cabin? Clothes? Built a swimming pool? I've never even been abroad.'

'That shows you're a real farmer,' chuckled Yosi. 'No one in this village knows how to enjoy life, including myself. Farmers don't like to spend money. They're too afraid of drought, locusts, mice. They've got their feet on the ground and their heads in the clouds, looking for rain – because that's the one thing that's free. Uri is the only one who was able to outgrow all that.'

'I'm just a watchman,' I said. 'I'm watching Grandfather. I promised I wouldn't let anyone take him from here.'

'My favourite story was the one about his saving you from that rabid jackal,' murmured Yosi. 'Our father made a bedtime story out of it. You were sitting in the yard throwing earth at some kittens, and Grandfather jumped on the jackal and broke all its bones.'

'It was a hyena,' I said. 'It even said so in the newspaper. Its skull is in the nature room at school.'

'If you feel that strongly about it, fine,' said Yosi. 'The point is that Grandfather saved your life.'

'I was in the yard by pure chance,' I said. 'Don't you think he would have saved yours?'

'If it had been me, there would have been no hyena. Don't you see that? Do you think it just happened to come along?'

I was flabbergasted. It never occurred to me that he might look at it that way.

'Sometimes, when we've been lying in ambush along the border night after night until I get so sleepy I hallucinate, I'm afraid that Shifris will turn up. I worry that he's going to set off a mine, or that some soldier will yell "Halt!" and that idiot who never halted in his life will keep on going and get himself shot.'

'He won't,' I said. 'He's just somebody Grandfather made up.'

'Grandfather was quite something,' said Yosi. 'He must have been a real heavyweight. Why else would they come from all over the world to be buried next to him?'

'That day with the hyena was a clear, bright summer day,' I said. 'Pinness made me remember everything by seasons.'

'Let's go for a walk,' he said. 'I'm getting cold.'

'Your father was born in early summer,' I told him. 'The double wedding was in the autumn. Grandmother died in the spring, and Rilov blew himself up in winter. That's when Tsirkin died too, but Fanya died in summer and Grandfather in autumn.

'I sat up with him for three days and three nights,' I said. For the first time in my life I was telling a story too. 'Your father kept coming and going. So did the doctor. Grandfather's friends were there too – Tsirkin, Liberson, Shifris, and Pinness. I was so tired I didn't know what I was doing.'

He lay in his bed, on his prickly mattress of seaweed, his pale skin clothed in new pyjamas. I rose heavily and stepped outside, onto the earthen paths that never failed me.

Autumn had descended on the village with the usual downpour of fallen leaves and the anxious, mournful cries of baby swifts baulking at their first migration. I followed the cart track to the fields, trampling the last yellow grass sticking up in the centre ridge. The titmouse and warbler nests were unravelling in the orchards and in the drainpipes of the cowsheds. Behind the stud pen I spied the cattle dealers' loathsome six-wheel lorry loaded with three dejected, stricken-tailed calves as it made its way among horse-drawn carriages and American limousines never seen in our village. Elegantly dressed men and women in high, round collars and children in shiny black shoes were walking up and down. I wondered who had told all these strangers about Grandfather's death, but I continued along the avenue of carob trees, whose heavy white smell embarrassed the visitors. 'The date and the carob are unisexual fruit trees. One male can pollinate dozens of females,' said Pinness in my ear.

I heard the whirr of the spring as it laboured to cool its late-summer trickle, and the fragrant fizz of delicate, ripely fallen fruit that lay rotting on the ground with soft drunken eructations. Every summer we stored yellow pears in bales of hay, where they gave off sweet fermenting fumes as they stewed. The fruits' flesh dissolved inside the peel, and by autumn they had turned into soft egglike lozenges swollen with intoxicating cream. Removing them gently from their hiding place, we pierced their skin with our teeth and sucked out the alcoholic nectar.

'I remember that,' said Yosi. 'It tasted like a liqueur.'

Dryness and finality were everywhere. The cicadas were long gone. The fierce, confident buzzing of heat-propelled wasps and beetles had subsided, and little piles of pebbles and chaff were the only signs of the dwellings of the harvest ants. And yet in the green groves the pistils of the oranges were swelling with a slow murmur and the grapefruits were fattening on their stems. Cells divided in the turkey eggs. Frozen sperm thawed in the wombs of cows. Milk and honey, sap and semen, were gathered up by the autumn.

There was a smell of watered earth in the air. The soil had been turned for autumn ploughing. It always smelled of rain before the first rains came. 'That's how the earth gets the clouds to water it,' said Pinness, who was walking by my side.

I felt a terrible sadness. For Grandfather, dying of his own incurable volition. For my own life. For the House of Mirkin, on whose windows love had stealthily tapped but once to die with my mother and father.

The blackberries were blooming by the spring. A baby bleated poems in their brambles. Strong as an ox, a barefoot boy with coarse features came towards me swinging cans of milk. 'Straight from the cow,' he bellowed, shutting his eyes for me to pat his neck.

'Let's get out of here, my child,' said Pinness, pushing me aside with uncharacteristic strength. 'Let's get out of here.'

It was autumn, and flocks of storks and pelicans were already wandering southward overhead, darkening the skies of the Valley with their giant wings. I knew that soon the robin would return to nest in the pomegranate tree, defending its home with loud, rosy-hearted clicks. Next would come the starlings, their thousands of spotted breasts spinning and whirling in great flocks, descending to blanket the earth of the Valley with their excrement.

My bare soles felt the huge snails stirring in the ground, waiting to be awakened by the first rains and tilt at each other with their siliceous blades. The bulbs of the autumn crocuses made bubbles in the surface of the earth. 'Soon the plover will arrive in our fields, wagging its pretty plumes and following the furrows,' called out Pinness behind me. I headed on into the hills, along the orphaned paths leading to the mountain. The farther I walked from the village, the stronger became the unruly smell of elecampane and the woodier the pads of thorny burnet. On the blue mountain where I had never been, the rubbery sceptres of the squill were already in bloom, and the speckled white blossoms of the caper plants hid sharp hooks that would tear at my flesh.

Green plains stretched beyond the mountain. (Not the sea, said the wind, not the sea, said the rustle of grain.) A wide river flowed there. White-breasted women bathed in its waters, and on its banks nestled little villages. Farther off the earth tilted and vanished with a motile, nebulous glow. It might have been white tundra wolves that howled there, or the wind tousling the birch trees. The land was broad, so vast it never met the horizon, which quivered high above it.

I turned and ran like a child who has opened a forbidden trunk.

And then the visions stopped rising from Grandfather's body and I knew that he was dead.

'That's an interesting way to determine clinical death,' said Yosi. 'Did you ever tell Doctor Munk about it?'

'Grandfather died when he had no more dreams,' I said. 'Doesn't everyone?'

# 50

After a few days Yosi went back to the army. When I shook his hand as he climbed into the jeep, it still prickled with wary suspicion. Uri stayed on and helped me out with some jobs. Tonya Rilov died that week, and when Uri and I lifted her up from Margulis's gravestone, there were not enough bees to fill the space she had left. Dani Rilov stood to one side, whimpering in a strange, high voice. 'Listen to him,' Uri said. 'He doesn't know how to cry. His father never taught him.'

The days that followed kept us digging all the time. Dani Rilov's little insect brain had hatched an unexpected problem – should his mother be buried next to her husband's boots or next to Margulis? He was so dense that he even went to ask Riva, who wrung out the cloth she was holding, pushed him off her freshly mopped stairs, and said that for all she cared we could open her husband's coffin and 'throw your mother and your father's filthy boots into it together'.

Each morning, confused and tearful, he came to tell me he had changed his mind. Surprised by such inner turmoil in a crude fattener of calves like Dani, I dug Tonya up and moved her back and forth five times despite the stench and the stings of angry bees. Even Uri, who normally could not have passed up a quip about this underground shuttle, remarked that Tonya deserved the utmost consideration 'for her devoted finger-sucking among the bees, rain or shine for so many years'.

Fortunately, Busquilla lost his temper in the end and said to Dani, 'That's enough! It's time to put an end to this farce. Who do you think you're dealing with here, a dead cat? Where's your respect for your parents?'

To me he said, 'What does he think he's doing? It's almost Yom Kippur!'

He invited Uri and me to spend the day with his family in the nearby town where he lived.

'You can come with us to the Moroccan synagogue,' he said. 'It wouldn't hurt you to see that there are real Jews in this country.'

'Let's do it,' said Uri. 'It might be fun.'

'You go,' I said to him. 'That stuff isn't for me. When did we ever make a thing about Yom Kippur?'

'I'm not going without you,' said Uri.

We stayed at home. That afternoon we were visited by Weissberg's little twins. Like two black-capped nightingales, they stood bashfully but proudly in the doorway of the cabin. 'You're invited to the meal before the fast,' they said, flying off with matched movements as if each were the other's shadow.

'I think we should take them up on it,' said Uri. 'Weissberg must have forgiven us.'

'Not me,' I said. 'That's not my cup of tea. And I don't like having supper at 4 p.m.'

'I'm going.'

'You can do what you want.'

At four o'clock, with the Day of Atonement soon to begin, I took off my shirt, stood in the middle of the yard, and split a few logs as loudly as I could. I stuffed the pieces into the wood-burning stove that stood against the cabin, making sure the iron door clanked, and took a steaming hot shower on Grandfather's little milking stool while Uri sat in his parents' house feasting his stomach on the cantor's food and his eyes on his beautiful daughter.

I scrubbed myself till I was red, hidden in steam as I listened to the deep purr of the chimney on the other side of the wall. I knew that the Weissbergs could hear the stove too and were doing their best to ignore the religious outrage.

Towards evening, when the cantor and his family went off to synagogue, Uri returned to the cabin.

'Aren't you going to pray?' I asked as caustically as I could.

'Not tonight. But I will go tomorrow,' he answered solemnly.

Although the second and third generation of villagers kept away from the synagogue, which was empty and abandoned most of the year, the old folk, after lapsing from the fiery free thought of their youth into subsequent indifference, had begun to take a renewed interest in religion. Some became greater heretics than ever, while others, falling prey to fears and penitence, took to praying regularly every Sabbath with great devoutness and even with tears. Eliezer Liberson referred to them as 'our bugbear comrades', a term whose exact significance escaped me, though its tone and intention were perfectly clear.

'What's she like?' I asked.

'Who?'

'The young cantoress.'

Uri laughed. 'She sat there like a heifer with its head in its feedbox. She just stared at her plate and didn't say a word. All I saw of her was a bit of forehead, a couple of fingers, and six yards of blue fabric.'

'She's beautiful,' I said.

'Since when do you notice women?' asked Uri. 'Has something happened? Do you want to tell me about it?'

I kept silent.

'I'm not really into all that any more, but there's still a thing or two I remember,' he said.

I woke him up in the middle of the night, and we went to the cemetery. In spite of myself I dug Tonya up one more time and moved her back to Margulis, although I left her headstone by the grave of Rilov's boots.

'Something tells me you're going out of your mind,' said Uri, who was sitting on Shlomo Levin's grave.

'A scarecrow like you would look better with a beard and sidelocks,' I said to him.

'You're beginning to annoy me,' said Uri. 'You're jealous, that's all. If you'd like to start up with her, go on. You can ask Pinness for a few good icebreakers from the Bible, go to the synagogue, and make eyes at her. I'll even teach you a few tricks myself.'

'I am not jealous,' I said, evening out the sides of the grave. 'And I doubt that your country-boy tricks would get me very far with her.'

When I awoke in the morning he was leaning out of the cabin window in his underwear.

'Quick,' he said, 'get up and take a look. What a sight!'

I got out of bed and looked out at the street. The Weissbergs were on their way from our yard to the synagogue, mother and daughter with coifs on their heads, the cantor in a shiny bright gown and huge skullcap. All had new white canvas shoes on their feet instead of the leather ones that were forbidden on the fast day.

'Don't they look athletic,' grinned Uri. 'Come on, team!' he called out to them.

They turned to look at him. His head and shoulders were out of the window, dappled sunlight falling through the casuarina tree onto his bare skin. Weissberg uttered a single syllable. The two gorgeous eyes stared back down at the ground, and the stockinged legs beneath the dress resumed their motion.

'Come on, let's eat something,' said Uri. 'Make me the Grandfather Special. Just – no colostrum, please.'

After breakfast he announced that he was going to the synagogue.

'They invited me yesterday,' he explained.

'I doubt they'll be thrilled to see you there after that crack of yours this morning.'

'It's not their private synagogue.' He left the cabin.

A long, boring day stretched out ahead of me. There was no special work to be done in the cemetery. I had no one to ask for forgiveness, and Uri's behaviour had annoyed me. After doing the dishes I walked around the yard for a while and then climbed the steps to Avraham and Rivka's house, crouching low as I tiptoed barefoot in the hope that some of the Weissbergs had returned to rest from the long service.

It was quiet. I opened the door and stepped inside, plunging into the unfamiliar smell that had already sunk into the walls. In Uri and Yosi's room the twins' clothes were neatly arranged on the backs of chairs. A white sheet had been hung over the bookcase to hide its forbidden books from sight. Two stern-looking suitcases stood in Avraham and Rivka's room, where the two beds had been moved apart. All the pictures in the living room had been turned around to face the wall. The impenetrable dark blue dress lay quietly folded on the cantor's daughter's bed. I knelt and buried my face in the thick weave, six yards of heavy blue fabric, until the horrid screech of a bluejay startled me and I ran back down the stairs and to the village centre.

The street was full of tractors as usual. No one ever made a fuss about the High Holy Days in our village.

'The hens do not stop laying on Yom Kippur, nor do the cows' udders go on strike,' Eliezer Liberson had written in the newsletter years before I was born.

Leaning against the wall of the synagogue, I listened to the supplicatory murmur of the prayer, which was interrupted by the merry shouts of playing children, the sharp whistles of swifts, and the purr of the refrigerator in the dairy.

I peered through the window. Weissberg was rocking back and forth like a huge owl. His wife and daughter were in the women's gallery along with some other unfamiliar females who were visiting relatives in the village. A few softly giggling girls walked in and out to stare at my cousin, whose handsome looks were enhanced by the embroidered skullcap on his head. The two little Weissbergs sat on either side of him, singing in thin, piercing voices. Uri followed their soft fingers, which led him over the sombre furrows of the prayer-book, helping him past the obstacles of the age-old words.

'For the sins we have sinned before Thee without knowing. For the sins we have sinned before Thee by our prurience. For the sins we have sinned before Thee by profligacy. For the sins we have sinned before Thee by our foolish utterance. For the sins we have sinned before Thee by our evil urge.'

Weissberg shut his eyes and crooned lamentingly, like Grandfather when he was bitten by the hyena.

'For all of these, O Lord of Forgiveness, forgive us, excuse us, absolve us.'

The sun dipped towards the blue mountain amid the last clamour of the youngsters splashing in the nearby swimming pool.

The clear, pleasant voice of the cantor carried through the synagogue windows. 'Open Thy gate as the gates are shut, for the day has passed, the sun will set and will pass, let us come unto Thy gates.' And the small congregation joined in. 'O Lord, we pray you, forgive us, excuse us, pardon us, absolve us, have mercy on us, atone for us, forget our sin and iniquity.'

The air was warm and still. There was not a breath of wind. Clear, round, and unblemished, the words went forth on their great flight.

Early the next morning I went to Pioneer Home. Uri was still asleep. Towards noon Busquilla arrived to announce that he had had 'a good atonement' and that it looked like we would have two funerals next month, 'a small one from abroad and a big one from Tel Aviv'. Efficient executive that he was, he sometimes went on reconnaissance trips to villages, hospitals, and old folk's homes and never erred in his predictions. 'He's gone to look over the merchandise,' Pinness would sneer whenever he saw the black vehicle kicking up dust in the fields.

From afar I saw the figures of the Weissberg twins and their sister heading down the gravel path towards the cemetery. In my embarrassment I tried to hide among the trees, but the two boys discovered me at once.

'We're going tomorrow,' they informed me. Their sister strolled among the gravestones, keeping her back turned towards me.

I felt an awful fear of my own body. 'Have a good trip,' I whispered to the boys, leaving quickly before I did something unforeseen. I had always felt at home in the dark, deep quiet of my flesh, and now, appalled and furious, I took off on the run for the cabin.

'What's the rush?' inquired Uri, coming towards me.

'I forgot something,' I said. Two minutes later, perched on the roof of the hayloft, I saw him open the cemetery gate.

That afternoon I went to see Pinness.

'Ya'akov,' I said, 'Uri was in the synagogue the whole day of Yom Kippur and prayed as though he had been bitten by a hyena.'

'There's nothing so terrible about that, my child,' Pinness said.

'Can I sleep at your house tonight?' I asked him.

'Of course,' he said. He kept a folding bed behind the door, and after supper he showed me where to put it.

'Cover me, Ya'akov,' I said. I wanted to talk to him, I wanted him tell me a story, to complain that he and Grandfather had never taught me to eradicate the pests in my own flesh.

His fat, ailing old body moved with difficulty. My skin tingled with pleasure and longing as he covered me with the thin blanket. He ran his hand over my face in the darkness, and then there was only the squeak of his bed springs and the soft murmur of his speech.

I awoke an hour after midnight. In the darkness I made out the hunched silhouette of the old teacher sitting awake on his bed. Without his glasses he looked like a frightened mole awaiting the thud of a hoe on its neck.

'What is it, Ya'akov?' I asked. 'What's wrong?'

'Shhh!' said Pinness sharply. 'Quiet!'

The air was still. A breeze as warm and light as a sleeping calf's breath whispered in the trees. Suddenly Pinness caught his breath and shuddered. Distinct and defiant, the fierce, perfectly formed words struck the earth like big drops of first rain, like the wings of thousands of locusts.

'I'm screwing the cantor's daughter.'

Then there was silence. I didn't know where to rush first – to Pinness, who had fallen off his bed like a feed sack, wheezing and gasping for breath, or to Uri up on the water tower, already encircled by shouts and the tramp of running feet.

'Help me,' groaned Pinness, who was an expert at detecting conflict in living organisms.

I laid him in bed and shovelled food into him, spoon after savage solacing spoon, pausing only to wipe his chin and mouth.

By the time I reached the water tower dozens of people were there. As pale as my American corpses, Weissberg and his wife were sitting on the ground. Burly farmers waited at the foot of the ladder.

All eyes were focused upward as my cousin appeared, hitched his legs over the metal railing, and began to descend the ladder with the bell-shaped silhouette of a dark dress behind him. Through their latticework of long stockings, the splendour of forbidden thighs flashed in the night. The crowd let out an angry growl. I stepped forward, pushed my way through it with the slow butting motion that every cattle breeder in the village knew well, and planted myself at the bottom of the ladder with my arms crossed over my chest.

Uri came down first, reaching up to help the cantor's daughter, and I walked protectively behind them until we got to the house.

The Weissbergs left the village that same night. Uri buried himself in Grandfather's bed, and in the morning Riva Margulis was awakened by a damp stench coming from outside. For a moment she thought that Bulgakov was back, fouling the yard with his breath. Yet when she skipped happily to the window, against which, smitten by transparency and yearning, bees crashed ceaselessly, and pulled back its spotless curtains to peer out, she saw that it was only Meshulam, who had smashed the big water meter in her yard.

Filthy animals were splashing around, splattering mud on the porch steps. Riva, who had even scrubbed the street outside her house on Rosh Hashana eve and made the tractors keep off it until it was dry, was the last living soul in the village to possess the ancient mixture of madness, faith, and uncompromising loyalty to principle. Without further ado, she joined the fray.

She had not been caught unprepared. In her husband's old shed, on shelves that were once stocked with fumigators, honey extractors, honeycomb frames, and jars of propolis, now lay thousands of neatly folded mopping cloths, while hundreds of brooms and fresh towels stood against the walls.

Armed with these simple tools and a visionary gleam in her eye, she sallied forth to the biggest mop-up of them all. The whole village turned out to watch the mocked old woman whose madness had lost her her husband and made her a public nuisance.

Riva's practised hands twirled the cloths with deft motions, each ending with a well-aimed splat as the cloth hit the ground. She first drove the swamp back from the house, and then, after pausing to rest, pushed on for the final battle. For three whole days she mopped Meshulam's swamp, wringing out the cloths in the wadi.

'Now this place looks clean,' she said contentedly when she had finished. She washed all the cloths, hung them out to dry, and went home to scrub the windows.

# 51

Uri did not go back to work for Rivka's brother. For weeks he lay in Grandfather's bed making horrible noises. Nehama, the cantor's beautiful, silent daughter, was taken home that same night. The Weissbergs did not even stay to pack their things.

The cantor refused to accept his pay, turned down all offers of a lift to the railway station, and rebuffed apologies and pained expressions of regret. Taking his wife and children, he walked them through the fields, stumbling in the dark on big clods of earth, scratched by autumn brambles.

For weeks I ministered to Uri, who was overcome with love and longing.

'I want only her, Nehama,' he groaned. 'No one else. I want you to go and bring her back from there,' he insisted. 'No one can stand up to you. Go!' he screamed. 'Carry her piggyback, sling her over your shoulder, hold her in your arms, do it any way you like. If you don't bring her to me, I'm going to die in this bed!'

I was scared. I didn't know where to begin. I drove to the village of the Hasidim, but no one would even talk to me.

'This isn't funny any more,' was all I heard from the old barber, who sat grieving on the ground, cleaning his cycle chain with a bowl of oil and petrol. 'It's not like our arguments with Eliezer Liberson. No fouler deed was ever done by Jew to Jew.'

Uri refused to wash, dress, or eat. All night he groaned and called Nehama's name. Spasmodically he plucked at his loins, groping and moaning and sniffing his fingers compulsively, searching for the musky smell of the girl, which had remained there like sticky drops of amber.

At first I tried to talk him into eating. Then, terror-stricken, I tried force-feeding him. But the spoon just bent against his teeth, and he threw up clear spittle on the sheet.

Five weeks later, by which time he had lost four stone and most of his pubic hair, Nehama Weissberg was brought to the village in the company of three mournful rabbis.

'She's pregnant,' they said, taking Uri back with them.

That was what took me to the city for the first time in my life. Uri and Nehama's wedding was held in a mouldy old courtyard. Weissberg did not invite many guests, and only Pinness and Yosi came from the village. Busquilla, who alone had remembered to cable Avraham and Rivka, came too. Uri's parents arrived straight from the airport. Avraham was tense and irritable, but his first glimpse of Nehama ironed the creases from his brow and made him beam. Rivka was suntanned, suspicious, and loudmouthed until Mrs Weissberg threw a heavy shawl over her head, which made her pipe down like a bird in the dark and sit quietly.

The ceremony was strictly Orthodox. The Hasidim wouldn't even let us bring the fruit for the banquet from the village. They also supplied the drinks and the wine and the greasy dumplings and the burnt noodle pudding. Two waiters served the food while the cantor cried non-stop in sweet, familiar tones.

While Nehama's pregnancy did not yet show, its soft velvety sheen lit up her face. Her opulent voice was surprisingly, almost magically rich. Although the Hasidim had shaved her head as is their custom, her veil gave off a good smell of damp earth. Even Weissberg and his friends, who were unfamiliar with such odours, understood that the bride would follow her husband to the village.

After the wedding ceremony a few self-conscious musicians played tunes that we all knew from the village, because they were the same as the ones the founding fathers used to sing on winter nights – 'Rabbi Elimelech', 'My Soul That Yearns for Thee', and 'On the Sabbath Day'. None of the band, however, could play like Mandolin Tsirkin, who had the knack of 'plucking the heart-strings along with the bowstrings'. Yosi, Avraham, and I stood in a corner with awkward smiles, watching the Hasidim dutifully go through the motions of dancing. A fatuously gay Pinness joined in loudly, while Busquilla was already deep in whispered negotiations with a pale bearded man. No one laughed when the wedding jester jumped on the table, or when Weissberg's fat brother balanced a chair with seven bottles of brandy on his forehead, all of which fell to the floor and smashed to pieces.

Later it clouded over and we rode home in a thin, pleasant autumn rain. Yosi drove, Avraham talked gaily all the way about marvellous tropical fruits and hot equatorial storms, Busquilla tried to tell jokes, and Pinness went on singing. Knowing I would soon be leaving the village, I kept silent. Uri sat in the back holding Nehama's hand, in which a small, protective kerchief was tightly clutched.

That winter I helped Uri cut down the ornamental trees in Pioneer Home, dig up the flower beds, and rip out the gravel paths.

Uri was full of enthusiasm. He wanted to bring two power saws to speed up the work, but I preferred to chop down the trees with an axe and drag their heavy corpses off myself, for once more I felt the old restlessness coursing through my body and the need for hard, violent work.

The bauhinias, the poincianas, the Judas trees, and the big hibiscus bushes fell under my blows, sappy puddles seeping into the ground. I cut the trunks and branches into fragrant cords of firewood and stacked them in the cowshed.

Avraham and Rivka gave the young couple their house. When spring came and Nehama went out to the fields in short hair and a maternity dress down to her knees, the sun shining through the thin fabric outlined the lovely roundness of her belly and the soft arched space between her legs. Yosi came home for a week's leave, and the four of us planted fruit trees and sowed fodder in between the gravestones. I liked the feel of the smooth little seeds of clover as they went slipping through my fingers.

Uri had all kinds of plans. Though he had no savings, his parents, his uncle, and I were glad to lend him all the money he needed. Nehama cleaned out Avraham's cowshed, and the cows filed back in their iron yokes to moo and listen to music while the milking machines whirred once again.

Late that summer we buried Eliezer Liberson. Some time before he had vanished from his room.

'He's out in the fields,' said Albert with a mysterious smile, adding a proverb in Ladino, though Liberson was not there to translate the soft, sure words.

Everyone knew that Liberson was wandering through the Valley, because the vagrant little dust devils his feet kicked up kept appearing in the most unexpected places, but the old man eluded his pursuers. Dying of hunger and thirst, he walked the land, too weak to open a water tap or pick the wondrous fruit on the trees. Although Daniel looked everywhere for his father, Liberson, like Grandfather before his death, was too small and light to leave tracks. He was only found months later, when the kibbutz corn harvester came across his bird-like bones.

Now I was waiting for Pinness. 'When he goes, I'll leave,' I announced, though Uri and Nehama assured me that I would make them happy by staying.

'Don't even think of it, Baruch. We want to be the last farm to use an ox along with the tractors,' Uri said.

I smiled, Nehama laughed, little Efrayim, who was feeding, gave a start, and Pinness, the oldest, illest man in the Valley, of which he was the last surviving pioneer, went on slowly chewing the stuffed spleen that Busquilla had officiously brought him. Pinness knew I was waiting for him and had kept his distance from me for several months.

'You can leave now,' he said to me with an effort. 'I wouldn't let you bury me in your cemetery even if you did it for nothing.'

Walking him home, I could feel the fear in his movements. He no longer talked about insects and fruits or put his hand on the back of my neck. He was saving up what little strength he had left for his last conscientious stand.

'You won't get me,' he said to me. 'You won't get me.' I did not answer. I knew that the School of Nature, which matriculated man and beast with equal randomness, was stronger than both Pinness and me.

'To Nature the flea, the cockroach, the hyena, the buzzard, the leopard, the cobra are as important as the dog who loves and guards you, the horse who understands and works for you, the young girl in her lover's embrace, the child at its mother's knee in prayer, or the mature man on whom depend the happiness and well-being of a gracious wife and a family of lovely children,' wrote Luther Burbank.

'Our self-love makes us try to ignore this obvious truth,' Pinness once said to me when I was a boy. 'We seek to palliate it with all kinds of religious fairy tales about Messiahs, other worlds, and superstitious Paradises.'

Now I trailed him like a pack of hyenas following a wounded ram, waiting for him to fall. I stalked him in silence. 'What a pitiful collector you are,' he said, turning to face me. 'You'd mount us all on pins if you could. But this is one series you'll never finish.'

In the middle of the night I saw him fumble in the drawer of his bedside table, take out the old key, and set forth. He covered the three miles in two days with me a few paces behind him, as once I had followed Liberson to the kibbutz factory. Every now and then he turned to look at me anxiously.

'You can wait for me there,' he said. 'You don't have to tag on behind me. You know very well where I'm going.' But I went on, carrying on my shoulders the memory of his old knapsack with its tweezers and jars of chloroform, the English wireless operator's pack he had been given by my uncle Efrayim.

The old iron latch, which had not moved in its groove for years, slid open as if newly oiled. Pinness stood in the entrance for a moment before turning around to smile at me. 'Being of clear mind,' he declared. 'Of clear mind.' He stooped and vanished. I waited for him to pay his last respects and step back out to fall into my clutches.

He stood for a minute inside the cave, breathing deeply. As the blind snakes of the past snuggled up to his legs and the ancient African wood lice cralwed possessively over him, I suddenly realised from my vantage point outside what was about to happen. I rushed forward with a shout and a howl, but the old teacher stumbled on ahead with surprising agility, groping, tripping, and skidding along the damp ground until he reached the great slab of slate that screened off the unexcavated depths. Taking a little hammer from his pocket, he searched for the fault line that the old stonemason from Nazareth had shown him.

Pinness raised a feeble hand. He was too weak to bring the hammer down with any force and let it drop on the rock's weakest point.

The loud chime could be clearly heard outside the cave. For a second nothing happened. Then came a gritty sound of crumbling from the heart of the rock, cracks appeared all over it with frightening speed, and it shattered like a glass plate. Pinness fell headlong, tumbling among the slivers as dozens of tons of earth from distant glacial epochs buried him with the antediluvian bones of his ancestors and his one-celled friends, the industrious bacteria, who pre-dated the swamps and the Creation of Light. More with the soles of my bare feet than with my ears, I heard the muffled echo rumble back to me.

A full moon punctured the sky, revealing the whole Valley at my feet, as clear and luminous as white silk. So, I thought, must Liberson have seen it before going wholly blind, when Fanya was alive and his cataracts still let the daylight through.

I looked around me. The sheets of plastic in the farmers' fields shone like great lakes of milk, the trees and haylofts loomed hugely in the dark, and here and there a big new puddle glistened among them. The fruit trees Uri had planted in my cemetery were still small, and among them the gravestones shone whitely like great birds of passage that had come down to rest on the surface of the earth.

Slowly I swivelled my head. The Little Owl, rejoining its rank fledglings, bowed to me with ancient mockery. I headed back to the village.

All night I tossed and turned without falling asleep. Towards morning, like a big bear, I climbed slowly and noisily up the casuarina tree outside their bedroom to say goodbye to Uri and Nehama. Huddled in the branches with a headful of jointed needles, I heard the sound of their breathing, followed by Nehama's voice, which still had its strange, rapid accent.

'And now,' she said to Uri, 'shout it again.'

The three of us laughed, Uri and Nehama in their room and I in the boughs of the great tree that still bore the shiny scars of the hammock my father and mother had hung in it.

Several weeks later Busquilla informed me that he had bought me a house and drove me and my moneybags to the banker's.

I am thirty-eight today, and my body is once more at peace. I will never be any bigger than I am, and my permanent weight, as I wrote in Grandfather's crumpled old notebook, is twenty stone or seven poods. Sometimes Busquilla comes in the black farm truck to drive me back to the village, where I visit Uri and Nehama and play with their four little children.

I was there last spring. I brought Uri some more money, and he gave me a weary hug. Nehama shook my hand and smiled, and the four children rushed at me with loud squeals, trying to knock me to the ground. After lunch I took them for a walk in the fields. I do that every visit. I put Efrayim and Esther, the two oldest children, on my shoulders, and carry Binyamin and little Feyge, who is always complaining about the old-fashioned name her parents gave her, under my arms.

We went to see the red flags of Nature, the little wildcats, and the hornet queens, and then we went to visit the graves of Grandfather and his friends. Uri has put poles as tall as ships' masts in the ground by every headstone, a strip of purple cloth hanging from each, because otherwise you could never find them among the thick cover of cotton and wheat, the crowded corn stalks, and the fruit trees.

Afterwards we walked barefoot along the paths that run through the fields and climbed the hill. The children ran around while I sat beside the rotting, bent old iron door, gazing at flocks of northbound pelicans, the chequered carpet of the Valley, and the wall of the blue mountain.

'Look,' said Feyge, pulling me by the shirt. 'Look, Uncle Baruch.'

Her brown eyes flecked with yellow and green squinted into the sun like an owl's mocked by the birds of day. Her great-grandmother's anxious smile, which never quite settles down, played over the corners of her mouth. With a tiny hand she pointed to the distant name of my mother. Daniel Liberson had ploughed it in the earth, and every year it is coloured by the spring in huge blue letters of cornflowers.